COLLEEN MCCULLOUGH was born in Australia. A neurophysiologist, she worked in Australia and the U.K. before joining the department of Neurology at the Yale University School of Internal Medicine, where she remained for ten years.

Publication of *The Thorn Birds*, her second novel, in 1977, saw the end of her scientific career. She moved to Norfolk Island in the South Pacific, where she lives with her husband, Ric Robinson.

COLLEEN McCULLOUGH

NAKED CRUELTY

A CARMINE DELMONICO NOVEL

McArthur & Company
Toronto

First published in Canada in 2011 by
McArthur & Company
322 King Street West, Suite 402
Toronto, Ontario
M5V 1J2
www.mcarthur-co.com

LIBRARY AND ARCHIVES CANADA CATALOGUING IN PUBLICATION

McCullough, Colleen, 1937-
Naked cruelty : a Carmine Delmonico novel / Colleen McCullough.

ISBN 978-1-55278-945-2

I. Title.

PR9619.3.M24N36 2011   823'.914   C2011-900709-6

Cover design by Matt Stanton
Cover images by shutterstock.com
Typeset in 11.5/18pt Aldine 401 BT by Kirby Jones
Printed in Canada by Webcom

10 9 8 7 6 5 4 3 2 1

For Ria Howell

The kindest person I know

Utterly devoted to her friends, all animals, and hard work

With huge amounts of love and millions of thanks

TUESDAY, SEPTEMBER 24
to
MONDAY, OCTOBER 14

1968

CHAPTER I

Didus ineptus permitted himself a slight laugh as he strode along the sidewalk of Persimmon Street, Carew. By the time that he reached the two-family house that was his target, however, his amusement had long gone. At just before five in the afternoon of Tuesday, September 24, in this Year of Our Lord 1968, the sun was still shining and the streets were relatively deserted. In another half hour the student and graduate ingress would be in full swing as young people poured out of classrooms and laboratories from Science Hill to the secretarial colleges on State, and the kerbs would fill up with VW bugs and clunkers as those too far afield to walk home grabbed parking.

No one noticed him as he turned off the sidewalk and trod coolly down the side of his selected house to its back door, open as most such were; he slipped in and listened intently at the downstairs door. A child was wailing, its mother's voice harried—no worries there. Up the rubber sheathed stairs silently to the tiny top landing, which Maggie never used. She came in at the front, always. Of course she shared the top floor with another girl, but Carol was away at a seminar in Chicago and wouldn't be back for four days yet.

Out came his lock picks. Expertly wielded, they got him inside within a minute. Now he could shed his knapsack—a relief, for it was heavy, weighed down by auxiliary equipment he didn't plan on needing. First he toured the interior of every room to make sure nothing had changed, paying particular attention to the area around the front door. She would enter, carry her attaché case to the work table not far away in the same room, then head for the bathroom and a pee. His women all saved their urine, too fussy to use a public convenience. So, he had ascertained on earlier visits, his best position was over there, behind a tall wing chair that Maggie or Carol must have brought with them to Holloman; it was not the kind of piece a landlord included in rented furniture. What significance did it have for its owner, that she had lugged it a thousand miles?

Having decided on his opening gambit in this delightful game, *Didus ineptus* carried his knapsack to the bedroom he knew was Maggie's. A tad unorthodox in its color scheme—he disliked beige women—yet extremely neat, the double bed made up as smoothly as a boot camp rookie's, the dressing table's oddments tidily arranged, the closet door and bureau drawers fully closed—oh, she was neat!

A chest stood against one wall, its big top free of objects—ideal for his purposes. Working swiftly, he put his tools on it in order before cutting off a piece of blue duct tape six inches long, then a yard long piece of thick twine. Everything was ready; he walked to the living room and its huge mirror, there to prepare his body, and finally positioned himself behind the wing chair.

Her key sounded in the lock at exactly the correct time: within three minutes either way of six o'clock. She'd had a good day, he could tell because he hadn't heard her on the stairs; a bad day meant she plodded, thump, thump, thump… In she came, attaché case in her left hand, and walked across to deposit it on the table, ready for some work later in the evening. That done, she aimed for the bathroom.

The duct tape was lightly fixed to the swelling curve of the chair back, and was across her mouth before she could think of screaming. In an extension of the same movement, he twisted her wrists behind her back and tied them with the twine, so cruelly hard that her face bulged with the pain of it. She was powerless!

Only then did he turn her around, only then did she see the man who had achieved this so quickly she hadn't had a chance. Tall and splendidly built, he was naked and totally hairless, his penis erect, engorged; her eyes filled with despair, but she wasn't done struggling. For about a minute his attention was fully taken up with subduing her, at the end of which she was utterly exhausted. He forced her into the bathroom, where he pulled her panties down and sat her on the toilet. Her bladder was bursting; she let the urine go in a stream, transfixed by a new terror: he *knew* she had needed to go!

He yanked her up and marched her to her bedroom, kicking her buttocks with what felt like all his might, then flung her on the bed and cut her clothes off with a wicked pair of dressmaker's shears. After that he drew a white cotton sock over each foot and taped it around the ankle to keep it on firmly. Next he rolled her over on to her stomach, sat on the edge of the bed and cut her fingernails down to the quick with proper clippers, indifferent to the blood he drew when he cut too hard. Out of the corner of one eye she could see his hands gathering the clippings into a small plastic bag, and see too that those hands were encased in the thinnest of surgeon's gloves.

Didus ineptus turned her over again. Beside herself with fear, Maggie stared up into a face concealed by a black silk hood secured around his neck—she couldn't even tell what color his hair was! Inserting himself between her thrashing legs, he pinched and poked at her breasts, her belly, her thighs. She kept on fighting, but her strength was flagging fast.

Suddenly there was a rope of some kind around her neck; the world swam, went dark, retreated, returned only to the pain of his brutal entry into a vagina hideously dry from terror. He worked the rope as if it were a musical instrument, cutting off her breath, releasing it to let her have one convulsive gulp of air, or two, or even five before he tightened it again and the world went dark. If he came to orgasm she didn't know, only that, after what seemed an eternity, he lifted himself off her. But not to leave. She heard him moving about in the kitchen, the noise of the refrigerator door, heavy footsteps in the living room. Then he returned carrying a book, sat down in her easy chair, opened it and started to read—if indeed he could read through a pair of narrow slits. Swollen with tears, her eyes sought her alarm clock: six-forty. Ten minutes to subdue her, nearly thirty for the rape and its asphyxiations.

At seven he raped her a second time. The pain! The pain!

At eight came the third rape, at nine the fourth.

She was sinking into a stupor by this, the rope around her neck doing its diabolical work faster and better—he was going to kill her! Oh, dear God, make it quick! Make it soon!

Between the rapes he sat in her chair and read the book—her book, because it had her initials painted on its spine in Liquid Paper—more naked than any man she had ever seen, so smooth and hairless was he. Not a scar, not a mole, not a pimple, anywhere. Oh,

Carol, why did you have to go to that seminar? He knew, he knew! There's nothing about me he doesn't know.

At ten he approached the bed with a certain purpose she thought new, closed her eyes and prepared through the waves of terror for her death. But he rolled her over on to her stomach and raped her anally, an unendurable pain that seemed to go on and on, for this time he didn't put the rope around her neck, and consciousness refused to go away.

At eleven he anally raped her a second time, using, she thought, his fist: she could feel tissue tearing, even worse pain. How to face the world after this, if he let her live?

Finally it was finished; he rolled her on to her back.

"Please kill me now," she mumbled indistinctly. "Please, no more, no more, please, please!"

He lifted something off the bed and held it up so she could see it. A neatly printed notice, meticulously measured off.

TELL ANYONE AND YOU ARE DEAD. I AM DIDUS INEPTUS.

The notice disappeared. She lay and listened to him making his departure at eleven-forty in the late evening, while there were still people walking on Persimmon Street.

Maggie waited five more minutes before she got off the bed and forced herself to stagger to the front door, where she turned around and managed to open its single lock, use both bound hands to pull it ajar. That done, she collapsed to her knees and crawled to the kitchen, where she knew her gas stove shared an exhaust vent with the kitchen downstairs. After resting, she got to her feet, seized her meat hammer in her bound hands behind her back, and lifted herself on tiptoe to beat on the vent.

When Bob Simpson from downstairs found her door open and came in to investigate, she was still banging away with the big wooden mallet, gagged, tied up, naked, and appallingly bruised. The warning notice loomed in Maggie's mind as Bob picked up the phone to call the cops, but Maggie Drummond didn't care. She wanted *Didus ineptus* caught, yes, but she wanted far more than that: she wanted him dead as a dodo.

Captain Carmine Delmonico saw her in the Emergency Room at the Chubb Hospital.

"She's been beaten, partially asphyxiated and raped a total of six times—four vaginal, two anal," said the senior resident. "No foreign objects except, we think, a fist for the last anal assault, which tore her up badly enough to need surgical repair. It's a bad one, Captain, but, all considered, she's in remarkable shape mentally."

"May I see her? It rather sounds as if I shouldn't."

"You have to see her, otherwise she'll give us no peace. She's been asking every two minutes for a senior cop."

The young woman's face was still puffy from weeping, and a crimson line around her throat told Carmine that the rapist had used a sleek, thinnish rope to apply his asphyxiations, but either she had passed beyond this most frightful of all ordeals, or she was made of sterner stuff than most women. Her eyes, he noted, were a clear grey in a face that, under normal circumstances, most men would call very attractive.

"There's no point in asking how you are, Miss Drummond," he

said, diminishing his height, bulk and masculinity by sitting. "You're extremely brave."

"Right now I don't feel it," she said, reaching for her water glass and sucking through a bent straw. "I was—I was petrified. I really thought he was going to kill me."

"What's so important that you've badgered the medical staff to let you see a senior cop?"

"I needed to tell the police while it's still fresh in my mind, Captain. That rope around my neck made me black out so often that I'm scared the asphyxia might have latent effects—you know, like damage due to cerebral anoxia."

Carmine's brows rose. "Spoken like a medical person?"

"No, but I am a physiologist, even though I specialize in birds. That's a part of why I wanted to talk tonight. You see, he called himself *Didus ineptus*."

"Which is?"

"The old Linnaean name for the dodo," said Maggie Drummond. "Taxonomically the dodo is now *Raphus cucullatus*. I assume the monster who raped me is trying to appear better educated than he actually is. He must have gotten that name out of a very old encyclopedia—prior to the First World War, say."

"Believe me, Miss Drummond, the monster's garotte hasn't harmed your brain," Carmine said, startled. "That's a detective's deduction, and a valid one. You think an old encyclopedia?"

"Some old source, anyway. The dodo has been *Raphus cucullatus* for quite a long time."

After a keen look at her face, which had, remarkably, grown less tormented, Carmine decided to stay for a couple more questions.

This was an amazing woman. *"Didus ineptus* or *Raphus cucullatus,* it seems an odd kind of name for a rapist. I mean, a dodo?"

"I agree," she said eagerly. "I've been racking my basic birds knowledge for an answer, but I can't find one. The bird really was what we think of modernly as a dodo—stupid to the point of imbecility. All animals trust men when they first run across them, but in no time flat they've learned to run, hide, fight back—whatever it takes to preserve the species. Not the dodo! It let itself be eaten into extinction, when you strip all the fancy language away."

"The island of Mauritius, right?"

"Right."

"So he's calling himself incredibly stupid, but why does he think he's incredibly stupid?"

"Don't ask me, I'm a bird physiologist," she said dryly.

"Another question. What did he wear?"

"A black silk hood over his head, not a stitch more."

"You mean he was naked?" Carmine asked incredulously.

"More than merely naked. He was absolutely hairless, even around the genitals, and his skin was flawless—no moles, spots, freckles, scars."

"No blemishes at all?"

"Not that I could see. It gave him an obscene look, somehow. He raped me at hourly intervals. Each rape lasted half an hour. In between he read a book."

"Did you see its title?"

"No, but it was one of my books. It had my initials on the spine, and no dust jacket. I always remove the dust jackets."

"What was his voice like?"

"He never spoke. He never even cleared his throat."

"So how did you find out his name?"

"It was written on a card that warned me not to tell anyone, or he'd kill me. It was signed *Didus ineptus*."

"Is it still in your apartment?"

"I doubt it. He was very organized."

"Don't answer this if you don't want to—did he climax?"

She winced. "How disgusting! Frankly, Captain, I don't know. He made no sound of any kind. The staff here found no semen, as I understand." She blushed a dull red. "I—I was dying to pee when I came in. Once he had me bound and subdued, he pushed me into my bathroom, pulled my panties down and sat me on the toilet as if he knew I had to go."

"Anything else, Miss Drummond?"

"He was there when I got home, and jumped me. I fought back, but I didn't stand a chance. He wore me out. After he had his rope around my neck, all the fight went out of me. Awful!"

"Everything you've told me indicates that the Dodo—we'll call him that—stalked you for some time before he acted. He knew your habits, right down to your need of the bathroom."

Carmine got up, smiling down at her. "Miss Drummond, you are what an English colleague of mine would call a brick. High praise! Try to get some rest, and don't worry about cerebral anoxia. Your brain's in great shape."

After a little more talk with Maggie—she was determined to instruct him about this and that, evidence of a methodical mind and a good memory—Carmine left the hospital in a dark mood, thankful for one thing only: that the Dodo had chosen a victim whose fighting back wasn't limited to their actual encounter. Maggie Drummond was such a fighter that she was genuinely thirsting to testify against him in a court. But she wasn't the first of the Dodo's victims. His act was far too polished for that. How many had there been, all too terrified to speak up? The Dodo—what a name for a rapist to give himself! Why had he chosen it?

"How many have there been?" he asked his two detective sergeants, Delia Carstairs and Nick Jefferson, the next morning.

"At least this answers the true purpose of the Gentleman Walkers," said Nick, a scowl on his handsome face. "Someone's girlfriend is out there in Carew too scared to report what happened to her, hence the Gentleman Walkers."

"We have to persuade the other victims to come forward," said Delia, "and the best way is to remove men from the cop equation as much as possible. Give me Helen MacIntosh and I'll guarantee to prep her well enough not to put her aristocratically narrow foot in her mouth. I'll go on Luke Corby's drive-home program this afternoon, and Mighty Mike's breakfast show at six tomorrow morning. By noon, I guarantee I'll have winkled almost all the victims out of the Carew woodwork. Between those two programs, I can reach every age group in Holloman."

"Oh, c'mon, Deels!" Nick exclaimed. "Take Madam MacIntosh as your assistant, and all you do is shoot yourself in the foot."

"Horses for courses," Delia said, looking smug.

"Save it, Nick," Carmine advised. "You can have your turn with our trainee over lunch today in Malvolio's—on the Division, so eat up. Helen's been living in Talisman Towers ever since she quit the NYPD eight months ago, so she has to know a bit about life in Carew, including the Gentleman Walkers."

"*Didus ineptus*! Hardly flattering," said Delia. "We still use the phrase 'dead as a dodo' in ordinary speech—is that what he's after? A glorious death shot down while raping?"

"We won't know until we catch the bastard," Carmine said.

"It's in-your-teeth contempt," Nick said. "Kind of like 'catch me if you can'. It's hard to believe he's done that to other girls and not been reported."

"I think Maggie Drummond is an escalation, Nick," Carmine said, "one more reason why we have to find his earlier victims. Until we see how he's progressed, we don't know anything about him. Delia, when you have time, I think you should talk to Dr. Liz Meyers of the Chubb rape clinic. She's going to have more work shortly, I predict."

"A naked rapist!" Delia cried. "That is so rare! Invasive rapists have to keep some clothes on in case they're disturbed. A man without clothes is so vulnerable, yet this fellow doesn't seem to feel at all threatened Was he wearing shoes?"

"Miss Drummond says not. It's possible, of course, that he has a cache of clothes somewhere, but he's still very vulnerable. What if he gets cut off from them?"

"His degree of confidence is extraordinary," Delia maintained.

"He takes fine care not to be marked or scratched," Carmine said. "Socks on their feet, fingernails pared and the clippings collected, Miss Drummond said. She described his skin as quite flawless—not even a freckle. He was tall and extremely well built. Like Marlon Brando, was how she put it."

"And no hair, even around the genitals?" Nick asked.

"So she said."

13

"Then he has his body hair plucked," Delia said decisively. "The skin there is too sensitive for depilatories and too hard to negotiate with a razor."

"Who in Holloman caters for that kind of hairlessness?" Carmine asked. "There'd be talk, and I've never heard Netty Marciano mention a beauty parlor half so adventurous."

"New York," said Delia. "The homosexual underground. They are beginning to come out of the closet, but not every kind. If the Dodo's been having the hair plucked for some years, what hair does grow back would be minimal. All he would require would be occasional touch-ups, and I doubt anyone in that world is going to assist in police enquiries."

Carmine's face twisted in revulsion. "Pah!" he spat. "This guy isn't a homosexual. He's not straight either. He's a one-off." He nodded a dismissal. "Spend the morning working on your tactics, but Nick, don't try to see any Gentleman Walkers. Lunch at noon in Malvolio's, okay?"

His own morning was spent with his two lieutenants. Abe Goldberg was in the throes of handing off the Tinnequa truck stop heist to the Boston PD and would proceed to a series of gas station holdups that had seen two men killed for reasons as yet not entirely apparent. Abe and his two men, Liam Connor and Tony Cerutti, were a good team firmly bonded; Carmine worried about them only as a conscientious captain should, because they were in his care and sometimes too brave.

Lieutenant Corey Marshall was rather different. He and Abe had been Carmine's old team sergeants, moved up to occupy a pair of lieutenancies only nine months old. For Abe, a piece of cake; for Corey, it seemed a leaden weight. Corey had inherited Morty Jones from the previous lieutenant, which handicapped him from the start; Buzz Genovese had just joined him after his second-stringer dropped dead at forty-one years of age, and while Buzz was a very good man, he and Corey didn't see eye to eye. Not that Corey valued Morty any dearer; he occupied his position as if he could work his cases unaided, and that, no man could do, no matter what his rank.

"Word's come to me," said Carmine to Corey in Corey's office, "that Morty Jones is both depressed and on the booze."

"I wish you'd tell me who your divisional snitch is," Corey said, his dark face closing up, "because it would give me great pleasure to tell the guy that he's wrong. You and I both know that Ava Jones is a tramp who screws Holloman cops, but she's been doing that for fifteen years. It's no news to Morty."

"Something's happening in that home, Cor," Carmine said.

"Crap!" Corey snapped. "I talked to Larry Pisano before he retired, and he told me that Morty swings through cycles with Ava. It's a trough at the moment, that's all. The crest will happen in due time. And if Morty chooses to drink in his own time, that's his business. He's not drinking on the job."

"Are you sure?" Carmine pressed.

"What do you want me to say, for Crissake? I am sure!"

"Every Thursday you, Abe and I have a morning meeting to talk about our cases, Cor. It's intended to be a combination of case analysis and a forum for bringing our problems into the open. Every Thursday, you attend. To what purpose, Cor? With what effect? If I can see that Morty is a drowning man, then you must see it too. If you don't, you're not doing your job."

The glaring black eyes dropped to Corey's desk and did not lift. Nor did he say a word.

Carmine floundered on. "I've been trying to have a serious discussion with you since you returned from vacation at the end of July, Cor, but you keep dodging me. Why?"

Corey snorted. "Why don't you just come out with it, Carmine?"

"Come out with what?" Carmine asked blankly.

"Tell me to my face that I'm not Abe Goldberg's bootlace!"

"*What*?"

"You heard me! I bet you don't hound Abe the way you hound me—my reports are too scanty, my men are on the sauce, my time sheets are late—I know what you think of Abe, and what you think of me." Corey hunched his shoulders, his head retreating into them.

"I'll forget you said any of that, Corey." Carmine's voice was calm, dispassionate. "However, I suggest that you remember what I've said. Keep an eye on Morty Jones—he's a sick man. And tidy up your part of our division. Your paperwork is pathetic and Payroll is querying your time sheets. Do you want me to have words with the Commissioner?"

"Why not?" Corey asked, a bite in his tones. "He's your cousin— once removed, second—how can I work it out?"

Carmine got up and left, still reeling at the accusation that he had favored Abe over Corey—untrue, untrue! Each man had his strengths, his weaknesses. The trouble was that Abe's did not retard his functioning superbly as a lieutenant, whereas Corey's did. I have *never* favored one over the other!

It was Maureen speaking, of course. Corey's wife was the root cause of all his troubles; get him drunk enough, and he'd admit it freely. A bitter, envious, ambitious woman, she was also a relentless nagger. So that was the direction her mischief was taking, was it? Easy enough to deal with when they had been his team members, but now that Corey was to some extent free of Carmine, Maureen's natural dislike of her husband's boss could flower. And there was nothing he could do about it.

Back in his own office, he wrestled with a different woman, a different feminine dilemma.

Commissioner John Silvestri had always dreamed of a trainee detective program as a way of injecting younger blood into the Detective Division. There were strict criteria governing the admission of a uniformed man (or woman) into Detectives: they had to be at least thirty years old, and have passed their sergeant's exams with distinction. Silvestri's contention was that they missed out on some of the advantages only youth could bring with it; his answer was to harass Hartford for a trainee program, admitting a university graduate with at least two years' experience as a uniformed cop into Detectives as a trainee who would be subjected to a formal program of classes and tuition as well as gain experience on the job. Since he had been harassing Hartford for twenty years about it, no one ever expected to see it bear fruit. But sometimes strange things happened …

No one in the modest, little old city of Holloman could escape its most influential citizen, Mawson MacIntosh, the President of that world famous institution of higher learning, Chubb University. M.M., as he was universally known, had one promising son, Mansfield, who never put a foot wrong. Mansfield was currently working in a Washington, D.C., law firm renowned for turning out politicians. As far as M.M. was concerned, one day Mansfield would also be a president—but of the U.S.A.

Unfortunately M.M.'s daughter, Helen, was very different. She had inherited her family's high intelligence and striking good looks, but she was stubborn, scatty, strange, and quite ungovernable. Having graduated *summa cum laude* from Harvard, she joined the NYPD, flew through the academy at the head of her class, and was at once shunted to traffic patrol in Queens. For two years she stuck it out, then quit alleging sexual discrimination. Working outside Connecticut had been a mistake; Daddy's influence waned across the border. New Yorkers weren't even true Yankees.

Helen applied to join the Detectives Division of the Holloman PD, and was refused courteously but firmly. So Helen appealed to her father, and everybody got in on the act, including the Governor.

Finally, after an interview with M.M. that saw John Silvestri paint him a picture of his inexperienced, too-young daughter dead in a Holloman ghetto street, the two men cooked up a scheme that saw the Commissioner's twenty-year-old dream become reality: Helen MacIntosh would join Holloman Detectives as its first trainee. M.M.'s share of things was to prise the money out of Hartford and guarantee that the trainee program would continue after Helen graduated from it. Silvestri guaranteed that Carmine Delmonico and his cohorts would give Helen great training and background for anything from three to twelve months, however long it took.

Madam had not been pleased, but when her father made it plain that her only chance to be a detective was to be a trainee one, she dismounted from her high horse and agreed.

Now, after three weeks in Detectives, during which she was

obliged to spend time in the uniformed division, as well as in pathology, forensics and legal, Miss Helen MacIntosh was starting to settle in. Not without pain. Nick Jefferson, the only black man in the Holloman PD, detested her almost as much as Lieutenant Corey Marshall and his two men did. Delia Carstairs, who was the Commissioner's niece as well as an Englishwoman, was sympathetic enough to act as Helen's mentor—a role that Helen bitterly resented as surplus to her requirements. As for Captain Carmine Delmonico— Helen wasn't sure what to make of him. Except that she had a horrible premonition he was a twin of her father's.

When he entered Malvolio's diner next door to the County Services building on Cedar Street at noon precisely, Carmine was pleased to see one of the objects of his morning's labors sitting in one side of a booth toward the back. Now all he had to hope was that she hadn't spent her morning at loggerheads with Judge Douglas Wilbur Thwaites, the terror of the Holloman courts.

He wished he could like her, but thus far Helen MacIntosh hadn't presented as a likeable person. Oh, that first morning! She had turned up for work looking like Brigitte Bardot or any other "sex kitten" as they were called. So inappropriately dressed that he'd had to spell out the kind of garb a woman detective ought to wear, from shoes that stayed on her feet if she needed to chase a fugitive to skirts that didn't drive men mad trying to see her "breakfast", as Carmine put it. She'd obeyed orders and dressed properly ever since, but it hadn't boded well. Nor had she seen the necessity of spending time with the uniforms to find out how the Holloman PD worked on all levels, and she was chafing at the bit to join an investigation, something Carmine had forbidden until she was better prepared. Worst of all, she put men's backs up. Three weeks into the program, and he despaired.

She was writing busily in her notebook—"journal" she called it, denying this indicated a diary.

"How did your morning go?" Carmine asked, sliding into the opposite side of the booth and nodding at Merele, who filled his coffee as she answered with a smile.

"Hard, but enjoyable. The Judge is so interesting. I've known him all my life, but doing law with him is an eye-opener."

"He's a nightmare for a wrongdoer. Remember that."

Her laugh sounded; it was a good one, neither forced nor unmusical. "I bumbled until I got used to him, then I did better. I wish the law teachers at police academy were in his league."

"Oh, he's forgotten more law than they'll ever know."

Delia came in.

Carmine patted the seat next to him. I always imagine, he thought, that today's outfit is the worst: then I see tomorrow's. Today was orange, green, pink and acid-yellow checks, over which she was wearing a bright scarlet waistcoat. As usual, the skirt finished well above her knees, displaying two legs that would do credit to a grand piano. Her hair, thank all the powers that be, had gone from purple and green stripes to peroxide blonde, below which her twinkling brown eyes managed to peer between what looked like tangled black wire. The great debate within the Holloman PD was whereabouts Delia managed to find her clothes, but even Netty Marciano, whose sources of gossip were legion, hadn't managed to find out. Carmine's private guess was New York City's rag district.

For three weeks he had been waiting for Helen to complain about Delia's appearance, but she hadn't said a word, just gaped at Delia upon first meeting. Perhaps even someone as rarefied as a MacIntosh could sense that Delia was exempt from criticisms about dress and appearance. Delia was a genuine eccentric, and apparently Helen had recognized the fact. Certainly when she opened her mouth and that mellifluous voice with its pear-shaped vowels and clipped consonants sounded, Delia was revealed as posh.

Nick appeared a moment later, and was bidden sit on the same side as Delia. Three of them now occupied one side of the roomy booth, with Helen, alone, facing them.

The lush, ice-pink lips parted, the vivid blue eyes glared. "Why am I in the hot seat?" Helen asked.

"You live in Talisman Towers in Carew, right?" Nick asked.

"Yes. I own the penthouse."

"I might have known!" Nick looked angry. "Completely exclusive, huh? Your own elevator and everything."

"Not quite exclusive. I use the same two elevators everyone else does. There's a slot for a key in them."

"Do you have any contact with your fellow tenants?" Delia asked. "*Any* sort of contact."

"I know a few of them, but the only one I'm on friendly terms with is Mark Sugarman. He's three floors down, on the eighth. His girlfriend, Leonie Coustain, lives on the tenth floor. She's French." Helen pulled a face. "She used to be vivacious and outgoing, but about three months ago she had a nervous breakdown. Now, not even Mark manages to see her. She's a snail inside its shell. The worst of it is she won't get any help, Mark says. He's very much in love with her, and I used to think that they were made for each other. Now—I really don't know. Leonie sure doesn't like him anymore, but he swears he doesn't know why." She flushed. "Sorry. That wasn't a good report—I rambled."

"Sometimes rambling is better," Carmine said. "I don't think Leonie fell out of love with Mark. She was raped."

The color drained from Helen's face. "*Raped*?"

"Yes, definitely," Carmine said, not yet prepared to mention the Dodo. "What do you know about the Gentleman Walkers of Carew?"

"The Gentleman Walkers?" she asked, sounding bewildered. "They walk," she said, and laughed. "Up and down and around and around Carew. They're a great group of guys."

"Do you know them as individuals?" Nick asked.

"Sure, some of them. Not all of them—Mark says there are over a hundred-forty of them. Mark's their head honcho."

"Good, a name," said Carmine. "A big group of men patrolling worried me—vigilantes. But so far they've kept well within the law, including when they apprehended a couple of peeping Toms and a women's underwear thief. Then last night a young woman named Maggie Drummond was viciously attacked and raped inside her Carew apartment. She notified us. Now we have sufficient evidence to act, including coming down harder on the Gentleman Walkers."

Helen sat, her face a mixture of horror and eagerness. "But I know Maggie Drummond!" she cried. "She goes to all Mark's parties—so smart! Well, you have to be smart to get post-grad work in bird physiology at Chubb. She's doing a Ph.D. in bird migration under Professor Hart—the world's authority." Her face softened. "Poor Maggie! Will it ruin her, Captain?"

"Scar her, certainly, but she's unusually resilient. She insisted on seeing me last night, while the ordeal was still fresh in her mind. He'd partially asphyxiated her multiple times, and she was worried that the trauma might cause her to forget details. She even gave us his name—*Didus ineptus.* That's the old term for the dodo, now known as *Raphus cucullatus.*"

"Can't I be of more use than giving you Mark Sugarman's name?" Helen asked.

"Yes, you can," said Delia, "provided you put yourself under my authority and do exactly as you're told. Will you?"

"Yes, of course," Helen said, face lighting up.

"Good. I suspect we're going to meet a number of the Dodo's victims, and it's vital that women comprise the front face of the investigation. Ever since their individual attacks, these young women can't cope with men, no matter how sympathetic. You and I, Helen, have to do all the victim contact until we can persuade them to seek help from Dr. Liz Meyers at the rape clinic. That means we spend as much time as we can this afternoon coaching you in how to behave— it's a matter of technique as well as feminine bonding. I'm hoping to be taking calls tomorrow after Mighty Mike's breakfast show, but it's possible we'll have some responses after Luke Corby. You're my shadow, Helen—wherever I go, you go. Understood?"

"Yes!" said Helen fervently. It was here at last, her first case, and she was going to make sure that Delia shone. Because if Delia shone, so did she.

Carmine took himself off to Carew and the eighth floor of Talisman Towers, the only ritzy block of high rise apartments in a district chiefly famous for its peace, prettiness, and hordes of women students at all levels of a tertiary education. Helen had explained that Mark worked from home, so Carmine fully expected to find him in his apartment.

"Like Helen, I own my condo," Mark Sugarman said, leading the way into a big room that had been intended as the living room, but had been turned into a studio. He indicated two hard chairs at a table, and went to the kitchen area to fetch mugs and a coffee pot, then sugar and cream.

In all visual respects he was a large-yet-medium man, from his height of just under six feet to his face and coloring. What saved him from obscurity were his eyes: long-lashed, widely open, and a vivid green. He was wearing baggy, faded jeans and a short-sleeved shirt whose two breast pockets bulged with items including pencils, cigarettes, a short steel ruler.

If typical artists are supposed to live in extreme disorder, he was not typical, for the room was immaculately kept; it was painted white and its natural lighting consisted of a whole wall of glass panes looking over the treetops toward Long Island Sound, dreamily blue in this lovely start to Indian summer. Rather than an easel, he worked on a drafting board, in front of which sat a bar stool. A tall table to either side held inks, pens, pencils, an electric pencil sharpener, various protractors and T-squares, a neat pile of rags, and a jar of water. As they passed the board, Carmine was amused to see that it held a black-and-white Indian ink drawing of a wacky-looking family of raccoons. It was very well done, its human element only subtly—but tellingly—suggested.

"I'm a book illustrator," Sugarman explained, pouring the coffee. "This one's aimed at a general market from teens to nineties, so the publisher wants classy drawings—no cheating with cross-hatching or other short cuts. Therefore, hire Mark Sugarman. Few art schools teach classical ink drawing, so I'm in demand. I learned in London and Antwerp."

"How long has the neighborhood watch been in existence?" Carmine asked, adding cream and sugar; the coffee was old. "I should tell you that Maggie Drummond was raped last night, and wasn't frightened enough not to call us. Her rape was atrocious—particularly brutal and demeaning—but I come from her with a request that you tell me everything you know. Maggie is very emphatic. She wants this monster caught."

The unusual emerald eyes had widened and shone with tears; Sugarman's coffee slopped. "Oh, Jesus!"

"Time to spill the beans about the Gentleman Walkers, sir."

"And that's a relief, Captain." He drew a breath, reached out automatically for a stack of paper napkins and wiped up his spill. "The first one we knew about was Leonie—my dear, sweet Leonie! I found her when I went up to see if she felt like a walk to blow the cobwebs away. She was—oh, a terrible mess! Not cut up or anything, but bruised and soiled. He'd raped her three times, once real pervert stuff. I wanted to call you, but she wouldn't let me, swore she'd deny the whole thing. Babbling about her family in France, the disgrace." He ground his teeth. "Nothing I could say would persuade her to change her mind."

"Did you believe Leonie was the first victim?"

"I did, but Mason Novak—he's my best pal—said his girl, Shirley Constable, had behaved so like Leonie that he was having suspicions that had never occurred to him before—he thought Shirley had had a nervous breakdown over her work, even though she loved it. After Leonie, he was convinced she'd been raped, but he can't even get into the same room with her, so—who knows?"

Carmine put his coffee down. "Mr. Sugarman, even if the women refused to co-operate, you should have brought your suspicions to the police, not organized a neighborhood watch."

"I see that now, Captain, but at the time neither Mason nor I did. I put an ad in the *Holloman Post* announcing that I was forming a walking club—Carew residents only need apply. And I was inundated with walkers! The Gentleman Walkers were an instant success."

"Without further stimulus than the rape of Leonie Coustain, which I presume you didn't mention? That sounds peculiar, sir."

Sugarman laughed, a wry sound. "Vanity, Captain. We'd found a way to keep fit—walking. Most walkers give it up because of the loneliness, while we walk in trios, always the same three men—we vary the routes. Guys sorted themselves out into trios of like mind, if you know what I mean. And a man walks each second evening, not every single day. It's enough to keep the waistline trim and the heart in good shape."

"And no Gentleman Walker has ever encountered a man who might be a rapist?" Carmine asked.

"Definitely not. The closest we came were the peeping Toms."

"You did a real service there, anyway. Peeping Toms who are never caught often become rapists later." Carmine cleared his throat. "I need a list of your members, Mr. Sugarman."

He rose from his chair at once. "Sure, I'll get it. I have full details of every Gentleman Walker, it's one of the club's strictest conditions."

Carmine conned the beautifully typed list in some awe. Names, ages, addresses, phone numbers, occupations, days rostered to walk: a painstaking and lucid timetable as well as a list. There were schoolteachers, an occasional physicist, chemists, tradesmen, medical doctors, dentists, plant physical workers, city clerks, technicians, biologists—146 names altogether, ranging in age from twenty-one to sixty-eight.

"You must be a very persuasive recruitment officer."

Sugarman laughed, disclaiming. "No, I'm the logistics man, not the demagogue. You want to talk to Mason Novak. He's the soul of the Gentleman Walkers, the one who keeps us inspired—and the one who took over from me as the ultimate authority."

Carmine found him on the list. "Mason Novak, aged thirty-five, analytical chemist with Chubb. Burke Biology Tower, or Susskind Science Tower?"

"Susskind Science. He's inorganic, he says."

"Do you have a meeting venue?"

"Mason requisitions a small lecture theater in Susskind."

"Um—today is Wednesday, so … Friday, six o'clock?"

"For what?" Mark Sugarman asked.

"Oh, come, Mr. Sugarman! A meeting between the Walkers and Holloman detectives. On Friday, September 27. Call the meeting and emphasize that every Gentleman Walker is to attend. Okay?"

"Certainly."

"It won't be difficult to assemble your troops. Listen to Mighty Mike's breakfast program. I predict that all the Walkers will be agog to discover what's happened."

Funny, thought Carmine as his beloved Ford Fairlane headed for home that evening, how troubles never come singly. I have to turn Helen MacIntosh into a first-rate detective when I'm not even sure she'll obey orders; I have Corey Marshall failing to make the grade as a lieutenant—who could ever have predicted that? Today I learned that our prettiest, most tranquil suburb, Carew, is harboring a particularly dangerous rapist. And my fantastic, six-foot-three wife has been defeated by a twenty-two-month-old child. *Desdemona!* Twice she's come face to face with killers and won the encounters, whereas a bullying, shouting, hectoring toddler has worn her down to utter defeat. My Desdemona, always hovering on the verge of tears. It doesn't bear thinking of, yet it has to be thought of. Not merely thought of: it has to be dealt with, and fast. Otherwise I might lose my wife forever.

He parked the Fairlane in the four-car garage's only free bay and trod down the sloping path to his front door, aware that his couple of visits after work had made him later than probably Desdemona needed. The house, a very big New England colonial with a square three-storey tower and widow's walk, stood halfway down two acres that backed on to Holloman Harbor; they had lived in it now for over two years and loved its every mood, from an idyllic summer's day to the wildest storm to encrustations of ice in a hard winter. But the spirit of the house resided in its mistress, Desdemona, and she was failing.

Nothing he could say had talked her out of a second pregnancy soon after her first; Julian was only sixteen months old when Alex was born. The boys were true fusions of nobly proportioned parents: from Carmine they inherited muscular bulk and a regal presence; from Desdemona they got bones that promised basketball players; and from both they took a high degree of intelligence that boded ill for parental tranquillity. If Julian was already so hard to take, what would it be like when Alex grew into the horrors of toddlerhood, from talking to walking?

The woman who had efficiently managed an entire research

facility had retired to a domestic world, there to turn into a superb cook and an indefatigable housekeeper. But ever since Alex's birth five months ago Desdemona had dwindled, not helped by Julian, a master of the filibuster, the harangue and the sermon.

Okay, he thought, opening the front door, here goes! I am going to do my best to pull Desdemona back from the abyss.

"It's good to see you, but even better to feel you," he said into her neck, crushing her in a rather frantic embrace. Then he kissed her, keeping his lips tender.

Understanding that this was no overture to passion, Desdemona put her husband into a chair and gave him his pre-dinner drink.

"Julian's in bed?" he asked.

"Yes, you tricked him for once. He expected you to be on time, but when you didn't turn up, he fell asleep." She sighed. "He had a shocking tantrum today, right in the middle of Maria's luncheon party. I told her I didn't want to come!" A hot tear fell on to Carmine's hand.

"My mother is sometimes not very bright, Desdemona. So I take it our son spoiled things?"

"He would have, except that Maria slapped him—*hard*! You know how I feel about slapping children, Carmine—there has to be a more effective way to deal with small children."

Sit on it, Carmine, sit on it! "If there is, my love, you don't seem to have found it with Julian," he said—reasonably, he thought. "Tantrums are a form of hysteria, the child takes no harm from being jerked out of it."

In the old days she would have flown at him, but not these days. Instead, she seemed to shrink. "It wore him out, at any rate. That's why he's in bed and asleep."

"Good. I can do with the peace and quiet."

"Were you serious when you threatened him with a nanny the other day? We can't afford a nanny, Carmine, and a stranger in the house would make him worse."

"First off, woman, I manage our finances. You shouldn't have that headache on top of two babies. We can afford it, and I didn't threaten Julian. I was warning him. It's going to happen, my dear love, though not for the reasons you think. Not for Julian—for *you*. You're permanently down, Desdemona. When you think no one's looking, you weep a lot, and you can't seem to find your way out of whatever it is plagues you. I went to see Doc Santini this afternoon because every time I insist you see him, you race in and out of his surgery pretending it's Julian or Alex is sick. Desdemona, honestly! If there's one thing Doc Santini's not, it's a fool. He knows as well as I do that you're the one who's sick. He says you're suffering from a post-partum depression, love."

She flung herself mutinously into her chair; when Carmine spoke in that tone, even God had to shut up and listen. And, she admitted as her anger died, there *was* something wrong with her. The trouble was, she knew it was incurable, whereas these men—what did men know about it?—thought it was physical.

"Apparently they're finding out a lot about women who become depressed after childbirth. It's nothing Freudian, it's a physical, hormonal thing that takes time and care to fix. You'll have to see Doc tomorrow morning, and if you ignore me, wife, I'll have you taken to the surgery under police escort. My mother is coming round to babysit—"

"She'll slap Julian!" Desdemona cried.

"Happen he needs a slap. Just because your father beat you as a child, Desdemona, doesn't make a slap for a transgression cruelty. Sometimes it's plain common sense. And let's not get on to Julian, let's stay with you."

The tears were running silently down her face, but she was at least looking at him.

"Doc doesn't want to put you on drugs. You're a borderline case and you'll get better naturally if we ease the pressure. In the main, that's Julian. And the answer for Julian isn't a slap, I agree with you there because once a slap loses its shock value, he'll ignore slaps. How am I doing so far?"

"Spot on," she said gruffly. "Oh, Carmine, I thought it was your work preying on you when you come home, but it's me! Me! I am so sorry! Oh, what can I do? I'm such a burden!"

"Desdemona, don't cry! I'm giving you answers for your pain, not reasons. You could never be a burden. That's a two-way street either of us could travel down. Doc suggested that I employ a young woman to help you. Her name is Prunella Balducci and she's one of the East Holloman Balduccis, therefore some kind of cousin of mine. She usually works for megabucks on New York City's upper east side. A couple of weeks ago she got tired of it and came home. Her savings account is loaded, so she isn't interested in taking a megabucks job. What she wants is to be near her mom and dad for a while. Once she's had a break, she's heading for L.A. and a different set of emotional cripples than New York's. By that, I mean that Prunella takes a job in an emotionally crippled household and gets its inhabitants organized enough for ordinary nannies and housekeepers." He drew a long breath. "On my way home tonight I called in at Jake Balducci's place and saw Prunella, who has agreed to come to us until Christmas. By then, she says, your troubles will only be a memory. We can afford what she's asking in Holloman, Desdemona, so money is not an issue."

"I don't—I can't—"

"Woman, of course you can! I am aware that you clean the house before Caroline comes, which is crazy, but you can't do that with someone who's staying here and eating meals with us and is really a part of the family, if only temporarily."

Desdemona gasped. "*Staying* here? Where? Which room? Oh, Carmine, I can't!"

"I also phoned my daughter at Paracelsus, ungrateful little puss that she is. Not a word to us in three weeks, but after I talked to her, I understood why, so she's forgiven. She's agreed to do her share toward your recovery by not coming home to sleep until Christmas. Prunella will live in Sophia's tower. Caroline can clean it tomorrow, I've booked her for the day. Prunella is coming next week."

By this, Desdemona was sagging in her chair, winded. "I see you have it all sorted out," she said stiffly.

"Yes, wife, I do. Prunella's chief task is to turn Julian into someone I look forward to seeing when I come home, rather than someone I could strangle for his treatment of you. At the moment he's power crazy—bossy, manipulative and obnoxious, and if he goes on developing like that, the only career he'll be fit for is a defense attorney. And I tell you straight, Desdemona," Carmine said, only half joking, "that I won't have a son who gets axe murderers and pederasts off. I'd be happier with a son who lived on Welfare. There are traces of a nice person underneath Julian's bluster, and now's the time to make sure the nice person wins. Do you hear me?"

"I hear, I hear," she said, trying to smile. "Was it Shakespeare who said, 'Let's kill all the lawyers!'? You are absolutely right, we can't produce a defense attorney. In fact, even a D.A. would be unacceptable."

"Then is it settled?"

"I suppose so. Yes, Prunella comes—but for Julian's sake, not for mine." Her face grew horrified. "What if I dislike her?"

"You won't. You'll love her."

"Will she spank Julian?"

"I think she has better ammunition in her arsenal than that, dear love. Try to move farther away from your own childhood and see Julian for what he is, not for what you were. He's only half you. His other half is tough Italian-American."

She climbed to her feet, a long way. "Dinner," she said.

No matter what her mood, and even when the meal was, as tonight, a simple one of steak, French fries and salad, Desdemona was a superb cook. She sprinkled the outside of the meat with a special salt before broiling it, and her French fries were out of this world—crunchy on the outside, feathery inside.

"Now," she said after they were finished, "tell me how things went today, Carmine. I heard Delia on Luke Corby earlier."

"It's too soon to know much about the Dodo—that's what we decided to call him, though he prefers the Latin—*Didus ineptus.* Any idea why he'd think like that?"

"Yes. He's a poseur."

"Who got it wrong. The term was a Linnaeus classification, out of date now."

"I don't think that bothers him. That particular phrase clicks with some idea in his mind. But the Dodo isn't what's worrying you," she said, sipping her tea. She had persuaded Carmine to switch from coffee to tea after dinner, and he was sleeping better. "Tell me, love."

"Morty Jones is drinking, and Corey won't see it."

"Ohh! Drinking is a firing offense, isn't it?"

"On duty, yes. Instant dismissal, the works—it's in our contracts. John Silvestri is an iron man about liquor, and the Holloman PD is famous—lushes need not apply."

"But Morty! He's a weak man, I know, yet …" Desdemona's plain face grew plainer save for her pale blue eyes, which Carmine fancied were the same color as pack ice, ethereal and slightly eerie; they grew moist. "I suppose it's his wife?"

"When isn't it? I caught him coming in to work Monday, and we had a talk. Seems their relationship came to a head last Saturday night when Morty found Ava sneaking to the spare room at three a.m. When he told her he'd had enough, she told him that his kids weren't his, and he decked her. On the floor, blood everywhere from a broken nose. Ava packed her bags and left him to the tender mercies of his mother—" Carmine threw his hands up and clutched fruitlessly at the air. "It seems he spent all of Sunday in the Shamrock Bar, so you can imagine what he looked like—and smelled like!— Monday morning."

"Oh, Carmine, that's terrible! According to Netty Marciano the boy—Bobby?—was fathered by Danny Morski, and Gidget belongs to the non-famous Holloman cop Harpo Marx. I must say the likenesses are speaking, but Morty never knew, did he?"

"Didn't want to, I guess. He's in denial, that's why he's drinking. Corey's playing ostrich, head in the sand. Morty's mom agreed to look after the kids for the time being, but told him to find a housekeeper."

"Oh, dear!" Desdemona's English accent wasn't as posh as Delia's, but it showed strongly on exclamations. And at least, thought Carmine, watching her, Morty Jones's troubles were giving her something other than Julian to think about. "What can you do, Carmine?"

"Keep talking to Morty and hope Ava comes home again. No other cop would put up with her out of a bed."

"Corey's bothering you in other ways, isn't he?"

"Clever chicken! Corey's jealous of Abe. He implied that I'm biased in favor of Abe. It was hard to take."

Why don't they leave him alone? Desdemona asked herself, all traces of depression burned to ashes in the furnace of her rage at Corey, Ava, Morty—anyone who didn't see her husband for the great and good man he was. I must get better, I must! The last thing Carmine needs is an emotionally crippled wife. But what her heart was telling her lay beyond her ability and capacity at this moment; Desdemona sat, huddled in her chair, without the strength to offer him any kind of comfort. All her little spurt of anger had done was to stimulate the ever-lurking tears. When she tried to blink them away, they overflowed, and again it was Carmine who had to summon up the energy to offer comfort.

By noon of the next day, Thursday, September 26, Delia Carstairs, in charge of gathering information about the Dodo's possible rapes, had accumulated a total of six young women she deemed highly likely to have been victims prior to Maggie Drummond. Done in the form of a dialogue between Delia and the host of the program, the radio broadcasts had proven astonishingly effective; Delia suspected that all six young women had yearned for somewhere feminine to go, and that, as was usually the way, it hadn't occurred to any of them that a medical school as prestigious as Chubb's would have a rape clinic rather than merely an emergency room. Delia used her accent to present as a very classy woman who really would, as she assured her listeners, see and talk to victims in privacy and without a male presence.

A delighted Helen was severely cautioned.

"Have you ever been raped?" Delia asked her.

"No, not even close."

"Then strictly speaking you're as ignorant as any man. All you have in facing these devastated women is your sex, which I require be used as a reassurance. Never appear indifferent."

"Are you implying that men dismiss rape as a fabrication?"

"A minority of men only. A few men have been falsely accused of rape—you'll never convert them. Some have been brought up to regard all women as liars and cheats. There is always an element of ignorance. Samson and Delilah is a good illustration—women are seen as stripping men of their power, their authority."

"Why tell me stuff I already know?"

Delia drew a patient breath. "I'm telling you this because it's a rare man who empathises with a rape victim, but Captain Delmonico is one such rare man. The Dodo case will be *worked*, and not just because the rapist is escalating."

"Why?" Helen demanded, eyes glistening.

"Don't take your mind there, Helen!" Delia snapped. "Don't go romantically endowing the Captain with a raped girlfriend, or anything even remotely so personal. No such person exists. What I am trying to get through your unversed head, Madam Trainee, is that you're extremely lucky to be working here."

"Yes, Delia," said Helen meekly. "What do I do?"

"If a victim chooses to come here, you sit in the interview room with her and me. If the victim prefers to be seen at her home, you accompany me to her home. You are purely a witness. You say not one word unless I indicate you may. You don't ask curious questions either, even if you believe your question will solve the case. You write it down, hand the paper to me, and I will decide. Our best advantage is that we're women, so don't blow it. Understood?"

"Should I take notes?"

"Unobtrusively, yes. None of them will consent to a tape recorder, unfortunately."

There were seven rape victims: Shirley Constable on March 3; Mercedes Mendez on May 13; Leonie Coustain on June 25; Esther Dubrowski on July 16; Marilyn Smith on August 6; Natalie Goldfarb on August 30; and Maggie Drummond on September 24.

When Helen offered to drive each young woman into County Services in a private car and return her the same way, Delia managed to persuade all six earlier victims to come in. Her trainee assistant, Delia noted when Shirley Constable appeared, had handled this most damaged of the victims with a cheerful insouciance that had revolved around her green Lamborghini sports car; she hadn't mentioned the coming interview.

The erstwhile Carew character had retreated so far inside herself that it took Delia almost an hour to get her talking, but when she did, it poured out. She had been a virgin for religious reasons and regarded herself as ruined for life; but that, Dr. Liz Meyers and the rape clinic would help. Delia had already been in touch with Dr. Meyers, a brilliant psychiatrist whose sole interest was rape.

What preyed more cruelly on Shirley's mind was her conviction that the Dodo would return to kill her, and a large part of her felt she deserved to die. Oh, we women have to get over this mind-set, Delia said to herself. The value society puts on virginity is a way to make sure a man fathers his children—look at poor Morty Jones.

Having assured Shirley that the Dodo was too busy moving on to bother going back and killing earlier victims, Delia sent her off with Helen to see Dr. Meyers.

"He's definitely escalating in method," she said to Carmine and Nick later, "but he seems to have settled into a three-week cycle. There were ten weeks between Shirley and Mercedes, then six weeks between Mercedes and Leonie. From Leonie on, three weeks, with a slight preference for Tuesdays and Wednesdays."

Carmine was scowling. "Then he's not a moon man or a sun man, Deels, and that means he's a real headache. He can switch his time span without feeling that he's offended the sun or the moon—I hate the ones without a planetary pattern."

"Then perhaps he's on a Mars or a Venus cycle. We won't know that until we check the astronomical ephemeris. I'll get on to it," Delia said. "However, if he sticks to three weeks, he's due to strike around October 16. A Wednesday. We should expect it, Carmine, sun, moon, or none."

"Does he have a physical type of victim?"

"No. Nor a racial one, nor a religious one. All colors of hair, eyes, Caucasian skin. Eastern European roots, Jewish, WASP, Latin-American. Things might pop out at us when we consider the events more dispassionately and conclude all the interviews. Apart from Shirley, all we did today was make their acquaintance."

Helen came in and sat down.

"Your impressions, Helen?" Carmine asked.

"Well, we didn't spend much time on our home visits—it will be better when I drive each of them in for a formal interview. I can say that the Dodo himself didn't vary much from victim to victim—did he, Delia?"

"No."

"Almost six feet, and extremely well built. Marlon Branda was the movie star they chose. Naked and completely hairless. No scars, spots, moles, pimples. A black, silky hood over his head. He never spoke. The warning and his name were printed on a piece of white Bainbridge board with a black marker."

"Thank you," said Carmine, interrupting smoothly. "Delia?"

"Shirley was raped twice, both vaginal. Mercedes also, but the second one was anal. And so it went, Carmine, escalating each time a little. My feeling is that with Maggie Drummond and the arrival of the garotte, or cord, or whatever, the Dodo is close to his kill point. That means it's imperative we catch him."

"I couldn't agree more," Carmine said.

"Have you any ideas about the Dodo, Carmine?" Nick asked.

"He's verging on unique, for starters. Through six rapes over a period of nearly seven months he managed to be invisible. If it weren't for the Gentleman Walkers, his attack on Maggie would have seemed the first. None of his earlier victims would have come forward of her own volition. The Dodo is a stalker who must know a great deal about the women he targets. It's my guess that he's working from a list, and that list might contain a hundred names," Carmine said grimly.

"Will he escalate to murder?" Helen asked, not having heard the first part of their conference.

"All multiple rapists of this kind eventually move up to murder, Helen. Asphyxiation is a give-away. That's why, as you women probe the earlier victims deeper and deeper, I want you to be on the lookout for anything suggesting asphyxiation. In a way, Miss Trainee, that never gives your victim any idea what you're doing. We don't want anyone feeding ideas, okay?"

The blue eyes were blazing, but Helen MacIntosh had learned more than merely police procedure: not a muscle moved in her face as she thought: how *dared* they treat her like a teenybopper! "Madam Trainee!" "Miss Trainee!" They were baiting her, but they wouldn't succeed in getting a rise. "Okay," she said aloud.

"The nakedness says the Dodo's ego is so big he's sure he can deal with the unexpected, like a room-mate coming home. His rape technique says he's never going to be a metal or a fire man, cutting, mutilating, even burning with a cigarette. He punches, pokes and pinches, but most of all he kicks. The assaults are erotic, in that they're directed at breasts, buttocks, belly, pubes. In an odd way, his actions are immature. According to Maggie, he sustained rigid erections for long periods, yet he can't climax. According to his lights, he has principles."

"You're describing an almost supernaturally cool, calm and collected man," Nick said uneasily.

"Not supernatural, but certainly highly instinctual. Has any victim reported seeing a weapon, Delia?" Carmine asked.

"Not so far."

"He must have brought a weapon with him and kept it close at hand," Carmine said.

Ask your questions, Helen, said their trainee to herself. If they make you seem ignorant, that's because you are ignorant. But you're here to learn, and sometimes they don't see the most basic questions of all—too much water under the cop bridge. "Why should so many sex murderers strangle?" she asked, eyes wide and curious. "I mean, asphyxiation is just one form of it."

Carmine looked pleased. "As against death by mutilation?"

"Yes."

"I don't know that anyone honestly knows, but the general feeling is that strangulation—hands, a garotte, a scarf—offers the killer about as leisurely a look at dying as he'll ever get. It can take minutes, depending, and especially if he's gotten his technique with a cord down so pat that he can drag his victim to the brink of death a dozen times before the *coup de grâce*. It also means no blood, and a good proportion of sex killers dislike blood as a component of murder. It's messy and unpredictable unless you're extremely well prepared to handle the mess. One errant drop can convict if the blood type's rare and the killer shouldn't have been there." Carmine's large, square, beautiful hands gestured. "One thing I can tell you, Helen. The Dodo isn't into blood. What turns him on is a woman's suffering."

Though they were sitting in a room without windows, it felt as if the sun had gone in; Helen shivered. *Suffering.* Such a terrible word. It occurred to her that in her twenty-four years of life, she had never truly witnessed suffering any closer than a television screen or news magazine.

"How can the Dodo do meticulous research on a bunch as varied as our victims?" Helen asked. "Shirley is an archivist, Mercedes is a dress designer, Leonie is a mathematician, Esther is a lecturer in business, Marilyn is an archaeologist in dinosaur research, Natalie buys women's wear for a chain of department stores, and Maggie is a bird physiologist. Where's the common thread, apart from the fact that they all live in Carew?"

"I doubt there is a common thread," said Nick; this is one case, he thought, where the women should be driving. "I do think we have to assume that the Dodo lives in Carew, and that under the black hood is a face well known to Carew residents. A face not only known, but trusted, maybe admired. He could be a Gentleman Walker. He could be that movie star guy you go out with, Helen."

She guffawed. "Kurt? Hardly likely, Watson! He's a contender for the Nobel Prize in physics."

"Yes, but do you see what I mean? Whoever the Dodo is, he leads a double life. I'd be willing to bet that he's invited to Mark Sugarman's parties—and those parties are something all the Dodo's victims have in common."

Delia squawked. "Nick! You stole my thunder."

"Did I? Gee, Deels, I'm sorry."

"It doesn't matter," said Carmine. "The fact is, you both noticed the parties. Sounds like you said a little more than hello and goodbye to the other five victims, Delia."

Her face went pink enough to clash with her orange ascot. "Um—well, yes. They were *dying* to talk, especially because the public nature of Maggie's rape told them they weren't in much danger anymore. They're very intelligent women."

"You don't give credence to the idea that the face under the hood might be disfigured?" Carmine asked.

Helen answered. "No. He has no hare lip, cleft palate or butterfly naevus, Captain. Nick was way off with his crack about my boyfriend, but I do know why he picked him. Kurt von Fahlendorf is a gorgeous looking guy who just happens to be a physics genius. There are three of them hang out together—Kurt, Mason Novak, and Mark Sugarman. They're friends with an old guy, Dave Feinman, and a couple of younger guys—Bill Mitski and Greg Pendleton. But I can assure you, sir, that none of them is harboring Mr. Hyde underneath Dr. Jekyll."

"We'll try to take your word for it—after we've investigated them," Carmine said gravely. "How many more Gentleman Walkers do you know, Helen?"

"Are they all Gentleman Walkers?" she asked ingenuously. "I know them from Mark's parties."

"Yes, they're all Walkers. There are one hundred-forty-six altogether."

"Do they have a uniform?"

"Apparently not." Carmine lifted his eyes to Helen's. "Is Mr. von Fahlendorf a neighbor?"

"Professor von Fahlendorf. No, he doesn't live in Talisman Towers. He lives around the corner in Curzon Close—the prettiest house in Carew."

"He's very pretty," said Nick, lip curling.

"He's very clever," she riposted. "He's a professor in the hardest form of physics—particles."

"Whoopee."

"Behave yourself, Nick," Carmine said with sufficient reproof in his voice to make Delia glance at him in surprise. "Is your professor a West German national, Helen?"

"Yes, on a green card. He works on sub-atomic particles in the Chubb bunker. Very highly thought of by Dean Gulrajani and a few other luminaries, though his nose is a little out of joint since Jane Trefusis joined the lab. It's really that he's not very fond of America, but it's where the work is, and that's actually what Kurt is all about—sub-atomic particles."

"What's he got against America?" Nick asked aggressively. "Funny, how none of these people have a good thing to say about us, yet they're happy to take our money and our jobs."

"I agree with you, Nick. It's mostly envy," Carmine said in calm tones. "They see their own cultures buried under American films, television and popular fiction. That must be hard, but their own people are in the forefront of promoting global American culture—the kids and the local moguls in particular."

"East Germany, or West?" Nick pressed.

"Well, it would hardly be East. Oh, you mean originally? Yes, the von Fahlendorfs were Prussian junkers, somewhere fairly close to the Polish border. His father skipped from East Germany in 1945. Now they're very wealthy."

"Including Professor von Fahlendorf?" Carmine asked.

"He's not hurting, sir. He drives a black Porsche and owns a lovely property. What's he like as a person? Stiff as a board and about as exciting as *Parsifal*. But I like Kurt. He has beautiful manners, and if he ever keeps me waiting on a date, I could safely bet my life that nothing less than an escaping muon has detained him. Kurt's a gentleman, and in case you haven't checked lately, sir, they're a dying breed."

"He sounds more and more like the Dodo to me," said Nick.

"Enough, Nick!" Carmine said sharply. "What do you know about Mark Sugarman, Helen?"

"Another of the dying breed," Helen said, a little tartly. "Like me, he owns his condo. An extremely organized person—in fact, the most obsessive man I know when it comes to work habits and organizing his life in general. Kurt's in the amateur league compared to Mark. He used to throw the best parties until Leonie Coustain got sick—raped, we know now." She shuddered. "To think that the Dodo invaded Talisman Towers! But Mark isn't the Dodo either, sir, truly. In the summer he uses the pool, and his chest is covered with hair. Kurt's hairy too."

"Haven't you heard of a chest toupee?" Delia asked.

Helen's jaw dropped. "You're kidding," she said hollowly.

"Anything but. It's seen as an indication of masculinity, so men who feel inadequate wear them."

"Thank you, Delia," said Carmine, eyes twinkling. "While you're about it, see if you can work out how a stark naked man left no trophy of himself behind in Maggie Drummond's apartment. Maggie told us he wears surgeon's gloves, but she had no answer for his lack of blemishes."

"He touched himself up with greasepaint," Delia said.

"*Greasepaint*?" Nick gaped.

"Think about it," Delia said eagerly. "I think we have to presume that the Dodo has beautiful skin—hardly a blemish. But no human being has absolutely flawless skin. If he's sandy or red, he has freckles. If his skin's olive, he has moles. And think of how many men have pimples on their bums. What flaws the Dodo has, he touches up with greasepaint. The Dodo is vain."

"Good girl!" Carmine said. "Three stars on your wall chart, Delia. We can add greasepaint to his repertoire, along with plucked body hair."

"Won't greasepaint come off?" Nick asked.

"Not very easily, if it's top quality. It may also be that his blemishes are in places that don't come in heavy contact with his victim. He may also wipe off any transferred greasepaint with an organic solvent—alcohol, xylene, chloroform."

"We have enough to develop a protocol for questioning the victims," Carmine said, looking pleased. "Girls, make sure you ask about smells, little scrubs of parts of their skins—you may get a clue as to where the Dodo wears his greasepaint from where he scrubs it off the victims."

Danny Marciano's last day as Captain of Uniforms had come and gone; today, Thursday, September 26, was Fernando Vasquez's first day in the same job. Though as he climbed the stairs Carmine's mind was not on Fernando Vasquez or the uniformed division.

What was he going to do with Corey Marshall? At their meeting this morning, Corey hadn't turned up. Worse than that, Abe was smelling a rat now that the Tinnequa truck stop heist was out of his hair and he could assume a more regular schedule. Like so many of Abe's cases, the gas station holdups were slow to start yielding pointers as to where a canny lieutenant ought to distribute his forces, and Abe was intelligent enough to go with the flow. So while Liam and Tony were out and about prowling, he was using his brain—and had sufficient vacant segments of it to notice something was up between Carmine and Corey.

"I got into the elevator with him yesterday," Abe said as the two of them concluded their business, "and he cut me dead. I wouldn't worry, except that lately he's been saying some hard things about you, Carmine."

"He feels as if the whole world's against him at the moment," Carmine said, knowing he couldn't palm Abe off with platitudes;

Abe was almost preternaturally sensitive to atmosphere in a way that, for instance, seemed to give him second sight about secret compartments. So while he wasn't in the slightest paranoid, he could see through evasions. "First, he inherited Morty while you got Liam and Tony, then Wes Cooper dropped dead—that's more than anyone's fair share of bad luck. And most of his cases haven't worked out well. You know Corey—he takes things to heart, Abe, without always seeing the best way to fix them."

"Say no more," Abe said with a wry smile, and took himself off to his own office.

What do I do about Corey? Carmine wondered, reaching the top of the stairs.

Having entered the Holloman PD straight from high school, Corey had been a cop for seventeen years, and spent the last five of them in Detectives: he knew the ropes. Yet he wasn't making it as a lieutenant. Most of the considerable paperwork was devoted to interviews, simultaneously a cop's nightmare and salvation; out of them came so many leads. But first, they had to be written down. If, for instance, a case went cold, like that triple murder at the railroad station in 1930, the written testimony was all that stood between continued frigidity and a case suddenly on fire. Regarding that old triple murder, pathetically inadequate reportage had stymied Carmine until he found a lead elsewhere. Morty Jones's notes were vestigial, and Corey's not much better. Nor did Corey have Morty's excuse, of working for Larry Pisano for nine years; his boss had been Carmine, a stickler. Now that he thought about it, Abe had done most of the writing up, but he had *seen* Corey put in his two cents' worth. Now he had to wonder if those had been the only occasions. Abe would never have told; that kind of pettiness wasn't in the man.

Corey's notes about the much vaunted Ziggy Taylor heroin shipment were unacceptable—*three lines*! Had it been a genuine tip from a snitch, or Corey manufacturing something more impressive than a series of bag snatchings and burglaries? Drugs had come to be regarded as Corey's turf, for no other reason than that Corey had laid claim to it with an elaborate network of snitches. It was also, Carmine well knew, the hardest area to police—free-wheeling and under the control of the lieutenant. I am being conned, Carmine thought, for no other reason than that Corey knows he can't hack it. He *knows* the lieutenant's job is too big for him, but he can't let it go.

What to do?

Silvestri's office loomed; squaring his shoulders, Carmine entered it.

Fernando Vasquez had come into a uniformed division fizzing with anticipation; no one knew what to make of a Puerto Rican boss after the crafty Commissioner had finally broken the news. The uniforms, stunned, didn't know at whom to be angry, or to whom they could go with their grievances when the time came, as come it would; Judge Thwaites got the blame for this bizarre appointment, and Commissioner John Silvestri said nothing to dispel the misconception. Sergeants like Joey Tasco and Mike Cerutti had filed every one of Captain Vasquez's qualifications in their minds looking for ammunition, the trouble-makers started assembling their troops, and the entire uniformed division was prepared for war.

At interview several months before, Carmine had been a little surprised at Vasquez, though very agreeably. Silvestri, he knew, was absolutely determined to bring in fresh blood of a different kind, for nothing escaped that black eagle's eye in his anything but ivory tower at the top of County Services. And he had set his heart on Fernando Vasquez.

Laying eyes on Vasquez again today only reinforced Carmine's conviction that this man would lose no battles, let alone the war. He looked like every super-efficient army major Carmine had ever seen: on the short side, ramrod straight, solidly built, radiating not so much confidence as determination. His dark face was handsome in a Silvestri mode, with a straight, blade-thin nose, a very firm mouth, and black eyes that looked clear through a man, exposing him for what he was. Not the kind of man you could lie to, and not a sympathetic type either. Get on the wrong side of him, and you'd wish you hadn't. Carmine liked the new captain, and hoped he had sufficient flexibility to sort the sheep from the wolves fairly painlessly. Mind you, Vasquez had a lot riding on this appointment: it was his first virtually autocratic command, and if he couldn't make a go of it, his career would inevitably dwindle.

There were going to be drastic changes, and immediately, Captain Vasquez announced. No more cosy sergeants' room, for one. In future, breaks shorter than meal breaks would be taken in whatever area a uniform inhabited, and meal breaks would be taken in the general staff canteen, or off the premises. There would be no more unofficial tenured-for-life positions. The new practice would be ruthless rotation of all duties; even the most senior cops would serve on the desk, in records, the cages, the cells, patrol, traffic, the myriad jobs uniforms did. Joey Tasco was already off his beloved desk and Mike Cerutti out of patrol, and revolution wasn't even a tiny storm cloud on the horizon; both men had been dumped immediately into equally responsible jobs they had to battle to learn without losing face. Some of the changes were shrewdly aimed at more junior men, suddenly given work they had despaired of ever getting. It was a kind of balancing act: for each old leader knocked down a peg, there was a young leader thrust up a peg. For, having got the job, the new captain had sent for copies of the personnel files, and had every one of his 200-plus men firmly in his mind on the day he started. Yes, he said cheerfully, there would be mistakes.

"Not with the old stagers who need a shake-up, however. It will be with the younger men moving upward. Only the job can reveal whether my guess was right."

After an hour listening to Fernando, Carmine felt exhilarated. What were his problems, compared to those of a man with such a huge group of men under his command?

"What's eating you, Carmine?" Silvestri asked suddenly.

Carmine blinked. "I didn't realize it was obvious, John."

"I've known you a long time. Spit it out."

"Corey Marshall's not making the grade."

"A shame, but no surprise."

"I chose the wrong way to go about settling him and Abe into their new jobs," said Carmine bleakly. "I really thought that after good tutelage in the basics, it was better to let them find their own way. It worked with Abe, but not with Corey."

"In what way?" Fernando asked, sounding interested.

"Organization, including paperwork. Except for Buzz Genovese, the reports from Corey's team are lousy. For instance, there was a drug-related murder of a prostitute behind City Hall a month ago—before Buzz's time. Corey handled it himself, but if I were a cop thirty years in the future trying to make head from tail of it, I couldn't. He hadn't taken enough photos and his description of the scene was pathetic. I chewed him out about it, but he never bothered to augment the report. There are a lot of Corey's cases done like that."

"Does he offer a reason?" Silvestri asked.

"Sure. It's not important enough to merit the time spent on the kind of report he would an interesting crime."

Fernando let out a breath. "Ah! He's an exclusive man."

"Excuse me?"

"Your lieutenant resents pedestrian cases, he wants glamor."

"Yes, exactly," Carmine said, nodding. "He dislikes routine of any kind as well, hence sloppy time sheets and poor rapport with his team members."

"No, he's okay with routine, believe it or not. How long did he work for you?"

"Five years."

"So he's okay with routine, otherwise you wouldn't have put up with him for five minutes, let alone five years. He wants exclusive-looking cases, not chickenshit stuff, and I'd be willing to take a bet he thinks your cases are much better than his. But he hexes himself—who's got his ear?" Fernando asked.

"His wife," said Carmine and Silvestri in unison.

"That makes it tough."

"Welcome to the Holloman Police Department," Silvestri said with a wide grin. "That's the trouble with small cities. No one can keep a secret. Within six months Netty Marciano will have you squared away too, Fernando."

When he stopped laughing, Carmine asked a question. "Is it true that you're going to reorganize the uniformed hierarchy?"

"Given the fullness of time, yes," Fernando said readily. "There are too many sergeants among the uniforms, which leads to confusion—who's senior to whom, et cetera. There's no hurry, Mr. Commissioner. It will happen when I'm ready." He stretched luxuriously. "Detectives is overloaded with chiefs as well. If the Holloman PD has a fault, it's lack of Indians. Your loots basically do the same work as your team members, Carmine. Your division sounds as if whoever structured it thought paperwork a terrible bogey."

"That was Johnny Catano," said Silvestri. "He was chief for years, but never captain. His belief was that each team of three men should be led by a lieutenant, with himself as the most senior. Carmine was made the first captain in 1966, more as a thank you than any change in structure."

"Mr. Commissioner and I are aware there are too many chiefs, but it's not easy to fix," Carmine said. "Tell me more about your changes, Fernando."

"I want three lieutenants, who will be promoted up from the sergeants. I need an executive, Carmine, so as not to fritter away my own time on—paperwork. I've been brought in to get this police department in shape for the stormy times that are coming. Two assassinations within three months are appalling. We can't let it happen again."

"Ah! Hence the rotation of men like Joey Tasco and Mike Cerutti. Under the old tradition, they would have automatically stepped into the new officer slots, though it's years since Joey's been anywhere but the desk, and Mike anywhere but patrol. It's brilliant. By the time you have to appoint your new loots, you'll know who are the best men."

"So I believe."

"You're right about stormy times," Carmine said. "I've had to put

Corey and his team on a case I wish I could take myself—is that an indictment of me, or Corey? Not of me, I contend. The Principal of Taft High found a cache of firearms in the gym. We have them in the cage already, but the kids aren't talking and we don't know why the cache was there. Both Taft and Travis, the two high schools, have disciples of Mohammed el Nesr and his Black Brigade among the pupils, but Mohammed is vigorously denying any BB connection."

"Lieutenant Marshall should do well," Fernando said. "It's potentially high profile and certainly important. What was in the cache?"

"The report will be on your desk, but it's scary. Twenty .45 caliber and ten .22 caliber semi-automatic pistols, as well as spare clips. A lot of people could have died."

Silvestri crossed himself. "As well for us that our high school principals are on the ball. If it's not the Black Brigade responsible, then who is? They're not the kind of arms high school kids have access to, and it's not some parent's collection. It's an arsenal cache, not an array of different guns. Just .45s and .22s, all the same make and model."

"It's their potential as automatics worries me," Carmine said.

"Kick ass, Carmine, including Corey's."

"Actually it's up his alley, if he sticks to procedure. My chief worry is, what's he *not* writing down?"

Carmine took time that Friday to drive around Carew, look at houses belonging to rape victims and Gentleman Walkers. Why did Nick have to conceive such a hot dislike of Helen? He couldn't pass up an opportunity to needle her.

Helen had been right when she called Kurt von Fahlendorf's house the prettiest in the district. It was a pre-Revolutionary saltbox with a pillared porch set in an acre of beautifully gardened grounds; a look around the back revealed a breezeway connecting the main structure to what, in the old days, would have been a kitchen annex. Now it was probably a guest house; someone whose family resided in West Germany would need adequate guest accommodation. The guy definitely had money, Carmine decided, between the address and the wages he must pay his gardener.

Mason Novak, the inorganic chemist whom Mark Sugarman had called the spirit of the Gentleman Walkers, lived in a small cottage on Curzon Close just two doors down from Kurt von Fahlendorf. A man named Dave Feinman lived in a neat little cottage on Spruce Street just around the corner from Curzon Close. He was a widower and was listed as a retired freelance statistician who still took an occasional commission.

No Walker seemed impoverished, and hardly any were married or lived with a woman. Probably because wives were not likely to want their husbands off patrolling for the benefit of other women when they had a woman at home. Privately Carmine thought that the reason for 146 unattached men in Carew lay in its hordes of young women. Carew was rich pickings for one kind of man in particular: a gentleman. And what else were the Gentleman Walkers?

Arnold Hedberg, a professor of history at East Holloman State College, lived his on-the-verge-of-forty existence in the bottom third of a three-family house on Oak Lane that he owned outright, no mortgages. Mike Donahue, a plumber with a thriving business, was young enough at thirty-one to live in a block of apartments he too owned, though he had a mortgage. He had plenty of women tenants under his own roof, but none had been targeted by the Dodo. Gregory Pendleton was a forty-five-year-old assistant district attorney; he occupied the top floor of a six-storey apartment block on State Street that he owned outright. Bill Mitski was another who lived in a private house he owned; he had an accounting business that specialized in taxation. And more, and more ... Few Gentleman Walkers were genuine bachelors. Most seemed to be men who had suffered so badly in the divorce court that they were once bitten, twice shy. Sugarman, Mitski, Novak and von Fahlendorf described themselves as "single"— which didn't say that they weren't towing more wives than Bluebeard. If his divorce was through, a man was legally single.

After due consideration Carmine decided that his entire team, including Helen, should accompany him to the Gentleman Walkers' meeting at six o'clock on the seventh floor of the Susskind Science Tower on Chubb's Science Hill campus. This was Henry Blackburn's brain child, and a good one. The President of Chubb just after the Second World War, Blackburn had sequestered 29 acres of Chubb land on Cedar to the east of the Green, and given it to the Chubb School of Architecture to turn into a science campus. Both the Burke Biology Tower and the Susskind Science Tower hadn't gone up until 1960, but there were plenty of smaller buildings dotted around, as well as the great truncated, grassy pyramid that was the physics bunker, where all work went on way underground in cooled and filtered air. This grassiness was a perpetual frustration as far as the Committee for Nuclear Disarmament was concerned; they had nowhere to paint their CND symbols, so had to content themselves by parading with placards that said BAN THE BOMB.

Having heard the widely disseminated news of Maggie Drummond's rape, all the Gentleman Walkers came to a venue Carmine thought ideal for an observer down on the podium, as every face was visible in the curved tiers of seats.

Delia and Helen sat on the podium flanking Mark Sugarman on one side, with Carmine and Nick on his other side. The Walkers stared hard at them, but hardest at Helen, whom most of them seemed to know. Probably, thought Delia, we don't look much like cops, between two women and a black man.

Mark Sugarman began. "I'm sure you know that Maggie Drummond has been raped, but what you won't know is that six other girls have come forward—I won't name names, but some of you will make educated guesses. You're here tonight to meet the police in charge of the case, answer their questions, and ask questions."

He introduced Carmine and his team, while Carmine's eyes continued to rove across the assembled ranks. Easy to decide who was Mason Novak and who Kurt von Fahlendorf; they sat together in the front row, together with a very elderly fellow of the kind Carmine always called a "Dapper Dan"—a bit like the 1930s movie star, William Powell, even including the little mustache.

Kurt von Fahlendorf was a looker in any language. Six feet tall, a good physique, and the kind of Nordic good looks a fan of Teutonic myth might associate with Siegfried. His crew-cut hair was so fair that it glittered as if made of frost—no fan of the fashionable Beatles-length hair here! His eyes were the same shade of ice-blue as Desdemona's, and his facial features sharply defined, including high cheekbones that made it easy to mentally put a Wehrmacht general's cap on his head. Odd, that he didn't look Gestapo. Maybe that's because I heard Helen on Prussian junkers? To Carmine he seemed cold in a scientific way; the eyes were extremely intelligent, but not involved as were the eyes of Mason Novak next to him. This was a passionate man, about the same height and physique as von Fahlendorf, but coppery in coloring and owning a face most women would probably prefer to the Prussian's; despite his facial irregularities, Mason was powerfully attractive. The heart and soul of the Gentleman Walkers? Yes, he looked all of that. The way he and Kurt sat said that they were very good friends who trusted each other, which said a lot about both men. Probably not the Dodo.

Mark then asked each Walker to rise and give his name; after driving around Carew and looking at records, this was a bonus Carmine hadn't expected. He had imagined that he would be obliged to demand identification, which would have put the meeting on a different, more antagonistic footing. Sugarman was a good guy. Feinman was a youthful sixty-eight, fit and appealing; he probably had no trouble pulling women. Arnold Hedberg looked studious, Mike Donahue looked as if he went rock climbing for pleasure, Gregory Pendleton was darkly handsome, Bill Mitski a "gold" man—hair, eyes, skin.

What all shared was remarkable physical fitness, and none was small in stature, maybe because small men would have found it hard to stay in stride with long-legged men: a man's height was in his legs, not his trunk.

"Our patrols are convivial because we always walk with the same companions," said Dapper Dave.

"Do you roster everybody?" Delia asked.

"Yes, for every second night, come hell or rainstorms," Sugarman answered. "We field twenty-four trios, with two men in reserve. As

Dave says, always the same three men in a trio. They sorted themselves out amicably during the first six weeks, and haven't changed since. So on any one night, we saturate the district. That's why we don't understand how we've missed him."

"You walk at the wrong hour, Mr. Sugarman," Nick said. "He starts earlier than you do, so by the time you're on the streets, he's already inside his premises of choice."

"Yes, but he has to come out!"

"If he were a run-of-the-mill rapist, sir, you're right, he would be leaving while you're patrolling. Unfortunately he makes a night of it," Nick said. "Instead of attacking and leaving at once, he remains—and rapes multiple times—for about five hours. So he's in before you start, and not out until way after you've all gone home."

"We're *useless*!" Mason Novak cried, voice breaking.

"No, sir, you're not," Carmine said in a strong, positive voice. "Look at what you know you've done! While you're on the streets patrolling, the women of Carew know they can walk safely. You've apprehended three potential rapists. And as long as you enjoy the exercise, keep on going. Your activities may not affect the Dodo, but they do make Carew safer nonetheless."

That made them feel better; they began to sit up straighter, murmur among themselves.

"You've saturated the district between six and seven-thirty," Delia said, "which is particularly important now that the days are drawing in. Do women ever approach you to walk with them?"

"The last couple of days, yes," Gregory Pendleton said.

"That's a trend will increase," Carmine said. "Believe me, the women of Carew are grateful for the Gentleman Walkers."

"Is there anything we can do to improve our technique?" Mark Sugarman asked.

"You could split into two shifts, the second one from seven-thirty until nine, but it's not going to affect the Dodo."

"Is that his police tag?" Bill Mitski asked.

"It's what he calls himself. *Didus ineptus.* The old Latin name for the Dodo. We're using the English form, Dodo."

Mason Novak scowled, displeased. "The media will love it."

"True, and that carries some advantages, Mr. Novak. We'll get publicity when we need it because the name is catchy. That may be why the Dodo picked it."

"He'll get publicity too," said Arnold Hedberg.

"If by that you're assuming the Dodo is a publicity hound, sir, you're wrong," Carmine said, fighting to remember his name. "The Dodo has been plying his craft in absolute secrecy for nearly seven months, which I think says loud and clear that he doesn't want publicity. Maggie Drummond was a mistake, Professor Hedberg, but he had no way of knowing how brave she is. He couldn't frighten her into silence. Now the police are aware of his activities, and his earlier victims have found the courage to speak up. Life is getting harder for the Dodo."

"Should we disband?" Mason Novak asked, despondent now.

Carmine looked surprised. "Now why would any cop want to disband a gentlemen's walking club? Haven't I already indicated what a good job the Gentleman Walkers are doing? Let's hear no more about disbanding, please." He's mercurial, Carmine was thinking as he spoke the soothing words; Mason Novak isn't quite stable, but luckily Sugarman knows it, and can handle him.

He spoke aloud again, but in a different voice: this one was stern, minatory, expressive. "I want all of you to remember one thing, sirs. The Dodo is not a peeping Tom, an underwear thief, or a simple stalker. He's the big cat of sexual predators—cunning, awake on all counts, innovative, and *silent*. There's a great deal more to him than meets the eye. The person his colleagues, friends and acquaintances know is usually impossible to associate with rape, torture and murder. I don't mean that you ought to look at everyone you know differently, I mean that sooner or later this extinct bird will crash because of a small mistake. If you think you've found a contradiction in someone that plain doesn't make sense, tell us."

"When may we see Maggie?" Arnold Hedberg asked.

"Not for a while, sir. We're taking her into protective custody. We don't think she's in any real danger," said Delia, who looked like a barber's pole tonight—diagonal red and white stripes, "more that there's no virtue in taking chances."

"The Chubb Medical School has one of the world's top rape psychiatrists in Dr. Liz Meyers," Carmine said as the meeting broke up some time later, "and she'll be running a special clinic for the Dodo's victims."

Kurt waited for Helen to come down from the podium.

"I didn't expect to see you," he said, ranging himself alongside her as the crowd moved toward the door.

"Since I'm a detective in the Captain's own team, why wouldn't I be here?" she asked in a discouraging tone. Now was not the moment for Kurt to assert ownership—in front of all these men, yet! Still, he was a pussycat, no argument there; his manners were impeccable, his kindness something he didn't need to prove to her after eight months of dating, and his genius was allied with a very rare quality: Kurt could get down to a layman's level effortlessly. What she found harder to admit to herself was that she loved Kurt's respect for her. Thus far she hadn't invited him into her bed, and he genuinely liked that. Why? Because he was looking for a wife, not a mistress; every date that ended in a few delicious kisses and strokes without going farther pleased both of them. He thought she was virtuous. She thought his search for a virtuous bride extremely convenient. Fighting off amorous boyfriends was not Helen's favorite pastime.

"You shouldn't associate yourself with this investigation," he said in a scolding voice. "This Dodo might see you."

"Oh, Kurt, honestly! I live in a security apartment, not the top floor of a two-family house," she said, exasperated. "I'm a cop! A professional cop who graduated at the head of the NYPD academy, what's more. The Dodo's not that stupid. Like all predators, he goes after prey he knows he can handle. I swear on your starched-up Lutheran God that he couldn't handle me."

"Do not take the name of God in vain!" he said, horrified.

"Bah, humbug !" she said, laughing at his seriousness.

Just behind them, Carmine and Nick walked with Mason Novak, and behind them were Bill Mitski, Mark Sugarman and Greg Pendleton.

"You were Shirley Constable's friend, right?" Nick asked Mason Novak.

"Yes."

"Have a talk to Delia Carstairs in about five days' time. She'll be able to advise you by then."

"I think Shirley's retreated too far to be saved," Mason said miserably. "She won't even let me be in the same room."

"Too pessimistic, Mr. Novak. We cops have seen Dr. Liz Meyers in action, and she's something else."

Didus ineptus heard that conversation as well as several others, and ground his teeth—but inaudibly. There was no point in belonging to the Walkers if he didn't utilize every asset this association of men owned. He hadn't been among the first to join, but he wasn't among the last either; to sit in the middle was ideal, for the middle was always a clump, a jumble, a crowd.

I should have killed Maggie Drummond, he was thinking. What's the difference between detection thanks to a woman too stupid to keep her mouth shut, and the discovery of her dead body? The body is preferable, but it's too late now. Because I left her alive, the cops know about me and my methods. Protective custody, eh? She's safe. Move ahead, *Didus ineptus!* Maggie Drummond had recognized the name, the taxonomy too. Would the cops deem him an untutored ignoramus, not to know about *Raphus cucullatus*? The wop captain was educated and intelligent, but was he subtle? It would take a very subtle man to unravel all the strands that tied and trussed the Dodo.

In his heart he'd known that Maggie Drummond meant trouble, but he had to have her. Such a glorious neck! Long and slender, curved like a swan's. The only one on his list whom he could bear to throttle first—all others paled. Yes, yes, yes, she was trouble! But if he kept her alive, he could go back for a second visit, do it all again. Work her throat to death then.

Whenever they had met he had actively disliked her, an emotion their conversations had revealed she reciprocated. And he had done battle with his extinct bird: fierce battle. It had won, and now the cops knew all about him. No, not all. Just far too much.

Waving and calling messages, he climbed into his car and drove away down Cedar Street toward Carew.

A disappointed and disgruntled Kurt von Fahlendorf turned into the blind little pocket of Curzon Close and put his black Porsche away in its garage. Having seen for himself that the electric door came fully down, he walked not toward his house but to a spot on the kerb where a gap in the trees permitted a view of the night sky. So wonderful! Yet not, he acknowledged, in the same league as southern hemisphere skies, free from humanity's lights and displaying the whole gauzy panoply of the Milky Way. After he gained his basic science degree it had been a struggle: did he pursue astrophysics, or particle physics?

Tonight he had felt like taking Helen to the Motown Café for a drink and dance, but she hadn't wanted to; this wretched detective's job of hers had eaten into her leisure a little. But if he star-gazed for a few minutes in peace and quiet, he would forgive her. He always did forgive her.

"Star-gazing, Kurt?" a voice asked.

Oh no! The Warburtons.

"Having been underground or indoors all day and evening, the rising winter stars are better than a glass of Moët," he said, keeping the annoyance out of his answer. If the Warburtons thought they were getting under one's skin, they'd never leave.

"No walking tonight?"

"At this hour? No, a Walkers' meeting. Why not join, Robbie?"

Came a whinny of laughter, curiously amplified; Gordie was there too—when was he not?

"Dah-ling!" Gordie exclaimed, coming to stand under the lamp. "So much Teutonic seriousness! Robbie and I would be as much use to the Gentleman Walkers as Dame Margot Fonteyn."

Kurt couldn't help his lip, which lifted in contempt. "You are correct," he said, his voice betraying only the slightest trace of an accent. "I will contact Dame Margot tomorrow."

"No Helen?" Robbie asked maliciously.

"Helen is in the police. Tonight she is on duty."

"Oh, my!" said Gordie. "A face that could launch a thousand ships, blue blood, and a mind in the Holloman sewers."

When they bunched into fists it could be seen that Kurt's hands were big; they bunched. "Retract that, you slimy worm, or I will insert Robbie's head all the way up your arse."

The twins backed away in a scuttle, only half afraid because that was their nature: pull the cat's tail and get out of the way of its claws. "Silly!" Robbie cried. "If your English were more locally colloquial, you'd realize what he said was a clever pun."

"In a pig's eye it was," said Kurt, demonstrating just how colloquial he could get. He turned on his heel and walked off.

The twins watched him go, looking at each other in glee.

"He's so thin-skinned," Robbie said, putting his arm around Gordie's waist and turning toward their house.

"Prussians were never my favorite people," Gordie said.

"How many have you met, sweetest?"

"Kurt."

"They say he's loaded. Oh, and that face! It's to die for. Why didn't Mother Nature give us Kurt's face?"

"Our face is fine, it suits our style," said Gordie. "We have *plasticity*! Kurt has the face of a marble statue."

"True, true. They say his papa has an enormous factory."

"Which little bird twittered that?" Gordie demanded.

"Babs, the waitress in Joey's diner."

"Is there anything Babs doesn't know?"

"The identity of the fellow WRHM and HN are calling the Dodo."

"A putrid fowl." Gordie shuddered.

They walked together through their red-lacquered front door and divested themselves of their jackets: a dark grey one for Robbie and an ecru one for Gordie.

"Dark—light—dark—light—dark—light," Gordie chanted, skipping nimbly from a black tile to a white one on the tesselated floor, a caricature of an over-sized child.

"Stick to the white," Robbie said, leaping on a black tile.

"Light!" said Gordie, on a white tile.

"Dark!"

"Light!"

"Dark!"

"Light!"

Which finished their dance; they had reached the living room doorway and encountered a geometrically crazed carpet in black and white. Laughing, they flopped into easy chairs, Gordie in a white one and Robbie in a black one, breathless and happy.

"Do you think it's time we told Aunt Amanda where we are?" Gordie asked.

"Patience, twinnie-winnie, patience."

"Our clown and check will go to San Diego, and you know we're renting the house to strangers. What if they pinch our present?"

But Robbie's mind still dwelled on their neighbor.

"There was a professor named Kurt

Who wore a plutonium shirt;

A mushroom-shaped cloud

Did Kurt really proud

When the garment proved far from inert."

"Very good, Robbie! I love your limericks."

"The Dodo's victims do have one thing in common," Delia said the following Monday, the last day of the month.

"Expound," said Carmine.

"None of the seven has what I'd call a menial job, though there are several thousand Carew women working at menial jobs. Shirley is an archivist—extremely thin on the ground. Mercedes is a dress designer, but not a struggling would-be. She's the chief designer of that famous boutique line, "Cobweb". Leonie's a brilliant mathematician, working at Chubb and surrounded by men who regard her as a freak. Esther was on a fast track at East Holloman State College teaching the more esoteric aspects of commerce— apparently her teaching abilities were outstanding. Marilyn is the one I'd call unlucky, in that she should have been in Alberta working the digs there—she came home unexpectedly. No, the Dodo didn't send her any trick messages, the summons was genuine. Natalie buys women's clothes from factories for Huxley's department stores. She has an unerring instinct for what women are going to want to wear, so Huxley's are feeling her absence severely. And Maggie, as we all know, is a bird physiologist at Chubb, no mean feat," Delia said.

"That's an impressive list, even for 1968," said Helen, taking over from Delia. "It suggests to us that the Dodo is well aware what his victims do professionally. He's an intellectual snob, and we're guessing that file clerks, waitresses and cleaning ladies are safe. Also undergraduates. All his victims so far have been old enough to acquire at least one degree."

"How does he find out their professions?" Carmine asked with a frown. "There's a list of Gentleman Walkers and their occupations, but the most Sugarman does with women is to write them down on his list for a party. Helen, your job is to check how many of them are on Sugarman's party lists. We can't hope for that from Mason Novak, he's too disorganized."

"He must be organized at work," Delia said.

"You're right, he must be. However, the Walkers have no idea from seeing a girl out and about in Carew whether she's a doctor or a file clerk. The Dodo must find out the hard way, by multiple break-ins. A woman's living space will tell him for sure. But it adds to the danger of discovery."

"File clerks don't carry heavy briefcases," said Nick.

"No, I believe the Dodo has access to records of some sort. What throws me off are the non-academics," Delia said. "Two of them, a dress designer and a dress buyer. Both women's wear, yet not really related. How does one find out about them?"

"Walk up to them in a shop and ask, with a very charming smile?" Nick said, half joking.

"He's a snob in all kinds of ways," said Helen, tired of Nick. "He doesn't use a foreign object during his rapes, except maybe his fist, but that's a part of his body. It interests Delia and me that the most strenuous tussles he had with his victims were *before* he put socks on their feet and cut their nails. We think he's taking precautions for later in the night, when he might flag a little himself. Those long, huge erections must take a heavy toll. I mean, sex is a pleasure, but it's also something you have to work at, especially the man."

"Has anything further turned up about the books? It seems weird to me that the victims don't remember a title," Carmine said.

What a pertinent way to change the subject, Helen thought. The boss could see my frankness made Nick uneasy, so Carmine to the rescue of a fellow man.

Delia answered. "The smallest library held three hundred books, and all of them contained at least a hundred novels. Most of the novels were old and hadn't been read in years. All the victims could have named a purloined textbook, but an old novel? They knew one had gone because the shelf held a gap where no gap had been before."

"That says it wasn't a beloved novel, like *Little Women*—its absence would have been noticed," said Helen.

Carmine caught the gleam in Nick's eye and got in first. "I estimate that we have a little over two weeks before the Dodo rapes again. If, that is, he sticks to his three-week cycle."

Helen jumped, suddenly very excited. "Captain, what if I set myself up as a lure? He might go for it."

The shake of Carmine's head was emphatic. "You're not thinking straight, Helen. This guy doesn't choose at random, he's working from a list he's already drawn up. It's not impossible that you're on it, but nothing indicates that. He'll know you're a cop, and I would have said that's not a profession he'd deem worthy of his attention." He grinned. "Sorry, but it's a fact."

She subsided. "Yes, Captain, you're right."

"If the Dodo also happens to be a Gentleman Walker," Delia said, looking businesslike, "then he can't be rostered for walking on an attack night. So I took all Mark Sugarman's rosters and went through them." She grimaced, revealing lipstick on her teeth. "No correlations, Carmine—not a sausage. I could have skimmed through the lot in less than thirty minutes if Mason Novak didn't do a good half of them—*untidy*! But there's nothing to find, except that I suppose nothing is something."

Carmine grinned, black brows flying high. "Who's a nothing that could be a something, Deels?"

"Sixty-one names that never occur on a Dodo night. However, some are bigger somethings than others," said Delia, smiling. "I mention Mark Sugarman and his two companions—er … Arnold Hedberg and Gregory Pendleton, and Kurt von Fahlendorf and his two—Dapper Dave Feinman and Bill Mitski. The list is on your table. Would you like me to try fishing for alibis?"

"For the moment, no. It's negative evidence at best, and the only guys who'll be able to supply alibis are the diarists. Work with the victims, you have their trust."

"What about me?" Helen demanded.

"Your schedule says you're with Lieutenant Goldberg and the armed holdups," said Carmine, sounding adamant. "It's suddenly gone state wide and is being worked from Hartford with Lieutenant Goldberg in command, so it will be invaluable experience."

"What about you?" Helen asked, then bit her lip: it had come out far too insolently. Oh, damn cops and their armed services style protocols! Why couldn't a person ask?

No change in Carmine's expression occurred, though Nick looked annoyed. "I have the Big Three to worry about," he said levelly. "Sugarman, Novak and von Fahlendorf."

"Oh, Kurt's all right," Helen said blithely.

"No one is all right, Miss MacIntosh, until *I* say so."

"Ow!" Nick exclaimed, laughing. Serves you right, you pushy little bitch, he thought.

CHAPTER II

The Glass Teddy Bear gift shop actually showed to best advantage after the Busquash Mall had closed its ornate doors and before the timer turned the shop's interior lights out. No customers disturbed the glitter from arrays of exquisite wine or water glasses, the sparkle from cut crystal vases, the gleam from transparent plates, cups, saucers, ornaments and paperweights. It was a cavern filled with pools and points of light arising out of mysterious shadows, an effect enhanced because every background thing was painted black, or covered in black.

All else paled in contrast to the glass teddy bear himself. He sat in the window on a black velvet box, all alone, glowing like a phosphorescent sea creature. His plump body, legs, arms and head were colorless, made of glass so flawless it held not a single air bubble. His legs stretched out in front of his body, the pads on the bottom of his feet a clear yet satiny ice-blue, each surrounded by stitches in glass thread of a darker blue. One arm was slightly forward of the body; the other was extended in mute appeal. Each had an ice-blue, satiny paw pad. The little round ears were lined with the same glass as his pads, and his face, mouth fixed in a joyous smile, bore two huge, starry eyes of a deeper blue. Though of itself the bulk of his glass had no color, this genuine work of art picked up the blue of paw pads, ears and eyes, and shimmered as if an invisible palest blue flame rendered him incandescent.

Most amazing of all was his gigantic size: about the same as a hefty three-to-four-year-old child.

Though to some extent the shop was still illuminated from the Mall, the lights inside the shop had been out for five hours when the unfaltering forest of pinpoints and pools shivered, some snuffed out, some diminished, others unaffected. The door from the service corridor into the shop's back room had opened, and remained open as a dark form passed back and forth through it, lugging plastic trash bags. This done, the door closed and a battery-powered lamp came on. From its position atop a filing cabinet, its rays lit up the curtain of glass beads, a frozen waterfall, that barred entrance to the shop itself. The dark form gathered the curtain up and tied all its fabulous ropes against the jamb. A trash bag disappeared into the shop, and came the noises of cans colliding, bottles clinking, boxes and cartons thudding, wet squelches from cascading organic matter. The bag emptied, the form went back to fetch another bag, empty it in a different place. Ten bags in all—more than enough.

The smell of decay was rising as the dark form moved then to the front of the shop, where the glass teddy bear sat on his black velvet box and the night lights from outside made him glow with a dimmer fire. *Whoosh!* A cloud of dust and debris flew from the smaller bag that the dark form held out and flapped; the glass teddy bear's luminescence was extinguished under a pall of sticky, grimy vacuum cleaner residue.

There were several more whooshes in other parts of the shop, then the dark form released the bead curtain, which fell into place with a series of chimes that plastic beads could never produce. A knife came out to slash the strands holding the beads; it hovered, undecided, then the dark form snapped the knife closed, and the bead curtain was safe.

The Vandal moved into the back room, collected his flashlight from the filing cabinet, and let himself out. A good exercise ... That idiot Charlie the Mall owners employed as their sole night watchman was on his coffee break, regular as the clock he consulted. How come such fools had the money and power to erect something as fine as this shopping mall, then didn't see the virtue of good night security? They asked for everything they got. And, come to think of it, he could do with a second visit tonight.

From the Glass Teddy Bear he went down to the Third Holloman Bank, whose premises, inside a very up-market mall, boasted little in the way of precautions like time-locked vaults—no need, in a venue where the clients were after cash or validation of checks. He disarmed the device in the service hall, let himself in, and went straight for the cage wherein Percy Lambert kept his cash ready for the morning. Who would ever have thought that these keys would prove so handy? People were so *careless*! The fifth key fitted the lock, the door opened; the Vandal strolled in and helped himself to $50,000 sitting on the table in preparation for apportioning to the tellers' drawers in the morning.

By four a.m. it was all over; the Vandal drove off just as Charlie was starting his rounds. He wouldn't even notice, thought the Vandal, taking a bet with himself. It would take Miss Amanda

Warburton and Mr. Percy Lambert to raise the alarm when they came in at eight.

Amanda Warburton smelled the damage before she set eyes on it, so stunned that she dropped the leashes in her left hand and ran into the shop feeling as if someone had cut off air to her lungs. Gasping, choking, she took in the enormity of this crime, and found herself unable to scream. Instead, she used the phone in her back room to call the Mall manager, Hank Murray. Because she was fifteen minutes earlier than Percy Lambert on this first day of October, Hank came racing with his bottle of emergency brandy and some paper cups oblivious to how bad his morning was going to get, intent only on Amanda.

"Oh, Miss Warburton, this is terrible!" he cried after one horrified glance into the shop. "Here, sip this, it will make you feel better. It's only brandy—the best thing for shocks."

He was a presentable man in his early forties whom Amanda had liked on her few meetings with him, so she sipped obediently and did indeed feel some strength flow into her.

"What did he do to the glass teddy bear?" she asked, tears coursing down her face. "Tell me the worst, please!"

Having assured himself that she wasn't going to pass out, he toured the glass shop, more astonished now than horrified—what was this guy about, for God's sake?

"Everything's covered in filth, Miss Warburton," he said, returning, "but it looks as if nothing's been damaged—not even a chip. The glass teddy bear is fine underneath his dirt."

"Then why—? What—?"

"I don't know, except that it's vandalism," Hank Murray said in a soothing voice. "Because your stock is glass, it won't suffer once it's been properly cleaned. I know a firm will guarantee to clean up your shop as if none of this ever happened, honest. All we have to do is catch the Vandal, who couldn't have done this if we had better night security." He squared his shoulders. "However, that's my business, not yours. Do I have your permission to get things rolling, Miss Warburton?"

"Yes, of course, Mr. Murray."

"Call me Hank. Are you insured for this kind of thing?"

"Yes."

"Then it really isn't a problem. Have you got a card for your insurance agent? I'll have to see him too, and he'll have to see this." He gave a rueful laugh. "I guess I sound cold-blooded, but I have to get things started for you, especially if Mall rumor says aright."

"What does it say?"

"That you're alone in the world."

"Except for a pair of very unsatisfactory nephews, rumor is true," she said.

"Are the nephews hereabouts? May I call them?"

"No, they're in San Diego. I'd rather you called Marcia Boyce— she's my friend and lives next door to me."

His hazel eyes showed concern for her, his attractive face very serious. "I'm afraid I have to call the police. Too much malice for simple vandalism, and I don't understand why, if the culprits are simple vandals, they didn't break anything."

"Nor do I, frankly. Yes, I have to notify the police."

Her phone rang; Hank answered it, growing stiffer by the second. When he put the receiver down he stared at Amanda in a new horror.

"You wouldn't read about it, the Third Holloman Bank has been robbed. Looks like the Vandal was more than a vandal. Will you be all right until I can get Miss—Mrs.—Boyce here?"

"Yes, Hank, I'm over the worst. You go. I'll call Marcia—she's Miss Boyce—myself. I'm okay, truly."

Only when Hank was gone did Winston make his presence felt with a long, highly displeased meow.

Amanda gasped. "Winston! And Frankie! Where are you?"

A growl in what sounded like a very big cat's throat took Amanda's eyes to a filing cabinet tucked in a corner; it didn't meet the wall, which was on an angle, and two pairs of eyes stared at her reproachfully. But they wouldn't come when she called—they were as upset as she was, obviously—so she had to go to them and remove their body harnesses; they walked on leashes with her to and from the car every day she opened her shop.

Winston, which had paws the size of a lion's, it seemed to people meeting it, promptly took its twenty pounds to the top of the filing cabinet and hunched there, a magnificent marmalade in color, with unusual green eyes. The dog, which most people judged a pit bull and steered a wide berth around, was black-and-white, its ugly white head adorned with a black ring around its right eye. In actual fact Frankie was a gentle soul utterly dominated by the cat, to which it was passionately attached. Both animals were males, and both castrated.

At the end of a ten-minute sulk, the cat gave the dog its permission to go to Amanda, who clutched at its muscular back as if to a lifeline. What had happened? Who hated her enough to do this? The stench turned her stomach, but she couldn't leave until the police came, and even then, she needed Marcia to drive her home, not trusting her own ability.

*　　*　　*

Two patrol cops arrived first: Sergeant Ike Masotti and his long-time partner, Muley Evans. Though Amanda couldn't know it, she had drawn the best team on patrol in the Holloman PD.

"Weird," said Ike to Muley after a cruise through the shop, "really weird, Muley. It's not kids."

"Nope," said Muley, who knew his place: agree with Ike.

"You got any enemies, Miss Warburton?" Ike asked.

"None that I know of, officer."

"It might be the glass. Some guys are kinky enough to see a shop full of glass as their ma's cabinet full of best glass and china, and maybe they hate their ma, but they're too afraid of her to break anything—just dirty it," said Ike.

"Right," said Muley.

"Only thing is, how does it fit in with the bank burglary?" Ike asked Muley. "Fifty thousand smackeroonies! He just picked 'em up and left. Locked the place behind him. Reactivated the alarm. Want to know what I think, Muley?"

"Yep."

"Two different crims. The guy that did this and the guy that did the bank are not the same guy."

"Uhuh," said Muley noncommittally.

"I like your animals, Miss Warburton," said Ike, approaching Frankie fearlessly. "What a great dog!" He pulled its ears and it groaned in ecstasy. He examined its collar and disc. "Your name Frankie, huh? Who's Mister Huffy over there?"

"Winston," said Amanda, who liked Ike Masotti a lot.

At which moment Sergeant Morty Jones came through the back door, reeking so strongly of booze that the two patrolmen exchanged a significant glance.

"Taft High kids," he said after inspecting the premises.

"You're wrong, Morty," Ike said. "A bunch of kids go to all this trouble? Never happen. They'd get their fun breaking glass, not covering stuff in filth. Did anyone else get vandalized?"

"Not according to Mr. Murray," said Amanda.

"Then this is a personal vendetta, right, Muley?"

"Right."

"In your ear it is, Ike," said the detective, turning for the back door and freedom; the smell didn't help his nausea.

"I'll write my report as I see it, Morty."

"You can write it as the devil sees it, Ike. Mine is going to say Taft High kids." On that note, and with a curt nod to Amanda, witness to the entire conversation, Morty Jones left.

"The detective goes, we gotta go, Miss Warburton. Sorry," said Ike in genuine regret. "You gonna be okay here alone?"

"Yes, I'm fine."

"That's one real nice lady," Ike said in the service corridor. "Why did we have to get Morty Jones? That was fresh booze on his breath, Muley, not last night's. If the Commissioner gets a sniff, Morty's out, and Ava wouldn't like that. I heard she's making sheep's eyes at young Joey Donaldson in Communications."

"I heard that too," said Muley, and offered a comment of his own. "We ain't snitches, Ike, but one day someone's gonna tell the Commissioner Morty's drinking on the job."

"The worst of it is that I remember Morty before he went upstairs to Detectives and Larry Pisano. He was a good cop," said Ike. "It's

Ava. How could she be stupid enough to tell Morty he didn't father his kids? I mean, he *loves* them! Who fathered them isn't the point. They're Morty's kids. I curse that woman, I curse her!"

"May she rot in hell," said Muley.

Thus Carmine didn't get a full report on the vandalism at the Glass Teddy Bear or the theft of $50,000 from the Third Holloman Bank. Despite the demands of the Dodo, both cases would have interested him.

Steaming, Helen MacIntosh went off to Hartford on that same Tuesday, October 1, in time to join Abe, Liam and Tony for breakfast in their motel; this was one case would not permit a commute, Abe announced, which didn't please the owner of a Lamborghini. Perhaps, she thought, speeding up I-91, I shouldn't have called Lieutenant Abe Goldberg ahead of time to ask for tips and a detailed description of what to expect, but how many women will there be? According to Goldberg, just me. He was curt and unforthcoming— I'd find out when I got to Hartford, why waste his time? He treated me like shit, the scrawny little guy—how did he ever make it into the cops at his size? Well, Lieutenant Abraham Goldberg, you are about to find out that no one from the wrong side of the tracks—or the right side!—treats a MacIntosh like shit. I will make your life such a misery that you'll send me back to Holloman, where I can do the job I'm suited to do—catch the Dodo.

Marcia Boyce drove Amanda Warburton home, Frankie and Winston, on their leashes, sitting royally in the back seat of Marcia's

Cadillac. Luckily Marcia knew Amanda's pets quite well enough to know that there would be no "accidents" en route.

Amanda and Marcia loved their condominiums, which were on the eighth floor just below the penthouse, and filled it entirely. They had bought off the plans, which had enabled them to custom-design their kitchens and bathrooms, an en suite bathroom for each bedroom, plus a guest toilet in the foyer. What luxury! What vindication!

As if all that were not enough, no sooner was the block of soaring glass up and its occupants moved in than the residents of Busquash, horrified at how it altered the antique patina of their world, fired the town Elders and put an iron-clad ordinance on the books that forbade the erection of anything over two storeys or modern in appearance. As the condos were dream apartments, they zoomed in value at once. What had cost a hundred thousand was now worth a million—and rising.

Marcia fixed a pot of English Breakfast tea and laced it liberally with cognac.

"Who would want to do such an awful thing?" Amanda asked, sipping with care: it was hot.

"Not high school kids," said Marcia emphatically. "Drink up, honey. That detective must have been a dope."

"You really don't think it was high school kids?"

"Too malicious in a plotty, planny way, if you get my meaning. Hank Murray told me that nobody else's shop was touched, and that baffled him. Everyone, even the dope of a detective, thinks the bank robber is a different person." Marcia sipped her aromatic tea with enjoyment. "Face it, honey, Hank and I both think this was personal, aimed at the Glass Teddy Bear and you."

Her bright eyes surveyed her friend affectionately—such a doll,

Amanda! Pretty too, with her streaky blonde hair and her big blue eyes. Why had she never married? Her figure was good, and her legs tolerated the current above-the-knee hemlines better than most women her age. Marcia herself was a childless divorcee in comfortable circumstances, but, she admitted, her chances of a husband to keep her company in old age weren't half as good as Amanda's. Marcia was plain, dark, and distinctly overweight.

"A lot of my pleasure is gone," Amanda said desolately.

"Huh?"

"The Glass Teddy Bear is all my dreams come true, but after this I feel—oh, I don't know—kind of violated. I sank all my available money into the Busquash Mall business—the shop and the mail orders. After all, I did well in my shop downtown, even though I couldn't display my better lines," said Amanda. "I leased off the plans at Busquash, and I was right—I've done amazingly well. Now—this! Why my shop? Why me? Some of the Mall antique stores leave my prices for dead."

Marcia listened, intrigued. Though they had been friends and neighbors since taking up residence in Busquash over two years ago, today was Amanda's first confidence. So she'd had a shop downtown? Where? My own business has been downtown for ten years, but I never remember a glass shop ... Yes! In the arcade that ran through to Macy's. Waterford, Stuart, Bohemian, Swedish glass and crystal, wine glasses, tumblers and vases, and a good price for top quality things.

"Do you have family, Amanda?" she asked, emboldened.

For a moment Amanda's face went expressionless, then she smiled and answered, her tongue loosened by the brandy. "Yes. Robert and Gordon, my late brother's boys. They live in San Diego." She frowned. "Not very satisfactory—they have such delusions of grandeur they remind me of patients in a book on psychiatry I read once." She visibly shuddered. "And the—the *affectations*! I dislike them."

"Oh, poor Amanda!" Marcia cried, moved. "It must be lonely for you." She looked brisk, smiled brilliantly. "Cheer up, my dear. On Friday you and Frankie and Winston are going to return to the Glass Teddy Bear to find it exactly as it was—a crystal cave of beauty and delight."

At the mention of their names the dog and cat stirred from their vigilant doze, but when the conversation didn't continue about them, they snoozed again. It had been an upsetting day, and the only cure was sleep.

Amanda Warburton smiled, an enormous effort. "I hope you're right," she said doubtfully. "The smell! The filth!"

Time to introduce another subject. "Hank Murray is smitten with you," Marcia said.

But that didn't have the desired effect. Instead of going coy or bridling with pleasure, Amanda looked grim. "I hope not," she said after a pause. "He hardly knows me. You're mistaking kindness for interest, Marcia—at least, I hope so. I'm not searching for a boyfriend, let alone a husband."

"Then you damned well should be!" Marcia said, astonished. "I wasn't implying love or marriage, Amanda. I just meant that Hank's a nice guy who'd like to know you better. Wouldn't it be fun to have dinner with a good-looking man at Sea Foam instead of with me at the Lobster Pot?"

"No, it wouldn't be fun!" Amanda snapped.

"But—"

"Leave it, Marcia! Just leave it!"

Marcia left it.

*   *   *

Expression flinty, Carmine stared at an unrepentant Helen MacIntosh as she sat on the opposite side of the kitchen table he preferred to a desk, with its drawers, knee-holes, modesty panels and nice wood tops. Who could ruin Formica, already?

Her pose was slightly insolent, slewed sideways on the old kitchen chair, legs crossed nonchalantly, one foot flopping up and down in its Ferragamo flattie, both legs on full display because she was in the shortest miniskirt Carmine had ever seen. A mane of hair flowed loose down her back, she was wearing enough make-up to put Delia in the shade, and her décolletage was—low. All told, his years of police training told him, she was flaunting about $3,000 in clothes, for nothing had been bought off the rack.

"What made you decide to join Lieutenant Goldberg in Hartford wearing exactly the kind of apparel I told you was inappropriate?" he asked, a hard edge to his voice.

"With about seventy cops in my immediate vicinity, *sir*, I figured I wouldn't need sensible shoes to chase any fugitives, or worry about what the public thought of my miniskirts," she said lightly, foot still jiggling.

"You were more than Lieutenant Goldberg's assistant, Miss MacIntosh. You were in Hartford representing the Holloman Police Department, on duty as a trainee detective, the first in a brand new program every police department in the state is watching. I did not send you to Hartford to model for Mary Quant, as you well know. Instead of looking professional and as unobtrusive as possible, you tricked yourself out as if your function in the Holloman PD is to tease cock, if not service it." Carmine's voice didn't change. "Who were you impressing? Or rather, to whom were you determined to give a wrong impression?"

Her cheeks were red, her mouth tight. "They stared at me like a dummy in a shop window. I knew they would no matter what I wore, so I decided to give them a thrill."

"And when are you going to learn that being a cop isn't about yourself, Miss MacIntosh? Did you stop to think what his peers and superiors would think of Lieutenant Goldberg, towing a sex kitten as his personal assistant? Under ordinary circumstances, Miss MacIntosh, there's only one reason a forty-year-old man tows a sex kitten as an assistant. If you'd been in Detectives longer, I would have let Lieutenant Goldberg figuratively strip you in front of seventy men, but you and he aren't acquainted yet. After this, you never will be. I hear tell that he simply looked you up and down, and told you to go home to Holloman. With, after you left, an apology on your behalf." The amber eyes blazed. "What a fool you are, Miss MacIntosh! I handed you an ideal opportunity to get to know the best detective in the division, and you screwed it up because of your own ambition. No wonder the NYPD did nothing with you. How long did it take them to realize that mentally you're on a par with any spoiled fourth grader? You're puerile! Asinine!"

Her hands were trembling, she had swung to sit upright on the chair, and the beautiful face was rigid—with rage or with mortification was impossible to tell.

"Am I to take it that you didn't understand the valid and necessary reasons for wearing sensible clothing on duty? That you have some scrambled feminist idea that I've put you down to feed my own masculine ego?"

"No, Captain, I got the message the first time," she said, eyes sparkling with unshed tears. "It's for my own safety and protection, I understand that."

"You will apologize to Lieutenant Goldberg. In writing, and in person."

"I'll be back there properly clothed in an hour."

"No, you won't. Lieutenant Goldberg doesn't trust you. You get your wish, Miss MacIntosh, and stay in Holloman. But not with the Dodo. Nick Jefferson will go to Hartford."

Her skin lost color, she gasped. "Sir, please!"

"No. The subject is closed, and we won't discuss it again."

"As you wish." Her shoulders straightened.

"However, I have a question to ask that I didn't when I interviewed you. What drives you to a police career?"

She had risen to her feet. "I avoided that at interview, sir, I know. I'm attracted to the armed services, but the very idea of trying West Point or Annapolis—brr!" She shuddered. "They really are institutions for men, and I'm not a committed enough feminist to buck those two fortresses. Besides, I have a funny feeling that being a cop is a more interesting life. I like working for solutions, I guess."

"I see." He stood, a powerful man whose muscular bulk diminished his nearly six feet of height. The face turned to look at his wayward trainee was both broad and angular, its nose imperious and its mouth's natural sensuousness disciplined into firmness. His eyes, as gold as brown, were widely opened and well apart, and had a fearless quality.

Why did I try that stupid stunt? Helen asked herself as she left Captain Delmonico's office. For the same reason, she decided as she climbed the stairs, that a little kid pokes a sleeping tiger with a stick.

*   *   *

"Very true," said Delia, in a frightful combination of acid-yellow and mustard-yellow with bright blue bows. "But in future, dear, do remember that poking a sleeping tiger is bound to see you squashed flat under one paw."

"Can't I help you with the Dodo?" Helen begged.

"No, dear, I have no desire to be pulp under the tiger's paw. You're with Paul Bachman in forensics for many days to come." Delia sighed wistfully. "I scraped into Detectives through the back door—a head for plans, lists, paperwork by the ton—and it didn't hurt to be the niece of the Commissioner, whose secretary I was. Before that, I had ten years with the NYPD in documentary fraud and anything else involving paper. But look at you! It really is a splendid program they've worked out for you. Everything we had to pick up on the job, so to speak, you're being properly taught. So don't you let my Uncle John down! If you do, you'll feel the size of my paw."

"The cleaners did a wonderful job," said Hank Murray as he emerged from the service elevator with Amanda Warburton on Friday, October 4. "You'll be able to open for the weekend." He produced his own keys and opened her back door, one of many on a broad service hall.

As they walked inside he sniffed, smiled. "Smell, Miss Warburton. Sweet yet a tad herby—I hope that you don't mind my picking the fragrance on your behalf. You'd never know that there was ever rotting garbage in here, would you?"

"No," said Amanda, sagging in relief.

"Come on, take a look at the shop," Hank encouraged as he steered her toward the shimmering curtain of glass beads. Then he stopped, so suddenly that Amanda cannoned into him.

"Dear God!"

She couldn't help herself. Amanda shoved the Mall manager aside and ran into the shop.

Almost every item had been moved to form a gigantic mound where her sole counter had been; it had been pushed, complete with cash register, against the only free wall, where her array of Lalique and Murano picture frames had hung. They too were in the huge heap displaying a corner here, an edge there. But the "yard" for drinking a yard of beer was still in place on the same wall high above, and below it, the entirely ornamental "half yard" of thick, heavy crystal was intact.

Tears pouring down her face, Amanda rushed to the front window to check on the glass teddy bear himself. Yes, yes, he was there, unshifted, unmarked, sitting on his black velvet box and apparently ignored by the Vandal.

What kind spirit had prompted her to leave her animals at home this morning? Fishing up her sleeve to find a handkerchief, Amanda Warburton knew in her heart of hearts that she had expected more trouble today; the dust and dirt of the previous assault had seemed— yes, definitely—unfinished. Today was a logical sequel to the first attack.

Having notified the police, checked that no other stores had been vandalized, and learned that the three banks the Busquash Mall harbored were all okay, Hank was now kneeling alongside the pile of glass, not touching anything, but eyes busy.

"Weird!" he exclaimed. "Miss Warburton—Amanda!—it is weird. As far as I can tell, nothing's been broken—or cracked—or chipped. Look for yourself. If I get the same cleaners back to pick up everything wearing gloves, you shouldn't lose much if anything. No, no, don't cry, please." He hugged her, trying to convey comfort and sympathy. Miss Warburton was a lamb, she didn't deserve this malice, this—this *cruelty*.

By the time Ike Masotti and Muley Evans arrived, Amanda was in the back room, with Hank Murray persuading her to have a little of his emergency brandy.

"I have to notify Detectives," Ike said on taking a look at the mound of glass. "May I use your phone, Miss Warburton? The air waves are full of flapping ears shouldn't be listening."

"Please do."

"There's definitely something weird going on," Ike said to the phone. "You'd better come take a look-see, Morty. This is definitely not high school kids."

They waited over an hour.

He couldn't help himself; he'd had to call in to the Shamrock Bar for a quick snort en route to the Busquash Mall and that persnickety bastard, Ike Masotti.

Nothing was improving, for all that Delia Carstairs kept telling him things had. She'd found him a great housekeeper, but he didn't want a housekeeper, and nor did the kids—*his* kids. They all wanted Ava back. Bobby and Gidget, the lights of his life, not his? It was typical Ava, that's all, to throw that one in. Only why had he decked her? So many years of knowing she played around—what was so different about that Saturday night? Except that he snapped at the taunt about the kids.

Now the kids cried all the time, he cried whenever he could sneak to the cells … He cried into his Jameson's too, and had to clean up in the Shamrock bathroom before he could nerve himself to do whatever Ike Masotti said at the Busquash Mall. His head was spinning, he had to stop and park for a few minutes to get some sanity back … Oh, Ava, Ava! Bobby and Gidget are *mine*!

When he shuffled into the Glass Teddy Bear the two patrolmen exchanged glances—the smell of liquor was overpowering, worse than it had been last Tuesday.

Morty gave the mountain of glass a cursory inspection and returned to the back room. "High school kids," he said, shrugging. And, to the cops, "You're wasting my time, guys."

"Less time to elbow-bend, you mean, Morty?" asked Muley when Ike wouldn't. No one made undeserved cracks at Ike.

"It's high school kids," Morty maintained.

"It is not high school kids!" Ike yelled, exasperated. "This is nasty, Sergeant Jones. It feels wrong. No way that high school kids would pile up all that glass without breaking some, and none's broken—not even chipped. This stinks of vendetta."

"I don't care what it stinks of, Ike. No real damage has been done, there's not enough here to put anyone up on charges." Morty licked suddenly dry lips. "I gotta go."

Blinking, Amanda sat listening as if in a drugged haze; she was conscious that Hank's hand on her shoulder had tightened its grip, and understood that the detective's indifference had angered him.

As Sergeant Morty Jones disappeared, she reached up to pat the hand. Thwarted, Ike and Muley followed Morty out, gazing at her in mute apology.

"Would you mind calling the cleaning firm for me, Hank?" she asked. "I'll have to stay to supervise them—they won't remember whereabouts things belong, now I tore the plan up." She gave a small squeak of distress. "To think I had to draw a plan even once! But to think I'd need it twice!"

"First, your insurance agent," Hank said firmly. "That lazy so-and-so of a detective didn't take any photographs, and someone should. If anything is damaged, you'll need proof." He pressed Amanda's fingers gently. "From now on the Mall is going to be protected by a professional security company, something I've been saying to deaf ears since the Mall opened. But no, the owners didn't want to spend the money. Now, they have no choice. A bank robbery and a vendetta against a tenant with fragile stock. I mean, what if the Vandal had decided to target Quattrocento, down on the first floor? You can clean the filth off glass, but not off a fourteenth century credenza."

"Who would do this?" Amanda asked for the tenth time, unable to get past her own violation.

"I have no idea." Hank paused, then said, very delicately, "It's going to be a very long day for you, and you shouldn't be alone this evening, Amanda. May I take you to dinner?"

"Thank you, I'd like that," said Amanda, sounding surprised.

The dinner with Hank Murray at the Lobster Pot went so well that the next evening, Saturday, he took her to Sea Foam.

Though she admitted that Hank was an ideal escort for a forty-year-old spinster, she wasn't about to let him put his shoes under her bed. An occasional man had enjoyed that privilege, but only one had mattered, and he was long dead. If her heartache was permanent, that was her business. Financially she was comfortable; she didn't need a meal ticket. Though, she couldn't say why, she had a feeling that Hank wasn't nearly as well off as the manager of a famous shopping mall ought to be. He paid the Sea Foam prices without a blink, yet when he fished for his wallet at the Lobster Pot, Amanda fancied that he was relieved she had indicated she preferred classy diners to up-market traps for gastronomes.

She had acquired Frankie and Winston, now three years old, as a deliberate ploy; with two cute animals in her window, her shop was visited by everyone who came to the Busquash Mall. No one else was allowed to have a pet; that Amanda was, was due to a clever sales pitch she had made to the Mall owners, a bunch of tightwads, combined with impeccably trained animals. At home the dog and cat were great company, though now that Hank had appeared, Amanda realized that no animal was a full-time substitute for a man. Hadn't Marcia said so? Yes, and had her head bitten off for her pains. Still, Hank might have worked out differently had he been a different kind of man—pushed for an intimate relationship, for instance. But he hadn't, and wasn't. Hank seemed willing to keep on an outer orbit, never close enough to get burned.

On Sunday night she worked late, though she hadn't told Hank. They hadn't made any plans for the evening because he was involved in the outfitting of a new shop only three doors down from hers.

It had been a dismal, unsuccessful outlet for vacuum cleaners—not the kind of thing people shopping at the Busquash Mall were after. Now it was going to be full of American Indian goods—blankets, ceramics, paintings, silver-and-turquoise jewelry. Hank had high hopes for it, and Amanda understood why. Buying Indian wares east of the Rockies wasn't easy.

At eleven o'clock she locked up. On her way to the service elevators she poked her head in the back door of the Indian shop to give Hank a surprise greeting, but the place was a zoo of workmen, materials, tools and noise.

Only when she reached her neat little black Mercedes did she realize that her car keys were on the edge of her desk in the back room of her shop—oh, darn! How had she come to do that? A rhetorical question: the reason was a brown-wrapped box about the size of a Benedictine box that she'd had to squeeze into her bag, only to find it sitting smack on top of her car keys. She'd taken the box out, retrieved the keys, put the box back—and forgotten to pick up the keys. Darn, darn, darn!

The security firm was coming on board tomorrow night, but there was so much light and racket from the Indian shop that her journey back to her own shop was shorn of most of its fears. What fears were left? Crates, tools, cables and items of shop furniture all over the service corridor.

She flicked on the switch that sat alone and illuminated the area just inside her back door; the car keys were there, right where she'd left them.

Came the unmistakable sound of breaking glass from her shop. Outraged, Amanda never stopped to think. Dropping her big navy leather bag on the floor, she ran for the bead curtain, screaming shrilly to summon help from the Indian shop. A black-clad form wearing a ski mask stood on the far side of her counter, surrounded by the shards of what had been—she knew it well—an Orrefors one-off bowl. Above his head he held a Kosta Boda one-off vase formed like a surrealistic cat.

What foiled her was the counter. As she ran to one side to get around it he threw the vase not on the floor but at her, turning her scream into a howl of pain as the heavy object struck her on the hip. Down she went, while the black figure raced for the big sliding door at the front of the shop. Men were spilling into her back room as the Vandal tore off down the Mall proper, and was lost in the shadows.

Hank! Where was Hank?

"Here, Amanda," came his voice. "What are you doing here?"

"Working late," she panted, and moaned. "Oh, he hurt me! Where were you?"

"Getting another plan from my office."

By this time the lights were on and Amanda realized that her glass stood in more danger from her would-be rescuers than from the Vandal.

"Please!" she cried, struggling until Hank lifted her to her feet. "Mr. Murray will deal with this now. Thank you, thank you for coming." I sound like a happy hostess after a dinner, she thought, and cried out in pain. Someone thrust her chair under her, and she sank into it, sitting side on, as the workmen gradually left.

"Luiz, there's your plan," Hank said, indicating a rolled up blueprint on the floor. Then, to Amanda: "Will you be okay while I use your phone to call the cops?"

"Wheel me with you," she said.

For some reason that amused him; he laughed. "Oh, Amanda ! What did he do?"

"Broke my Björn Wiinblad bowl—a one-off," she said, her hand grasping his belt as he wheeled her at her side rather than from behind. "He threw the Kosta Boda pussycat at me, so I suppose that's broken too. Oh Hank, this is awful!"

"He might have killed you," Hank said grimly, making her as comfortable as he could. "Ambulance first, then cops."

"Make sure the ambulance uses the service corridor!" she cried in alarm. "I won't have a gurney in my shop." A small pause, then: "And I won't have Sergeant Jones."

Hank picked up the phone. "Nor will I," he said.

The call was patched through to Carmine at home. Though as a captain he was on permanent call, he and his two lieutenants took turns on matters that came in after hours, and tonight chanced to be Carmine's turn, a double whammy: he was taking Abe's calls as well until he returned from Hartford.

"Captain Delmonico."

"Oh, thank God, someone senior! Captain, I absolutely refuse to let Miss Warburton have any further dealings with that drunken moron, Sergeant Jones!" said an irate voice. "I understand that a detective will have to come to the Busquash Mall—just don't send him. The previous attacks were vandalism and so is this one, but tonight Miss Warburton was injured. I want the bastard caught, and all Sergeant Jones can catch is a cold."

Carmine finally managed to get a word in. "Your name, sir?"

"Henry—Hank—Murray, manager of the Busquash Mall, and a

personal friend of Miss Warburton's. It's her shop, the Glass Teddy Bear, that's been vandalized. And the first time the Vandal struck, we had $50,000 taken from the Third Holloman Bank as well. Sergeant Jones is supposed to be dealing with that too, but he's done nothing."

Carmine decided to go himself; if the theft of $50,000 from a bank was being neglected, his division was in big trouble—why didn't Corey mention it? I've seen not a word on paper! What is going on with Morty Jones? "Drunken moron" sounds as if he's drinking on duty. By rights I should send Corey, but I have a feeling matters have already gone too far for that. Nor can I be sure that Corey would give me a truthful account of Morty's situation. The only one who tells me anything is Delia.

"Must you go out?" Desdemona asked in the hall. "If Julian wakes and realizes you're not here, he'll get up."

"At a quarter of midnight? He won't wake, lovely lady."

"He might."

"Think best, not worst." He kissed her. "If he does wake, tell him I'll be back in five minutes with a switch."

"Carmine!"

"It won't happen, Desdemona. Go to bed yourself."

I can't wait for Prunella Balducci to arrive, Carmine thought as he backed the Fairlane on to East Circle. Why didn't I sense that my wife was as green as grass when we had Julian? She was stuffed full of theories, and that's what they were—theories. Julian needs far more exercise than he gets, but Mommy is stuck with a second baby. Now she's lumbered with an under-exercised, strong-willed child who pushes her around because she's permanently tired. Nag! I never understood that toddlers could nag until I met my own son. Julian the defense attorney.

By the time he reached the Busquash Mall, Carmine had girded his loins to hear the worst about Morty Jones, and could only be thankful that Mr. Henry—Hank—Murray hadn't called Silvestri. Not that he, Carmine, was prepared to shield Morty from official retribution; more that he wasn't as yet convinced that Morty was beyond redemption. "Drunken moron"—an interesting reading of Morty's character. If he was drinking on the job, it was more recently than when Carmine had seen him ten days ago. That had revolved around Ava's swearing that the kids weren't Morty's. He loved those kids, loved them far more than selfish, nympho Ava did. Why did she screw cops, and no one but cops? But if the poor guy's inebriated condition was obvious to civilians, it must be obvious to Corey. Who wasn't lifting a finger.

Amanda Warburton was shaken and in pain, but quite capable of speaking for herself. "I lost my head when I heard the glass breaking," she said. "He'd busted my Björn Wiinblad bowl into pieces, and he had my Kosta Boda cat over his head, ready to do the same. Then he saw me, and threw it at me."

Carmine stamped the floor with his foot: it was covered with a deep-pile black commercial quality carpet. "I'm surprised the object broke," he said.

"It's concrete underneath, and while a short drop wouldn't harm it, it would have sufficient momentum if he pitched it from above his head, which is where he was holding the cat."

"You know your glass, Miss Warburton."

"Yes, it's been my life. But he knows it too, don't you think? No short drops."

Hank Murray butted in. "That idiot Sergeant Jones kept insisting the culprits were from Taft High," he said angrily. "None of us agreed with him, even the two patrolmen—now they were great guys. Better detectives too. When he wouldn't change his mind after the second attack, Miss Warburton and I lost all confidence in him. He stank of booze! So this time I wasn't going to let Mr. Jones near the place."

"I'm taking the case myself, Mr. Murray," Carmine said, his voice calm. "Any reason Sergeant Jones was so set on Taft kids?"

"Vandalism in the neighborhood, apparently, but Taft's neighborhood isn't anywhere near Busquash apart from its easterly situation," said Hank.

"What about in this mall? Apart from the Glass Teddy Bear's vandalism and the robbery at the Third Holloman Bank, have you suffered any kind of crime wave, as the papers put it? Pick-pockets, bag snatchers, gang hazes?"

"You'd know if we had, Captain."

Or should, thought Carmine grimly. "No, sir, I guess I need to phrase that better. I meant activities that weren't reported to the police. I presume, for instance, that you have a security company patrolling?"

"No," said Hank, scowling. "Finally, after nearly three years and half a hundred requests to the owners, Shortland Security will start patrolling tomorrow, Monday, October 7. It took three vandalisms and a bank robbery to succeed, but at last I have."

"I see. Why the surprise that the Vandal broke your bowl?"

"Because on his two earlier visits," said Hank Murray before Amanda could answer, "the Vandal never so much as chipped one thing. That was the weirdest part."

Two ambulance medics walked through the back door, and all hope of further conversation with Amanda Warburton ceased.

"I'll send two forensics technicians over first thing in the morning," Carmine said as she was wheeled out, "but if by some miracle you're discharged from the hospital tonight, don't come in tomorrow. No one is to touch a thing, understood? Mr. Murray, I'll see you at ten tomorrow morning about the bank robbery."

Carmine thought Hank heard, but it was debatable; he was busy assuring Amanda that he'd go to her apartment to feed her animals, and taking custody of her keys. Besotted.

Before he left at a little after one a.m., Carmine picked up Amanda's phone and dialed the number in his notebook. A sleepy voice answered. "Miss MacIntosh? Be at Paul Bachman's lab before eight tomorrow morning. At eight on the dot you will accompany him to the Busquash Mall and a shop called the Glass Teddy Bear, which has been a prey to vandals or a vandal. Paul will take care of the physical evidence, whereas you will take care of the detective's duties. I expect you to make full enquiries at the neighboring shops, and also ascertain, if you can, the number of vandals involved. Pay particular attention to a shop three doors up that's being fitted out to sell American Indian goods—there may be witnesses. Take a close look at the Glass Teddy Bear's goods—how up-market are its lines, for instance? You can report to me later on Monday."

She couldn't not ask it: "Is this connected with the Dodo?"

"Absolutely not."

There! You might have wangled yourself back to Holloman, Miss MacIntosh, but no way are you working the Dodo. In fact, I couldn't use you on the Dodo if you were a model trainee rather than a pain in the ass. The Dodo case is going nowhere.

*　　*　　*

Carmine's first task on Monday morning was to visit the County Services property registry, which necessitated a plod up and down several flights of stairs and the negotiation of several halls that made him feel as if he passed from one country to another, instead of from one municipal function to another.

Without evidence he couldn't look at Kurt von Fahlendorf's bank accounts, but there was one way he could check whether the Carew gossip was right about the German's wealth. How valuable was his property, and did he own it outright? Half expecting the deeds of 6 Curzon Close to be buried under X or Y Holdings, he found them openly listed: K. von Fahlendorf owned 6 Curzon Close free and clear. At one acre, it was a significant Carew property, especially given its extreme age. That antiquity made it costly to maintain, as every rotted board in its siding had to be replaced with a board of the same age and kind, and every roof shingle had to be hand split. A tiny cul-de-sac, Curzon Close, just six houses on it, and two were owned by Gentleman Walkers: Mason Novak owned 4 Curzon Close outright. Dapper Dave Feinman lived first house around the corner on Spruce Street. Coincidence?

"Ebenezer Curzon had owned and farmed fifty acres of Carew," said the chief conveyancer to Carmine, delighted to have a captive audience. "It was sold off gradually, of course, all but the farmstead itself. That passed out of Curzon ownership in 1930, when the Depression was at its worst. It's had a number of owners since, and I'm sorry to see it in foreign hands." Her spatulate fingers tapped the floor plans of 5 Curzon Close. "Now this one, I'm pleased to say, has recently gone to what sound like real Yankees. Robert and Gordon Warburton."

Poised to plead an emergency—the chief conveyancer would talk all day—Carmine propped.

"Warburton? Robert and Gordon?"

"Yes. They bought 5 Curzon Close eight months ago."

"Do they live in it, or was it an investment?"

"That, Captain, I do not know." She leaned across the counter conspiratorially. "However, I can tell you that there was an awful fuss when they started to paint it."

Hooked, he leaned forward too; their foreheads nearly touched, like caryatids doing without a lintel. "Fuss, Aggie? Cough it up, or it's back to dancing in the Rockettes for you."

She giggled. "Would you believe, Carmine, that they began to paint it in black and white, board by board," she tittered. "I had to drive out and see it. Like a zebra! Naturally the Council wouldn't permit it—we were inundated with protests. I mean, right next door to Busquash, where you can't even have a colored Christmas light showing outside? Carew is a part of Holloman City, so the ordinances can't go that far, but they can be interpreted as forbidding black-and-white-striped houses. The Warburtons were livid and tried to launch a lawsuit, but not even Isaac Lowenstein would buck the town ordinances. Well, can you *see* Judge Thwaites hearing it? In California, the Warburtons said, anything goes. In which case, was the consensus of opinion, go back to California."

"Well, dog my cats!" said Carmine feebly. "I guess staid old New England would be a shock after California, huh, Aggie? What was I doing, that I didn't hear of it?"

"The race riots after Martin Luther King Junior?"

"Yeah, right." He gave the chief conveyancer his most charming smile, and vanished as quickly as a pricked bubble.

He just had time on his way to Busquash Mall. Fortunate.

When the Fairlane pulled up outside 5 Curzon Close, Carmine tried to envision the lovely white clapboard house painted in black-and-white stripes. Why on earth would anyone want to do that? It stood in about half an acre of land, and bore evidence that at least one tenant of it was prepared to put in the hard work English-style flowerbeds demanded; they had been mulched for winter, and about next May would be a picture. No, real gardens didn't fit with zebra striped houses. The only touch of color the house now sported was a red-lacquered front door. Not paint, lacquer. Carmine ended in concluding that Robert and Gordon Warburton had been pulling a few tetchy New England legs. Jokesters and pranksters, not Philistines.

Out of the Fairlane, up the flagged path toward the red door; before he was halfway there the red door had opened to disgorge two men who shut it firmly behind them. Perhaps five paces apart, Carmine stopped and they stopped, each side examining the other.

What Carmine saw were two absolutely identical men about thirty years of age. They had the kind of streaky brown hair that suggests tow-headed toddlers; it was well barbered, thick, and wavy. The face they shared had regular features and an enquiring expression, with greenish, grape-like eyes contributing most of the enquiry. As they stood side by side on the path, Carmine could not put one a fraction taller, heavier or wider than the other, and their physiques were exactly alike: narrow shoulders, slim waists, no hips, though the feet were splayed like a ballet dancer's. They wore the same knitted shirts, casual trousers and loafer shoes, except that one twin was clad in black, and the other in white. Had they not worn different colors, it would have been impossible to tell them apart, and that was very strange in mature men: identicalness diminished with the years.

He pulled out his gold badge and introduced himself.

"I'm Robert Warburton," said the black clad twin. "You'll always know us apart by the colors we wear. Robbie dark, Gordie light. We thought it had better be black and white today in case you've come about our black and white house that was."

"So you already know I'm a policeman?"

"You have been pointed out to us, Captain."

There was the faintest suggestion of femininity about them; Carmine found himself wondering if, had he not been known to be a cop, the slight suggestion might have been a downright scream.

"Are you related to Miss Amanda Warburton?" he asked bluntly.

They gave a stagey jump, perfectly synchronized. "Yes, we are," said dark Robert, apparently the spokesman.

"She never mentioned you last night, though I would have thought she'd stand in need of relatives."

"You saw her last night? Not a date, obviously. Actually she wouldn't have mentioned us." He giggled. "She doesn't know we're living in Carew."

"Any reason why, sir?"

Robert and Gordie shrugged in unison. "Not really, just the way families are, Captain. Amanda's our father's generation—our only aunt—even if there aren't many years between us. A pity, I feel. The three of us are the last of the Warburtons. One reason why we decided to have a house near Amanda."

"And then not tell her."

Both pairs of skinned gooseberry eyes opened wide, but neither twin answered.

"I'd appreciate your letting Miss Warburton know," Carmine said. "Your aunt is the victim of a weird kind of persecution, gentlemen. Her glass shop has been vandalized three times in a week, and Miss Warburton was injured last night during the third attack. A motive is hard to find, hence my visit to you."

"Ooo-aa!" Gordie squealed.

"You mean we're suspects?" Robbie asked sharply.

"Yes. Have you been in Holloman all week?"

"Well, yes," dark Robert admitted.

"Are you gainfully employed, sirs?"

Both faces lit up identically. "Are we gainfully employed? Are the Marx Brothers a success? Are Olivia de Havilland and Joan Fontaine sisters? We are movie stars!" Gordie announced.

"Glad to hear you can speak too, sir. May we go inside?"

"A Californian's home is his castle," said Robert. "No, Captain, we stay out here."

"What's inside? Dead bodies? Stuffed dodos?"

They understood the reference to dodos, but ignored it. "Whatever it might be is our business until you produce a legal warrant," Robert said, chin out. Gordie's chin was out too. "I note that New Englanders are not a trusting bunch, so why did you think Californians would be?"

"It's Miss Warburton concerns me," Carmine said, rather enjoying this interlude. "I hope you're planning to tell her you're here, like today or tomorrow?"

"Don't you want to hear about our career as movie stars?" Gordie asked, sounding injured.

"I don't go to the movies," Carmine said solemnly. "There are three repertory companies in Holloman, and American Shakespeare is just down the road at Stratford."

"Yecch!" gagged Gordie. "Stage is phoney."

"Film is phoney," said Carmine.

"Twins! Identical twins!" cried pale Gordie.

"Huh?"

"And there you have it, Captain," said dark Robert. "We are identical twins who can *act*. We fence. We're expert riders. We can sing and dance. After we did *Waltz of the Vampire Twins* last spring, the offers have been rolling in. Right age, right sex, right look— we'll never be Cary Grant, but we've found a way to live pretty well."

"And that's just the tip of our iceberg !" shrilled Gordie.

"Shut up, Gordie!" Robert snapped.

"How can movie stars live in Connecticut?"

"Paul Newman and Kirk Douglas do," said Gordie.

"We have two more houses, Captain," said Robert; it was clear that he was used to cleaning up after Gordie's indiscreet remarks. "One is in San Diego that we rent out, and one in the Hollywood Hills is our residence while we're on the West Coast. Work in California, rest in Connecticut."

"Does either of you keep a diary?" Carmine asked.

"It's a joint effort," they chorused.

"Now why doesn't that lay me flat on the ground in surprise? Bring yourselves and the joint effort diary to the County Services building, Police Department, tomorrow morning at nine. And make sure your diary goes back to the beginning of March."

"Why? What have we done?" Robbie asked.

"Just helping with enquiries, sir. There's a rapist loose in Carew." He nodded to them and retreated down the path, the Warburton twins staring after him in horror.

*   *   *

Hank Murray was waiting in his VIP's office, rather than the one where he kept plans, records, mountainous files and his secretary.

"A man your size could hardly move down there," he said, seating Carmine in a green leather chair. "This one is for my clients and members of the Board. Cappuccino? Long black with cream? Ursula's waiting for the order."

"Cappuccino," said Carmine.

"Danish?"

"Would not go amiss, Mr. Murray."

Within five minutes Hank's secretary appeared with a loaded tray, including his favorite, apple Danish.

"Fill me in on the bank robbery," said Carmine.

"A definite inside job, Captain. Whoever stole the money had a set of keys. They came in the back door off the service corridor, and had keys to the strong room."

"Do you have keys to the strong room, Mr. Murray?"

Hank gasped. "Lord, no! I have keys to the service door, of course, but to nothing else in any Busquash Mall bank branch."

"Did Sergeant Jones ask you?"

"Uh—no. I wasn't with him when he went to the bank."

I hope it's when, Carmine thought as he found the emergency stairs and went down a floor. Avoiding elevators was one of the ways he dealt with Desdemona's cooking.

Having declined Hank's company, he walked around to the Mall proper and entered the bank through its front door.

A nice little branch, floored and walled in a streaky marble of pink, white, green and grey. The tellers were behind a fine counter of the same marble, and probably each was equipped with an alarm button beside the right knee placed so it wouldn't be knocked accidentally but was easy to reach. There were five teller slots, but only two working; several—customers?—clients?—patrons?—were inside, but no line had formed.

His gold badge admitted him through an electric gate in the counter, and he was conducted to a large desk in the far left corner where Mr. Percy Lambert, the manager, sat looking gloomy.

"Captain, I'm so glad to see you," said Lambert, a tall, thin man with scant hair and the facial lines of one who suffered chronic indigestion.

Carmine sat in the client's chair and looked competent. "I gather the money that was taken was your cash reserve for the next day?" he asked. "Answer me as if I know nothing, it's my usual technique. Sometimes repetition jogs the memory," he explained smoothly.

"Yes, it was the next day's cash reserve. Under ordinary circumstances it's sufficient to get us through, but if we have a heavy run on cash, I call head office in Cromwell Street and get more," said Mr. Lambert.

"Does that happen often?"

"No, as I usually cater for known periods of high demand, like holiday weekends. Weekends I have to keep additional funds in house, as all our other branches are closed. The Busquash Mall is special. The Fourth National has a branch here too, and we alternate weekends. Holiday weekends, we're both open."

"I see. Was there anything special about the money, sir? Was it sequentially numbered? New or used?"

"Used bills, non-sequential." The long face grew longer. "Ideal for a robber. It wasn't marked in any way."

"Show me where and how."

The back right-hand corner of the big premises had been cut off from the general area by an extremely pretty cage of gold bars adorned with curlicues and simple lacework. The area inside it was ten by ten feet, its rear wall taken up by a series of safes with heavy, branched handles and numbered dials. A console sat against the front row of bars, and the entrance door was to the only free side, the left.

"We changed the lock immediately," Lambert said as he turned a key several times back and forth, "but it's being converted to a proper combination lock whose numbers will be changed daily."

"You're insured, of course."

"Oh, yes."

They walked in, a squeeze for Carmine, who vowed to check his weight at the police gym that very day.

"We have no safety deposit boxes or facilities for really big sums of money," Lambert said. "I guess if I expected any kind of robbery, it was a holdup."

"And none ever happened?"

"No, none, even aborted."

"Has Detective Sergeant Jones been back to see you?"

"No," Lambert said, sounding unconcerned. "I told him at the time that I didn't think he'd solve it. I've racked my brains, Captain, and can't ever remember the keys to the strong room out of my hands, let alone gone missing."

"Do you carry them on your person?"

"No, I can't. They're heavy—the tellers' drawers are on the same ring, and several keys to those safes back there."

"So they're in your desk? Known to be?"

"Not quite. They're in that safe in my far corner—under the imitation fern. And I'm the only one with its combination."

"Then your security is good, Mr. Lambert. Just keep your eyes peeled for anyone who reveals knowledge about the bank's locks, and particularly your safe combination." His voice remained dry. "Were you satisfied with Sergeant Jones's conduct, sir?"

"Have you any reason to think I might not be, Captain?"

"No, it's a routine question. But I would like a frank answer," Carmine said.

"Well, he was pleasant enough, and he knew how bank robberies usually go down. If I have any complaint, it was the smell of liquor on his breath. But he apologized for that, said his wife had just left him and he'd gone on a bender."

"Thank you for your understanding, Mr. Lambert. I'll keep in touch," said Carmine, and departed.

So Hank Murray was ruled out, and who else was left? No one. Murray had seemed a shoo-in for a while, listening to him on the subject of parsimonious mall owners and their reluctance to hire proper security; had it stopped with Amanda Warburton, Hank was a good bet, as the vandalisms had brought him into closer contact with a very attractive lady he clearly doted on. It would have enabled him to kill two birds with the same stone: get to know Amanda better, and bring Shortland Security on board. But to Carmine, the same man committed both crimes. In fact, the Vandal, whoever he was, had probably never intended more than that first, most bizarre invasion of the glass shop—garbage, yet! The two that followed were less imaginative, even if it had taken him some hours to pile up all the glass on the second invasion. The Warburton twins, perhaps? No. They were poseurs, and the idea of vandalism would most likely horrify them. Who, who, *who*?

*   *   *

A glance at his watch said that perhaps his forensics team were still at the Glass Teddy Bear; since he was on the premises, he may as well see what, if anything, had been discovered.

"The cleaning firm put paid to any chance I had of collecting evidence right up to this moment," Paul said, packing up his gear in the back room. "It reeks of commercial fluids under an air freshener, and the carpet was shampooed within an inch of its life. The Vandal must have ruined the place. So to get it back to normal took real work. I asked Mr. Murray if it was Whistle-Clean, and it was."

Since this firm contracted for the worst messes human beings could make, Carmine simply grimaced. "Never mind, Paul. The poor lady needed to be cheered up. How did Miss MacIntosh the sex kitten do?"

Paul's fresh, round face lit up in amusement. "I wish I'd seen her! She turned up in a gaberdine pantsuit that wouldn't have looked out of place on a nun. She did very well, Carmine. Went the rounds with her notebook and pencil, charmed the men and made the women like her. I guess the rocket you tied to her tail did the trick."

In she came, notebook, closed, in her right hand; when she saw Carmine she gulped, almost saluted, then contented herself by standing to attention.

"At ease," Carmine said solemnly. "What did you find out, Miss MacIntosh?"

"Nothing worth a thousand words of notes, sir, but there is one very interesting thing I'd like to show you," she said, and moved toward the shop.

Carmine followed, waving goodbye at Paul.

Down to the front window, where the glass teddy bear sat in all his glory; Helen pointed at his face. "Did you ever see such eyes?"

she asked. "Stars in them. And such a gorgeously rich blue, like the Pacific at its deepest."

He inspected the glass teddy bear's blue orbs intently. "Uh— they're lovely," he said lamely. "Is that it?"

"Yes, sir, that's it." Her face became serious, awed. "Sir, this glass animal is a wonder of the world. If you look closely at the little round tail—teddy bears don't usually have tails—you'll see the artist's signature—Lorenzo della Fiori. He was the acknowledged master, the best in anyone's memory. Based in Venice, but on Burano, not on Murano. Ten years ago he was murdered—thirty-four years old! God knows what treasures the world lost when he died untimely."

Carmine was staring at her, stupefied. "How do you know this, Miss MacIntosh?"

Her lashes lowered, she assumed the demure look he supposed was a part of her customary repertoire when talking to men. "Art history and art appreciation at Miss Procter's School for Girls, Captain. They may not have taught us much science, but they stuffed us full of art, literature and music. Miss Procter's theory of education is that a Miss Procter's girl will marry so well that one day she'll be a patron of art, literature and/or music. After all, there's only so much of a schoolgirl's day that can be devoted to etiquette and the Blue Book."

His lips twitched, but he maintained his calm. "You're saying this thing is worth a fortune?"

"Several fortunes, actually. Look at its eyes again. Each is as big as an over-sized marble, and its color is a rich, slightly opaque, cornflower blue. You can't call the glass cloudy, because that implies wispiness, whereas this is uniform. It really is an eerie opalescence, isn't it?"

"Yes," he said, fascinated. Where was she going?

"What really makes each eye so mesmerising is the six-pointed star in its depths. I mean, the star isn't anywhere near the surface, yet if you could turn the big marble over, it would give you the same impression. The star kind of floats in space. Fabulous!" she cried.

"It must have been very hard to get the stars in its eyes."

"That's just it—he didn't!" Helen said excitedly. "No human hand made those eyes, Captain. They're star sapphires."

"Jesus!" He stepped back involuntarily. "What are we looking at in pedestrian terms like dollars?"

"First, sir, you have to understand that this matched pair of gems is unique," said that remarkable young woman. "Star sapphires are a dismal blue-grey color that detracts hugely from their value. The perfect color for a sapphire is cornflower blue, and star sapphires don't come in cornflower blue. They just don't. Except for this teddy bear's eyes. Their value is inestimable, but if I had to put a price on a wonder of the world complete with two huge, matched, cornflower-blue star sapphires for eyes, I would go into the double millions. *High* double millions. Put it on display for two years, and you'd earn your money back. This is a true museum piece, but the only way you or anyone else would find out what it's worth is to send it for auction."

He grinned. "Does Miss Procter's teach gemology too?"

"Captain, really! Did the Russians get into space first? Gemology is number one on the Miss Procter's syllabus—name me a debutante who doesn't have a jeweler's eyepiece in her evening bag to check out any offered diamonds."

"Quite," said Carmine, keeping his mouth straight. "So a museum piece sits unprotected in a window with a vandal on the loose. Except that the Vandal has a carefully laid plan. And were it not for Miss

Procter's syllabus, we wouldn't know that the teddy bear is anything other than very lovely and moderately expensive. The Vandal must have had a shock when Hank Murray succeeded in hiring Shortland Security. They're the best, so getting the glass teddy bear out is now almost impossible."

"Do you think he's what the vandalisms have been about?"

"It begins to look that way."

"According to Mr. Murray, Miss Warburton will be back in the shop tomorrow. Her injuries were slight."

"What did she lose in breakage?"

"Just a one-off Orrefors bowl made by someone called Björn Wiinblad. Her books give its retail price as a thousand dollars."

"The other piece wasn't harmed?"

"No, sir, it survived. It's cute, if wacky. Art glass is highly individualistic—there is no other substance can be worked in so many different ways than glass," Helen said.

"This is shaping up as a peculiar case," Carmine said. "I want you to cultivate a friendship with Miss Warburton if you can, and work other aspects of the case as well. I want a full report on Robert and Gordon Warburton, ex San Diego. That means all the way back to times before their birth. And investigate Amanda Warburton's life too. How did she come to get possession of the glass teddy bear?"

Helen looked at Captain Delmonico's obdurate face and made an intelligent decision: not to hope for the Dodo.

"Yes, sir," she said, looking willing. "I can do that."

On his way into the County Services parking lot, Carmine got lucky; Morty Jones was arriving too, and because a captain rated a better spot, he was able to trap Morty as he walked past the Fairlane everybody knew was Carmine Delmonico's unmarked—a crotchet that the Commissioner condoned. Morty made the mistake of assuming the Fairlane's driver was gone; when Carmine opened his door and leaned out, Morty gasped.

"Get in," said Carmine curtly.

There was no escape; Morty slid on to the passenger's seat

"You can smoke, Morty," Carmine said as he slewed sideways to examine the sergeant, eyes busy. Yes, no doubt he was drinking. Not so much the stink as the trembling hands, the rheumy eyes.

He'd been such a promising cop, Morty Jones, twenty years ago; Danny Marciano, not a dinosaur then, had put in as much work on Morty as he did later on Nick Jefferson, bullied him into taking a degree from West Holloman State College at nights, and put him in patrol with Virgil Simms, another great guy.

All the girls were after him. He was going to have a big career in law enforcement, and he was easy on the eyes: tall, a graceful mover, handsome in a dark and broody way he used to joke branded his ancestors as Welsh. He passed his sergeant's exams with distinction, and, armed with his degree and a new wife, applied to join Detectives. The move had upset Captain Danny Marciano as much as his choice of a bride, but nothing could budge Morty: Ava said a detective was better. He was wild about her, would do anything to please the woman all his friends knew was a tramp—only how to tell Morty? It couldn't be done.

By the time he made it to Detectives he was the father of a son, Bobby, an event that predisposed him to like his whole world, including Larry Pisano, the lieutenant to whose team he was posted. Not a good boss for Morty Jones. Elderly and embittered, especially after he was passed over in favor of Carmine Delmonico as head of the division, Pisano lived for only two things: his looming retirement, and creating as much trouble as he could for Carmine. Among other ploys, he set out to ruin Morty Jones's roseate life by informing him of Ava's extramarital activities. Morty hadn't believed him, but the seed of doubt was sown; the cheerful, enthusiastic cop gradually lost his good humor and—worst of all, in Carmine's view—his interest in his work, which he continued to perform, but sloppily.

"I know what your troubles are, Morty," Carmine said in a warm voice, "but the drinking has to stop."

"I drink on my own time, Carmine."

"Horse shit you do. Right at this moment your boozing is so consistent that they're thinking of giving you your own stool in the Shamrock Bar. The Shamrock Bar, for God's sake! A cop bar! You're like a man in a car with no brakes at the top of the roller coaster's worst hill—you won't pull up when you get to the bottom, you'll wind up mangled in a heap of broken parts—the parts that make up your life, Morty! I know about the bust-up with Ava, and it's bad, but think of your kids. You owe them a duty. What happens when the Commissioner finds out, huh? You're out on your ear, no pension, no references to help you get another job. You're on contract, have you forgotten?"

"I'm not drinking on the job," Morty maintained.

"Have you talked to Corey?"

"No, he's got his own problems."

"Then talk to me! I want to see you the kind of guy—and cop!— you used to be. Try to see your life on the job as the one place where you can forget your personal problems, bury yourself in the work. It's a good technique, Morty, and it's not beyond you. But while the alcohol is swilling around in your brain, you can't think straight.

That's why it's number one priority—stop drinking entirely, *please*! I could go to John Silvestri now, and you'd be gone in less than an hour. I choose not to, because I don't believe you're too far in to climb out. Delia found you a great housekeeper to give you a decent home life while you fight this battle, so fight it. Fight it!"

But Morty's response was a sudden bout of despairing tears; Carmine watched and listened in his own kind of despair.

The story came out again; the accusation that his kids didn't belong to him, Morty's striking her, how awful it was to exist without Ava. His kids cried, he cried …

"If I can't get through to you, Morty, you'll have to see Dr. Corning," Carmine said eventually. "You need help."

"The department shrink? I won't go!" Morty said.

"You will go, because I'm seeing Corey and making sure of it," Carmine said. "Doc Corning's a good guy."

In answer, Morty opened the car door and bolted.

Which left Carmine to see Corey.

Who was in his office, apparently having some kind of argument with Buzz Genovese.

"Later," said Corey, glancing at Carmine's face.

Buzz gave Carmine a smile, and vanished. Carmine sat down; not the right moment to tower across a desk at a seated man.

"What do you want?" Corey demanded, sounding truculent.

"Dig out HPD Form 1313," Carmine said.

"*What*?"

"You heard me, Cor."

"Why, for God's sake?"

" 'Who' would be a better question, but you know who. Morty Jones. It's time you and I referred him to Dr. Corning."

It had always been the team joke that the Jew Abe Goldberg looked like a WASP, and the WASP Corey Marshall looked like a Jew. The older they became, the truer the statement became. Corey had lost weight—Maureen was on a fad diet—and his long, Semitic face had fallen in a little more, giving the scimitar of a nose additional prominence and the permanent black beard shadow on Corey's jaws the appearance of charcoal stage make-up. His dark eyes blazed into anger.

"That's crap, Carmine! There's nothing wrong with Morty."

"Oh, come on, Cor, where are your eyes? Where's your sense of smell? Morty Jones is drinking on the job, and he's gotten himself into a terrible mess," Carmine said, keeping his voice level, dispassionate. "If I can see it, you must see it—he's your team member."

"Yes, and my business!" Corey snapped. "I don't need the captain sticking his oar in. As soon as Ava comes home, Morty will go back to normal—without the need for a psychiatrist."

"My sense is that Ava's not coming home. She's going to file for divorce, and we have to act before that happens. Dig out the form, Corey. That's an order."

"Only if I agree with you, and I don't. In my opinion, to send Morty to a psychiatrist would be the end of him."

Carmine's hands clutched at the air. "Oh, Jesus, where do you guys get your mistrust of psychiatrists from? Dr. Corning has saved at least half a dozen cops from losing their jobs—and worse, their lives. The murder rate is rising nationwide, which makes cop suicides look less, but that's a false statistic, and you know it. It's my considered opinion that Morty is very depressed. He may need medication— but not Jameson's whiskey."

"I'll undertake to deal with the booze myself, Carmine," Corey said, adamant, "but I will not sign your form."

Carmine got up and left. True, to mention suicide was to give Morty's situation undue significance, but it was imperative that the drinking stop, and he didn't think Corey was capable of that kind of therapy. Why *did* they hate psychiatrists?

Delia trotted in late that afternoon. "I've finished the interviews," she said, "save for the twins tomorrow morning. Do I get to do them?"

"You can sit in, but I'm having the pleasure," Carmine said.

"And I'm off to see what noisome things I can find under the California stones," said Helen lightly, waved at Delia, and left managing to look as if she were intrigued by her task.

"Anything interesting?" Carmine asked Delia.

"Only what Miss Marcia Boyce does for a crust," Delia said, perching on the chair Helen had vacated.

"Expatiate."

"Miss Boyce runs a secretarial agency on Cromwell Street. Her girls are skilled in abstruse forms of executive assistance like typing specifications for space rockets, Nobel standard papers in physics and organic chemistry, medical dissertations, mathematical hypotheses— you name it, Carmine, and Marcia Boyce has a secretary who can do it. It costs heaps to hire a Boyce secretary, but those who do can be certain they'll have no errors in transcribed dictation or deciphered scribbles. Most hirings are to Chubb or U-Conn, but there are lots of out-of-state universities hire too. Educational institutions rarely hang on to a Boyce girl for more than six months—a federal grant runs out and Miss Boyce has her girl back. However, professors who have already won a Nobel Prize hang on to their Boyce girls for years. Miss Boyce doesn't care which way it goes—she takes a healthy cut as personal profit."

Delia paused to sip her mug of cop coffee, grimacing. "Of course if Richard Nixon becomes president in November, there won't be nearly as much research money available. Republican presidents are notoriously anti-research unless it's armaments related. Pure research will die one of its little deaths because the dodos in Washington don't understand that applied research sits on a solid foundation of pure research, so ... According to Miss Boyce, at the moment everyone is using up LBJ's lavish research money rather like condemned men eating a last meal."

"The topic's fascinating, Deels, but not relevant."

"Oops, sorry!" The eyes twinkled within their stiff mascara hedges. "Miss Boyce is genuinely worried about Miss Warburton, but she can't offer anything concrete. Even when the Busquash residents made such a kerfuffle over their skyscraper and sacked the town Elders, Miss Boyce says there was no sort of emphasis on Miss Warburton as a tenant. The word Miss Boyce is fond of is 'evil'—she says Miss Warburton is being persecuted—her word again—by an evil presence, someone out to torment Amanda in a sadistic way. Marcia doesn't believe the Vandal is interested in the glass. She thinks his obsession is Miss Warburton herself."

"How does Hank Murray figure in her ideas?"

"No, it's not Hank is the Vandal, at least according to Miss Boyce." Delia gave up on the coffee with a sigh. "The trouble is, Carmine, there seems to be no motive apart from a psychopathia."

"And there, Miss Carstairs, you and Miss Boyce are wrong." Carmine filled her in about the glass teddy bear and his eyes.

"Ooh!" Delia exclaimed. "And *Helen* found all this out?"

"Thanks to Miss Procter's School for Girls—or so she'd have you think. There's an element of leg-puller in Miss MacIntosh, but I confess I like her the better for it. We can safely put the bear's value in the high double millions."

"Does Miss Warburton know?"

"It would seem not. I've shifted Helen to the case to see what she can learn. Obviously our trainee is going to do much better on cases that have an up-market nature."

"Stands to reason," Delia said. "I miss Nick!"

"So do I, though I wish he'd make more of an effort to like Helen. Still, Abe says he's doing fantastically well in Hartford, and he's a minority representative for us."

"How can a little boy from the stews of Argyle Avenue come to like M.M.'s daughter?" Delia asked. "Especially given her personality? In time she'll lose some of the hauteur, the unconscious exclusivity, but it must be very hard for Nick in particular to stomach. He's had to work so hard to get what he sees as falling into her undeserving lap."

"I know, Delia, I know."

The Brothers Warburton announced their advent before they actually appeared; the County Services parking attendant buzzed to say that this pair of spooky twins refused to leave their car on the street; until their Bentley was safely garaged, they were not getting out of it. The attendant was told to let them park, and shortly thereafter the Warburton twins materialized in Carmine's office looking insufferably smug.

They were exquisitely dressed for a chilly fall day. Both wore what were probably Hong Kong copies of Savile Row suits: Robert's was a navy three-piece pinstripe with a striped Turnbull & Asser shirt and a Stanford tie; Gordon's was a pearl-grey silk with a white silk shirt and a self-embroidered white silk ascot. They wafted a hugely expensive cologne, and bore shaves so close the skin gleamed like satin. Even their eyebrows were thinned and brushed, Carmine suspected. A pair of sartorial dazzlers.

"What color's your Bentley?" he asked, curious.

"Pewter," said Robert, "with white leather interior."

Having introduced Delia, Carmine escorted the twins to the largest of the interrogation rooms, sat himself and his papers down opposite the Warburtons, and put on a pair of reading half glasses that gave him a professorial air. Their diary was full-page size, one day to a page, and its cover was a hairy faux zebra skin; the year, 1968, was emblazoned in gold numbers an inch high.

I am fed up with all this light and dark nonsense already, thought Carmine, conscious of a burning desire to cause mayhem. Fire a twelve-pounder shot at this catamaran, hole both hulls!

"I should inform you," he said, "that I have a very old and dear friend in L.A.—Myron Mendel Mandelbaum."

The effect of this projectile was extraordinary. Both the brothers assumed an identical look of mingled awe, astonishment, delight and—speculation? The skinned-green-grape eyes had somehow acquired the kind of stars Carmine had last seen in the eyes of a glass teddy bear. Now I know, he thought, what the phrase "stars in their eyes" truly means.

"Mr. Mandelbaum assures me that you are indeed—er—'hot property' in Hollywood. Apparently it's far cheaper to pay real actors a high salary than incur the costs of blue screen doubling the same actor through many scenes. Also, two real actors give additional flexibility, Mr. Mandelbaum says. I've also talked to your agent, who assures me that you've arrived at a point where you can choose your film roles. TV commercials as well."

They proved what superb actors they were by managing to look simultaneously proud yet humble, worthy yet unworthy.

"How divine to be vindicated by luminaries like the great and powerful Myron Mendel Mandelbaum," said Robert, winking at tears. "A Zeus, he dwells atop Mulholland Drive, unattainable, a thousand titans as his lackeys, his world spread out before him in a myriad million lights!"

"Obliterated by smog, more like," said Carmine. "Okay, let's can the crap. March 3 this year—where were you?"

Gordon flipped the pages, Robert read the entries.

"In Holloman," said Robert.

"Both of you?"

They looked identically appalled. "We are *never* apart!"

"May 13?"

"Holloman. In between, we were in L.A. filming our greatest screen triumph, *Waltz of the Vampire Twins*."

"But B-grade. June 25?"

"Holloman."

"July 12?"

"In the air from L.A."

"August 3?"

"On vacation in Yosemite National Park."

"Can you produce proof? Receipts, for instance?"

"Of course."

"August 31?"

"Alaska, filming a TV commercial for an after-shave."

"Why Alaska?"

"Coo-oo-ool," Robert drawled.

"September 24?"

"Holloman."

"Have you left Holloman during September?"

"Not after we returned from Alaska on Labor Day. We decided to stay in Connecticut for the fall colors."

"In Connecticut, try October for those."

"We are now aware of that, thank you."

"Why Yosemite? You don't look outdoorsy, sirs."

"You can't tell a book by its cover," Gordie piped up.

Robert glared at him.

"Do you like books?" Delia asked.

"Easy come, easy go," said Robert.

"Novels?"

"If there's a film of the book in the offing," Robert said.

"If you saw a wall of shelves containing a thousand books of all sorts, sirs," Delia persisted, "what would you look for?"

"A *thousand* books? That's a library. There'd be indicators. I'd go straight to movies."

"That rapist in Carew is heavily into books," Carmine said.

The inevitable As One reaction: horror mingled with terror.

"Captain, you cannot possibly think of us as rapists!" cried Robert, gasping in perfect unison with his twin.

"Seriously, sirs, no, I don't. What I do want to know is how much of the simultaneous everythings is real. You may be as homozygous as homozygous gets, but you're not inside the exact-same skin."

Carmine's voice became menacing. "There must be all kinds of differences between you, but you've turned eliminating them into an art form. You're actors by trade, and actors by nature. I'll grant you some invisible connections, even a minor ability to read each other's minds, but you are *not* the same person. How about dropping the identical role for a moment and letting me see the quintessential Robert versus the quintessential Gordon? I can tell you this much— Robert is the one thinks before he speaks, and Gordon is the one speaks before he thinks."

They smirked—identically.

"Captain Delmonico! Is that a valid observation?" Robert asked. "Perhaps the speak-think is a function of our clothing? Perhaps the one in pale clothing, no matter whether it be Robbie or Gordie, is the twin speaks before he thinks? Colors have such strong vibes, you must know *that*! Who knows what the City of Holloman did when it forbade us to balance the exterior of our house between the forces of Dark and Light?"

"Oh, piss off! Get out of here!" Carmine said, tried beyond endurance. "You may not be the Dodo, but you're sure cuckoo."

Amanda returned to the Glass Teddy Bear limping a little from a sore hip, but basically unharmed. She had insisted on driving herself in and had Frankie and Winston with her; Hank was waiting at her named parking place to help her out, make a fuss of the animals, and bring her upstairs.

"Luckily I have another Björn Wiinblad original in stock—not a bowl, but a vase," she said, pointing to a stack of big cardboard cartons against the back wall of her office. "If you can get it for me and unpack it, I'd be grateful."

So by the time Hank left Amanda had settled down, the new original was in place, she had adjusted the Kosta Boda pussycat to her satisfaction, and the dog and cat were ensconced in the window. Hank had put the partition up that prevented any customer reaching in to pat them and disappeared through the front door with a wave. He was bringing Chinese over for dinner in her apartment, and she didn't expect to see him until it was time to go. Why couldn't she learn to love him? Marcia was right, he was ideal for a lonely woman. Yet she couldn't seem to love him as more than a friend, and wished there was some way she could at least demonstrate that much to him.

The morning passed fairly quietly; she sold several lots of wine glasses to customers with very different ideas—one was after the impossibly thin blown crystal of utter plainness, the other after Waterford hobnail, and a third after Murano edged in gold. Wonderful, how tastes varied.

When her stomach rumbled she realized that she hadn't brought any lunch with her—well, she hadn't had the energy yet to shop. Never mind, it wouldn't hurt her figure to skip lunch.

At which moment the door gave its glassy tune; she looked up in time to see a tall, very beautiful young woman clad in a business pantsuit of burgundy gaberdine erupt into the shop with both hands full.

"Is there a space on the counter?" she demanded, steering a skillful path around pedestals and tables.

"Yes," said Amanda, startled.

"Good," said the young woman, whose striking mass of apricot hair seemed likely to snap her slender neck off, it looked so heavy. Down went brown paper bags and a thermos. "I suppose there's a place in the Mall where I could have gotten us lunch, but not knowing, I brought everything in from Malvolio's, including coffee. Have you any plates, or do I have to pirate some glass ones, wash them, and use them?"

By this Amanda didn't know whether to laugh or back away in horror, but the pets decided for her by effortlessly leaping the partition and crowding around the visitor begging for attention.

"I'm Helen MacIntosh from Holloman Detectives, and I'm here to grill you. I hope you like hot roast beef sandwiches."

"Indeed I do, and I'm hungry, and I forgot to pack lunch." Amanda got up from her chair. "I'll get plates, mugs, and whatever you recommend in cutlery."

The lunch was delicious, Helen MacIntosh such good company that Amanda hated the thought that, as soon as she had answered some questions, this feminine sun would vanish to shine elsewhere.

But it was a very leisurely interrogation that lasted for several hours and through a dozen customers, during which intervals Helen pretended to be a staff member.

"I have a message from Captain Delmonico," Helen said after the lunch things were cleared away and the shop deserted.

"He's very different from Sergeant Jones," Amanda said.

"Try comparing Veuve Clicquot to rubbing alcohol. Anyway, he said to tell you that your nephews, Robert and Gordon, have been living in Carew for over eight months."

She was shocked: "I don't believe it!"

"True."

"Why haven't they told me? Visited me?"

"The Captain thinks it's the way they're made—pranksters. Every day you live in ignorance of their proximity, they have a giggle at your expense. It's no more malignant than that, he says. They're not the Vandal—the wrong kind of prank."

"Have you their number?"

"Sure. I'll give it to you before I leave." Helen gazed around. "This is the most gorgeous shop, I love it. It's solved all my Christmas shopping problems. That glorious massive urn over there with the peacock feathers actually incorporated in the glass—it's so hard to get glass to assume those iridescent, metallic colors. My father will adore it, he's got a vacant pedestal in his office."

Amanda went pink. "Um—it's very expensive, Helen—a one-off Antonio Glauber," she said in a small voice; here was a blossoming friendship going west before it really got started.

"What's expensive?" Helen asked.

"Fifteen thousand dollars."

"Oh, is *that* all? I thought you were going to say a hundred thousand. Put a red sticker on it."

Amanda's eyes had gone as round as the glass teddy bear's. "I—are you—can you honestly afford it, Helen?"

"The income from my trust fund is a million dollars a year," she said, as if it meant little. "I don't spend wildly, but it's so hard finding things for parents who can also afford to buy whatever they fancy, price no consideration. And that urn is really a beautiful piece—Dad will love it."

"It's for sale, of course, but I never expected to see it go," Amanda said huskily. "One gets so attached to the original pieces. Still, I've done so well since being in Busquash Mall that I'll have to take a buying trip next summer."

"I can understand why there's a NOT FOR SALE notice beside the glass teddy bear. It's a museum piece."

"Yes. I'd never sell him."

"No one could afford it. What have you got it insured for?"

"A quarter-million."

Helen's vivid blue eyes glazed. "Uh—that's crazy! You must know what it's really worth."

"He's worth whatever value I care to put on him, Helen. If I insured him for more than that, he'd have to go into a vault and never be seen. That's not why Lorenzo made him. Lorenzo made him for me, my own one-off, never for sale."

There was iron in the voice; Helen desisted, choosing to sit on the floor and play with the dog and cat. She had begun her work, but it was far from over. Here was her best source about the twins. Twice a week, lunch. That should do it. And what a change, to find she really liked the person under the detective's microscope.

"Do you believe all that?" Amanda asked Hank over Chinese in her apartment that night. "Eight months, and never a word! I phoned Robert up and gave him *such* a chewing out! Oh, they'll never change! Narcissistic, self-centered—the tragedy, Hank, is that they're so clever. I mean really, really clever. Robert plays with words the way a cat does with a ball of twine, and Gordon is a brilliant artist. They're both artistic, they should do something with their talents, but do they? Never! All they do is hang around movie studios grabbing work here and work there, silly projects—Oh, I am *mad!*" Amanda's voice changed, dropped to a growl. "They murdered their parents."

The noodles fell off Hank's chopsticks; he put them down and stared at her, astonished. "Excuse me?"

"You heard me! They pushed their father down the stairs when they were eight, and put arsenic in their mother's food as soon as they didn't need her anymore."

"Wow!" Hank fished for more noodles; he was hungry. "I take it they escaped retribution?"

"Yes." She sighed. "What do I do with my estate?"

His laugh sounded zany. "My mind's spinning in circles, Amanda. You mean your will?"

"Yes. The only blood kin I have are a pair of crazy twins. But if I disinherit them, who is there? The ASPCA? The Humane Society? A farm for broken down donkeys?"

"Or an indigent mall manager," he said with a grin.

She gasped, clapped her hands together. "Yes, that's it! I've had a funny feeling—are you really indigent, Hank? Trust me! I'd like an honest answer."

He looked hunted, swallowed convulsively. "For what it's worth, I'd trust you with my life, Amanda. My ex-wife is permanently institutionalized, and I'm permanently broke keeping her there. The fees are astronomical. Funny, your health insurance will pay for anything except a mind, just as if something that can't be seen can't be broken."

"Oh, Hank! That's terrible! What happened?"

"The divorce was through—acrimonious on her side, not on mine. Her moods—well, they frightened me. Then she came back on some pretext—a forgotten picture, I think it was."

"You don't remember?"

His hunted look grew worse. "According to the psychiatrists, human beings have a tendency to forget just what they ought to remember. Anyway, it was a pretext. She went for me with a knife, and I defended myself. We were both wounded, and there was nothing in it between our stories. That the cops tended to take my word over hers wasn't popular with her friends—she had some very important ones. In the end it never came to trial because her mental condition deteriorated terribly. But I got the hint. Unless I paid to keep her in a private asylum, there might be a trial—mine. I knew it was the easy way out. I'm pretty sure I would be acquitted at trial, but I can't be a hundred percent sure. There's no statute of limitations on murder, and she's way past seeming dangerous. Any jury looking at her now would see a shriveled up scrap of scarcely human flesh. So I keep on paying."

"Hank, Hank!" She rocked back and forth. "I knew there was a big trouble there, I knew it! Go to trial, Hank, please. You would have to be acquitted. Besides, there was no murder, just an attempted murder."

His shoulders hunched. "I can't bear to open that can of worms, Amanda, I just can't!"

He's a lovely man, she was thinking, watching him, but he's timid, and I suppose that side of him will show at a trial. If indeed there is a case to answer—he won't even find that out. Her friends are having a kind of revenge in keeping him poor ...

"I wish there was something I could do," she said, sighing.

"There isn't. One day Lisa will die, and my troubles will be over. She's developing kidney failure."

"Would you consider a loan?" she asked. "I could afford to help you keep her institutionalized."

His hand went out, clasped hers, and his gentle brown eyes sparkled with tears. "Oh, Amanda, thanks, but no thanks. I'm not much of a man, but I won't let you do that."

"I have a good cash income and over two million dollars in assets," she said warmly. "I'm not in love with you, but you're my very dear friend. Leave it for the moment if you prefer, but let me ask again six months from now. And if she does go into kidney failure, you'll have huge medical bills as well. Please don't hesitate to ask, okay?"

There had been a subtle alteration: Hank Murray looked more cheerful, stronger. He squeezed her hand. "Okay," he said, lips turned up in a smile. Then he lifted her hand and kissed it.

TUESDAY, OCTOBER 15

to

MONDAY, NOVEMBER 4

1968

CHAPTER III

Prunella Balducci was in her late twenties, slim, fashionably dressed, and very pretty. Since she arrived at two in the afternoon, Carmine wasn't there to take the edge off Desdemona's awe: how could someone who looked like this earn a successful living managing emotionally crippled families?

A little tongue-tied, she took Prunella to see her quarters, the high square tower with its widow's walk.

"Oh, this is wonderful!" cried Prunella. "Are you sure your daughter doesn't mind not being able to come home until Christmas?"

"She's a freshman pre-med at Paracelsus and doesn't want it known that she's a local," Desdemona explained.

"And of course she's busy making the adjustment from high school to college. Wise girl. Who's her room-mate?"

"A black girl from Chicago, there on scholarship, poor as a church mouse. Another inhibition for Sophia, whose stepfather has dowered her with an enormous amount of money. Our girl is super-sensitive about appearing privileged, but she's not allowed to give her money away. This is the first year that Paracelsus has taken women, and there are fifty of them—you must know that Chubb is finally admitting women?"

"Oh, sure. Go on, Mrs. Delmonico."

"Desdemona, please. Half the freshman intake at Paracelsus has been women. I think Sophia's glad she has Martina for a roomie. They like the same music—the Beatles, the Rolling Stones, Elvis, a whole lot more I don't know or remember. Music seems to be a great bond. They both want to be surgeons, and you must know how impossible a dream that is for women. I suspect we'll get Martina for Christmas—air fares are a problem."

Desdemona put the suitcase she was carrying in a corner and smiled at her new colleague. "Coffee before I wake my monsters? For once in his life, Julian felt like a nap today, but I warn you! The moment Julian wakes, peace vanishes."

In Prunella, Desdemona soon saw, Julian had met his match. Smart enough to know the effect of his eyes and his smile, he turned them and the charm on as soon as he woke.

"Oh, great!" he exclaimed. "I don't have to go rowing."

"Rowing?"

"Yes," said Desdemona, who had forgotten all about the rowing and now came down with a gasp, a look of desperation. "I must explain to you, Prunella, that Julian hoped to sleep his way out of rowing, and that in turn would have meant Julian awake tonight." She glared at her elder son, who seemed as innocent as any cherub Raphael ever painted. "Last year," she went on, "things happened that made me realize I'd lost my physical fitness, but getting it back through a pregnancy and another baby proved impossible until Carmine came home with a two-man kayak. I used to hike, but shepherding Julian is beyond me—I'm too tall for toddlers, they kill my back. Carmine thought rowing would be feasible, and he was right. I sit in the back space, and both kids sit in the front space in special harnesses. Julian swims like a fish anyway, and I make him use a paddle, it's good for developing his arms and shoulders Alex lies in a weeny cradle. The trouble is that I've not had the energy or the enthusiasm to do it regularly. I did tell Julian this morning that if he wasn't a good boy, we were going for a paddle."

"Does this mean, Julian, that you haven't been good?" asked Prunella in bored tones.

"I'm never good," he said solemnly.

"Then you go rowing, Desdemona. I know you don't feel like it, but you need the fresh air and the exercise," said Prunella.

"Yes, Mommy, go rowing," Julian said, voice like honey. "I can stay here with Prunella and do things I like."

"No, you're rowing with Mommy. Alex gets to stay behind."

The huge feet planted themselves firmly apart on the floor. "I don't want to go, so I won't go!"

"That's not good enough," said Prunella. She seized Julian by one hand and looked at Desdemona, who was on the verge of tears. "Lead on, Mommy, to the kayak. No one's getting out of this."

Digging his heels in didn't work, nor did much roaring and yelling; relieved of the authority but hugely comforted by the fact that it had not passed to Julian, Desdemona led the way down the path to the boatshed and unearthed the kayak. At sight of it Julian decided to get physical, and kicked out at Prunella's shins: the next thing he was sitting on the hard ground with a thump, and Prunella was *laughing* at him!

"Do get up, Julian," she said cheerfully. "You look silly."

"Mommy, she tripped me up!"

"You deserved it," said Desdemona, and gulped. Somehow it was easier when she had another adult to back her, and that adult was an acknowledged expert on how to deal with recalcitrant children. Prunella had managed to wound Julian's dignity, his rather inflated idea of himself, and that part of him would continue to smart long after his bottom ceased to pain him.

In record time Desdemona was launching her craft, with a very co-operative Julian doing his share instead of whining; he was not about to be laughed at again by a stranger.

Who, by the time she had supervised his bath and clad him in pajamas, had already given him to know that she'd stomach none of his tricks. Mommy, she informed him, was sick, and he wasn't helping any, so until Christmas he'd have to make do with her, Prunella. The trouble was that he quite liked her; she had such merry eyes, eyes that made him want to get on the right side of her. Mommy's eyes were always dreary and uninterested—why hadn't he seen that she was sick? He wasn't very old, but he could well remember an interested, jolly Mommy.

"It's too early for bed," he said after a six o'clock dinner.

"Why?"

"I'm not sleepy."

"Oh, good! Then you can exercise your imagination after you go to bed. I'll be there to listen."

"Listen to my what?"

"Your imagination, silly! Everybody has one, so that's your first task after you hit your bed—looking for it. When you've found it, I'll help you exercise it."

"Oh, not more exercise!"

"Exercise for your mind, Julian, not your body."

His eyes should have been as dark as the rest of him; Julian Delmonico had taken after his father in bulk and coloring, and sported a mop of black curls as well as rather thin black brows and impossibly long black lashes. A remarkably handsome child, he had discovered that his looks could win him favors and treats—not to mention excuses for bad behavior. But it was the eyes that put the finishing touch on a striking appearance: the color of weak, milky tea, they were surrounded by a thin black ring that made them piercing, compelling. Well, thought Prunella Balducci, his mother and I have to inculcate some humility and sensitivity into this unpromising material, otherwise he'll king it at St. Bernard's Boys' School and be ruined.

He's had his first lesson: Mommy's sick, and he didn't see it. Now let's see what imagination can do.

"What does an imagination look like?" he asked, curious.

"Anything you want. You'll know it when you find it. Until you do, lying in bed is awful, isn't it? Like a desert, dry and sandy. Once you find your imagination, you won't mind going to bed, even if you're not tired."

"I still want to know what it looks like."

"Imagination makes the desert vanish, become all kinds of places. Maybe it disappears and a depth-diving submarine appears—that's imagination. During the day," said Prunella, warming to her theme, "you and I will look at books full of pictures your imagination might like to hide in. Looking at books is like piling wood on a fire when the world's all snow—the fire burns brighter and brighter. You're going to love books, Julian."

I don't believe it, thought the listening Desdemona. She's hooked him already, and she hasn't even unpacked her bags.

When he walked in at six-thirty that evening, Carmine got a loving, intensely grateful kiss; his elder son was pestering Prunella to go to bed. Wasn't it time yet?

For answer, she presented him to his father and mother for a goodnight kiss, then took his hand and led him away. "Phase two—a walk around East Circle to get the sleepy-bugs biting—and no, Julian. The more you badger me, the longer our walk."

"Wow!" said Carmine, following his wife into the kitchen. "Doc Santini told me she was ruthless. Has Julian eaten yet?"

"Yes. Prunella insists on six o'clock for the children, so Alex gets a breast and Julian gets meat or fish and three veg. At least on his food I didn't fall down. Prunella gave me full marks. I don't over-cook the veg, nor give him bloody meat—blood can turn kids off their best source of protein, she says."

"What about us?"

"We eat at seven-thirty. By then, Julian will be sound asleep. That, I'll believe when I see it. She made me take him out in the kayak, but he's not tired."

"He will be. What's for our dinner?"

"Swedish meatballs and mushroom risotto. And a salad."

"Prunella's going to want to stay forever. Did I tell you today that I love you?"

Her beautiful smile lit up those cool eyes. "Every day, as soon as you smell the dinner. I love you too. And thank you, thank you for Prunella."

She was making up her "pickle solution" as she called it; he pressed his lips against her flushed cheek and stole away to visit the nursery.

His younger son was slumbering peacefully in his crib; when Carmine leaned down to kiss him, inhale the inimitable smell of properly cared for babies, two chubby arms came up to touch his face, and the eyes opened, too clouded with sleep to arouse fully. Daddy smiled into them, and they closed; the arms fell. Both his sons had strange eyes, Alexander James Delmonico's even more peculiar than Julian's: silvery-grey, with that black ring around the irises made them piercing, unsettling. Alex's eyes reminded Carmine of Kemal Ataturk's, exactly the same in an even darker face. Not an unpleasant similarity; Ataturk was regarded as the founder of modern Turkey, and had beaten a British army nearly half a million strong at Gallipoli during the First World War. Well, Alex wouldn't have that tortured man's life, but it was interesting. Blame Desdemona, really. Her extreme fairness had to show somewhere in her sons.

And back to the little sitting room adjacent to the kitchen, where they sat to have a drink before dinner and unwind. I am blessed, thought Carmine, taking the glass Desdemona held out.

He couldn't wait any longer. *Didus ineptus* let himself into Melantha Green's second floor apartment with his lock picks, then gazed around familiarly: he had been in here before. Melantha was another neat and tidy girl—he loathed mess!—who lived on her own and considered that her black belt in judo gave her all the protection she needed. So while other girls were fitting more locks, Melantha had decided that one dead-bolt was fine. As indeed it was, provided that the predator was an amateur with locks. Whereas this predator was an expert.

Today's methodology was different. The piece of duct tape for a gag remained, but in place of twine there were manacles and chains. Appropriate, really. His first black woman, and his first venture with chains—chains probably not unlike those that had encumbered her slave ancestors. A fresh thought, not the one that had prompted him to switch to chains.

When the bedroom yielded no surface he could use, the Dodo located a folded up card table in the living room and carried it to the bedroom, there to employ it as a place to put his tools, neatly arranged. The silenced .22 went under a bed pillow, the duct tape, manacles and chains accompanied him back to the living room. There he began his careful transformation from just another guy into *Didus ineptus*: folding his clothes in a stack on top of his tennis shoes, removing a few items from his body, and then, admiring himself in the full-length mirror on the bedroom door, touching himself up with the greasepaint, a perfect color match to his skin. On went the surgeon's gloves, after which he cleaned his prints from everything he had thus far touched.

Finally, about a quarter of six, he was ready, black silk hood over his head, poised behind the front door. He knew this one was a self-defense expert, so it was important not to give her any chance to use his body weight against him. She came in at five of six. The tape was over her mouth and the manacles snapped on her wrists within seconds; then he struck her on the jaw with a clenched fist. Her knees buckled. He propelled her, semi-conscious, to the toilet, pulled her panties down and sat her in place, a part of him astonished to see that those panties were sexy red lace. She groaned.

"Piss, Melantha," he said. "You don't move until you do."

Sagging forward on the seat, she urinated. Didn't the news programs say he never spoke? Why was he speaking to her?

The idea of the chains had come to him when he first set eyes on her bed, an old-fashioned brass one with stout posts and bars. While she was still groggy he tethered the manacle chains to the top of the bed.

"Manicure time," he said.

Her feet went into socks, her fingernails were clipped down to the quick and collected. After which he left her bedroom and went to look at her bookshelves: hundreds of books! Melantha was a final year medical student at Chubb. There! That one was great, just right for his collection. He brought it back to the bedroom, drew up a chair, and sat down.

Melantha moaned; he was there at once. "Waking up, are we?" he asked, slapping her face. Her dark eyes rolled, then cleared; she gasped.

"Yes, I'm *Didus ineptus*," he said, "and I've come to do all kinds of things to you."

She couldn't scream or talk back to him. The duct tape was in place. But she didn't need to ask him her most important question; he had already answered it by speaking. *Didus ineptus* intended to kill her.

He raped her for hours, vaginally and anally, with penis and fist, using his cord around her neck time and time again, retiring to his chair to read, returning for another assault. He pinched, pummeled, pounded.

"I am not a pervert," he said to her. "My only instruments belong to my body."

Melantha's mind began to wander as the strangulations went on; so intent was he on what he was doing that he almost missed the change begin in her eyes. She was lying half on her stomach, but this next one would be the last. He flipped her over—the chains allowed that—and pulled the hood from his head. The eye slits were too frustrating to retain it at such a moment. When she died, her eyes must be looking into his face. And, in case this was the ultimate of all experiences, he paused to snap on a condom. Buried in her, choking her, eyes locked on hers, he watched the life slowly die until he understood that all he had left was her shell. The bitch had escaped him! The orgasm never came.

As he left the bed, tossing the unfilled condom on to the card table, the front door lock gave a dull thunk as the dead bolt turned and fell back. The Dodo's hand went under the pillow and emerged holding the .22 pistol.

"Melantha? Hi, honey," said a man's voice.

He was halfway across the living room when the Dodo shot him in the throat, and he collapsed, dying, in a gurgling heap. But that was not satisfactory. Reaching him, the Dodo stood over him and shot him between the eyes.

That taken care of, the Dodo unchained the lifeless girl and replaced everything in his knapsack, tucking his souvenired book down in one pocket. The load was heavier now that he had added chains to it, but on the whole the weight was worth it. He had almost come inside her; that he would definitely come later as he held the book he knew, but it was a disappointment nonetheless.

At four in the morning *Didus ineptus* stole out of the place, wriggling on his elbows across the grass of the backyard until he reached the shelter of the side fence, down which grew a row of small pines. There he waited long enough to be sure that he was undetected, then he crawled on hands and knees to the front boundary. On his feet now, he ran across the road and into the deep shadows of the street's maple trees. From there, it was a short run to Persimmon Street, where his car was parked. As soon as he reached it he got in and put the knapsack on the back seat floor. But he didn't drive away. No, he'd wait until other cars were growling into life; only then would he drive away. A good night, all considered. He had always wondered how he would cope with an intruder. Now he knew. No sweat.

The bodies were not discovered until noon, when a friend had gone to see why Melantha hadn't attended the morning's rounds; she was meant to be presenting a case to Prof. Baumgarten—*important.*

And Helen was back with the Dodo.

"It isn't a question of your winning any victories," Carmine said to her icily, "it's simply that I need manpower, and you know the case. But don't you ever play another trick like the one you did on Lieutenant Goldberg. If you do, you're out one second later, and your father will know why."

She said nothing, just hastened to report to Delia; her luck that Nick's wife had succumbed to a critical illness, and he was on compassionate leave. Knowing how he disliked her, she shrank from their confrontation once he was back at work. Oh, pray Imelda Jefferson was okay! The Dodo's victims were *black*!

With two women as his team, Carmine drove to Spruce Street in Carew. One corner of his mind yearned for Nick, but that was impossible. Black victims? It made no sense.

For Helen, the crime scene came as a shock that she was too professional to betray, and she was relieved to learn that her stomach was a strong one. A patrolman had been forced to race outside and throw up, but not Helen MacIntosh!

"Tell me what you see, Helen," Carmine commanded.

"A black male, mid to late twenties, shot first in the throat, then finished off with a bullet to the brain. If the head shot had been first, he wouldn't have needed the throat shot. Whoever did it is a top marksman who made a mess of this guy's throat from fifteen feet away, to silence him, obviously. He administered the *coup de grâce* standing over the victim—entry is straight in, not angled," said Helen. "I guess this is her boyfriend and that he has a key. I can't hazard much of a guess as to time of death. Have we beaten the Medical Examiner?"

"Just," came Patrick O'Donnell's voice from the doorway. He took a liver temperature and examined both wounds. "I'd say he died at two in the morning, cuz. No earlier, but not much later." He fished in pockets until he found a wallet and gave it to Carmine, then vanished toward the bedroom.

"Dr. Michael Tolbin," said Carmine. "From his library card, a general surgery resident. Jesus, the waste! The country can't afford to lose two young doctors—senseless!" He went in Patrick's wake, the women following.

A worse shock for Helen. Melantha was lying stretched out on the bed in an X position, belly up, covered with the crimson marks of forming bruises. Around her wrists were angry rings that didn't suggest any kind of twine or wire; they were too broad and indistinct. Her face was blue and congested, the tongue protruding, the eyes open and so dark that it was difficult to discern an iris.

"She fought for every breath," said Helen huskily.

"That she did," said Patrick. "She died about the same time as the young man in the living room—a matter of minutes between them, I'd estimate. She was restrained with handcuffs, probably connected to chains, but her legs were free. This bed screams S & M—not that I'm implying that, only that it served the Dodo's purposes admirably. Melantha probably thought it was unusual in a pretty way. There are other pieces of Benares brass. Feet in socks, nails pared down—it's definitely the Dodo. He's escalated—this isn't accidental, he arrived to kill. That probably means he spoke to her, may not have worn his hood. Is there a book missing?"

"Impossible to tell," said Delia, coming in. "The shelves are overflowing. Oh, the waste! Their whole lives ahead of them, so much work to get this far! Melantha would have had her M.D. in six more months. Her thesis is on meningococcal meningitis. She's twenty-five. Chubb Medical School! That means she was one of the best of her year nationwide."

"As today is Wednesday, October 16, he's still on a three-week cycle. What a way to die," said Helen.

No one answered. Helen drew a long, sobbing breath. "I'm okay," she said. "Just spitting mad."

"Delia, you'll have to stay here after the bodies are removed and go over this apartment with a fine-toothed comb," Carmine said. "Keep Helen as assistance."

He left; Delia looked at Helen. "Tell me what you see."

"On the girl? Greasepaint, there. And there?" She looked puzzled. "If he uses greasepaint, I don't understand how he doesn't leave slathers of it behind." She went red, but labored on. "I mean, sex with her, skin on skin? Even if it's a rape, sex is intimate physical contact. He's naked and she's naked. So why isn't there more greasepaint?"

"He cleaned her up with xylene," said Patrick, packing his case. "It's an effective reagent for something oil-based, but it also says his own skin is on the delicate side. He's probably not of Mediterranean origins. Why not alcohol for his delicate skin? Because it's overrated as an organic solvent, and he's careful. However, he's neither a chemist nor a pharmacologist. Maggie had no Dodo administered drugs in her system, and I'll bet this girl won't either. He does it on surprise, brute strength and, for want of a better word, *natural* techniques. In one way he's a colossal psychopath, yet he uses no metal instruments of torture. Fingers, fists, feet. I suspect he despises rapists as sickos and doesn't think of himself as abnormal. The strangling ligature has to fit within his definition of normality, so I'm guessing it's made from human hair."

"His own?" Delia asked.

"More likely his mother's." Patrick picked up his cases and departed.

"Why did Dr. O'Donnell call the Captain 'cuz'?" Helen asked.

"Their mothers are sisters," said Delia.

"I never knew that! Does my father?"

"I have no idea," said Delia, sounding bored.

The two women worked in silence, each taking half of the bedroom, the floor of which was covered in one of those annoying carpets that show every mark. Helen stared at it closely.

"Delia, take a look at this."

Delia came, inspected. "Something with four legs sat here."

"That's what I thought. Don't tell me he brought his own dinky table!" Helen said, a little incredulously.

"More likely that he transported a table from somewhere else in the apartment—don't leap to the madder conclusions first."

This time Helen's flush was pure mortification; lips tight, she left the bedroom to search for a table that fitted the marks. When none did, she checked again, and found the card table tucked in a niche to one side of the living room window. "Bingo!"

They opened it and stared at its green baize, which bore a number of marks and stains; there was still a faint reek of xylene. Smears of greasepaint marred the baize in several places.

"Paul will be able to get enough to match the color," said Delia in quiet triumph.

"What's this?" Helen asked, pointing to a spot that also showed marks, but these were colorless. She sniffed. "Condom lubrication, do you think?"

"I do, but there's no trace of semen. His mutton gun jammed." Delia began to fold the table. "We'll take it with us," she said. "I wonder what else is here? We have to find it before the fingerprint boys arrive."

But the apartment yielded nothing else.

"Where did he wait for her?" Helen asked.

"Behind the front door, I suspect. With Maggie Drummond, it was a wing chair, but there's no hiding place in Melantha Green's living room. He jumped her literally as she was entering, which might suggest that these photos are right—Melantha had martial arts skills."

147

"Do you think three weeks is his cycle, Delia? *Do* you?"

"It seems likely, but that's speculation best suited for one of the Captain's think-tanks, if you mean the direction his future assaults are going to take."

"Think-tanks? I'll be excluded!" Helen cried. "I want my own think-tank here and now, with you, Delia—with you! Why do we always wait for the men to lead, tell me that? It's obvious to me that this girl wouldn't have had time for a party since last year, if then. Added to which, she was in a serious relationship with a surgical resident who wouldn't be going to parties either. They would have met on the ward, not at a Mark Sugarman party. Nick's wrong, but he's a man, so he's believed."

Delia was watching her, and frowning. "Stop thinking about this murder for a moment, Helen, and think about your own conduct. What you're doing right now is passing the buck to Nick for your exclusion from the Captain's inner circle, just as if he's not entitled to have one. You're restless, impulsive and ambitious. I don't blame the Captain for keeping you in your place, silly girl. You push too hard. There's one American saying that I just love: shape up, or ship out."

A silence fell; Helen's face was beet-red. "I'm sorry."

"I hope so."

Suddenly Delia looked indignant. "I love and esteem our boss, but he can be thoughtless. He's buzzed off in our wheels. We are stranded."

"No, we're not," said Helen in a more cheerful voice. "I did a deal with the cop who got sick—if he brought my Lamborghini here, I promised not to breathe a word about his weak stomach."

"Clever chicken! Just answer me one question: how are we going to get a card table into a Lamborghini?"

"We aren't. I asked my queasy cop to hang around in case we had any bulky evidence to transport."

At six that evening, dressed in the shortest of miniskirts and with her wonderful legs sheathed in shimmering lilac pantyhose, Helen was sitting on a stool in Buffo's Wine Cellar waiting for Kurt von Fahlendorf. None of the staring young men would have believed for a second that this glorious young woman had spent her afternoon pursuing the aftermath of a particularly brutal murder. It was very unlike Kurt not to be doing the waiting; he was obsessed by gentlemanly conduct.

He came clattering down the area steps not two minutes later and perched himself on the vacant stool next to her, leaning to kiss her on the cheek. "Sorry I'm late," he said. "Muons."

"Of course it's muons. It's always muons," she said with a smile, and leaned to kiss his lips, which pleased him. "Are there any other ill-behaved sub-atomic particles?"

"Loads of them. That's the thrill—finding new ones. We do, all the time. What are you drinking?"

"The house red, but I haven't tasted it yet."

"A glass of house red," he said to the bartender. "You look amazingly lovely, Helen."

"Do I? Good lord! I wonder if that makes me a ghoul?"

"I wish you wouldn't make remarks that mean absolutely nothing to me. What is a ghoul?"

She ignored the question. "Do you know a light-colored black medical student named Melantha Green, Kurt?"

His brow creased. "Melantha Green? From Mark's parties would be the only place, but … No, I do not remember a light-colored Negro girl. Well, you know there are Negroes at Mark's parties—this is New England, not the South. But though I have been going to Mark's parties for years and you, for eight months only, someone with a name like Melantha would be memorable."

"That's a pity, we need background. Melantha was raped and strangled by the Dodo last night."

Even in Buffo's dim light Helen could see that Kurt had gone pale. He was not a morbid or prurient type.

"Oh, Helen! The poor thing!"

"A thing is certainly what the Dodo made of her. Try to imagine it, Kurt! All the fire and energy a black woman must have poured into her life, then a sick psycho just—ended it! Put a cord around her neck and throttled her in stages as he raped her over and over. And I never knew that black skins can show bruises—oh, it was awful!"

Kurt retched, clapped a hand over his mouth. "Helen, *please*! I know these things happen and I know you deal with them, but I—I cannot bear to hear of them!"

"I'm sorry, Kurt, I didn't mean to upset you. I get angry and indignant about some things, especially rape."

"Drink your wine—Buffo has uncorked a good red for a change. And let us alter the subject, eh? I am not very strong of the stomach," he said, his English becoming more stilted as he grew more upset. "I will not ask you about your day, but about your mother and father. Are they perhaps well?"

She laughed, humor restored. "'Perhaps' is a word you can't apply to that pair," she said, chuckling. "They're never unwell, especially with a presidential election scant weeks away. Dad is terrified that Richard Nixon will get in."

"Why is that necessarily bad?" he asked.

She eyed his noble, impassive face in some amusement, then shook her head. "You're too foreign to understand," she said.

"Tell me about your father, Helen. I am aware that to be the President of Chubb is a prestigious position, but your papa seems more important than that."

Helen shrugged, blew a rude noise with those fabulous ice-pink lips. "Dad's a perfect illustration of the fact that the job can make the man, but that the man can also make the job. He's got the word they applied to John F. Kennedy—charisma. No matter how important the men in a room might be, when my father walks in, they pale. Something *in* him, not something anyone can cultivate. Added to which, he's got genuine ancestors—something most Americans have to scratch for. Not merely one of his antecedents, but three of them came over on the *Mayflower*—well, he couldn't be President of Chubb without a *Mayflower* connection. And Mom has connections too—she's Cleveland, Ohio rich, like a bunch of great American families." She stopped, grinning. "There! Does that help, Kurt?"

"Yes, I think so. You must arrange a dinner with your parents, Helen. It's time I met them."

Her heart sank, then soared. What did meetings matter?

"Sure," she said, and sipped her wine.

"Have you time for dinner? We could eat here, or anywhere else you fancy."

"Here would be fine," she said, keeping her sigh of despair inward; what was the sense in dating Kurt von Fahlendorf, when he all but threw up at the mere mention of rape or murder?

I need a cop or a doctor for a mate, she told herself—a man who'll relish my telling him all about my day, a man who understands danger, blood, death. Kurt likes things that whizz around at near the speed of light and collide—which makes him far more dangerous than anybody else I know, though he'd never see that.

And what was he talking about now? Oh, no! No, please, no! He was on a ponderous fishing expedition to find out which precious stone she liked best—diamond, ruby, sapphire, emerald?

"Listen here, Kurt," she said pugnaciously, "don't you dare go getting ideas about buying me a ring! When I put a ring on my finger, I'll do the choosing—hear me? The man's sole function will be to pay for it." She gave a giggle. "There! That's tidied up. Let's look at the menu, I'm starving."

Heavens! he thought. Rape and murder all afternoon, and she is hungry!

Food, however, soothed them both. Buffo's wasn't one of Holloman's top restaurants, but it served well-cooked Hungarian fare; Buffo was a Hungarian who had fled after the Russians crushed the 1956 rebellion, and was still a passionate patriot.

Stomachs full of schnitzel (Kurt) and goulash (Helen), heads pleasantly buzzing from the wine, the couple left at ten.

"Do we leave your Lamborghini here, or my Porsche?" Kurt asked outside. "Let it be the Lamborghini, my darling Helen! Come home with me for coffee."

She shook her head in the way he had come to associate with an unbendable negative. No matter how he pleaded or what new, brilliant argument he produced, Helen didn't want to prolong the evening. A fair man, Kurt could understand why; her afternoon must have been traumatic. So he watched her leap nimbly into the car, and stood as she roared away down South Green Street. Other open sports cars didn't survive ten minutes on a Holloman street, yet Helen's Lamborghini bore a charmed life.

Shoulders hunched, Kurt walked the half block to where his metal-roofed black Porsche was parked, unlocked it, took the steering wheel lock off, and finally, after several adjustments to the dashboard, drove away.

"There goes Professor von Fahlendorf's Porsche," said a patrol cop to his new (and rather stupid) companion as they cruised the other way up South Green Street.

"Do we chase it?" the jerk asked.

"What for? He's not speeding or weaving."

Which little incident made them the last people to see Kurt von Fahlendorf, who never made it home.

She was obliged to do it, she admitted. On that same mild Wednesday evening Amanda Warburton invited her nephews over to her apartment for a home-cooked meal.

Things went better than she had expected; when she descended to let them into the garage beneath Busquash Condominiums she found herself gazing at a pewter-colored Bentley, and had to admire it. No more clunkers for the twins, obviously!

"It's ten years old and it guzzles gas," said Robbie as they walked to the elevator, "but we should worry! Gas is dirt-cheap. We like the lines of this model."

"Rightly so," she said. "You have good taste."

She continued this theme as the twins dutifully gushed over her huge apartment. "Having good taste," she said as she led them from her burgundy and pink bedroom, "why the drama of black and white? I would have thought a trying color combination to live in the middle of, surely?"

"Shock value," said Gordie, sitting where he could see the view, illuminated by a waning moon.

"Explain that to me."

"We're movie people," Robbie said, uncorking wine, "and we understand the importance of the personal image. A key element is difference—be unusual, eccentric even, if your talents are not those of a Paul Newman or a Rock Hudson."

"Where do your talents lie?" she asked, moving around her kitchen. "I hope you don't mind, boys, but I had our dinner catered by Sea Foam—shrimp cocktails and roast beef."

"Wonderful!" chorused the twins.

They ate, she noted, with an appearance of enthusiasm, but left a good amount uneaten.

"We have to watch our weight," Gordie confided.

"Let's go back to your talents," she said, pouring coffee—at least she could make that! Except, she discovered, that it wasn't something called decaffeinated, so they drank very little. She was beginning to gain the impression that West Coasters were riddled with dietary superstitions that, if Robbie and Gordie were anything to go by, did not have the imagined effects.

"Talents," said Robbie, drinking camomile tea. "The one that's appreciated at the moment is our acting, but we have scads of aspirations." He looked coy. "We can't talk about them—it would tempt Fate." One boneless-looking hand waved around. "All we can say is that we have a very big project coming to fruition."

"Does it require me to put in money?" Amanda asked warily.

The gooseberry eyes opened wide. "Amanda dear, no! We need millions! In other words, we need a top Hollywood producer."

"Gordie, are you sure you wouldn't like some camomile tea?"

Robbie put his cup down and rose. "We must be going, dear Amanda. You're sure you don't mind our dropping the 'aunt'?"

She laughed. "Since I'm only a few years older than you, I prefer not being an aunt." While Gordie gathered their coats, she looked at Robbie. "Where are your hearts?"

He understood immediately. "In our prosperity. The Bentley. Flying first class. In walking down the red carpet at a premiere and being cheered by the crowd."

"General fame and fortune," she said.

"In a nutshell, yes. But I didn't mention the biggest. In winning the first twinned Oscar."

"It's laudable, and I wish you very, very well."

After the twins departed Amanda sat at her glass wall and thought for a long time, chiefly about her money, her will, and the glass teddy bear.

She picked up the phone and dialed. "Did I wake you, Hank? Then how about coming over for some coffee and devil's food cake?"

He arrived in twenty minutes, smiling broadly. "Don't the twins eat dessert?" he asked.

"They eat very little of anything except things I didn't have—what a world the West Coast must be! I mean, why drink coffee at all if you want the caffeine removed? And if you strip all the fat off meat, it doesn't roast well, and why would you want to fry a bean twice? I gave up." She looked down at the dog and cat, sitting at Hank's feet. "Frankie and Winston are glad to see you. Robbie and Gordie squealed and ran away. I had to put the animals in the spare bedroom."

In answer, he picked Winston up—a struggle. "Winston, you have been conning Marcia into thinking Amanda isn't feeding you—I swear your weight's gone up to twenty pounds."

They sat at the plate-glass window. It was after midnight and the half moon was overhead, pouring an intangible, gold-hued light down upon Busquash Inlet; the leaves of the trees glinted with colored highlights, fully turned now in preparation for a season's sleep. Some sea creature broke the burnished surface of the water in ominous, ever-widening ripples, and a romantic soul with a yen for the fires of winter had lit one, its smoke writhing in delicate tendrils toward the stars. Even here, eighty miles from New York City, they were dimmed and the sky yellowed by a million urban lamps. Lovely or ugly, according to your tastes.

By mutual consent they turned away from the window. Hank gave Amanda his customary tender kiss, smiled at her, and started for her front door.

"See you tomorrow," he said.

On Thursday Nick came back from his compassionate leave looking worn and harried, but Imelda had come through having an aneurysm on the non-dominant middle cerebral artery clipped, and seemed to have no others to explode in the future. The Jefferson clan had rallied, so that, the operation itself over, Nick was free to go to work. Two grandmothers had moved into his house to prepare it for the invalid, and he was underfoot.

"I can't even do the marketing," he complained to Carmine.

"Here, you're definitely useful," said Carmine.

"What's Helen's status?"

"Delia thinks she's been punished enough, so I returned her to duty as a full trainee yesterday, when Melantha was found."

"Fair enough," said Nick, grimacing. "What's with the Dodo and a black woman?"

"No one knows, nor can the psychiatrists come up with a theory," Carmine said, frowning. "I am assured that in the few cases of multiple murder that we know of, the killer has never crossed a racial frontier, though rape is cloudier. But now this sicko is killing, so how do we categorize him? Admittedly his rape victims have been of all persuasions and all Caucasian origins, but Melantha is a black woman, avowedly so. It doesn't seem to have fazed him—my feeling is that to him, her color isn't even important."

"Christ! He is sick."

The two women were summoned as soon as Nick was fully up to date; Nick found enough amusement to smile, eyes resting on a remarkably restrained Delia, wearing rust, navy and black.

"Why won't you listen when I talk about the source of the Dodo's knowledge about Carew women?" Nick asked, sounding exasperated.

All eyes swung to him. "Hit us," said Carmine.

"Parties. Delia and I keep telling you that Carew is famous party country. Until Leonie was raped, Mark Sugarman gave regular parties. Mason Novak was another party giver, usually in conjunction with Dapper Dave, as their backyards abut. Von Fahlendorf is too exclusive to be a collaborator, but he has thrown an occasional party. Those four are all Gentleman Walkers, but there are other famous party givers too."

"Right on, Nick," said Delia, beaming.

"You've got my ears, Nick. Keep on going," said Carmine.

"For starters, tongues get loose. The booze flows, and there is always pot. The men are in charm-the-women mode, there are loads of couples huddled in corners or on sofas letting their hair down about themselves. I'm not describing orgies. No one tries to find a place to engage in sex—sex follows after a couple has left the party, if you get my meaning. The party itself is a gab-fest. Talk, talk, talk. Cheap wine or spirits, finger food, loud music, a chance to unwind among like-minded souls. It's amazing what people say about themselves under the influence of intoxicants or hallucinogens, even when people don't know each other. What if the Dodo goes to Carew parties, cruises in search of women he fancies, then gets them in a corner and quizzes them, all charm and honey like a psychiatrist?"

Nick stopped, greeted by a profound silence.

Finally Carmine spoke. "That's a valid theory, Nick. It makes sense. We've found no common threads that would give the Dodo information on any official level, and we know he has his victims summed up. Maybe he can learn enough about a woman at a party— it's surprising how much information can be exchanged in a half hour. He'd also be in a position to steal keys, or take wax impressions of them. All the victims have been outgoing women before they were attacked, and some know Gentleman Walkers well. Mark Sugarman might keep invitation lists—dollars to dimes, he's a hoarder."

"Well," said Delia, looking as if she regretted her dreary choice of colors, "pounds to peanuts, the Dodo is a charmer."

Carmine's eyes creased at the corners in amusement. "Do tell, Delia! C'mon, give us more."

"He has sufficient animal magnetism to attract whomever he

fancies," she said, cheeks flushed with pleasure, but not forgetting to give Nick a look of intense gratitude. "He gets her into a corner, and persuades her to tell him the story of her life, complete with enough personal details for him to identify her. She tells him about her obsessions—all his victims have been anal types, according to Freud. Perhaps they aren't the full obsessive-compulsive disaster, but they're definitely on the cusp. For instance, none of them would use a public toilet. Hence the Dodo's marching them to their toilets—he knew they'd be dying to go. And that suggests an extremely skilled technique as he quizzed them at a party. He presented as no threat, yet as a masculine man. That's a difficult act."

"I don't think he sounds very masculine," Helen said.

"No, dear, you're wrong," said Delia patiently. "He must be stuffed with masculinity, otherwise women would deem him creepy or slimy. I imagine that he waited until the girl was tiddly, stoned— whatever—before he made his move, so that her tongue was loose and her brain not sufficiently alert to remember the encounter the next day. He's clever, Helen."

Patrick O'Donnell walked in, his blue eyes bright, his fair and freckled face sober. "Good work finding the table, ladies," he said to Delia and Helen. "It confirms his techniques, though it doesn't give us any fresh information apart from the condom. Paul is trying to match the color of the greasepaint."

"Was she drugged?" Carmine asked.

"All the results aren't in, but there's nothing in her blood relevant to the attack. The number of rapes is impossible to tell, but he used his fist more this time. She is shockingly bruised and torn, particularly around the anus. Though it seems he does not attain orgasm, he must be an extremely fit man to sustain so many erections. Fist plays an increasing part, but we know from his living victims that he uses his penis constantly."

"What about the chains, Patsy?" Carmine asked.

"As he cases their apartments ahead of time, it may be that the brass bed gave him the idea, so we can't write cuffs and chains down as a permanent change in his method. If there is a next time and the bed's an ordinary one, he might use twine."

"The Dodo is a forensic desert," Carmine said gloomily.

"Yes, cuz, I'm afraid he is."

Carmine's phone rang as the meeting broke up. "Don't go!" he barked at Helen as he hung up. "There's a parcel for you at the front desk," he said. "I've asked that it be sent up. In the meantime, do you have a report on the Warburton twins yet?"

She jumped. "Yes, sir! They're in my notebook."

"Fetch it, please."

Her answer was to heft the shoulder bag onto a chair seat, scrabble, and triumphantly produce a thick exercise book bound in navy-blue, with the Holloman PD coat of arms on it. "Here, sir. I put it all in my notebook."

"Good," he said, surprised, skimming through it. "What's with the colored inks?"

"Oh!" she exclaimed, looking confused. "My own convenience, Captain. Black is for straight narration; crime scenes are in blue, significant facts are red, anything environmental or chemical is in green, and my own theories and hypotheses are in purple."

He glanced up, face expressionless. "Original," he said, "but I can see why it's a help. Keep this one for the glass teddy bear, but use a separate notebook for the Dodo. And don't hesitate to get empty ones from Stores."

"No, sir." He was curious about her parcel—well, good! She was livid. Which one of her friends was playing a joke? A young cop came in, holding a package not much larger than a matchbox, though he was clearly unsure whether to give it to its addressee, Helen, or Carmine, her boss. Carmine nodded at her, which the cop took to mean he should give it to her. "Sit down, Helen, for God's sake!" Carmine said. "I won't chew you out for opening your parcel. Sit, sit!"

She did so, clumsily, having forgotten her bag was on the chair, but eventually she got herself organized, and sneaked a peek at him as he flicked the pages of her notebook. It was entertaining him. She could see what the unknown joker had sent her. Very well wrapped! Corners squared, the whole exercise done without any scotch-tape— just string, expertly tied. When she got the paper off, she found one of those big matchbox tins that held proper matches—the kind a cowboy used to light by scraping the match on his boot. *Who?* She struggled to open the tin, seeing the point of Carmine's contention on her first day that long nails were not for women cops unless they were Delia's—now her nails, he had explained gravely, could double for crowbars.

Carmine was caught in Helen's narrative—whatever it did or did not do, Miss Procter's taught excellent English: Helen had style. Came a strangled gasp, a choke; he looked up immediately, and in alarm.

Face drained of color, she was staring at him blindly, a sheet of paper in her right hand, the box still in her left.

Carmine moved around his table and took the box before it could fall. Its lid was flopped open, he gaped at an amputated finger.

The brown wrapping paper was tipping off her lap, that had to be rescued first.

"What is this?" he barked.

She mutely handed him the paper.

WE HAVE KURT VON FAHLENDORF. YOU HAVE HIS LEFT LITTLE FINGER. INFORM HIS FAMILY THAT THEY ARE TO DELIVER THE SUM OF TEN MILLION AMERICAN DOLLARS TO THE SWISS BANK ACCOUNT WHOSE NUMBER IS ATTACHED. THE SUM MUST BE LODGED BY FRIDAY, 25TH OCTOBER, AT NOON, GREENWICH TIME. IF IT IS NOT PAID, KURT VON FAHLENDORF WILL DIE.

He put the box down on his table carefully. "Have you any reason to believe this finger does belong to Kurt?"

"I don't know," she whispered.

Carmine picked up his phone, dialed an extension. "Paul, bring your fingerprint gear to my office right this second." A keen glance informed him that his trainee wasn't going to pass out; her color was returning, awareness filling her eyes.

"Kurt is on a green card, right?" he asked.

"Yes."

"Then his prints will be on file with Immigration and Naturalization in Washington, D.C. That means we can identify the finger as his or not his very quickly. I think it's best we do this before notifying anyone, from Kurt's family to the FBI."

"Sir, isn't that weird? *The note was sent to a cop!* It says nothing about not notifying the FBI! Don't they care?"

"It seems not. I agree, Helen. Very weird kidnappers."

Delia and Nick came in together and froze at once into attention;

Carmine gave them the gist of the matter in a few sentences, by which time Paul had arrived.

"Facsimile the print, his name and social security number to the exact right number at Immigration and Naturalization—Nick, get that done, please."

"Have you had breakfast, Helen?" Delia asked.

"Uh—no, just coffee. I usually wait for morning coffee break and have a Danish."

"Then there's nought to do until we get word about the identification of the fingerprint," Delia said briskly. "Paul has the letter, we have a xerox of it, and I suggest we repair to Malvolio's to discuss our moves. Please, Carmine?"

"A good idea," said Carmine.

The diner was fairly crowded, but they got a big booth down the back and enough privacy to talk. Carmine studied the note. "Typed on an electric machine. The only prints will be yours and mine, Helen. Nor will the wrapping paper yield any information. Delia?"

"It's not an IBM," said Delia positively. "An Olivetti, I'd guess. The phraseology is educated—succinct and with some attempt at style. The date is European—day ahead of month—and how many Americans are familiar with Greenwich Mean Time? West Germany is an hour ahead of GMT, as I remember, but daylight savings might be a muddle, as various countries finish at quite different dates. The writer is specific—we have Kurt's left little finger. The kidnappers use plural number, but that's usual. Solo kidnappings are mostly women who snatch babies left in buggies at supermarkets."

"What I want to know," said Carmine, eating an apple Danish, "is why the ransom note came to you, Helen. The letter makes it clear that Kurt's family hasn't been told—you're to do that. Are you and

Kurt so hot an item that his family knows about you? Come on, eat another Danish. You need your strength."

"I don't know what Kurt may have told his family in Munich," Helen said soberly, "but here in Holloman we're just an item, rather than a hot one. For instance, we're not lovers, and most of Kurt's colleagues know that. He's thirty-four and looking for a wife, not a mistress."

"Would his family be under the same impression?" asked Nick.

"It's possible. Last night we had dinner together, and he dropped heavy hints about what kind of engagement ring I'd like. I flew right at him! I'd choose my engagement ring, I said—all my fiancé had to do was pay for it. Typical Kurt, he took that literally. It didn't even cross his mind that I might have been turning his proposal down." Her eyes filled with sudden tears. "Oh, I'm hard!"

"If you don't want him, hard's better," said Delia.

"Well, I think we have to assume that Kurt's family deems you his future wife," Carmine said. "If Delia's right about the note, then the kidnapping is German-orchestrated."

"The Swiss bank account confirms that," said Nick. "How would an American gang of kidnappers get inside the fortress of a Swiss bank? Answer: they couldn't. And ten million dollars? That's a massive ransom! The kidnappers must know that we won't get any information out of the bank. I mean, even Nazi gold is still sitting in some Swiss banks, even though everyone must know it will never be collected. Wow, the interest it must have accrued in twenty-plus years!"

"Have you accepted the fact yet, Helen, that if the finger belongs to Kurt, you're going to have to call his family?" asked Carmine. "Is his father still alive?"

"Yes, the Graf is still alive, and I have realized it."

"Is Graf a first name?"

"No, it's a title. The English equivalent would be Baron. But I won't be calling him, he's too senile. Kurt's sister, Dagmar, runs the family now," said Helen.

"Fill us in a little on the von Fahlendorfs, Helen."

"The Graf's first name is Erich. After he escaped from the East he finally got a chance to do something with his Italian wife's fortune—they kept very quiet while Hitler was in power. The Baroness financed the Baron's first factory, in Munich. He was a genius chemist who invented a process for dying synthetic fibers. Now, twenty years later, Fahlendorf Farben has a dozen factories scattered all over West Germany."

"How come the Baroness kept her money ungarnished through the Third Reich?" Nick asked, frowning.

"Her father deposited it in a Swiss bank, of course. The day after Mussolini signed the Pact of Steel with Hitler. The Milanese nobility seem to have run rings around Mussolini."

"More Miss Procter's history, Helen?" Carmine asked, smiling.

"Oh, definitely, sir."

"Where does Kurt come into this?" Nick demanded.

"Helen's getting there," Carmine said softly.

"Kurt's aptitude for mathematics showed very early, though he's not musical, and as he grew older he inclined to physics. It was Dagmar took after the Baron, had the chemistry. She's five years older than Kurt, and went from university into Fahlendorf Farben as a research chemist. She's better than the old man, so Kurt was free to do what he loves—particle physics. The Baron consented when he was told Kurt was potential Nobel material."

"Are they snobs, then?" Nick asked.

"Insufferable snobs," said Helen without hesitation. "Old Prussian junker stock, very conscious of the bloodline. They were Catholic Social Democrats, hence the disapproval of Hitler."

"Is Dagmar married?" Carmine asked.

"Yes. The Baron and Baroness dislike him—he's low-born. More importantly, he's not in Dagmar's class when it comes to the chemical innovations Fahlendorf Farben must produce if it's to stay ahead of the competition—insecticides, fertilizers, new plastics, oil substitutes. They met in Bonn, at university. In 1951, a year after they were married, Josef changed his name to von Fahlendorf, and struck a deal with the Baron, who wasn't senile then. In return for changing his name, he'd be paid a fat salary, no questions asked, no accountability. Kurt loathes Josef, mostly because he's hurt Dagmar so badly. No mistresses—fraud. She caught him selling her trade secrets in unpatented formulae to Fahlendorf Farben's chief rival. Luckily she found out before the papers were handed over. Josef was sent to the Fahlendorf Farben equivalent of Siberia, though he still has an office and a fat pay check. That's because his name is von Fahlendorf, as far as I can gather, and the old Baron tends to protect him for the sake of the grandchildren."

"How many children do Dagmar and Josef have?" Carmine asked.

"Four. Two boys, then two girls. Aged between fifteen and seven. The youngest, a girl, is by far the most intelligent. The children have been taught to despise their father," Helen said.

"What was Josef's name before he became a von Fahlendorf?" Delia asked.

"I haven't been able to find out, I think because the family is busy playing ostrich—they want the world to believe that the guy really is a von Fahlendorf cousin of some kind."

"Could you find out, Deels?" Carmine asked.

"If it were in Britain, yes, sir, but not in either of the Germanys. Just what are you thinking?"

"If this could possibly be a family job."

"Nothing would surprise me," said Helen, trying to sound cool.

"Ten million dollars!" Delia exclaimed. "Can they raise that?"

"I honestly don't know! How do I break the news?"

"As a cop does," Carmine said. "Sympathetically, warmly, yet dispassionately."

"But will they be able to raise the money, Captain?"

"It's a perfect scheme," said Delia. "Kidnappings inevitably disintegrate over payment of the ransom—it's so difficult to retrieve from the drop spot undetected. Whereas here there is no drop spot, just a Swiss bank account number. The money never enters the U.S.A., and the Swiss will never divulge information about their clients."

"Once the money's deposited, we can't touch anyone," Nick said. "The whole thing sucks."

Carmine slid out of the booth, reaching for his wallet. "No, this is on me."

Helen didn't speak until they reached Carmine's office. "I've made up my mind, Captain," she said then. "I'll talk to Dagmar, but I'm not going to drop any hints that the kidnapping might be a family job. Dagmar is the logical one."

"A good decision," said Carmine, sitting down.

Nick came in on their heels. "The finger belongs to Kurt von Fahlendorf," he said. "It's been verified twice over."

The phone rang: Paul Bachman. Carmine put it on the speaker. "There are no prints except yours and Helen's on the package," Paul said. "Patrick says the finger was amputated eight to nine hours ago. There are no drugs in the blood, so they cut it off cold turkey. No cauterization either. Kurt will have lost some blood, though not a major bleed. Patrick suggests that the only first aid might have been to pack the hand afterward."

"They mean business," Carmine said. "If we don't find him, he's a dead man. Payment of the ransom won't alter that. They've taken a mature, highly intelligent man trained to look for things smaller than atoms. They daren't release him." The amber eyes stared into Helen's soul. "You can't betray this when you speak to Dagmar, Helen. The family has to make its decision as to payment or non-payment in the belief that there's a chance Kurt will be found alive. You're not empowered to communicate what we might know is fact, as fact. At this stage, nothing is proven."

"I understand," Helen said, staring at the railroad clock on the wall facing Carmine. "It's nine a.m. here, which means it's three p.m. in Munich." She reached into her huge bag and drew out a black notebook: her own property. "I have Dagmar's work number as well as her home one. Kurt gave them to me in case anything ever happened to him." She laughed wryly. "He meant a car or a skiing accident, not a kidnapping."

"Fred's rigged up this red phone through a tape recorder," said Carmine. "On speaker, we'll hear every word said. The recorder switches on automatically the moment the receiver's picked up. Go to it, Helen, and don't let us put you off. We have to be here." He handed her the red receiver.

Dagmar was at work, and answered the phone herself; the number Kurt had given Helen was a private line.

The von Fahlendorf daughter's initial reaction was incredulity, followed by all the emotions associated with a practical joke. Only when they had worn themselves out did Dagmar begin to suspect that her caller was serious. At the same moment Helen reached the end of her tether

"Listen, ma'am," she said, "I'm handing you over to our chief of detectives, Captain Carmine Delmonico. Maybe you'll believe him—he's a man!"

She subsided muttering while Delia patted her soothingly and Carmine talked to Dagmar, who, perhaps because she associated police with men, now seemed to understand Kurt's situation and peril thoroughly.

"What's concerning all of us in Holloman is the size of the ransom," Carmine said. "Have you any hope of raising it?"

"Oh, yes," said the clear voice in its German accent, "it is already collected."

"No kidding! How did that coincidence happen?"

"It is the foundation of a trust fund for my children," said Dagmar. "My mother has retired from the company, and the ten million represents her capital, which she insisted be put into American dollars. Of course it will go to pay Kurt's ransom—we can always set up another trust fund for the children later."

"I see." Carmine's mind was racing. "First of all, ma'am, I do assure you that your brother has been kidnapped. His finger established his identity, as the kidnappers knew it would. I must warn you that the odds of getting Kurt back alive are not good, but there is a chance. The Holloman end will be devoted to a search aimed at finding him, because we have our doubts that the kidnapping masterminds are in America. We think they may be German, and that the kidnappers don't care who is brought in to solve the American end because it can't make any difference to the ransom. That's going straight from Munich to Zurich."

"Typically American!" she said in an icy voice. "Blame anyone but yourselves."

"There's no blame attached to us, Frau von Fahlendorf!" said Carmine, voice equally icy. "We're the whipping boy. What's your husband's real name?"

"Von Fahlendorf," she said.

"No, before he changed it."

"That is no one's business except his."

"For someone whose blood brother is in terrible danger, you seem to have strange priorities, ma'am."

"Don't call me ma'am!" she snapped. "Helen, what is the account number, and the name of the bank?"

Carmine shook his head vigorously. "Oh, no, ma'am, you don't get that information until it's time to pay the ransom."

She hung up.

"What a bummer!" Nick exclaimed. "The Dodo escalates to murder, and a day later a foreign national who is a Chubb professor of physics is kidnapped. It stretches us thin, boss."

"Too thin," said Carmine grimly. "I'll have to go see the Commissioner in a minute, but first—priorities. The Dodo has to be worked, even though his victim is dead. We don't know if von Fahlendorf is dead yet, so we proceed on the assumption that he's alive. That's not impossible, because a lot of kidnappers kill passively by imprisoning their victim somewhere impregnable and then not giving them food or water. Three days without water, three weeks without food. Not a terribly accurate rule of thumb. If the prison's insulated, sheltered and full of air, the victim will survive at least a week unwatered. Therefore our first priority is searching for Kurt." He hunched his shoulders, sank his chin onto his chest and thought for what seemed an eternity; it was probably three or four minutes. Then he sighed. "I can' t run the Dodo and the kidnapping," he said flatly. "As a completely new case, the kidnapping goes to Corey and his team, with Helen tacked on to liaise between us and Kurt's family as well as with other agencies like the FBI."

Helen's face betrayed her dismay, but she had learned from her conflict with Abe Goldberg; she nodded willingly.

"When and if Abe and his team can be freed up, we'll have two teams spearheading the search for Kurt. Helen, keep me in the loop at all times. You're my trainee, not a part of Corey's team—understand?"

"Yes, sir." She looked directly at Carmine. "Will the FBI be a help or a hindrance, Captain? Cops dislike them."

"They won't bother the Holloman PD," said Carmine, unfazed. "If the kidnappers were known criminals, the FBI would be a big help, but we know they're not. I'd be willing to take a hefty bet that they're German nationals who visited the U.S.A. with only one purpose—to snatch Kurt. Further, the kidnappers knew that Dagmar von Fahlendorf had liquidated her mother's investments to form a trust fund for the grandchildren. Again, it screams a German operation. Our real task is to find Kurt before the ransom money has to be paid."

"Do you seriously think that she's involved?" Delia asked.

"No, but I don't trust her security, Deels. If she leaves the name of the bank and account number lying around, and the kidnapper has access to the ten million, the transfer might take place ahead of time. So—she doesn't get it until her Friday twenty-five ."

"What if the FBI tell her?" Helen asked.

"After I've explained, they won't."

From Silvestri's office Carmine went to Corey's, two floors down. He was on his own.

When Carmine entered Corey looked up, grinned, and pushed a file across his desk. His long, dark face was suffused with triumphant content.

"The Taft High arms cache case," he said. "Closed."

"That's great, Cor. Fill me in."

"It wasn't as bad as we originally thought, though Buzz is still muttering that there's more to it. All I can say is that if there is more, we can't find evidence of it, including Buzz. The story as we have it is that someone in the Black Brigade got spooked into thinking there was a raid coming, and gave his little brother the cache of guns he had in their home. The kid hid them at the Taft High gym, and, as you know, Principal White found them."

"Why does Buzz think there's more to it, Cor?"

"He believes the Black Brigade has thrown off a splinter group composed of less patient, more violent soldiers who don't think Wesley le Clerc is doing it any more than Mohammed el Nesr. Both le Clerc and el Nesr preach that violence for the sake of violence is a waste of manpower, but the splinter group is tired of waiting for the country's entire black population to erupt. The guns weren't supposed to be at the school for more than a few hours in transit—they'd been bought with the proceeds of a bank holdup in Middletown, and there are a shitload more than were found."

"But there's no proof?"

"None whatsoever."

"Then the case is closed. But keep an eye peeled, huh?"

"Sure, always. What have you got for me now?"

"A kidnapping."

Corey sat bolt upright, staring at Carmine as at the Angel Gabriel. "*A kidnapping*?" he squawked, gasping.

"Yes, and not a baby snatching outside a supermarket." Corey following avidly, Carmine told him the story of Professor Kurt von Fahlendorf, including the direction his own theories were taking.

"Is it possible that von Fahlendorf himself is a part of it?" Corey asked.

"No, I don't think so. I'm picking his brother-in-law, but I don't expect to get much co-operation from the Munich cops." He leaned forward across Corey's desk. "I'm giving you Helen MacIntosh because she knows Kurt better than anyone else here, and because she's the liaison between Kurt's family and all the cops on this side of the Atlantic."

"He's already dead, Carmine."

"I agree, but we have to pretend he's alive. And, Cor?"

"Yeah?"

"Keep decent notes. That's a direct order. This case has the potential to wind up in a civil court with the State or the County accused of some kind of malfeasance. And don't glare at me! You've brought cautions on your own head. If Morty Jones takes a drink, he's off the force. Understood?"

Corey managed to nod civilly, but the anger burned inside. "Sure, Carmine." He thought of something. "I guess the FBI will be here to trip us up?"

"Is assassination the flavor of the year? Sure the FBI will be here. I expect you to co-operate with its agents, okay?"

"We'll give them whatever we get."

"Good," said Carmine, knowing it was a lie. "Helen will be here shortly to fill you in on the details." He walked out, very relieved that Corey was finally shaping up.

A kidnapping! The ultimate crime, the hardest to solve, the most satisfying yet frustrating case to run, thought Corey. He frowned. What was this about, he, a lieutenant, having to wait to be briefed by a lowly trainee? Still, he knew Carmine. If the boss said she knew the most, then she did. Unwilling to sit waiting for her like a patient for his doctor, Corey got up and went to the office of his two team members.

Buzz was filling in the despised time sheets, a task Corey had handed to his precise second-stringer when he realized that the guy actually enjoyed filling in forms. When told what was in the offing, Buzz swelled in satisfaction.

"Where's Morty?" Corey asked.

Buzz Genovese shrugged. "Try Cells. Virgil Simms is in charge since Vasquez shifted everyone around, and Virgil's an old pal of Morty's. I'll call if you like."

"No," Corey said quickly. "I need some exercise, I'll go find him for myself. You can go to my office. We have to wait for the princess."

The cells and the offices attached to brief incarceration were on the ground floor of the County Services annex, which had been due for demolition ten years ago but was still waiting—and still functioning. It contained all kinds of antique gear for long-abandoned police techniques, like two massive bathtubs wherein raving lunatics were once submerged until the men in white coats could come and remove them to the asylum. The record of every drunk held overnight was on a file card in a special room together with arrests on more serious charges of everything from arson to murder.

There were twelve terrifyingly white cells, each twenty by twenty feet, equipped with a toilet and inadequate bench-bunk-beds covered in stained mattress ticking down three of the walls. The whiteness, achieved by tiles, dated back to the turn of the nineteenth/twentieth century, and meant that the slightest hint of dirt showed up like neon signs in a black void. It was general practice to put the night's takings in as few cells as possible; less mess to clean up later.

No place, however, for a woman. Of the weaker sex the Cell Sergeant saw few; when one did arrive, she was put in a proper room, albeit one easy to clean and not good enough for a lady. It had a toilet with a seat on it behind a screen, a wash basin, and three proper single beds, though the mattress ticking didn't vary. She was issued with a towel and bed linen. No mirrors, of course. Usually these poor creatures were plunged into a despair so deep that a shard from a broken mirror would have spelled freedom in death. Few of Holloman's whores were arrested; the female intake varied from wives who had killed their husbands or lovers to child abusers.

A man pushing forty, Sergeant Virgil Simms was sitting in his office wading through the mountains of paper this new Captain of Uniforms was generating. When Corey came in he sighed, and inclined his head toward the women's cell.

"Sleeping it off?" Corey asked.

"I doubt that," Simms said loyally; he and Morty had gone through the academy together, served on patrol as partners, kept up their friendship. "The new housekeeper's giving him hell, so are his kids. The only place he seems to be able to sleep is down here. Sorry, Cor."

"Not your fault. Thanks for helping. Our boss isn't very sympathetic."

Corey walked into the women's cell to find Morty sprawled on one bed in an attitude that suggested either booze or bone-tiredness; he didn't stink of Jack or Jim, so maybe Virgil was right, he couldn't sleep in the hell of his home.

"Morty!" Corey called, shaking his shoulder. "Morty, it's time to wake up. Have a shave and comb your hair—we've got a new case, and it's a doozy. I need you alert! The Captain's going to be watching us, and he's put a spy with us—Princess Helen. She'll be reporting everything to him. And go home later, find a clean shirt. You look like something the cat dragged in."

He caught the elevator upstairs; he'd been gone twenty minutes. Buzz strolled in and sat; Morty, looking reasonable, entered on his heels. All three men were waiting when Helen, looking flustered, came in.

"You're late," said Corey: put her in her place, tell her that she wasn't going to be the kingpin around here.

"My apologies," she said, but offered no excuses. Then she proceeded to give them a description of the case that, Corey had to admit, could not be faulted. "I'm here with you because I know Kurt very well, and the kidnapper is using me as the go-between. Beyond that, I'm strictly a trainee," she said, winding up her presentation.

"Thanks." said Corey, "First, I want you to come with me to an interrogation room—yeah, yeah, I know the Powers That Be want them called interview rooms, but the old name suits me fine. Whatever you know about Kurt von Fahlendorf and his family is best put on tape and transcribed. We're going to have the FBI all over us, and I want something to slap on my desk in front of their head honcho. It'll save us a lot of time as well. Buzz and Morty, listen in and ask your own questions."

Off they went, Helen's head spinning; Corey's detecting techniques were certainly different from Carmine's!

Nor was Corey easy on her, either because she was one of their own, or because her father was the President of Chubb University and she had a trust fund five times bigger than the von Fahlendorf ransom. He grilled her mercilessly for two hours as to her relationship with Kurt—thank God she wasn't sleeping with him! Who his other friends were, how much she knew about the people he worked with, why the son of an industrial chemist had gone into particle physics, what his habits were, his favorite colors, his favorite music, why he'd bought a pre-Revolutionary house—it went on and on. She answered calmly and lucidly, and was sufficiently intelligent to keep the threads separated in her mind—no contradictions or uncertainties in Helen MacIntosh's testimony! To her surprise, she was asked to read the typed version and sign it as an affidavit. Smiling slightly, she obliged. Corey was loading both barrels for the advent of the FBI by giving them twenty tangents to fly off on.

"Shrewd, but it won't answer," she said. "By the way, Corey, has anyone told you recently what a prick you are?"

Looking taken aback, Corey took her affidavit and left; she was not surprised to find that he chose to go to lunch with Morty and

Buzz. The word was getting around too. Soon the papers, radio and TV would be sniffing, and the kidnapping would go public.

Delia was eating alone; Helen slid in opposite her and ordered a burger and fries.

"I just told Corey Marshall he was a prick."

"Accurate," said Delia, enjoying Yankee pot roast.

"He grilled me for two hours, then brought in these people to rubber-stamp my statement as an affidavit."

"You could have said no."

"Wasn't worth it."

"Carmine had to break into Kurt's house," mumbled Delia through a mouthful of mashed potato. "The Porsche was locked in the garage, and his keys and wallet were on his hall table. That means he got home." Her eyes followed Carmine as he entered Malvolio's, sought out Corey. "Corey's being told now."

Helen put her pager on the table. "In case Munich calls."

"I hope they don't call you in the middle of the night."

"Doesn't matter," Helen said cheerfully as she bit into her burger. "I go back to sleep in seconds."

Carmine slid into the booth next to Helen. "Is it usual for Kurt to leave his keys and wallet on the hall table?" he asked, his body language telling those who watched that it was Delia he questioned, not Helen.

Who got the message and picked up a French fry. "Yes, sir, it's usual. Just as he always locks up the Porsche."

"You'd better come with me as soon as you're finished eating, Helen. I want you to check Kurt's house, including the guest quarters, with particular regard to foreign presences."

"How do I explain my delinquency to Lieutenant Marshall?"

"I already have."

"Then as soon as Delia is finished, I'm ready, sir."

"No one has stayed here, Captain," Helen said to Carmine after touring Kurt's premises thoroughly. "Nothing is out of place. It also looks as if Kurt's wearing the outfit he wore when we went to Buffo's last night."

"How long have the von Fahlendorfs been planning to set up this trust fund?" Carmine asked as he locked the front door.

"It's a mystery to me. Kurt's never mentioned it."

"Would you have expected him to under normal circumstances?"

She paused halfway down the path. "Yes, I think I would.. Kurt's not secretive. I don't mean that he runs off at the mouth, but a trust fund is an important thing. Yes, he'd discuss it."

"Which means one of two things: that he wasn't told, or that the idea is a very recent one. Does Dagmar tend to cut Kurt out because he's elected to live in a foreign country and pursue a foreign career?" Carmine asked.

"I think Dagmar loves Kurt very much," Helen said slowly, "but I also think that a part of her condemns him for leaving the Fatherland. When Kurt talks of her, there's always an underlying tone of sadness. Once he told me that the family felt that if he was brilliant enough to be a Nobel contender in physics, he could have done the same in chemistry."

"And could he?"

"No!" she said scornfully. "Kurt's narrow, and his gifts are mathematical. Chemistry is *terra incognita* to him."

"They should have had a Prunella Balducci when Kurt was less than two years old," said Carmine.

"Eh?"

"No matter."

"How intensive is the search for Kurt going to be, Captain?"

"That depends on the FBI. They take the lead in kidnappings."

"Are they on their way?"

"They'll be at County Services by the time we get back."

Robert and Gordon Warburton came galloping down the path from their house just as Carmine and Helen were about to climb into the Fairlane.

"Captain, Captain!" said Robbie breathlessly, "is it true?"

"Is what true?"

"That Kurt's been kidnapped."

"Yes, it is. Did you see him last night?"

"Not see," said Gordie. "Heard."

"What did you hear, Gordon?" Carmine asked.

"The Porsche coming home about one in the morning— Wednesday to Thursday, that is. Late for Kurt!"

"Why did you hear it and not Robert?"

"I'm on Kurt's side of the house. Robbie hears Mason Novak come and go—his garage is in his backyard."

"Are you sure you didn't look, Gordon?" Carmine pressed.

"Wellll ... When he grated his gears, I confess I did get up to have a look, Captain. I mean, Kurt *never* grates his gears!"

"An observation I confirm, Gordon," said Helen.

"What did you see?" Carmine asked.

"Not Kurt, for sure! Two people, a woman and a man. They got out of the Porsche and played with the remote as if they'd never seen one before. When the door went up, they got back into the car and drove in. I went back to bed," said Gordie.

"Did you get a look at them?" Helen asked eagerly.

"Since there's a lamp post there, yes. The woman was about forty, the man younger. She wore what looked like dark red, but she had a hat with a veil on her head, so her features were a mystery. I think her hair was dark. Certainly she had a good figure. The man deferred to her. He had thick, wavy dark hair and a handsome face, but don't ask me to identify him in a line-up because I couldn't do it." He giggled. "Handsome is as handsome does, Captain."

Carmine growled. "Keep on like this, Gordon, and you won't be half as handsome."

"Ooo-aa!"

"Did either of you see Kurt on Wednesday?" Helen asked.

"Yes, around five-thirty. The Porsche was parked on the kerb and he came running out of the house dressed for a date, we thought," said Robbie. "Very smart!"

"They're weirdos," said Carmine as he and Helen drove away. "At first I thought they were bent. Now I don't think the homo act is real. Though they're not straight."

"Think of pretzels," said Helen, grinning.

"Let's both write reports, huh? That way, yours will end up with Corey Marshall, who'll shove it at the Feds."

"Anything you say, Captain."

"Your journals are excellent, by the way."

She went pink. "Truly?"

"Oh, yes. I especially like the colored inks."

"Well, I'm long-winded, so having different colors makes it easier to find a specific passage."

"I may adopt it myself."

She went pinker.

Of course the case was huge, not to mention very complicated. The person kidnapped was a foreign national resident in the United States; his father, who was paying the ransom, lived in West Germany; and the ten million dollars were bypassing the United States on a much shorter journey between Munich and Zurich. Worse, none of the police forces involved had any jurisdiction over a large and prestigious Swiss bank.

"It's brilliant," said Carmine to Desdemona that night as they got ready for bed. His eyes, at once appreciative and caring, had noted that his wife looked calmer, fresher, more alive.

"If you put that nightie on, it's only going to get ripped off," he said, climbing into his side of the big bed.

She giggled and draped it over a convenient chair. "There! I can grab it in an emergency. Having children rather inhibits nudity." She slid into bed and gave a luxurious stretch that had him wanting her more urgently than he had planned; he groaned, rolled over and buried his face in her neck.

"Carmine, stop! You know that drives me wild! I want to say something," she said in a low voice, yanking at his head until he gave up and lay still to listen. "Now I understand why the second child can be perilous. You were right to want to wait a year or two longer. Prunella says some women need quite an amount of time to get their hormones back to normal, and she thinks I am one such. I've been—I've been down in the dumps since Alex was born, and I got myself in a terrible muddle. It all went to Julian, I haven't given Alex the attention he should have. But, you know, I couldn't see it! Not until I had a few heart-to-hearts with Prunella, anyway. Normally I'm efficient enough to cope with whatever comes along, so these past six months have been a shock. But I'm getting better now, dear love, I truly am. With Prunella to take the brunt of Julian and teach him a routine, I have enough time and energy to love Alex the way he has to be loved. He's not a scrap like Julian, and this time with him is vital." She sighed, stroking Carmine's hair. "Our elder son is a handful, and I now understand that old saying better—there's no training for politics or parenthood."

"Well, it's not hard to see that you're feeling much better," he said, zeroing in on her neck again.

"No, no, *wait*! I want to thank you, Carmine, for being not only understanding, but finding the answer to my depression. East Holloman is one vast extended family, you have access to all sorts of people. And I thank you for setting the network in motion. How else would I ever have found a Prunella?"

"Finished?"

"Yes."

He went back to driving her wild by kissing her neck, his arms around her, her legs around him. How great it was to make love to a six-foot-three wife!

Though wives of any kind were far from Carmine's mind the next morning, when the FBI hit town. No Ted Kelly this time, of course, as espionage was not on the menu; this team was led by Special

Agent Hunter Wyatt, a very different kind of man and investigator. Of medium height and build, he moved well; his face was studious down to a pair of wire-rimmed glasses behind which genuinely grey eyes regarded the world with what appeared to be a deep-rooted skepticism. Carmine liked him, and took him off to Malvolio's for coffee.

"Beats cop coffee," he explained, "and you'll be getting plenty of that. Unless you have an expense account bigger than a Holloman cop's, Malvolio's is the best place to eat."

"This suits me fine. Fill me in," said Hunter Wyatt.

Privately deciding that if you had a name like Hunter Wyatt you were a shoo-in for a career in law enforcement, Carmine filled him in. "Tell me my bones are wrong," he ended.

"I can't. Your bones are right. Number one, this isn't an American operation. The kidnapping occurred here, but it was carried out by foreign nationals. Number two, I think we have to suspect that Herr Josef von Fahlendorf is the mastermind, even if he didn't leave Munich. Number three, we're not going to find Kurt von Fahlendorf alive, the usual way—he'll be left in an impregnable prison without food or water. That might be a car trunk or a cellar or something so weird that its nature hasn't occurred to us. They don't dare leave him alive because he's a mature man of undeniable genius. He's used to looking for the tracks of unknown particles on backgrounds that are one mass of loops, whorls, curves and paths, which makes him the kind of guy who'll notice a tiny bump in a smooth wall or the faintest seam where a door used to be. He probably has superlative hearing, and who knows what sounds may have percolated into his prison?"

"You're the expert, Hunter, so what kind of prison might Germans have chosen?" Carmine asked.

"Not a car trunk, I'd say. They'd gravitate toward something like a cellar, except that ordinary cellars conduct sound, so it would have to be isolated from things that produce noise. I'd go for a quarry or some underground prison. I notice that this coast on army maps is riddled with old gun emplacements—very German! My guess is that the guy is in Connecticut, and not far enough away from Holloman for the kidnappers to need an Interstate. If Gordon Warburton is right and the kidnappers are a man and a woman, that reduces their physical strength. Either there are three or four of them, the unknowns male, or the duo you picked is strange. Why a woman? When we know that, Carmine, we'll know it all."

"Yeah, especially given that Kurt wasn't drugged. If they needed to render him unconscious, they did it with a blow or blows to the head," said Carmine. "They chopped off his finger while he was out to it, and by the time he woke up, he was imprisoned."

"An hour," Wyatt said immediately. "He was seen by your two patrolmen at ten on Wednesday night. By eleven-thirty at the latest, he was locked up, one finger gone. Why no drugs?"

"My guess is that they're amateurs," Carmine said. "Their German experience didn't include garage doors opened by a remote, and their lack of drugs suggests that they labored under the misapprehension that our customs people might have searched them scrupulously. People always assume that the unknown world behaves exactly the same as the world they know. German customs is very severe, especially if there's a suspected link to East Germany. So let's assume there is a link to the East."

Hunter Wyatt had been scribbling in his notebook; he looked up with a smile. "Want to join the FBI, Captain?"

"And lose the network my wife admires? No, thanks."

"It seems to me," Hunter Wyatt said, "that we should expend our energies on finding Kurt von Fahlendorf."

"I couldn't agree more. Has Corey Marshall given you all our information?"

"Yes. He's a good cop—has to be to grill the girl the way he did, considering who she is. She has to be a good cop too, because she co-operated all the way. The kidnappers aren't afraid of being found, or of Kurt's being found. What kind of guy is von Fahlendorf? A jock? A nerd? He looks like a movie star."

"He does look like a movie star. But according to Helen MacIntosh he's not into how he looks. In fact, he seems to be what his profession would indicate—a nerd."

"Then every available law enforcement individual in Holloman should be looking for Kurt von Fahlendorf. If we find him alive, he'll be an ideal witness."

"If," Carmine cautioned, "he remembers people and events."

Leaving Hunter Wyatt with Corey and his team, Carmine went to see the Commissioner.

Who had already held two press conferences, but, typical John Silvestri, played his cards shrewdly; the action, he pointed out, would certainly be in and around Holloman, but also as far afield as Munich and certain huge American cities.

"As far as the journalists are concerned, there's a certain thrill to this case," the Commissioner said. "It's big money, foreign nationals, German involvement, da de da de da. I led the sharks a dance."

"You can also feed them people like the Terrible Twins Robert and Gordon Warburton," Carmine said, finding a grin. "As the twins are actors, they'll relish the publicity attached to living next door to the kidnapped man."

"Thank you, thank you," said Silvestri with a purr.

"Now I have to discuss what we're going to do, John. Hunter Wyatt agrees that we're not going to find the kidnappers here in America, so he's willing to join forces with Holloman and other police departments who volunteer to look for Kurt. I don't know how you want to publicize this, but our aim is to find Kurt alive, before lack of water kills him. So I need the uniforms, of course, if Fernando's willing. We divide the county up into blocks and allocate searchers to every one of them. If people like the Gentleman Walkers want to volunteer, I can do with them. But it has to be a search under rigid control, or we'll miss sections and repeat others. If Fernando's willing, I'd like him to take charge in conjunction with Hunter Wyatt. Detectives is not in a position to assume command—among other cases, we still have the Dodo."

"You won't have opposition from Fernando," the Commissioner said in the voice that told Carmine he, and no one else, would be in overall command. "I'll start by getting the cops of neighboring counties on the job in their territory."

And that, thought Carmine, hurrying away, is why I love John Silvestri. He never pussyfoots around, it's straight for the throat. Unless, that is, he's holding a press conference, when he's smoother than Marzullo's butter-cream.

Next, Corey Marshall and his team. At first Corey was inclined to take the news of searching as a demotion, but after some persuasive talking, Carmine managed to make him see that locating the victim was actually more praiseworthy than apprehending the kidnappers, and was also a task that the FBI did not feel beneath it. It was highly likely, Carmine hinted, that in finding Kurt, they would have a fantastic lead to the kidnappers, sitting smugly in West Germany.

Morty Jones, he noticed as he left, was looking ghastly. Carmine rolled an eye at Helen, who unobtrusively followed him out.

"What's with Morty?"

"He was served with papers from a lawyer's office yesterday, but he won't open them. Just lugs them around."

"They'll be divorce papers. Why won't he open them?"

"I honestly don't know. Those three guys hate me. They think I'm your spy or snitch or something."

"Ignore that, and keep me informed."

"I feel like a snitch," she muttered.

"Don't. You aren't. I'm worried about Morty."

"Okay." She went off to the Ladies—yes, she was smart! Corey wouldn't know she'd snitched to the boss. But humiliating for her, Carmine thought, having to slink around corners. She *was* a snitch, but of the noble kind.

On the surface, things were going well for Morty Jones. Delia had come through with an excellent woman to keep his house in far better shape than Ava had, he was forced to admit. Milly worked eight to five Mondays to Fridays, did the washing and ironing, left a hot meal for them at night, and in a very few days had washed or sent to the cleaner's every drape, curtain, blanket and bedspread his home possessed. All of which made his kids happy. She was a cheerful person who asked about their day at school as if it really interested her, and saw to it that they did their homework. Milly also cooked delicious food.

But she couldn't make Morty happy. She wasn't Ava—sloppy, self-absorbed Ava, so glamorous as she flitted around in satin and feathers and high-heeled mules, bestowing kisses and apologies on the kids because she hadn't made their lunches or found them clean clothes—oh, Ava, Ava!

He had no idea what was in the envelope the process server had dropped on him yesterday afternoon, but his heart was leaden. So leaden, in fact, that he couldn't nerve himself to open the packet no matter how he tried. All Thursday night at home he had stared at it, then brought it in this morning still intact. He must open it, he must!

"Cor, I don't feel well," he whispered as soon as he had a little privacy. "I got to open these papers, but not here, not with that nosey little bitch sniffing around. Can I go down to Virgil? He's on, and I got privacy there."

"Sure," said Corey absently, only half hearing.

Virgil was busy discharging a tank full of drunks, but nodded toward the women's cell and left Morty to what he imagined was a much needed nap; the guy looked fucked.

But the papers and photographs that spilled out of the cheap brown envelope were not conducive to a nap. Ava was suing for divorce alleging cruelty, and asking for full custody of the kids, who, she stated, were not fathered by Morty. She was also asking for every cent he had in the world. Apparently it didn't matter that everything was in his name!

There were two groups of photographs, both in color: one was of a full length, naked Ava covered in hideous bruises, particularly nasty on her lower trunk and private parts; the other consisted of head shots showing a taped up nose in a swollen face black with bruises and cut around the mouth. Oh, Jesus, had he done *that* to her? She'd gone to the hospital emergency, then she'd found herself a lawyer. She wanted the kids! She wanted the house! She wanted his income and his savings! And there it was in full color, what he had done to her. Supported by, said a letter, witnesses as well as many photographs.

His career was over; Captain Delmonico had an absolute loathing for men who beat their wives. His chances of happiness were over. Oh, Ava, Ava! Why did you screw around? Who will believe that I only ever touched you that once, you whore, you sad bitch, you any man's cunt? They'll believe you. They always believe the woman. They'll say I made up the screwing around. Oh, Ava, Ava! Why?

He sat down on a naked bed, buried his face in his hands and wept, wept, wept …

Virgil Simms looked in, sighed, and went back to his work.

"We won't wait for Morty," Corey said. "He's not well, went to lie down. The sooner we start to search our block, the sooner Fernando will allocate us a fresh slice."

"May I have my own wheels?" Helen asked.

Corey eyed her warily; she was too pushy, reminded him of Maureen. "Is that stupid little wop car wired to base?"

"Naturally," she said, brows rising haughtily.

"Okay, then—but keep in touch, hear me? Buzz, you want to ride with me, or go on your own?"

"On my own," Buzz said quickly. "We're just looking, we don't need brute strength. If one of us finds something, it's a find for the whole team."

"I can live with that," Corey said, moving doorward.

"Sir, may I check up on Morty first?" Helen asked.

She really was a pest! "Okay, okay, whatever!" he snapped, and departed.

Helen clattered down the stairs in her nun's shoes—not very silent, for all their practicality—and crossed the courtyard that led to the old annex and the cells

She pushed open the door and beheld Virgil Simms in his glass-fronted office, head bent, working away.

"Hi, Virgil," she said. "How's Morty?"

"Asleep by now, I guess. His wife served him divorce papers and he's real cut up."

"Oh, poor Morty! Did he tell you?"

"Didn't need to. The papers were all around him on the bed. He's much better off without the bitch, but he refuses to see it. It's more than his loving her. I think he's terrified she'll take him to the cleaners. Morty's tighter than a fish's ass."

The roar of a .38 going off in an enclosed space destroyed their conversation; they went rigid.

"Morty!" Virgil cried, leaping around his desk.

He was out the door and running down the hall in a flash, toward a door at its end. He charged through it and stopped, Helen cannoning into him.

"Jesus, Morty!"

Helen shoved him to one side so she could see Morty Jones sitting on the edge of a bed, sagging forward, his .38 still in his hand, his brains a surreal pattern on the wall behind him.

"Get out of here, Virgil," she rapped, pushing him through the door and closing it on two uniforms hurrying toward them. "You," she said to one of them, "go back and guard the main entrance. No one is to come into Cells. And you," she said to the other, "stay here outside this door. Don't let anyone in."

Virgil Simms looked on the verge of collapse; Helen got him into his office chair and picked up the phone.

"Captain Delmonico? Please come immediately to the Cells, and bring Captain Vasquez with you. There's been an accident."

Carmine and Fernando arrived together five minutes later, staring in some amazement at the young woman who had apparently assumed command.

"No one's come in or gone out, but I haven't called the Medical Examiner yet," she said, forehead dewed with sweat. "Sergeant Jones ate his gun five minutes ago. Sergeant Simms and I heard the report. There was nothing we could do for Sergeant Jones, so we closed the door on him, came here, and called you at once."

"*We?*" asked Captain Vasquez.

"Yes, sir, we," Helen said steadily.

"Why are you here at all, Miss MacIntosh?" Fernando asked.

"I was worried about Sergeant Jones, sir, because I thought he had been served with divorce papers."

"Why look for him here?"

"I understand that in his shock he came looking for Sergeant Simms, sir. Or so my enquiries indicated."

"When Morty appeared I thought he was going to pass out, sir, so I told him to rest in the women's cell," said Virgil Simms.

"Let's look," said Fernando.

The two captains gazed at the ruin of Morty Jones, whose body still remained as it had been when he put the gun in his mouth and pulled the trigger. The door opened and Patrick O'Donnell walked in.

"Jesus, Carmine, didn't anyone suspect this was coming?"

"Yes, I did," said Carmine. "Unfortunately I was howled down by his lieutenant." He peered at the papers on the bed, drew a glove out of his pocket and picked up the full length photograph of Ava Jones. "Someone's touched this up," he said to Fernando Vasquez.

"The poor bastard!" Fernando said. "Why didn't he wait until he had a legal opinion? The touching up is amateurish, it would never hold up in court."

"Too late now," Carmine said. "Did he suffer, Patsy?"

"I would say, not at all, cuz. The bullet went through the vital structures of the brain stem, from the exit wound."

Fernando drew Carmine aside. "What's with his being allowed to use the women's cell?" he asked.

"I have no idea," said Carmine with complete truth. "I can tell you that Morty and Virgil Simms have been pals since academy days. They worked a patrol car together for years, too. Simms hasn't been down here more than a few weeks, I understand?"

"True. But we do have a sick bay, Carmine. I'll have to question Miss MacIntosh."

Carmine stared at him blankly. "Why?"

"She was down here at the time."

"Under specific orders from me. I asked her to keep an eye on Morty after I learned he'd been served with papers I assumed were divorce. Miss MacIntosh is needed where everyone we can spare is needed, Fernando—looking for Kurt von Fahlendorf."

The Captain of Uniforms thought for a moment, then nodded. "Very well, I'll take your word for it."

"You'd better!" said Carmine, none too pleased. "I'm not used to its being doubted, and nothing gives you the right to doubt it.

New brooms ought to save their bristles for genuine corruption. This is not corruption, it's a tragedy."

He jerked his head at Helen as he passed the Cells office on his way out, his expression flinty; Helen scrambled to keep up as he strode away.

"Did you fix Virgil up with a watertight story?" he asked. "If Captain Vasquez suspects liquor's involved—"

The eyes gazing up at him were limpid blue pools. "Yes, of course, sir. It's too complicated for a new captain of uniforms."

"Good. Now go do what you were going to do."

While I, he thought, clean up the shambles that the death of Morty Jones is going to make. He will have died intestate; men like Morty don't make wills, or plan for the future. That means his cop-fucking wife won't get everything, though if he'd made a will he would probably have named her sole legatee. His kids will inherit at least half, and Ava is no stranger to Child Welfare; they won't let a court give Ava power over the kids' share. Oh, Jesus, what a mess!

That stupid, horny wife! Why did Morty love her?

When Carmine tried to find Corey, he was told that Lieutenant Marshall was out searching for Kurt von Fahlendorf.

"I failed to take adequate precautions," he told Silvestri a few moments later.

"Nonsense, Carmine! It's a rare cop who's killed in the line of duty, though the statistics are creeping up every year, whereas cops who eat their gun are common. The work's hard, and all too often thankless. How many women do you know who can put up with a police marriage? Damned few! My Gloria, Danny's Netty, your Desdemona, Abe's Betty. Looks like Fernando's Solidad. A few yeah, but it's worst for the cops with unsuitable wives."

"You're right, John, it's Ava at fault. Screwing cops for a hobby! I wonder what her real name is? Bertha? Gertrude?"

"You don't think it's Ava?"

"The only Ava I know is Ava Gardner."

"A movie star. But stop blaming yourself, Carmine. If a rookie like Helen MacIntosh could see this coming, Corey should have. Helen's turning out a good girl."

"Far better than I'd hoped. The NYPD lost a fine detective when it stuck her in Traffic. Resourceful too."

However, Carmine didn't inform the Commissioner that her resourcefulness ran to concocting leakproof stories for cell sergeants moved by pity to break the rules for an old friend.

"I'd better find an address for Ava," Carmine said.

There was a bunker light in the ceiling just to one side of the trapdoor; a dim bulb burned behind extremely thick glass and a steel cage, though Kurt's keen eyes discerned faint hints of more powerful wiring. The original light hadn't been this one.

He was hungry, but far thirstier. As best he had calculated, he was somewhere in the second twelve hours of his captivity; his watch was on his wrist, but broken. Vaguely he remembered skidding on Persimmon Street and getting out of his car to see if he had collided with anything. Then came a hard blow to his head, and then— nothing. The most horrifying part of a painful arousal had been the throbbing in his left hand, roughly bound in his own handkerchief— his little finger was gone! Amputated! Dislodging the blood-soaked linen to find this out had started the stump bleeding again, and he had wrestled to seal it using his right hand and his teeth; but it ached badly, and the fabric was wet again. Why had they done that?

There was no food of any kind, but a half-gallon container of water was sitting on the ground in one corner, and an empty bucket in another. Without thinking he had drunk deeply, even spilled some of the water down his shirt front before suddenly realizing that when it was gone, he had no guarantee of more. His head pounded, his eyes felt gritty and sore.

He could hear nothing. No wind whined or howled, no fluid coursed through pipes or a stream bed, no traffic roared either near or far, no 60-cycle hum came from overhead wires or buried power cables, no rattle of jack-hammers or ponderous grope of caterpillar tracks came to his ears. Nothing. *Nothing*! Nor could he feel even the faintest flutter of vibration. As for sight—without the bunker light he would be blind.

How long he sat huddled in a corner he couldn't know, save that he dozed, even slept deeply once. Then he got to his feet and began to pace, up and down, up and down, up and down … A wasted, futile activity! Faltering, he sat down on the concrete floor with a thump that hurt his sacrum, and started to weep. But that accomplished nothing either; sniffling, he rummaged in his hip pocket for his other handkerchief. It wasn't there, they must have used it on his hand, then thrown it away. A pencil fell out, rolled a tiny distance, and stopped; swiping his face with his bound hand, Kurt considered what the pencil had done, and concluded that the floor was almost perfectly level. At least in that spot.

Checking the level of the floor took some time; he felt occupied, at least. One hand out, he stroked a wall. Plaster, quite smooth.

Unpainted, which was interesting. Who would go to so much trouble to plaster a wall, then leave it unpainted or unpapered? Another mystery. From that he passed to emptying out every one of his pockets: three in his jacket, one in his shirt, five in his trousers. No wallet or keys, though he had had them in the Porsche after Buffo's. His plunder was typical, he thought wryly: a total of fifteen German-made 2B pencils; four red ball-point pens; a Faber-Castell eraser; a notebook on a spiral wire; a Swiss Army knife; a set of jeweler's screwdrivers in a clear plastic case; and a bottle of Liquid Paper white-out.

A consuming thirst was drying out his mouth and he was finding it increasingly difficult to wet it with a new secretion of spit, so he shut it as tightly as he could. He wasn't a physiologist, no, but he did understand that an open mouth was drier than a closed one. Since he was alone and had no need to speak, he would keep his mouth permanently shut. Until, he thought ironically, death ensued. For he knew now that he was meant to die.

How to pass the time? That was the worst, the vainest question of all—until he really looked at his treasure trove of pencils and pens, his eraser and white-out.

I will use the walls to do mathematics! he thought, suddenly excited. I will go back over all my equations and check that they are right. Some of my peers insist I am wrong, and I have refuted them in the comfort of my study, using proper blackboards that must be erased. But here, in this place, I cannot do that. I'll write very small, and not erase one single step. By the time I am too weak to hold a pencil, I will have left my entire career behind on these walls. And when my pencils grow blunt, I will sharpen them with my Swiss Army knife. I may never need the implement that gets a stone out of a horse's hoof, but I will make great and fine use of the blade.

He stood in the center of the room and surveyed his prison keenly: where to begin? Yes, that far left-hand corner! One wall at a time. He was so excited that he knocked his left hand against a wall as he spun around; the bleeding increased. Sparing it no more than an angry glance, Kurt von Fahlendorf ignored it as he went to the designated spot and started below a very large infinity sign written in red ball-point. His chapters would be in red, a little like Helen and her colored journals.

"When I heard," said Desdemona, tramping through the forest alongside Carmine, "that almost everybody was working alone, I decided that it wouldn't do Julian or Alex any harm to spend a few days with Prunella. It's impossible for me to hike these days, so don't you dare send me home."

She had topped the ridge in front of him like a glorious figurehead on a mighty ship of the line, he had thought, winded; as he watched her come down the slope to join him; his knees went weak, it was all he could do to stay upright. What a woman! A goddess! And she's mine!

"Today is one day I don't need to be alone," he said. "I guess you've heard about Morty Jones?"

"Yes. Netty Marciano called me. So did John Silvestri, who says you're blaming yourself too much."

"How do people box themselves so tightly into a corner that the only way out is to eat a gun?" he asked.

"Suicide is the ultimately selfish act, my love, you know that. Think what a mess Morty's left behind. No will, even, so Netty says. He and Ava should have made wills on their wedding day as we did.

Quitting this earth is complicated when there are children and property involved, and worse with a vengeful, greedy wife. Though Ava is going to have to look elsewhere for lovers than the Holloman PD, according to Netty. The ranks have closed against her. The poor little children are in a bit of a limbo—Ava's more interested in what money she can get."

"And here was I thinking that when Danny retired, Netty's sources would dry up. I'm glad they haven't. Many's the time she's given us a lead." Carmine sighed. "Like you, I grieve for the kids. I sometimes think people should have to have a license to produce them. Whatever, it shouldn't have happened to Morty, he didn't have the strength to deal with Ava. The thing is, how do I approach Corey?"

She paused, shading her eyes; the sun was past its zenith. "Is that a shack down here?"

"It is. It won't yield anything, Desdemona, but we leave no stone unturned."

"You approach Corey as you ought," she said as their pace increased. "He's earned some censure, no doubt of that."

"I dread bad feelings. Stay back behind this tree until I make sure the coast is clear."

"Of course you dread bad feelings!" she shouted at his back. "You're a good boss, and good bosses are soft as well as hard. I suffer because I have to watch you suffer, but I'll do what I can to help. Like a favorite dinner," she said slyly.

"Terrible woman! Food is not uppermost in my mind."

"It will be, by dinner time."

They examined the shack, long decayed; it had no cellar or stouter compartment.

"We're working toward North Rock, aren't we?" Desdemona asked as they walked on.

"Yes, into the cleft where the deserted mansion is."

"Do you think—?"

"We'll reach it tomorrow, but we won't find Kurt there. Would you use it if you were a kidnapper, knowing it will be gone over the way a chimpanzee picks for lice? A whole week has to elapse between demand and ransom payment—no, they've stashed Kurt in a place virtually impossible to find."

"Oh, Carmine!" she cried. "People are so diabolical—and so greedy! I can understand the Dodo better, killing for sexual urges he can't control. But greed? It's—it's despicable, and that's worse than monstrous!"

"Murder of any kind is diabolical." Carmine gave his wife a shrewd glance. "The shadows are too long, lovely lady. Let's go home to our kids."

CHAPTER IV

"We're searching on a proper grid, Frau von Fahlendorf ... That makes it more likely that we'll find your brother's prison, but we're working in ignorance ... I don't think you need fear that our police efficiency isn't up to the task ... Yes, ma'am, that is correct, but we cannot tell our journalists what to say. We have freedom of the press, and the trashier ones tend to make things up if the story isn't dramatic enough ... I agree, this is one story doesn't need embroidering, but ... Thank you, Frau von Fahlendorf ... Good afternoon."

"Phew!" Helen exclaimed, putting the phone down. "They really do think they're the only ones can do anything, don't they? She's an autocrat, the Frau. She either suspects or knows that the kidnappers are German, so she's on the defensive. Was I okay, sir?"

"You did well," said Carmine. "What intrigues me is that the family von Fahlendorf hasn't sent someone to Holloman, though they've had the weekend to do it. It's where Kurt is, no matter where the kidnappers are. That raises some possibilities: one is that Dagmar knows Kurt is already dead, and another, that Dagmar knows they're going to get Kurt back alive. I ask myself, is someone in Germany, acting for the kidnappers, in direct contact with Dagmar, who would rather trust villains from her own part of the world than good guys from a country she doesn't know? A country, moreover, that stole her beloved Kurtchen. She's forgotten it was his choice to emigrate."

"To me, the most important point," said Delia, "is why the family hasn't sent someone here? What if we find Kurt alive? The poor chap won't be greeted by one family face, and that positively stinks. Even my potty papa would come for me."

"That tells me they know he's dead," said Nick.

"They're going to refuse to pay the ransom?" Helen asked.

"It kind of looks that way," Carmine answered.

"In which case, why does Dagmar keep trying to get the bank and account number out of us?" Delia asked.

"So they can say we gave it to them," Carmine said.

"They could say that anyway," Nick said.

"That's true," from Delia. "The other answer is that there's no one to send here. Dagmar must suspect her husband is behind it, the Baron is senile, and the mother is retiring and giving her money to the grandchildren. She might be senile too."

"That flies," said Nick.

"He tried to steal her industrial secrets once. I imagine Dagmar must suspect Josef of the kidnapping," Carmine said.

"She genuinely may not suspect him." Helen squeezed her hands together. "Oh, I wish I knew the family! I wish I was there!"

"I couldn't agree more, Helen," said Delia. "Not knowing the suspects, how can we solve the case?"

"What about the FBI?" Nick asked. "They have better foreign contacts than the police department of a small city."

"Not a brass monkey, according to Hunter Wyatt," Carmine said. "Like us, he's convinced it's a German job."

Corey and Abe came in.

Corey was looking haggard. Everyone in Detectives knew why; he had to face an enquiry over Morty Jones's death, and he had also to face Carmine. Both were postponed until the search for Kurt von Fahlendorf was over, but that moment was drawing closer with every tick of the clock.

"Anything?" he asked.

"Nothing."

Abe Goldberg didn't look hopeful, and that was a bad sign. As he had an uncanny instinct for hidden doors and vents going nowhere, he was Carmine's secret compartments expert; for that reason Carmine had allocated him a strip of territory to the south and west of Holloman Harbor, an industrial wasteland beyond the airport where functioning factories and workshops were mixed with buildings and sweat shops long abandoned. Though it had streets, it was a wilderness of sorts, bounded by the Holloman jail and I-95.

"Not a sausage, as you'd say, Delia," Abe said. "I've been searching for four days without a twitch or a tremble, and that's bad. I don't think he's there, but I haven't finished, so I'll keep on going, Carmine."

"You do that, Abe. If he is there, you'll find him."

Today was Tuesday, October 22, and the search had been in full swing since dawn of last Friday. Desdemona was taking his place today, allowing Carmine time to check up on the Dodo. The first phase of this consisted in a short walk to the Medical Examiner's;

Patrick was in his office. When his first cousin came in Patrick's face lit up and he pointed at the coffee pot. "Just brewed," he said, putting his pen down.

"The autopsy on Melantha Green," said Carmine, sitting with a mug of fresh coffee. "The last of the bloodwork hadn't come through when Kurt von Fahlendorf was kidnapped, and we've been on that non-stop ever since. What goes?"

"Nothing helpful," Patrick said, pouring himself coffee. "She had amphetamine in her bloodstream, I suspect self-administered to keep awake and on top of a crushing workload. There was no other substance present. His anesthetic was crude—a clip on the jaw that probably stunned her but didn't knock her out. She was known to have a black belt in judo, hence the clip, which wasn't hard enough to cause any meningeal bleeding. Her death was due to asphyxiation." Patrick sipped. "The young man was killed by someone who can shoot. The throat shot was perfect, the second bullet overkill. He used a .22 pistol."

"No one heard the shots, yet the other apartment was tenanted and its inhabitants were actually awake—the wife was sick to the stomach," Carmine said. "He used a silencer."

"Must have done, but not a home-made device. I doubt the Dodo was interested in the young man. Two shots, then he went back to cleaning up after Melantha."

"Did he wash Melantha with soap and water?"

"No, he simply wiped her down with xylene. That you know."

"Good coffee, cuz, but bad news," said Carmine, smiling. "Anything else on any other case?"

"No, but something else on the Dodo. I think you should go talk to Nick and Delia."

"I just left them!"

"Sorry about that."

"Shit!" Carmine put his half drunk coffee down. "Maybe I can catch them before they go searching their grid."

But it was Corey he encountered in the parking lot. His lieutenant flinched, but had the sense to stop.

"You're in big trouble, Cor."

"I don't see why."

"A man on your team is dead."

"That's not my fault."

"In one way, it is. Several other people noticed that Morty was depressed, and I even spoke to you about it. You sneered."

"Now isn't the time to have this, Carmine. I'm going to my search area right this second."

"You're only piling up demerits, Cor."

"Fuck the demerits!"

Carmine watched him go, then got into his Fairlane and drove off toward the shoreline of Busquash Bay, where his list said Nick and Delia were searching on the far side of the peninsula from the Inlet and getting close to the neighboring district of Millstone, home to Delia.

He found them walking along the rocks at the base of the low Busquash cliffs, and paused to take in the sight before they knew he was in the offing. Nick had changed into shorts, a tee shirt and tennis shoes, but Delia possessed no leisure apparel in her lavish wardrobe. She was paddling along bare-legged, her miniskirt hitched up a few inches, something like a multihued crab with two pallid rear legs; her dress was marbled in bright green, orange, cyclamen and ultramarine blue.

"Hi!" he yelled. "It's lunch time, see you in the Lobster Pot—Nick, you're okay dressed like that!"

"What on earth do you hope to find literally foot-deep in water?" he asked when they were settled in a booth.

"Old gun emplacements," said Delia.

"They went years ago, Deels."

"You'd be surprised. How many have we found, Nick?"

"Four so far, east of the Carew-East Holloman boundary. Ben Cohen and his team found nine in East Holloman, on the point, mostly. The guns are all gone, the emplacements are cunning," Nick said. "I guess no one sees them, so no one bothers about them."

"The things you learn!" Carmine said.

Nick and Delia were ravenous, and made short work of their lobster rolls; Carmine let them eat in peace. Over coffee he broached the reason for seeking them out.

"Patsy says you know something about the Dodo."

"No, about the kidnap," Nick said, lighting a cigarette and inhaling luxuriously. "Tell the man, Delia."

"We think we found the spot where the kidnappers jumped Kurt—not really important, as it offers no clues of help, but interesting. We can show you if you like."

One hand waving for the check, Carmine looked eager. Nick and Delia piled into their unmarked and Carmine ranged his Fairlane behind them, forcing himself to a sedate pace as the two cars headed for Persimmon Street in Carew. There Nick and Delia pulled into the kerb, Carmine following suit. Once he joined them Delia pointed to the intersection with Spruce Street. Curzon Close was clearly visible two hundred yards away.

"It was here, on this corner," Nick said. "See the skid marks? I checked, the tires are Michelin and the right size for the Porsche. Von Fahlendorf's a good driver, he came out of the skid slowly, and left us some pattern. See here? Glass from a Porsche parking light, forensics told us. And see this? It's blood, the same type as Kurt's."

"Look at these bushes," said Delia, leading Carmine over to the corner house, where tall smoke bushes grew along the edge of the sidewalk. "They pounced when he got out of his car, and he must have reeled before he lost consciousness. Someone landed heavily in the bushes. We took photos of everything."

"Why haven't you mentioned this?" Carmine asked.

"Since we're looking for him, we couldn't see a good reason why," said Delia. "We dealt with the forensics in case it was ever needed in the future—you had enough on your plate, boss, when this blew up."

"How could the kidnappers stage their abduction between ten and ten-thirty on a busy street in Carew?"

"Persimmon and this side of Spruce are concealed and dampened by trees," Nick said. "All they needed were a couple of minutes."

"But the collision?"

"Was staged, we think. Someone stepped out in front of Kurt, he braked in a well driven skid, and when he got out of the car, they jumped him. The blood is his, whether from a head blow or the finger amputation, who knows?"

"Well done," said Carmine. "Kurt was loaded into their car, one of the two drove the Porsche, and they accomplished whatever they had to do in two and a half hours. By one, both of them were putting the Porsche in Kurt's garage. All they needed to do then was walk around the corner to their own vehicle. A pity Gordie Warburton went back to bed."

"It looks like two kidnappers to me," said Nick.

"And to me," said Carmine. "The gall! Whoever they are, they have superb confidence in themselves."

Mention of Gordon Warburton prompted Carmine to go and see Amanda Warburton, who was in her shop and looking well.

"I continue to enjoy a trouble-free existence," she said.

"Did you get a museum expert to look at the glass teddy bear, Miss Warburton?"

"No," she said, and laughed. "Even if he is as valuable as you say, Captain, he's as much a fixture in my window as Frankie and Winston. People don't believe that he's priceless."

"Business is good?"

"Very good."

"And the twins? How are you getting on with them?"

"What a shock when they turned up! I don't have any idea why they moved to Holloman and then didn't tell me, except that it's not money, I gather." She smiled. "To answer your question, I'm on good terms with them. Perhaps they're not ideal nephews, but now they've confessed that they're down the road in Carew, they are behaving delightfully. I've decided to leave them in my will as my heirs, which solved a dilemma."

He concealed his alarm. "You didn't tell them, I hope?"

"No, Captain, I won't do that. Let it come as a surprise—oh, thirty years from now."

"Take care of yourself."

"I do, honestly." Her eyelids dropped, she looked a little inscrutable. "Hank Murray is a great help to me."

He left carrying an image of her pretty, smiling face, and decided to see Hank Murray before he left the Busquash Mall.

Hank was dressed casually in jeans and an open-necked shirt; Carmine caught a glimpse of a sparsely hairy chest, and decided that if he himself were to wear a chest toupee, it would sport better hair than Hank Murray's! Hank's chest hair, he concluded, was the real thing.

"You look as if you're going on a picnic," he said.

Hank grinned. "No, Captain. I've been out searching for Professor von Fahlendorf. Captain Vasquez roped in quite a few local men to comb the vacant lots and houses of Carew. Mark Sugarman, Mason Novak and I all volunteered. Kurt was a friend."

"How's Miss Warburton?"

"She's well." Hank went red. "I see her most evenings—just dinner and a board game or cards. She and Marcia Boyce don't have many friends, which I guess is the fate of single women working every day. It's especially hard for Amanda, working weekends. As Tuesday is the slackest day, we both take it off, and go somewhere."

"That's good. Have you met the twins?"

"Pah! What poseurs!"

"Interesting word, poseur. If they present as that, what do you think they are underneath?"

"Something creepy, Captain. Or slimy—words like that. Amanda was in two minds about them, but of late she seems to be coming down on their side. They've managed to impress her."

"Well, they're blood kin after all. Maybe they're late bloomers." Carmine went to the door. "Keep in touch if you have any worries, Mr. Murray."

"Any news about the bank robbery?"

Carmine shrugged, "Not a thing," he said.

And more than that he couldn't do.

Now it was off into Dodo territory. Mark Sugarman would probably be home.

Mark Sugarman was. He looked tired, and not a lot had gone on at the drawing board.

"Searching for Kurt?" Carmine asked.

"Yes, but also walking, Captain. If the Dodo strikes within his usual three weeks, we're running out of time. October 15 means he's due to pounce up to and including the presidential elections. A lot more people vote in presidential years."

"I'm beginning to realize that."

"An omen, huh?" Sugarman asked.

"No, not that, Mr. Sugarman. More that there's likely to be increased foot traffic around polling stations."

"How's Maggie Drummond?"

"Pretty good," Carmine said. "The Chubb psychiatrist has made a difference to all the Dodo's victims already."

"Tell me about it!" A look of content came over Sugarman's attractive face. "Leonie trusts me again—she's behaving more like her old self. I wish she'd seen Dr. Meyers earlier."

"Better late than never, pardon my hackneyed comment." Carmine walked over to the big windows displaying Spruce Street. "Sir, were you up last Wednesday night about half after ten?"

"I think so," said the President of the Gentleman Walkers, looking puzzled. "I'd made supper for Leonie, and delivered her back upstairs around ten. Even after the hassle of checking all her locks, I would have been back down here by ten-thirty."

"Did you hear the noise of a collision at the intersection of Persimmon and Spruce?"

"No, not a collision, Captain. I did hear a screech of brakes and some yelling—it happens all the time at that intersection."

"Thank you," said Carmine, looking pleased.

"Will you find Kurt?"

"We're all praying so, sir."

"Good afternoon, Frau von Fahlendorf," said Helen at seven on Wednesday morning, October 23. "No, I am afraid not ... That is unfair, ma'am! We have tied up huge resources in the search for your brother—as you would have seen for yourself if you or any member of your family had come here ... No, I am not rude, I am fed up—indignant, do you understand that word? Good! ... At midnight tonight, American Eastern Standard Time, Special Agent Hunter Wyatt of the FBI will telephone you on your home number and give you the details of the Swiss bank and account number, but I entreat you not to pay the ransom early! To do so won't make any difference to his chances of surviving ... Special Agent Hunter Wyatt will also forward you a written report on our activities ... Thank you, ma'am. Goodbye."

The receiver went down with a bang. "Bitch!" said Helen. "She has the hide to blame us—*us*! I could cheerfully kill her."

"She's under great stress, Helen," Carmine soothed. "We still have two full days of search—well, one full day and a few hours. Time zones are a pain in the ass."

Corey and Abe came in.

"Corey?" Carmine asked.

"The most suspicious things we've found are a few cow pats, but we still have sheds, barns and bunkers to deal with on the north side of North Rock. Old Ray Howarth has a bomb shelter, or so I'm told."

"Actually we've found quite a number of bomb shelters," said Carmine. "I never realized how paranoid some people are about The Bomb. I saw one the day before yesterday that had Persian carpets and air conditioning. It hadn't occurred to the owner that if The Bomb went off, electric power would be cut off. He was expecting to run his shelter on mains."

"Like my potty papa," Delia said. "If Richard Nixon gets in, he's moving permanently into his shelter—he's convinced that the first Nixonian presidential action will be to push the button."

They all rolled their eyes at each other, but the light moment faded fast.

"Abe?" Carmine asked.

"I just have to check around the outskirts of the jail," Abe said. "Nothing so far."

"Have you heard what Patrick found in the Porsche, guys?"

"Nothing—it's so clean it might have come from the dealer's showroom," said Nick, "except that there's some gravel wedged in the tire tracks. Nonspecific, but not the kind of gravel you'd get from a crumbling road base. No asphalt component."

"Which says they drove the car somewhere off-road, but it could have been anywhere. Holloman is full of gravel, even has three quarries. Does it come from them?"

"Some of the uniforms checked them, but didn't think to take samples," Corey said. "They asked me, but I couldn't see any virtue in sending them back to do it."

"What color and size is it, Carmine?" Abe asked.

"Pink granite, so it's not from our quarries. It sounds more like something you'd find in a monument mason's yard."

"File that in case you see it. Incidentally, Joey Tasco, who had that section to check, told me that none of the quarries had a septic tank. They use chemical toilets, so don't go back there, Corey. Keep on into virgin territory."

It might have been because Carmine said "septic tank", but when Abe Goldberg, Liam Connor and Tony Cerutti reached the West Holloman industrial estate, Abe wasted a good hour going back to check that they hadn't left an old, buried septic tank unexplored. They had not; Liam, who understood how Abe's mind worked, did not grudge him the wasted time, but Tony, younger and a more restless type, was inclined to grumble until Liam shut him up by treading heavily on his foot.

They had emerged from the streets and functioning factories into a relatively vast area that had been demolished in the aftermath of the Second World War with the intention of building a prison. Beyond it sat Holloman Jail, which was a jail, not a prison. Short-term, that is, lacking the architecture and facilities necessary for the high security confinement of intractable criminals. These were sent up-state, but from time to time new noises were made in Hartford to go ahead with Holloman Prison, an institution no resident of Holloman wanted. Bad enough to have a jail!

The area did not resemble a war zone, unless that war be an atomic one; there were no shells of buildings, just gigantic heaps of stony detritus that rose and fell like the foothills of a red rectangular mountain range, the jail.

"We need a minidozer with a blade," Liam said. "A bucket as well, but not attached. If there's anything under the edge of one of these piles, we'd never find it unless we have something to move the crap around, but a bulldozer might be too heavy."

"Good idea," said Abe, who was feeling a little dizzy. "I'll radio the Captain, see if he can arrange a miniature dozer."

Tony Cerutti produced a set of blueprints from the back seat of their car. "These are the plans of the mooted prison as they saw it in 1948," he said, spreading the huge sheets on the hood and anchoring them with hunks of old brick.

"Did they actually get as far as starting to build?" Abe asked, staring fascinated at several pentagons connected by thick passageways. "Make a good Meccano project." His sons were avidly into Meccano, and buying it was keeping him poor.

Came a squawk from the radio. When Abe returned to the plans he looked content. "We'll have a little dozer here in about an hour, blade attached, bucket in reserve, backhoe just in case. In the meantime, guys, we walk. Liam, you go toward the east end of the jail. Tony, take the middle. I'm going west."

Tony laughed. "Yeah, a long time ago!"

Liam and Tony set off; still conscious of an alien dizziness, Abe lingered to take another look at the plans of the west side. He didn't know why he felt so strange, except that in some way it was important. Then the headache hit, and Abe fell to his knees.

Two walls were full, Kurt had moved on to his third wall; he had sharpened ten of his pencils down to stumps, but the last five were the longest and best, deliberately saved. His mouth was utterly dry and his ears rang on an internal sound, but the excitement of putting his life's work on his tomb walls had not faded. Egyptian pharaohs were reduced to pictures of their lazy existence, interspersed with an occasional battle, but not one of them could equal his feat! Not one of them could display a life so filled with intellectual incident and triumph.

The bucket his captors had left him for his bodily functions had not filled, but it stank. Though the room was cold, Kurt had sacrificed his coat to throw over it, blanket the stench. They said a human being got used to smells, but so far he hadn't. At least the chill meant that he lost no moisture through sweat, but Kurt was conscious that it was becoming difficult to stand. His back ached intolerably and he was forced to lie down at increasingly frequent intervals, but the work went on.

Time for a break; he sat gazing around the closely written walls, the smile on his lips spontaneous. Thank God for work! What if he hadn't owned the mentality or the professional training to occupy himself through what he was sure had mounted into days? How would someone who processed copies of the same form for a living manage to survive this imprisonment ending in death without going mad? He believed devoutly in a properly Catholic God, but few people had the kind of mind that could dwell upon God day in and day out, especially with death as its conclusion. That seemed a contradiction, but no man was ever ready for death unless he were a saint, and Kurt knew he was no saint; modern men could never be saints because modern living negated the concept.

But I, thought Kurt, head spinning, have never harmed the world, even by my nuclear research. The damage is done … He lay flat out, his head too heavy to keep aloft, a mist swirling before his eyes. Slowly they closed; he slept, woke with a jerk, saw the third wall almost pristine, got to his feet and picked up the equations where he had left them. His body was failing, yes, but his mind was still capable of seeing mathematical truth.

I wish, he thought, pausing, that I could hear some Bach one last time!

The headache disappeared as suddenly as it had come. The plans, the plans, Abe thought in a quiet frenzy. A number of straight, parallel lines traveled from the prison itself toward a square that said in tiny print that it was a sewage holding tank. Much larger than a septic tank, this thing was the size of a Holloman PD drunks' tank cell.

Suddenly Abe stiffened. His skin began to prickle in a way it never had, and he understood. This is the first time I've looked for a living, fully grown man! The life in him is big enough to affect me! I am staring at a prison—a *real* prison! They built this holding tank, they probably put in some of the inlets, the outlet, the vent—it's there, under a thin layer of rubble. He's there! Kurt von Fahlendorf is there!

Abe had a whistle on a cord around his neck; he put it to his lips and blew a shrill blast. Liam and Tony came at a run, while a guard toting a rifle on his back leaned on the railing of a watchtower atop the jail wall and followed their antics.

"We have to find the sewage holding tank," Abe said, "and I'm not waiting for machinery. But first we find the gravel—the tank won't be far from the pink gravel."

A more confused directive than they were used to from Abe, but neither Liam nor Tony misunderstood. All three men went in different westerly directions.

"Here!" Tony shouted, appearing around a huge hillock.

And there it was, an expanse of pink rubble about a hundred feet long and fifty feet wide. Beyond it lay more flat ground, but smothered in ragged pieces of concrete.

"They stopped on the pink because this concrete's sharper," Liam said. "What happens now, Abe?"

"We look for pipes or vents," Abe said, the master at this kind of work. "Watch around your feet, you won't see anything from a distance. My vibes say von Fahlendorf is alive, which means the vent is open and you'll see it. You remember that rain storm we had last Monday and cursed? Well, it might have shifted things hereabouts, so look. *Look!*"

Abe found it, a round four-inch hole that originally had been covered by a concrete slab that had slipped off it in the brief but torrential rain; the signs were unmistakable, for whoever had put the little slab in place was no construction worker. It had probably never done its intended job, to block the ingress of air.

"A gap is all that's needed," Abe said, that terrible daze vanishing just as the headache had.

The little bulldozer arrived, but by then Tony had raced to the jail and phoned in their find to Carmine; soon the wasteland in front of the jail was crawling with cops and machinery.

"He's alive!" came Patrick O'Donnell's voice from below.

A cheer went up, men hugged each other.

"Carmine, you have to see what's down there," said Liam in an awed voice, emerging.

Carmine squeezed through the trapdoor in the holding tank roof and climbed down the few steps of a ladder to join a jubilant Abe. Cameras were flashing constantly.

"Holy shits!" Carmine whispered, staring at the many hundreds of penciled equations. "What the hell is it?"

"The unified field theory, for all I know," said Abe. "The work, Carmine, the work! Von Fahlendorf can't have the original, but he'll have to have photographic copies. What a feat!"

"How many Masses have you committed me to, John?" Carmine asked the Commissioner an hour later in his office.

"Fifteen, the old-fashioned way."

"I'll wear my knees out!"

"So will I. So will Mrs. Tesoriero, God bless her. She's been praying night and day. When I commit you to Masses the old-fashioned way, Carmine, the cause is very urgent. But you and Mrs. Tesoriero always come through. Miraculous!"

"It's Abe Goldberg comes through, and he's Jewish."

"That guy is spooky, I admit. How does he do it?"

"He doesn't know. He says he gets a feeling, but not always."

"A pity cops can't claim rewards. Without Abe Goldberg, von Fahlendorf would be dead and ten million bucks would have wound up in a Swiss bank account." Silvestri assumed his cat-got-the-cream expression. "I did explain to Frau von Fahlendorf that she could show her deep appreciation for the excellent work of Lieutenant Goldberg by setting up a college fund for Abe's sons. Really bright boys, from what I hear."

"I forgive you, and I'll do the Masses the old-fashioned way, down on my knees instead of a donation."

"That means all three of us will be in St. Bernard's for the next fifteen mornings. Oh, my arthur-itis!"

"We'll never nail his kidnappers," Carmine said.

"I know. Tell me why it's a German operation."

Carmine leaned forward, hands clasped between his knees. "Too unnecessarily complicated, John. Like a German motor—over-engineered. Americans would have used a car trunk, whereas these bozos went to the trouble of finding that sewage holding tank. Who got the prison plans from County Services? Why stand out in the open with surveyor's gear to pinpoint its location? The way they see the world tells them that complicated is better. The risk taking isn't seen as risk taking, but as normal activities. They're too obsessive to be American kidnappers. Simple is better."

"I do see what you mean." Silvestri sighed. "In which case, we haven't the hope of a snowflake in hell of nailing them."

"The important thing is that we got von Fahlendorf back in one piece, and the ransom wasn't paid. So now I'm free to ask questions and expect answers."

"A minute ago you were the soul of pessimism, Carmine. What's changed inside that minute?"

"I've just realized that I have a weapon, John. The adorable Helen MacIntosh—or, at least, Kurt thinks she's adorable. I happen to know that she has an income of a million dollars a year, so a trip to Munich isn't going to bust her bank. Kurt has ideas of marrying her. What if I could persuade Helen to talk Kurt into making a visit home with his fiancée on his arm?"

"You devious schemer!"

"She wouldn't like committing herself maritally to Kurt, but she'd wear it for two reasons. The first, she's quite cold-hearted in a MacIntosh way, so it won't grieve her overmuch to break the engagement on her return from Munich, and the second, that she's panting to run her own case. If she has three or four days in Munich, she has a chance to find Kurt's kidnappers. In fact, if she takes Kurt into her confidence, she needn't promise to marry him in reality. He's livid enough to co-operate."

"You get more devious by the second!"

"I do, don't I? Well, think about it, John. Two shits we don't know had us running in circles and spending a lot of money we'll never see again. The von Fahlendorfs will keep their ten million, but the several million finding Kurt cost us—goodbye!"

"Do it, Carmine, do it."

"Will you be in it, Helen?" Carmine asked his trainee the next morning. "I know you'd have to fund your trip yourself, but would you consider the expense worth it if you could find the kidnappers?"

Her eyes were shining. "Captain Delmonico, I'd walk up the Spanish Steps on my knees to get iron-clad evidence on Kurt's kidnappers! And he'll co-operate, I know he will. He was a little disappointed when no member of his family was there to see him come out of his cell, but Dagmar managed to sweet-talk him around. In fact, she seems to have sweet-talked him so efficiently that he's already muttering about taking a trip home to check up on the folks."

"Then you have a case, Helen, that entirely depends on you for a solution. If you can't crack it, no one can." Carmine nodded at a chair. "Sit down, sit down! It's going to take some time to organize. In the meantime, what have you deduced?"

"They did their homework, sir, that's foremost. They must have known that green card holders have fingerprints on record in Washington, D.C. They knew enough to get the prison plans from County Services archives. They knew how much money was going to be freed up as a trust for the grandchildren, and the date it was happening. They knew enough to allow a week for the gathering of the ransom, for no other reason, I believe, than that they assumed people like the FBI would expect a week for such a huge ransom. In actual fact, they could have made their time span an hour. But that would have pointed toward Germany and away from America. A lot of their information about how things are done here came from movies and television." Her brow creased. "However, there are anomalies, sir. The air vent wasn't closed firmly enough to survive a downpour, which says the villains are not familiar with downpours. Or it may be saying that one of the two didn't really want to see Kurt die. He was left water that would have lasted longer if he hadn't guzzled some and spilled some. Was it a form of torture or a hope that Kurt would be found before he died? One of the two is a real hater, Captain, but the other is a weakling. And which one left a bucket? You don't leave a bucket for someone you expect to die, though I don't think the bucket had anything to do with Kurt's living or dying. I believe that whoever left it knows Kurt personally, and didn't want him to endure the indignity of looking at his own excrement. If there is a personal link, then both kidnappers know Kurt. The weakling is under the domination of the hater, but doesn't like how he or she feels. It may be that cutting Kurt's finger off tipped the balance, hence the water and the bucket. The hater can't have realized their significance, or maybe the weakling threw a tantrum, as weaklings can." She stopped. "How did I do?"

"Very well, but I'm a pussycat," said Carmine with a grin. "It's Kurt you have to fool, Helen."

"When do you think we should go?"

Carmine frowned. "Today is the twenty-fourth, and the Dodo is due to attack Tuesday or Wednesday of election week. Provided he's on schedule, you have time to go before, though I'm not sure what his schedule is going to be now he's killing."

"Yes, if it's two weeks, he's due next week," Helen said. "If we go tomorrow, Friday, we can be back by Monday night."

"Passport? What if you need a visa?"

"Sometimes it's handy to be my father's daughter. I can get whatever I need, and Kurt's all set up."

"That doesn't leave you much time for investigations at this end, Helen."

"I have this afternoon. It's enough."

"You realize you're off the Dodo until I can close the kidnappers, even if the kidnappers are never arraigned?"

"Yes, Captain."

"Then I won't delay you any further."

The Captain's departure left Helen pondering her logistics; this afternoon she had to buy two airline tickets to Munich, and that meant Lufthansa, not TWA; then she had to find out how the kidnappers got hold of the Holloman prison plans. She saw her way about the travel almost immediately, and picked up the phone to dial a number she knew better than her own—her father's. But not to speak to him. She wanted his secretary. Ten minutes of cajoling later, and it would all be done for her, though she still had one thing to do on that front; she called Tiffany's and had them send the dear woman a pair of ruby earrings.

Next, a call to Kurt, home from the hospital.

"Darling," she cooed, "how about I bring over Chinese tonight and we have a quiet evening?"

"Helen, yes, please!"

"Six o' clock, with a bottle of Moët?"

"Yes, please!"

Good, that was organized. Slinging her bag over her shoulder, Helen set out for a different part of the County Services building to find out who had obtained a copy of the prison plans.

After drawing a blank at three of the five sections holding those plans, she hit paydirt at Correctional Institutions, the new euphemism for places where people were incarcerated apart from society in general. It included juvenile detention centers and the parole system, but it also housed penal archives.

A middle-aged clerk manned the enquiry counter, a mournful fellow who, thought Helen, would remember nothing of the people fronting up to his desk. But when he beheld this beautiful young woman in her immaculate, tasteful clothes, every memory cell in his brain opened in a flood of information. Shabby lawyers and desperate parents did nothing for him, but a girl with stunning apricot hair that never came out of a dye bottle—!

"The lady who asked for blueprints of the prison plans? Oh, yes, I remember her, officer. Who couldn't?"

"What made her memorable, apart from asking for those particular blueprints?" Helen asked, smiling seductively.

"Well, she was such a lady. Beautiful clothes in a maroon shade that suited her. She even wore a hat and gloves, both in the same shade of maroon. The gloves were finest French kid, and the hat screamed Paris. Not *vulgar* clothes, like modern trash," the clerk said, warming to his theme. "Her suit looked like Chanel or Balenciaga, and her shoes were Charles Jourdan."

"You're amazingly conversant with women's fashions, sir."

He simpered. "My wife is a keen follower of fashion, Miss. She and I design clothes as a recreation."

"I wish more of our witnesses did! What was her face like?"

"Hard to see—her hat had a maroon net veil that covered the top half of her face, and it had little furry bobbles on it. *Stylish!*"he exclaimed, sighing. "Her lipstick was maroon and didn't really follow the outline of her lips—she preferred being in fashion to anatomical accuracy, I guess. Her hair was a light brown and beautifully cared for."

"Did she have an accent?"

"Yes. Foreign, more northern European than southern."

"Like German?"

"Exactly!"

"Would you know her again, sir?"

"By her clothes, anyone would."

"Who is the best-dressed woman in the world?"

He looked amazed at Helen's ignorance. "The Duchess of Windsor, even if she is getting old."

"What about Audrey Hepburn?"

"Can't hold a candle to Her Highness," he said fervently.

Hmm, thought Helen, leaving Correctional Institutions. So a very *haute couture* woman collected the plans! A German accent, as we suspected. No real description of her face. We have two kinds of cases on our files at the moment. One is prompted by sex, and the other by greed. So far greed hasn't led to murder, since Kurt survived, but why do I think it will? I mustn't forget the glass teddy bear, a reason for greed too. And nothing is what it seems! The German woman isn't poor—that funny little guy knew enough about fashions to put what she was wearing at about five thousand dollars. Per annum a Chubb technician lives on that.

She still had some time, and two Holloman watchtower guards had information to offer.

"A man and a woman appeared several weeks ago with surveyor's gear and measured up the vacant ground outside," said the first guard. "They concentrated on the gravel area and the ground beyond it. Must have been there most of a day."

"Can you remember the date?"

"The week of September 16 to 20."

"Did you put the glasses on them?"

"No need for the binocs, officer. They were two surveyors in coveralls with city lettering on the back. One was a man and one was a woman. Women do all kinds of jobs these days."

"I saw one of them baby bulldozers pushing rubble around," said the second guard. "The date was September 30—I know because it was the last day of the month and it fell on a Monday. My wife works at Chubb, only gets paid twelve times a year, on the last day of the month. Lousy system!"

"Yes, Chubb workers do it hard on long months. What do you think the baby bulldozer was doing?"

The guard shrugged. "We figured they were going to start building the prison, except no one heard nothing on the grapevine. And after that one day, no one never came back."

So, said Helen to herself as she unearthed her latest notebook, I now know that the kidnappers went to considerable pains to locate a cell for Kurt, and that they made their on-site preparations so far back that no one would associate two surveyors and a baby bulldozer with Kurt von Fahlendorf's disappearance. On the night they drove in quietly and without headlights; the cars were hidden from the jail by mounds of rubble, and they're undoubtedly not the only cars to use the area—it's a great place for steaming up the windows. Kurt was unconscious when they arrived, and they were probably not there longer than ten minutes. Holloman Jail isn't a high security institution. Its wall guards are slapdash unless there's genuine trouble, when they snap to attention efficiently enough, the Captain says.

One of the two surveyors was a woman; women occupied all kinds of jobs these days, the first guard said. Indeed they do, sir! Look at me.

Her journal was open, her colored pens arranged; Helen began to write, quite a lot of it in purple for her own theories.

At six o'clock she rang Kurt's bell, laden with Chinese food and a jeroboam of French champagne; she had decided that the huge bottle was more seductive than several ordinary ones, which had to be opened—a noisy procedure with champagne. The jeroboam meant one kept on pouring from an open vessel.

Her first impression was that Kurt looked wonderful, rather than someone who had suffered over five days of imprisonment, most of it without water, all of it without food, and enduring pain as well as blood loss from a hacked off finger. His pale blue eyes were dancing with life; even his flaxen hair sparkled, and his tanned skin was smooth and supple.

It was no hardship to kiss those full red lips; Helen was tall enough not to need to stand on tiptoe for a near six-footer, and fitted her mouth into his with pleasure, if not with passion. Why wasn't there any passion? That was something she wondered about a great deal without so far finding an answer. In all her life, she reflected, no man had ever stirred her to passion. She had never had an orgasm; M.M.'s children would have died sooner than masturbate. Auto-eroticism was hideously shameful; it was, besides, unnecessary. Somewhere in the world lay that elusive state called a climax. She could wait.

"Ice bucket, if it will fit," she said, breaking the kiss. "Are you hungry? Shall we eat now, or heat the food up later and eat then?"

"Later," he said, busying himself with an oversized ice bucket and then opening the bottle. "Is this designed to get us drunk?" he asked. "If so, I'm all for it, my beautiful Helen. I miss the days when you wore your hair loose, therefore I have no love for your police career. So I shall get you drunk and undo it."

"Glass for glass," she said with a challenge in her voice.

He poured; they toasted with clinking glasses.

"I know they're going out of style, but I much prefer these saucers to the flutes," he said, savoring the wine. "Neither you nor I has a big nose, admittedly, so we could drink comfortably from flutes, but think of those who do have big noses!"

"Good lord!" she exclaimed. "You have a sense of humor!"

"Of course I do."

"Well hidden." She sipped. "Oh, I do love champagne! And, Kurt, I can't think of a better reason to wallow in a saucer than celebrating your liberation. You look so good!"

"I feel good," he said.

"What went through your mind during those nearly six days?"

The handsome face hardly changed. "My life's work. I had no room for anything else, and I never did finish. They have promised me a photographed wall—I do not know how else to say it, but I gather they connect each small photograph to those all around it in a way which makes it look like wallpaper. Then I can finish, and I will. I had never realized how important it is to have every single step of my research mathematically expressed as a continuum. I had reached within my last year, and so far I now *know* I have made no errors in my thinking. When my results are spread over three dozen papers, often repeated to make a paper legible, it is easy to lose track. To miss that one little step makes sense of it all." The face had grown animated, enthusiastic. "If there are errors, they are in this last year of research, but I do not think so. I am right, Helen, I am right!"

"Well, at least you've shown me where your priorities are."

"In the proper place, yes."

"So it wasn't the specter of death loomed largest?"

"Yes—and no. I just wanted to get my work completed before I died. Work was more important, even if death was certain."

"No wonder your colleagues admire you so much."

"You exaggerate," he said.

"No, I don't. I've spoken to them throughout this business, and every last one of your colleagues is consumed with admiration for your passion—" She stopped, looked astonished. "Of course! That's where the pass ion is! In our work!"

"You have lost me."

"I know, and I'm going to leave you lost. Drink up, Kurt."

Three glasses, she decided, were optimum for her purposes: Helen struck.

"Do you feel vengeful?" she asked as he took off her shoe and stocking; she had come garbed for seduction, no pantyhose.

"At this moment," he said, dunking her forefoot in his champagne, "I am more concerned with limiting my drinking by sucking champagne off your perfect toes."

She squealed and giggled. "Kurt, don't! I'm ticklish!"

"Wriggle away. I love it," he mumbled.

"Okay, but only for five minutes."

At the end of the five minutes she counted him down to zero, then grabbed his ears and pulled his head up.

"Ow!"

"If you had longer hair, I could use that, but a crew cut means it has to be your ears. No, sit up, Kurt, and pay attention to me! I want to be serious for a moment."

He obeyed, curiosity aroused. "Okay, my lovely Helen."

"Do you feel vengeful about your kidnapping?"

"Yes, *natürlich*. Not so much for the inconvenience they caused me as the grief and anxiety they caused my family."

"Do you have any ideas or theories about who did it?"

He looked puzzled. "No, not really. I was too consumed with writing my work on the walls."

"I have some ideas and theories."

He had reached for the jeroboam, but jerked his hand away. "No, I must not drink more. Tell me, Helen."

"Captain Carmine Delmonico isn't just another small-city policeman, Kurt. He's a fine detective—fine enough for me to choose the Holloman PD for my training as a detective. He came to conclusions that I share. The first is that your kidnappers are German, not American."

She had caught him; he was staring at her, confounded. "But that cannot be! *German*?"

"Accept the fact that when it comes to crime, you're a very ordinary guy," Helen said. "Delmonico is the expert and I'm learning to be one. Believe me when I say that American kidnappers would have behaved differently from yours. And if they're German, by extension they know you personally. Otherwise they wouldn't have fixed on you, we think. With Baader-Meinhof running around in Germany, local kidnapping thinking would be going in quite a different direction. There's also the fact that they knew when this trust fund for the grandchildren was going to be set up, and, compounding that, they have the pull to open an account with a prestigious Swiss bank. Riff-raff they're not."

"Josef," said Kurt in the back of his throat.

"As to that, we don't know. We're not in a position to do any detective work in West Germany. Unless …"

"Unless what?" Kurt asked, attention pricking.

"Unless you conspire with me in a scheme that may not get any hard evidence, but will identify them."

"I am interested."

"First off, when are you due back at work?"

"Whenever I feel up to it, Dean Gulrajani said. I said, at once." Kurt grimaced. "I need to finish my walls."

"How about next Tuesday? "

"Why? That's four full days away."

"Four full days during which you and I can fly to Munich and I can do some investigating." Her eyes, a much deeper blue than his, caught and held them. "I know your family would love to see you. It's so small that there was no one to send here while you were missing, damn it, so I know they'd love to see you. And I know that you're always telling Dagmar that you want to marry me. Well, I don't say I will, but I am willing to go to Munich with you pretending to be your fiancée. It gives me a perfect reason to be with you. While we're there, you can manufacture plenty of excuses to be alone with your family for hours at a time. I can use those hours snooping, but not in a way that will alert the Munich cops. On that, you have to trust me."

Kurt had listened the way highly intelligent people did, processing the content of what Helen said as she said it; now that she was ended, he had already made up his mind.

"That is an excellent scheme," he said, smiling, "but I am afraid we have left our run too late. Plane bookings have to be made, and tomorrow's plane may be full."

"Plane bookings are made, the tickets are in my bag, and the plane isn't full in first class," said Helen.

"*First class?*" He looked aghast. "Helen, that is wasteful! I do not mind traveling coach."

"You stingy old Scrooge! You're a rich man, you can afford first class."

"It is a principle," he said stiffly.

"Then isn't it lucky I'm paying? Miser! That's a good reason not to marry you."

"You have your own money, it would not be a problem."

"Does this mean that if we were to visit Paris, you wouldn't take me to the Tour d' Argent?"

"Most assuredly," he said with that typical, slightly wrong choice of phrase. "Paris is full of restaurants just as good but far less expensive."

"I hereby serve you notice, Kurt, that if in future we ever need to fly together, I'll be in first class and you in coach."

"I do not understand you, Helen."

"You don't have to. Will you call Dagmar first thing tomorrow morning and tell her that we're coming for the weekend?"

"Of course. And, Helen?"

"Yes?"

"It is an excellent scheme."

"You mustn't tell any of them, even Dagmar."

"I understand that. She is wonderfully loyal, but some of that loyalty is given to Josef. Were it not, she would have sent him packing when she found out about his industrial espionage."

"Good. Shall I heat the food?"

"I think so. Your news has stimulated me to hunger."

"I'll need a car," she said later, as they ate.

"You can use my Porsche."

"I might have known you'd have one stashed over there!"

CHAPTER V

N ow that Kurt von Fahlendorf was safely flying off to Munich with Helen MacIntosh, Carmine could turn his attention back to other matters. Though the Dodo stood at the head of his list, it also contained Corey Marshall. His own enquiries into Morty Jones's death could not be postponed a moment longer, though the official enquiry was set for November 11, a week after the elections; by then, memories would be blurred, attitudes hardened.

When he poked his head around Corey's door at five after eight, Corey wasn't in; not a crime, but Carmine expected his lieutenants to be in before their men, and Buzz was there.

Delia, he noted, was already hard at work, obviously celebrating Kurt's survival with more festive raiment than usual: a frilly dress in shocking pink, yellow and black stripes, a matching bow on the back of her head. How she managed to type so rapidly and accurately with such long, manicured nails, he had no idea. Today they were painted shocking pink, and as always produced a secondary sound as she hammered away at the electric IBM with the heavy touch of one who had worked for years at manual machines. Hard on the heels of the wallop of the finger striking the center of the key came the click of the nail colliding with the edge of the key. Boom—click, boom—click, like a man in a lead boot with an aluminum knee joint. Wasted on the Dodo, Carmine thought, watching her; she needs one of those cases we don't have at the moment, saturated with paper, lists, tables and computations.

Even before he checked Corey's office a second time at eight-thirty, Carmine could feel the sinking sensation invade the pit of his stomach. If there had been no love in what he felt, it would have been easier to bear, but there was love, and love meant hurt, broken bits of dreams, memories of days gone by when Corey had been magnificent.

He was there, setting up his desk for the day.

"What's my new case?" he asked as Carmine walked in.

"Time to talk about cases after we've talked about Morty," Carmine said, sitting down.

Corey hunched his shoulders. "There's nothing to say. He hid his depression well."

"Oh, Cor, come on! I noticed, my team noticed, Abe and his team noticed. How can you sit there saying you didn't notice, when I came asking you to fill out HPD Form 1313? I wanted him to see Dr. Corning, you overruled me as Morty's immediate boss, the one who'd notice most of all. A mere trainee, Helen MacIntosh, was left to go in search of him that morning. It should have been you, and you know it. What I don't understand is why you chose to adopt that attitude to Morty. He was a sick man."

"It's been blown up out of all proportion," Corey said, voice hard. "There was nothing much wrong with Morty. What made him eat his gun was the sight of Ava all beat up, nothing else."

"You won't save your skin by wearing a blindfold, Cor."

"What would you know about it, Carmine? I've been listening to Morty whine about Ava for ten months—it was nothing new, I tell you! Her leaving was the best thing could have happened to him—no more looking at every Holloman cop and wondering."

"I'm going to have to mention Form 1313 at the enquiry."

Corey gasped, staggered. "Carmine, you wouldn't! It was internal, a discussion between the overall boss and the immediate boss—nobody's business but ours."

"Everybody's business, when the object of the discussion took his own life two weeks later," Carmine said.

"It was *internal* I tell you! You can't mention it! Morty did not act depressed, and he had the drinking under control."

"Then how come he was almost never here?"

"He had a bolt-hole in the cells."

"To sleep it off."

"No! To get away from that housekeeper Delia Carstairs found—he hated her."

"But the kids liked her fine, Netty Marciano reports. I know Morty used to say they cried for Ava all the time, but that was Morty confabulating," said Carmine. Time Corey realized how far the gossip about Morty and his domestic situation extended.

"Jesus, is nothing sacred?"

"Not where Netty's concerned, Cor. You know that."

"He went to the cells to see Virgil Simms," Corey said, desperate to get Carmine off his back. "They've been pals since academy days. It's not surprising that Morty would have gone to cry on Virgil's shoulder, open his divorce papers there."

"I see." Carmine got up, still seething.

"Hey! Cases? And who's to take Morty's place?"

"There won't be a replacement until after the enquiry panel gives its findings, so you and Buzz will just have to jog along a man short until then," Carmine said over his shoulder. "I want the pair of you back on the Taft High weapons cache. There are rumors that there's a smoke and mirrors element. Put your hat on properly, Corey, and find out the truth."

"I think it was only a matter of time," said Sergeant Virgil Simms. "Morty didn't have any luck. He was Sad Sack. Whoever he married would have turned out like Ava because Morty wished it on himself. He always had a yen for a tramp, maybe as a reaction against his mom. She's one of those hard, selfish women who never miss going to church on Sundays."

"What's going to happen to the kids?" Carmine asked.

"Ava's taking them and moving back into the house, but Morty's mom is complaining to Child Welfare that Ava's not a fit mother."

"Does she genuinely want custody?"

"Hell, no! I can't come to the rescue, Captain—my wife's not an Ava lover."

"No wife is. I take it trouble's brewing?"

"Definitely. Neither mother nor grandmother wants the kids."

"It's hard to believe that Kurt von Fahlendorf's been found," said Mark Sugarman to Bill Mitski as they prepared to walk.

"Great news," Bill answered. "Holloman has good cops."

"Does that mean you think they'll nail the Dodo?"

"Yeah, it does. The problem all along has been randomness, but the crimes have to be getting less random, if only because there have been more of them to take into consideration."

"Oh, I hope you're right!" Mark said with fervor. "Then we could all relax."

"You wouldn't give up the walking?" Bill asked, alarmed.

"No, I wouldn't. It's too good for the heart and the waist, Bill." Mark laughed and slapped his belly.

"Who's that up ahead?" Bill asked suddenly.

Mark's lip lifted. "The Siamese twins," he said, groaning.

"You're right, they should be joined at the hip. They even walk like it. Repulsive!" Bill shuddered.

"Good evening," Mark said politely, coming abreast of Robbie and Gordie Warburton.

"And the top of the evening to you, sirs," said Robbie.

The twins stood to be introduced to Bill Mitski.

"Out for a constitutional?" Bill asked, trying to still his crawling flesh.

"Tonight, yes," said Robbie. "Such soft weather! I love a New England Indian summer, don't you? Days in the eighties, nights around freezing, this time of night perfect for walking."

"Do you walk often?" Mark asked. "I've not seen you."

The twins tittered, sounding effeminate.

"Heavens to Betsy, no!" Robbie cried, and moved on, Gordie automatically moving in time with him.

"Toodle-pip!" Robbie called.

Mark and Bill continued to stand for a moment.

"They give me the creeps," said Mark.

"They give me the shits," said Bill.

"Toodle-pip! Who does he think he is, Noel Coward?"

The pair resumed their walk.

"You know what I feel like?" Bill asked as they turned on to Cedar for the east-west segment of their route. It was busier here, cars driving up and down, people on the sidewalks.

"No, what?"

"A party. One of your wing-dings, Mark."

Mark sighed, shook his head. "After Melantha? No, Bill, I don't think so. Her death would hang over us like a miasma."

"One sick bastard is all it takes to wreck things! Carew used to be such a great place to live."

"It will be again, but not until after the Dodo is caught."

When he had a little time to spare, *Didus ineptus* liked to review his plans, and the plans for this next woman were looming larger and larger in his mind as the gap between the fingers of time grew ever narrower. Would it be three weeks, or would he go at the end of two weeks? They thought it had significance for him—what idiots they were! When he moved was simple self-preservation, nothing else. The thing is, did he want to share his glory with a pair of buzzards like Hubert Humphrey and the feral Richard Nixon? That was three weeks. He could be ready to go in two weeks, when the stage would belong to him entirely.

She lived on Cedar Street, and that was perilous. But not impossible. He just had to conduct his expedition accurately. The place he wanted was right next door to the Hochners, who lived in a private dwelling, whereas his target was an apartment block of four storeys that held eight tenants. Were the Hochners not next door it would have been an unattainable goal, but the Hochners were the boy who cried wolf; they were forever calling the cops to complain about the neighbors, and the cops had given up coming to investigate. Of course the Hochners complained about *that*, but even new broom Captain Fernando Vasquez had tumbled to them, and dealt with their whines by writing them flowery letters.

The Dodo's quarry lived on the first floor and out the back on the Hochner side; her name was Catherine dos Santos, she was a devout Catholic of unimpeachable virtue, a dark and lovely girl with the look of a Raphael madonna.

He had been saving her through nine others. Oh, there were more deposited in his account for future forays, but Catherine was very special. For one thing, though her hair was midnight-black, her eyes were a striking violet-blue, large, round, fringed by lush lashes, owning an expression of perfect tranquility. She had never been in love, she had told him at the party, and was saving herself for her husband.

She had bars on all her windows. Not imitation bars, but authentic jailhouse bars, an inch in diameter and solid iron. They were bolted to the inside of concrete block walls—no way in except to cut them with a torch, and the Hochners would see the first spit of a spark. Her doors were solid core, only two in number. One, a fire escape, was two doors down on the Hochner side of the building, and bolted top and bottom. The entry door was in the middle of the back wall and held three separate locks, all different.

He had the keys. Even virgins have to pee, and she had gone to Mark Sugarman's guest toilet not precisely drunk, but a little too light-headed to be bothered lugging her big bag. The keys were in it. While Dave Feinman did a wicked impersonation of Senator Strom

Thurmond, he had taken wax impressions of all five keys on her ring. In the middle of a night he had tried the five and found the three he needed, labeled them. Except that he had learned they triggered many sets of tumblers per lock, which was why he came back at exactly the time she was due home. He had to see her open the door.

Using the jungle behind which lived the Hochners, he worked his way to the back of the apartment building and sat in the boundary hedge, absolutely concealed, to see Catherine enter.

She came down the side path so physically close to him that he could hear her pantyhose hissing as her thighs brushed against each other: six-thirty on the dot. Top lock first: three turns right, two left. Then the bottom lock: six turns left, no right. Last, the middle lock: four turns left, three right. All of that done, she leaned her left shoulder against the door and gave it a powerful shove. It came open just enough for her to slip inside. Then came the sound of a big steel bolt slamming home at the top of the door and another at the bottom: only after that did she close the three locks. Fort Knox was ready and armed: what a woman!

His window of opportunity was tight. In Catherine's case he knew he would have to be inside and waiting before she arrived home, but the Hochners had a small deck outside their back door and could be found on it every afternoon drinking iced tea until six-fifteen, when they retired. No doubt they would soon make their al fresco interlude terminate at an earlier time, but he couldn't risk bringing that into his calculations. Fifteen minutes were all he would have, though he would be there at six just in case.

He could feel his heart pumping faster, the adrenaline begin to flow at the mere thought of how dangerous this one was, right there on busy Cedar Street. A small, thin voice kept urging him to abandon hope of Catherine, but he suppressed it angrily. No, he would do it! They were getting so *boring*! In Catherine lay a challenge, and he could never resist a challenge. Whatever the obstacles, he was going to rape and kill Catherine dos Santos.

Next Tuesday evening. Two weeks. They wouldn't count on that. A week later, and Commissioner John Silvestri would have Carew saturated with cops.

"I want to pull you in, Fernando, because I want to flood Carew with cops on election night and the night immediately after," said Carmine. "It will be three weeks since Melantha Green, and his cycle is a three-week one. If I'm wrong, I won't ask for another date, because he'll have gone to some unpredictable cycle only God could solve. We have to be seen to be doing something to protect the community, and this is the best suggestion I have."

"Have you talked to the Commissioner?" Fernando asked.

"Not yet. If you have a better idea, I'd rather know now."

That was the trouble with having new feet in Danny Marciano's shoes; Carmine didn't know Fernando Vasquez well enough yet to divine which way he'd jump in any given situation. Danny had jumped the way he was pushed by Silvestri or Carmine, but those days were gone, and had had their bad side; too many empires were built, too many perks and privileges were sanctioned. In time Fernando would settle down and settle in, but his Latin roots were Spanish, not Italian, which made a big difference. This was his first major job in a non-Hispanic area, and he was still groping for the right way to go about things.

"We can't have young women raped and murdered," Fernando said. "I've read enough about this case to know that no stone's gone unturned. The guy's like a ghost—but sex killers always are. No familiar tracks."

"Now he's killing, he'll never stop," Carmine said, "unless he's caught. One day he'll make a serious mistake. I want to flood his victim area with cops to help push him into making that mistake. Will you give me uniforms?"

"As many as I can spare." Fernando held up one hand, a beautiful member, square in the palm, with long, tapering fingers. "But one thing I ask, Carmine."

"Ask."

"Let's not notify my guys until election day midday, when I'll call in extra men. I'm not saying there are leaks in my division, but I'd rather make sure the Dodo has as little time as possible to prepare. Agreed?"

"That's a good idea. I won't mention it in Detectives either. That way, if the Dodo is planning to go Tuesday night, he'll have no reason not to until Tuesday afternoon. He may decide then to abort, but it's short notice, and he doesn't strike me as the kind to change his plans unless he absolutely has to. A longer wait might spook him, a short one is less likely to."

"Have you a plan?" Fernando asked.

"Nothing to rival Alexander the Great, no. I just need as many men as possible in cars and on foot."

"I can give you ten cars—I daren't make it more. Thirty foot patrols of two men each. That skins me dangerously, Carmine. If anything unrelated happens elsewhere in Holloman, bearing in mind what kind of year the country's had, things could explode."

Despite his pessimistic words, Fernando looked remarkably cheerful. "But they won't. If anything happens, it will be earlier, and you won't get any reinforcements at all."

Carmine reached out a hand. "Thanks, Fernando."

It was shaken warmly. "My thanks to you, Carmine. If you didn't have a weird and quirky detective named Abe Goldberg, all my uniforms would have meant nothing to Kurt von Fahlendorf. I suggest we go see the Commissioner."

It would not have surprised Helen MacIntosh to learn that Captain Delmonico had deliberately sidelined her to West Germany and Munich, though why she should suspect him of ulterior motives lay deeper than her consciousness. After nearly two months in Detectives, she had concluded that the Captain's unit was so tightly knit there might be some activities he didn't want her to know about. These activities were concerned with personalities rather than events, which meant she honestly didn't care one way or the other about them, but she was sharp enough to sense that he might perceive her differently than she did herself.

By far the hottest item on her secret agenda was the uncovering of the von Fahlendorf kidnappers. Why not the Dodo? Because the laurels for catching him would inevitably be scattered among several detectives, with the Captain himself at the top of the pyramid. Not good enough, just not good enough! Helen was intent upon winning all the laurels for herself, which negated the Dodo. So when she was offered the chance to investigate the von Fahlendorfs in Munich, she leaped at it.

The most uncomfortable part of the expedition was Kurt's attitude to her; though she had told him explicitly that she was pretending to be his fiancée, by the time they boarded their plane he had somehow become convinced that the engagement was as real as the plane itself. A nuisance, but one she was prepared to suffer considering the prize.

With time differences, they arrived close to midnight at Munich; she wouldn't get to meet the family until breakfast of Saturday, probably. A large Mercedes car met them, but again, no representative of the family came with it; the uniformed driver informed Kurt in German that it was past the family's bedtime. The worst feature of the trip, Helen reflected as she climbed in, was that she spoke no German, and had to take Kurt's word for it when he translated. Kurt himself grew more jovial the closer to his home he got, and seemed to regard the family's absence as normal.

What she could see of the house when the car drew up an hour later told her that it was huge by American standards; more a palace than a mansion. Her two bags were whisked inside, Kurt kissed her in the vast foyer, and she was conducted up a curving flight of purple Levanto marble stairs to her quarters, a better word than bedroom, as she had a sitting room and a little kitchen as well as a bedroom, and her bathroom looked as if mad King Ludwig of Bavaria had designed it, between the marble swans, dolphins and seahorses that swooped, frisked and floated all over green marble weeds and pink marble shells.

She let the maid finish unpacking her bags, bestowed a ten-dollar note upon the astonished girl, pushed her out the huge double doors, and sat down at a desk in her sitting room to enter her journal, as she wasn't very tired. Like Kurt, Helen had the knack of sleeping on planes. First class helped, if only he'd admit it, the skinflint.

She met them at breakfast, though no one had told her what time it was served, or where; her answer was to venture out of her quarters at seven, and start to wander A chance meeting with the butler, who spoke good English, established a valuable friendship. Clearly enchanted by her youth and beauty, he beamed.

"You are too early, *fräulein*," he said. "The maid would have brought you coffee at eight, and breakfast when you wanted."

"Oh, I'm a lark, not an owl," she said, losing him with the metaphor. "I'll eat with everyone. What's your name?"

"Macken, *fräulein*."

She glanced around the blue, cream and gilt of the room and looked conspiratorial. "Meet me here after breakfast, Macken, then you can take me on a grand tour."

"But Herr Kurt—"

"I intend to give him plenty of time with his family."

And off she went, following Macken's directions, to a small parlor wherein the family breakfasted at seven-thirty.

Five people sat at a round table, in the center of which stood a big basket of crisp white bread rolls whose aroma assailed the hungry Helen's nostrils as truffles did a hound's, a plate of assorted cheese slices, a plate of sliced German sausage, and a plate of salami. At each place—there was a sixth—sat a bowl of butter. Breakfast, it seemed. Alien, but tempting.

The men rose; Kurt performed the introductions, delighted that his Helen had risen early.

She smiled at everybody, sat down, and drank her first cup of coffee at a gulp. It was refilled as promptly as Minnie did a mug at Malvolio's.

They were strikingly handsome. Kurt set the family pattern: tall, a strong physique, frost-fair hair, pale blue eyes, the kind of features a few movie stars were lucky enough to have, as they obviated any requirement to act. Though she was not really a von Fahlendorf, the Baroness too was very fair, but sleek and exotic, with green eyes. The dark one was Josef, who quite took the breath away: thick black hair, large and dreamy black eyes, the face of an Adonis.

"My dear, I am so glad to meet you," Dagmar said. "Kurt has written so much about you. Mama, what do you think?"

The Baroness smiled with all the enigma of a cat. "She is beautiful indeed, Dagmar." Then, to Helen, "I always knew that American cosmeticians were superbly clever. Which company makes your hair dye and what is it called?"

Mouth full of delicious fresh bread roll and butter, Helen blinked, swallowed in a hurry, coughed, almost choked. Oh, hell! she thought. Aristocrats come in two flavors—bitter and sweet. This bunch are so sure of their bloodlines and wealth that they say and do exactly as they like. Bitter? They'd make a lemon feel syrupy by comparison. I am in for a rough ride.

Aloud she said, "I don't dye my hair, Baroness. It's my father's family's color. My brother has it too."

The two women exchanged a glance that said they didn't believe a word of her answer.

"You see," said Dagmar, nibbling at a roll, "Fahlendorf Farben is contemplating a cosmetics branch, a line to be called *Domina*. That means—"

"Lady!" said Helen with a snap. "I'm well versed in Latin *and* Greek, ladies. In fact, I graduated *summa cum laude* from Harvard—a great university, I'm sure you know."

"Helen's father," said Kurt, looking bewildered, "is the president of another great university—Chubb."

"Really? How nice," said the Baroness.

She, thought Helen, must have a pedigree that makes the von Fahlendorfs look like hayseeds and yokels. I bet Catherine de Medici was an ancestress, right along with Lucrezia Borgia. I am going to have *fun*!

Josef was opposite Helen, and gave her what was probably his most charming smile. "Breakfast is a hurried meal," he said, his English more heavily accented than that of his in-laws. "I look forward to a more leisurely conversation at dinner, Helen."

"No more than I," she said, trying to simper; Josef looked like a man who would succumb to a simper.

He gave her another smile, got to his feet, bowed, and clicked his heels before leaving.

"Oh, dear, flog the in-laws, eh?" said Helen, crunching her roll. "What a delicious breakfast! Nothing sweet in sight, yet nothing slimming. I love it. Is the sausage bologna?"

"No, kaiserfleisch," said Kurt, who seemed to think it was his job to keep the peace. "It is more delicate."

"It's yummy." Helen piled some on to another roll, well buttered. "I could get fat on this breakfast, Kurt. Seriously, though, is Josef off to work?"

"We all are," said Dagmar, a touch of ice in her voice. "Dinner is at eight, but we assemble in the red drawing room for an aperitif at half past seven. Macken will send someone for you, otherwise you might get lost."

"Good thinking," said Helen, on her third roll. "Kurt, do go with your sister, please. I'm off for a drive later anyway."

He smiled at her and hurried after Dagmar's retreating form.

Not much of a dresser for a rich woman, Helen was thinking as she watched them; her skirt, sweater and coat hadn't come from Chanel or Balenciaga. In New York, I'd pick her as shopping at Bloomingdale's, not Bergdorf's. She wouldn't bother driving to Boston to do Filene's basement either. *Not* a clothes horse. Therefore, who is the mysterious woman who can rival the Duchess of Windsor? The Baroness is sartorially up to it, but she's too old. And there's something about her … A flaw in what looks like a perfect stone until you really look …

Macken was pottering around the blue, cream and gilt room when Helen walked in at a quarter of eight.

"What does a German butler do?" she asked as he led her down a long, fussily decorated hall. "My father has a butler at Chubb House, but he's more a superintendent of staff than anything else. He doesn't open the front door unless he happens to be passing, for instance, and he doesn't have a pantry full of silverware. We hire an indigent scholarship student to polish the silver."

She chattered on, apparently oblivious to Macken's horror at her familiarity, until, passing into the ballroom, she decided she had softened him up sufficiently.

"Macken," she said earnestly, her eyes on his seamed face rather than the splendor of a room that would have done credit to any palace, "you must understand that I'm far more your class of person than I am of the von Fahlendorfs. And no, I am not going to marry Kurt, so there's no indiscretion involved. I'm here because Herr Kurt had a horrible time while he was kidnapped, and he needed company to come home. In other words, I'm everybody's friend, nobody's fiancée."

His eyes were grey and keen; they regarded her with liking and respect. "I understand, Miss Helen."

"Good! We're supposed to fly home on Monday, but don't be surprised if it's tomorrow—Sunday. Kurt's unhappy here."

"Yes. It is Herr Josef. Kurt cannot forgive him for the injuries to his sister."

"What was Josef's real name?" she asked, not varying the amount of curiosity in her voice. "Was it aristocratic?"

"No, not at all. His name was Richter," said Macken.

"Where does he come from? His accent in English is different."

"I do not know, Miss Helen, but I think East Germany." He swept his hand around in pride. "Is it not a beautiful room?"

"For a family of five, I think it's downright hedonistic," Helen said tartly. "I know the family is very wealthy, Macken, but this place must cost a fortune to keep up."

The dam wall was broken; the old man loved her, and would have told her almost anything. "Indeed, indeed, Miss Helen! It is killing them, but Graf von Fahlendorf will not hear of selling Evensong—that is its name in English."

"Pretty soon Swansong, sounds like."

They left; it was a long trek to the front door.

"Do you miss Kurt?" she asked.

"Yes, and no. His work has always interested him more than the factory or life anywhere, I think."

"Is the factory actually open on a Saturday?"

"Not the factory itself, but Herr Josef and Miss Dagmar go in to the office. It was a wonderful thing, that you found Kurt before the ransom was paid."

"Why, particularly?"

"Because it was the Baroness's money, her dowry for the grandchildren." He opened one leaf of the front door. "Kurt has left you a map in the car, Miss Helen, with the factory and Evensong marked on it."

She looked at the high blue sky, the sun bathing the park around this palace in warmth, and smiled. "What a shame to have to slave in an office on a day like this," she said, laughing.

"Herr Josef does not," Macken said, insisting on escorting her down the great bank of steps. "He leaves the office at noon to visit his mother."

"Do you know her?" Helen asked, looking at the black Porsche parked exactly where the door would coincide with her knees as she came off the bottom step. Trust Kurt! Control was his middle name.

And there she was, free in tons of time to get used to the Porsche's quirks, even time to get lost. But driving in Munich wasn't difficult the way driving in Great Britain had been, with traffic on the wrong side of the road. Germans drove on the correct side, the right. That was the Brits, though: island mentality.

Traffic was light compared to New York City, lighter even than Holloman; clearly not every Bavarian owned a car as yet, or maybe there were fewer two-car families? She cruised around contentedly, taking in the sights, but by half after eleven she was parked outside

Fahlendorf Farben at the entrance she had decided looked like the one to the offices.

If Josef came out, she had a good chance of catching him here. What chewed at her was that if he didn't use this entrance, she'd lost her only chance to investigate Josef as an entity divorced from the von Fahlendorfs. However, her instincts said that he was the kind who detested seeming soiled or working class; if her reading was correct, then she would succeed. At first the showy Porsche had worried her, but after a couple of hours in the city, she had seen enough Porsches on the roads to believe Josef wouldn't notice her, parked far down the block and behind a cheap Ford. Come on, Josef, prove me right! .

At noon precisely he came through the imposing glass doors and strode across the wide thoroughfare to a dark red Mercedes she hadn't noticed until that moment. It must have just pulled up. Dark red ... She couldn't really see, but she suspected that the driver was a woman. Slipping the Porsche into gear, she watched the Mercedes ease into traffic, and followed it at a distance that put two cars between it and her.

It proceeded at a pace well within the speed limit and turned off the main road within a kilometre. From that point the red auto drove with purpose, behaving as if its driver had no idea she was being followed. Traffic became sparse so Helen had to stay well back, but she never stood in any danger of losing her quarry. Right into one street, left into another, always moving out of the city central. At no time did the Mercedes navigate a poor district; quite the contrary. When it stopped at last, thirty minutes later, the street was affluent and the house that apparently was its goal was as imposing as the rest. Not in an American way, this affluence, but the three-storeyed and well painted residences were all situated in reasonable gardens.

A young man ran down the ten steps from the front door and across to where a self-contained garage had been constructed at a later date; he used a key on its padlock and then rolled up the door. Very dark, very handsome, very like Josef to look at. The car drove in, but no one came out. There must be a walkway to the house, Helen concluded, easing the Porsche into a vacant space two hundred metres away on the same side of the road.

Now what do I do? Get a closer look at the young man and the woman who might or might not be the woman who obtained the prison plans from Correctional Institutions.

The street was fairly quiet, but not deserted as it would have been in America. People were out and about, walking their dogs, all on leashes. The sidewalks were mined with dog turds, so she would have to be careful where she stepped—gross! It was going to be hard to access the house as each residence was surrounded by an iron rod fence topped with spear heads, and each had a big bay window looking down on the front fence.

Helen took to the sidewalk herself, cursing her jeans and windcheater: they looked wrong in a place where every woman was in grey or brown tweeds and snappy little hats. If she was accosted, she'd pretend to be an English au pair girl; they wouldn't believe an American au pair girl, popularly supposed to throw the baby out with the bath water. Or so Helen's friends had assured her when they swapped yarns of life's adventures.

"Mausie! Mausie!" she called, as if searching for a small and delinquent dog.

Where the garage stood—most houses seemed to make do with kerbside parking—was a little gap, like a side passage; Helen ducked into it quickly and ran toward the backyard, expecting to be brought up short by a connecting corridor. But no such existed. Around the back she discovered why. The house had a fourth floor half buried in the ground; these were by far the most private rooms, as the windows were almost at ceiling level.

She looked down on three people sitting at a table: Josef, the young man, and a woman of about forty. As they were speaking German, she couldn't have understood what they were saying even if she had been able to hear it, which she couldn't. The room was insulated, probably air-conditioned: a rarity for Munich. It was also expensively furnished and attractively decorated—a lot of money had been spent on this basement flat. Presumably it was designed for Josef and his visits, which meant the house's occupants didn't want the neighbors looking in to see Josef. Well, well …

But this was definitely the woman who had obtained the plans, because she was dressed to rival the Duchess of Windsor, and did. Her outfit was dark red rather than maroon, but it was French and extremely expensive. What were the odds? It *had* to be the same woman! A beautiful face perfectly made up, as dark as Josef's—was she his sister, then? And who was the young man, a son or a nephew? He was about eighteen or nineteen years old, Helen estimated, and he was stylishly dressed in the European idea of casual. They were, in fact, a trio any couturier would die for.

She had Kurt's and Dagmar's phone numbers and there was a call box at the end of the road, but she decided not to call them. First, see what ensued at dinner tonight.

When the woman in dark red Dior dropped Josef one street over from the factory, Helen learned something else: unless incest was in the equation, she wasn't Josef's sister. They exchanged a passionate kiss before Josef transferred from her car to his, a top of the line

BMW. So they were lovers. Richter, Richter … Though there was another possibility, given that this youth was about four or five years older than Josef's eldest by Dagmar. What if Josef and this woman were husband and wife, the marriage to Dagmar bigamous? That would *not* please a toplofty clan of Prussian junkers with an Italian aristocrat thrown in the mix!

The family dressed for dinner, which Helen, no novice, took to mean black tie for the men and evening gowns for the women. Well, no long dresses for her! Helen climbed into a miniskirted dress of amber with an amber lace overdress—I'll drown those two bitches in this color! Sheer gold pantyhose and gold shoes, a gold bag, and down her back the famous MacIntosh apricot hair. Out of a dye bottle, indeed! Eat your hearts out, you anemic, skinny blondes!

The look on Macken's face said he hadn't seen anyone look like this since Aphrodite, and two footmen in dark green livery stood gaping until Macken barked at them. A smile fixed to her face, Helen swept into the crimson, cream and gilt drawing room, where the three male von Fahlendorfs gaped at her.

The Baroness, exquisitely garbed in charcoal grey with white touches that displayed and vanished as she moved, came up to Helen and brushed cheeks. "My dear, such beautiful legs! You must have done ballet and gymnastics."

"Track and field, actually," Helen drawled, vowing that Miss Procter's would be proud of her.

"We have a perfect table tonight," said Dagmar, brushing in her turn. "Three couples."

She was wearing, Helen noted, a dowager-style dress of beads and billows in an unflattering pastel blue—why do blondes wear blue? It diminishes them. The dress screamed Hong Kong and made her look sixty—oh, Dagmar, Dagmar!

The Baron, who thus far hadn't really impinged on Helen, served sherry or Campari as an aperitif and wandered around the room with Helen in tow, showing her his favorite paintings.

"I would wish for Delacroix or Rossetti, but the museums have them," he sighed.

"That's where I'm lucky," Helen said, grinning evilly. "I get to borrow some of the Chubb collection, though it's more Impressionist. One of these days the Parsons Foundation will have to cough up its el Grecos, Poussins and whatevers, but until then Dad refuses to build the Chubb art gallery."

The Baron, she saw, was lost; wasted ammunition. The old man lived in a dream world, and she felt sorry for him, dominated by his wife and daughter. Yet, she noticed, he didn't seem at all comfortable when marooned with Kurt—I must remember to put that in my journal, she vowed mentally. Kurt sets them on edge, he's too alien, with his muons and particles. It's The Bomb, of course. Europe's in the first line of fire, so to speak, and they're really paranoid about The Bomb. Look at how they hoped John F. Kennedy would save them. His death meant more over here, and now the von Fahlendorfs have spawned an atomic scientist. Brr!

The children came as a shock. A dowdy little governess shepherded them into the drawing room like clockwork dolls; it had horrified Helen to learn that they shared no meals with the adults— oh, think what she had learned at Dad's table as a child! They were so stiff and polite—the two boys bowed and clicked heels, the two girls curtsied. Amazing! Even the fifteen-year-old boy, with fuzz on his legs, wore short pants and knee socks. Astounding! Martin and Klaus-Maria, older than the girls, were also darker, though none of the four was as dark as the father. Annelise looked as if she might give the governess trouble, but, Helen was assured, it was Ursel, the youngest, who had inherited the genius. A promising research chemist of the future.

From her tiny conversation with the children, she learned that the family was Roman Catholic—why had Kurt led her to believe they were Lutherans? Because I assumed it, and he just couldn't be bothered correcting me. He's a physicist, he believes in time and timespace, whatever that is, and he told me that there is no life after death, it flies in the face of the laws of physics.

Even with all its leaves removed the dining table was too big for six people, especially since the Baron chose to sit at one end and the Baroness at the other. There was more than a yard of space between her and Dagmar on one side, Kurt and Josef on the other; she faced Josef, Dagmar faced Kurt.

"Where did you meet your husband, Dagmar?" Helen asked as a mediocre soup was removed.

"At the polytechnic in Bonn," Dagmar said, it seemed willing to view this question as permissible. "We were in the same year, and both doing chemistry."

"Had you done a general degree first? Arts? Science?"

"No. I knew what I wanted to do, so why waste time?"

"Um—you don't think that four years of college can put a polish on whatever you want to do later on?"

The arctically blue, cold eyes surveyed her from the gold of her head to the hand-made gold lace of her dress. Contemptuously. "A foolish waste of time, which is the most precious article in life. Before you know it, you will be an old woman."

Especially wearing a dress like that, said Helen's eyes. "Nothing's wasted that broadens a life, I believe. Look at me—a Harvard graduate one moment, dealing with Queens traffic the next. Harvard was a help."

"The Queen has traffic?" Dagmar asked blankly. "In what?"

Her laughter broke all conversation into a transfixed stop-motion; everyone stared, and Helen realized that one didn't howl with laughter at a von Fahlendorf table. Too bad. "No, you misunderstand. Queens is a borough of New York City, and I was a traffic cop there for two years."

Someone pressed the button: movement resumed.

"An extraordinary job," said Josef, dark eyes admiring. "I think you left it, yes?"

"Yes, to train as a detective in Holloman, my home town."

"Such unfeminine work," said the Baroness, looking itchy to leave even though the fish was just coming in.

"Work is work," said Helen in a flat voice, staring at the glaucous eye of a sole above its pursed little rubbery lips. "People give work a sex, when it shouldn't have one. Detection of crime is eminently suited to the talents of women."

"Why?" asked Kurt, smiling.

"Because women are naturally nosey, Kurt, love."

"It cannot pay much," said the Baron, scraping one side of his sole down to its skeleton and eating with relish.

"I don't need to worry about money, Baron. I have an income of a million dollars a year from a trust fund."

Stop-motion again.

"You are enormously rich!" said Josef on a squawk.

"Not for my family," said Helen, laying knife and fork down together to indicate that she found the fish inedible. "The thing is, we made our money several generations ago, and thanks to good management, we've been able to do useful things with it. My father is a famous educator, my parents have brought my brother and me up to regard philanthropy as necessary, and we work to benefit our family reputation, our home state, and our country."

"Didn't I tell you Helen was wonderful?" Kurt demanded.

The Baron flipped his fish over to enjoy the more buttery, lemony underside. "What we do not know," he said, scraping away, "is who kidnapped Kurt. Your getting him back unharmed and saving our money were laudable, Helen, but the crime is not solved."

"Actually," said Helen, waving at a footman to take her plate, "it is solved. I know who kidnapped Kurt and tried to steal your ten million, Baron."

"Nonsense! How could you?" Josef asked sharply .

"Not nonsense, Josef, as you well know. She must be a most expensive mistress, the woman who lives with the young man in that big house. Is he your son too?"

The silence was palpable; the four genuine von Fahlendorfs were staring now at Josef, trying to seem unaffected.

"A joke, Helen?" Kurt asked, face the color of ashes.

"Unfortunately, Kurt, no. It's the truth. Josef masterminded your kidnapping, which was carried out by a cruel and ruthless woman who is either Josef's mistress or his real wife. Her assistant—a rather unwilling one, I think—was the young man who looks too much like Josef not to be his son," said Helen.

Josef broke into a stream of German that dried up when the Baron smacked the table with the palm of his open hand.

"*Halte die Klappe!*" he roared. "Speak in English, or not at all! Since the day you married my daughter, you have been a leech! I have tolerated you because of Martin, Klaus-Maria, Annelise and Ursel—" Suddenly he floundered, eyes rolling wildly.

Dagmar was howling noisily and Kurt fully occupied in trying to calm her, but the Baroness was behaving most strangely of all, scratching at her chin and throat. The brilliant light of the overhead chandelier showed the beads of sweat breaking through her careful make-up; Helen saw the light. The Baroness was a junkie. Morphine, probably.

It was Macken and Helen who took charge. Kurt was ordered to take his sister away and help her in her own rooms, and the Baroness's maid summoned to deal with her mistress and her habit.

"Brunhilde knows what to do," said Macken, revealing that at least the senior staff knew the family secrets. "My lady had a back operation several years ago, and cannot deal with the pain," he said smoothly.

In a pig's eye, thought Helen. "Josef can't be allowed to communicate with his woman," she said to Macken, "and that means locked in guest quarters like mine, with all the phone jacks unplugged and no one in contact with him who might be susceptible to a bribe. It's up to the family what they do with him and his accomplices, I'm butting out—going home, I mean."

"This is all nonsense, Helen," Josef said as two footmen prepared to march him away. "You spied on me and discovered my sister and her son."

"Sister?" Helen laughed. "I saw the lip-locker you and Frau Richter—shall I call her that?—exchanged this afternoon."

Kurt walked in, looking grim. A swift conversation passed between him and Macken; Kurt looked relieved. "You are a woman in a million, Helen," he said to her. "I must take Papa to his room. He will recover in a moment, then we will decide what to do with Josef. Poor Dagmar!"

"I'm going home tomorrow," she said.

"I will be coming with you," said Kurt, and led his father away: a curious business. The old man shrank, muttering about bombs— that much Helen got, even in German—then seemed to cave in and allowed Kurt to assist his faltering attempt to walk.

"You're a treasure, Macken," she said to the butler when they were the only people left in the room.

"Thank you, Miss Helen."

"What did your father do to make a living?"

Macken looked surprised. "He was butler to the Graf."

Old retainers! "And your son or sons, Macken?"

"One son. He is the head of a government department in Bonn."

Dagmar begged for admittance as Helen was packing the next morning. "I must thank you," she said stiffly.

"It's not necessary. You realize, I hope, that I'm not going to marry Kurt? I came to see if I could solve the kidnapping."

"That relieves me. You would drive my Kurtchen insane." She sat on a chair out of the way and watched the jeans-clad Helen work, smoothly and swiftly. "We will save the family name, that is all-important."

"I figured as much," said Helen dryly.

"Josef asked me to split two of the ten million off and give it to him," said Dagmar. "I took it as selfishness, but of course he wanted it for his natural son. His request was denied."

"May I offer you a word of advice?" Helen asked, stopping to look at Dagmar very seriously

"No doubt I will resent it, but offer it anyway."

"Josef's mistress dresses like the Duchess of Windsor—both very expensively and in very good taste. You dress like old Queen Mary, with whose appearance I'm acquainted thanks to an English colleague. You're a frump, Dagmar, but you needn't be. Put yourself in the hands of one of those faggy guys always hanging around rich women and let him work a Pygmalion. The best revenge is to live well, so while the Richter woman rots in a German prison, you can flaunt it. You'll be a happier woman, betcha."

The sheer insolence deprived Dagmar of a retort.

Helen packed on tranquilly until she finished.

Dagmar spoke again. "Did you mark the woman's house on your map?" Dagmar asked then.

"Yes," said Helen, surprised.

"May I have the map? I will need it for the police."

Helen reached into her enormous shoulder bag and withdrew it. "Here it is, complete with the wrong folds." She opened it and pointed. "There you are."

"Well, at least I know what Josef did with his salary."

"Speaking of houses, this one—" Helen began.

"Will be sold," Dagmar said with finality, and got up. "I will not see you again—ever, I hope. But thank you."

*   *   *

Helen and Kurt flew home together on Sunday, and parted in the foyer of Talisman Towers undemonstrably.

"I am tired," said Kurt, brushing her chin with one hand.

"Worse than being kidnapped?"

"Infinitely. My poor sister! She is heart-broken."

"Give her my compliments when you talk."

"I will."

And, thought Helen, gazing around her attractive but austere bathroom, it may not look like mad King Ludwig of Bavaria, but I like it all the more for that. Something in between would be nice.

"Bigamy!" said Carmine on Monday morning. "It fits. Yeah, it fits like Frau Richter's hand in her French kid glove. The brother-in-law did it to provide for his legitimate son, since his bastards had so much—and were getting more."

"Bigamy can happen when a once-whole nation has been split ideologically, and the two parts don't talk to each other. I daresay the von Fahlendorfs didn't ask, and Josef sure as hell didn't say," Helen said to Carmine, Nick and Delia.

"They won't prosecute," Nick said.

"Definitely not," Delia said.

"They have to do something," Helen said. "Honor has been insulted, and the Baron's not the man to suffer that without lashing back. Nor is the Baroness. And Dagmar's even worse."

"Well," said Carmine, leaning back in his chair, "thank God whatever they do is German business, not American. Note, however, that the family pushed Kurt back to our side of the Atlantic with indecent haste."

"Protecting him from whatever they do," said Nick.

* * *

"Have you seen the evening papers?" Desdemona asked on Tuesday night when Carmine got home.

He was on edge; there was a faint possibility that the Dodo would strike today. "No," he said, taking his drink.

Prunella came in and sat down with a breathless sigh. "I wish Julian had less imagination, now that he's found it," she said, smiling. "Captain Nemo is rather wearing. Did you know that a race of fish men live in the deep ocean right at its bottom? I could bear that if they hadn't invented this whizz-bang, super-duper death ray."

Desdemona handed her a glass of red wine, and gave Carmine the New York evening papers; Holloman's was a morning one.

"It's in both papers," said Desdemona, sitting. "The *Post* has the bigger article."

It was front page, and headlines: Josef von Fahlendorf, brother-in-law of kidnap victim Professor Kurt von Fahlendorf, had been shot dead outside the von Fahlendorf factory in Munich on this Tuesday at dawn. "Holy shits!" Carmine exclaimed, still reading. What Josef was doing there at that hour no one in authority at Fahlendorf Farben seemed to know, including its managing director, Dagmar, who hadn't even been aware that Josef was gone from their bed. According to the sole witness, a Volkswagen car eased up behind Josef and the two men in it cut him down with automatic pistols. Heinrich Müller was a factory worker on his way in to Fahlendorf Farben to fire up some new equipment, and he behaved heroically. Instead of seeking shelter, he tried vainly to help Josef, who died in his arms a few minutes later. "Kurt!" he said several times, quite clearly. Müller said the men looked like Turks, had spoken a few words in Turkish. Enjoying this news item immensely, the by-lining journalist said it was evident that Josef thought he had been mistaken for Kurt.

"What do you think?" Desdemona asked.

"That it's as fishy as Julian's fish men." He got up.

"Off to Helen's minus your drink?"

"Hell, no! She can wait until tomorrow. I'm going to see Delia. Give her a call for me, please? With this news humming on the aether, every hammer and teamster in creation will be tuned to the cop band, so let's keep my movements secret."

"Dinner?"

"I should be home in time. Otherwise, save mine."

"Luckily it's steak, so we'll wait. Prunella, looks as if this might be a night for the girls to get blotto."

"That's a good chambertin—don't guzzle."

Since she didn't mind the half-hour commute, Delia lived in Millstone, where she could afford a spacious apartment on the waterfront of Busquash Bay. Having chosen a divine color scheme of rust, blue and pink, Delia had stuffed every room with furniture imported from Oxford, where it had graced her grandmother's home. The walls were a permanently open photograph album of Carstairses, Silvestris, Ceruttis and Cunninghams, the occasional tables boasted lava lamps next to Dresden china lamps, and there were lace-edged, daisy-embroidered doilies everywhere. It was *home*.

By the time that Carmine got there she had read the newspapers and listened to the local news radio station, WRHN. She also had his drink ready.

"So who did it?" Carmine asked.

"I'm not quite sure, Carmine dear. Whoever, it's carefully orchestrated. Heinrich Müller was there accidentally on purpose, of that I'm positive. They had to have a witness to point out that the culprits were Turks."

"Why Turks?" he asked, sipping.

"Because Germany's filling up with them," Delia explained. "Turks find German much easier to learn than other European languages, and penniless Turks gravitate there in search of work. I predict that in the future the trend will escalate, but it's already marked enough to have created a degree of resentment in working class Germans. Turks make convenient whipping boys."

"I see. And Heinrich Müller?"

"Will get a big fat promotion. Oh, he was there! I'm also sure the men he saw looked like Turks, may well have been Turks. But I very much doubt that Josef died with Kurt's name on his lips—or that he died so slowly. I don't know how clever Müller is, but he's probably clever enough to suspect that he was given this special job in order to be there as a witness. If he earns a big fat promotion out of it, I predict that he won't care who set it up or for what reason. Dagmar had him pegged as promising."

"So who do you think set it up, Deels?"

"A von Fahlendorf. Which one is the brain-teaser. Not our Kurt, of that we can be sure, I think. The family was anxious to get him out of Europe. But whether it's the Baron, the Baroness or Dagmar, I don't know. My choice is Dagmar."

"Broken heart and all?"

"The broken heart makes her more likely, in my book. A woman scorned and all that stuff? According to Helen, Josef is—was—a gorgeous looking bloke, smooth as satin, charming as Cary Grant. She'd already forgiven him an attempted scam and must have been positive he wouldn't err again. But to think he'd kill her baby brother—! Ooo-aa! That's blood versus love," said Delia with a shudder. "I'd choose blood over love every time."

"So would I, I think. What will the German cops think?"

"That some Turks did it. That it was Turks planned the kidnapping too."

"In which case, why kill Josef?"

Delia pursed her lips. "Some abstruse Ottoman mind-set? A peculiar eastern revenge? I think the German cops will be so grateful to have a solution offered to them that they won't ask too many uncomfortable questions."

His glass was empty; Carmine declined a refill. "Thanks, but no. I have to get home for dinner."

"There's a chance the Dodo will strike tonight."

"I know. That means early to bed."

TUESDAY, NOVEMBER 5
to
SATURDAY, NOVEMBER 30

1968

CHAPTER VI

He hadn't struck a week early after all; when push came to shove, he just hadn't felt like it. What was the point in moving up to murder if simultaneously he made life easier for himself? The big, muscular cop Carmine Delmonico was a hazard he knew he was capable of beating, but the victory must be worthy of Catherine dos Santos, she of the prison bars and multiple locks.

She had told him the story as they huddled together on Mark Sugarman's couch, giggling.

"The realtor told me," she confided, violet-blue eyes shining. "Such a joke! Simons built the apartments and reserved mine for himself. He hoarded money, you see. Can you imagine it? No one tried to rob him because no one knew he hoarded money, so when he died, the bars and bolts became his executioners. The firemen took *hours* to break in. And there he was, on his bed, surrounded by stacks of bank notes, swollen up—disgusting!"

"You don't mind living with that history?" he asked, smiling.

"Heavens, no. I'm safe, that's the main thing."

One by one he had picked the necessary details out of her; when the party broke up he saw her to her car like the gentleman he was, lightly kissed her hand, and never bothered to see her again in case she remembered what they had talked about. Had she cried for him? Sat by her phone hoping that he'd call? If she had, a fruitless wait. In those days he had merely been making up his list, hadn't even started raping in the clumsy, amateurish way he'd tackled Shirley Constable. Well, a man had to learn by experience, didn't he? And the list had to be complete, so far back in the past that none of the women would remember.

When *Didus ineptus* parked his Chevy on Persimmon Street in its usual spot on election day, Tuesday, November 5, his mind was filled with his own brilliance. No coincidence that he had begun his career on a leap year and a presidential election year: luck favored the bold, and he'd sensed what a disastrous year 1968 would be.

He always parked there, yes; he had been doing so for long enough now for his fellow Persimmon Street parkers to recognize his car. The moment he got out, he couldn't help but see the cops. They were everywhere: cruising in squad cars, strolling the sidewalks in pairs, holsters open, cuffs easy to get at. As he turned in the direction of Cedar Street he had a sudden impulse to abandon his foray, then grew angry at his own cowardice. Plan A was clearly impossible, but Plan B was just as good. He limped down Persimmon Street dragging his right leg, and in the instant when no cops were visible he leaped off the sidewalk into Plan B's bushes, which flourished in fits and starts right along the back fences of the blocks facing Cedar Street. The sun was lowering, a month and more past the equinox now, and the shadows at ground level were heavy, darkly dappled.

His blood was pumping hard; the thrill of the chase had invaded him, and he knew how and where he was going better than these uniformed idiots could imagine. In a gap, he lay full length and walked it on his elbows, his combat camouflage ideal, until the next profusion of low-slung leaves permitted him to rise to a squat, peer toward Cedar Street or the back of a building. Catherine's apartment block lay nearly 300 yards from Persimmon Street, but the worst of it was that the Hochners were beyond her, closer to Cranberry Street. His shelter was thickest where he could not use it, with Plan A discarded.

Mountain laurels grew along the back fence of Catherine's block—good, sturdy evergreen bushes that no one tended. And there, right opposite him, was Catherine's door at last! He put on his ski mask just in case, eased his back with its load of knapsack, and pulled the three keys from his pocket. The Hochners, he saw, had finished their iced tea and were going inside, and the cops weren't smart enough to extend their patrolling off the street sidewalks. He would have to trust to his luck that while he ran from the bushes to the awninged back door, no one upstairs was gazing into the backyard.

The sun plunged down into the foliage of an old oak growing behind the Hochners, and with its going the light decreased; the Dodo checked using his peripheral vision, saw nothing, and ran for Catherine's door. The keys went in and turned in the same order as hers; he felt the last lock relax and did what she did, leaned his shoulder heavily against the door and pushed it open.

AAA-OOO-GAA! WOW-WOW-WOW-WOW-WOW! AAA-OOO-GAA!

The world erupted into noise. Deafened, stunned, the Dodo stood for perhaps three seconds leaning against the door, then leaped for the bushes alongside the Hochners and went to earth, trembling, eyes blinded by sweat, those abominable alarms still shrieking and wailing in his ears. What was it? What hadn't he done? The wretched woman had tricked him! He, *Didus ineptus*, had fallen for a trick!

Plan C. He had to get away from here before the area swarmed with cops like flies on carrion. The knapsack was shrugged off, the ski mask, the jacket and the pants. From the exterior of the knapsack he pulled a series of aluminum tubes, screwed them together, and worked to make sure that his ordinary slacks were well down over his socks, not tucked in anywhere. Then, as the noises continued, he wormed his way around the back of the Hochners, who had emerged and were standing at Catherine's door. Like a snake he slithered across the exposed ground bordering their back deck before burying himself in their bushes again. Then, down their far boundary to Cedar Street, where he crouched and watched the cops thunder by until, in a temporary lull, he appeared on the sidewalk supported by his crutch, limping along. The next bunch of cops rounded the corner from Cranberry Street, split up to pass him on both sides, and left him to make his way to Persimmon Street and his car.

He was stopped twice, asked if he had seen anyone; he looked bewildered, said no, and was allowed on his way. The crutch was genuine, he was dressed in yellow checkered slacks and a red jacket, and he seemed a little simple. He never came under any suspicion, even from a stray squad car minutes later.

The bitch! The fucking bitch! How had she tricked him?

* * *

Carmine gazed about in amazement. No one, looking at the fortress from its outside, could ever have believed how beautiful Catherine dos Santos's apartment was. None of the bars showed; instead, there were ceiling-to-floor falls of frail silk curtains that shaded from palest green gradually through to the dark green of a pine forest, then began to fade to pale again, all around the room, a gradual color waxing and waning. The carpet was dark green, the ceiling palest green. Chairs, tables, occasional furniture were carved mahogany upholstered in vivid peacocks.

"I rarely spend time in the living room," said Catherine. She had shut off the alarms; no one else could. "He must have watched me enter, but of course he couldn't see me deactivate my alarms—I press a section of the door jamb and paint it again when it wears." She led them farther into her artificially lit retreat. "Between the bars and the four bedrooms, I was lucky to find this place. In here I paint," she said, showing them a studio with a half finished oil of dried flowers on the easel.

"In here I sew and embroider," showing them a second room.

Shades of Desdemona! thought Carmine, staring at a priest's chasuble on a dummy. Is that what all spinsters do?

"And in here I illuminate manuscripts," Catherine said. "I confess it's my greatest pleasure. You'd be surprised, Captain, at how many institutions and people want something illuminated."

"So you sell your work?"

"Oh, yes. It's my hedge against an indigent old age."

"Do you ever go to parties, Miss dos Santos?" Helen asked as they returned to the living room.

"Only Mark Sugarman's. The last one was four months ago."

"Did you meet anyone memorable at a Sugarman party?"

She concentrated, then nodded. "Yes, I did. A very nice man! We had a long, pleasant conversation, but he didn't hit on me. I don't think he gave me a last name, but his first name was Brett. I said that sounded as if he'd been named after a movie star, but he laughed and denied it. It was a family name."

Helen stifled her sigh; there was no Brett on Sugarman's party lists.

"Did he have an opportunity to rifle your bag?"

"Only when I went to the toilet. I wasn't gone long."

"Have you seen Brett since?"

"No, never. That's not surprising, Captain. I have no need of people, either at work or at home. Everything I do is art of some kind. I like solitude, I guess."

"Don't you feel—well, imprisoned?" Helen asked.

Catherine dos Santos laughed, a high, clear sound of true amusement. "Good lord, no! Detective, in here I feel *safe*! No one can get at me. That's always the terror of women who love living alone, that they'll be targeted by a predator. I love my bars, which is why I went to a lot of trouble over my weak point—the door. Noise is the best deterrent—really loud, siren noises. They always deter. I installed the sirens myself, bought them in an electronics hobby store." She smiled jubilantly. "I'm especially fond of the one that sounds like a submarine. With the Hochners for neighbors, I'm safe, believe me."

"Oh, I believe you," Helen said. "What I find hard to credit is that you really like your life."

"You were at Mark's party—how do you live?" Catherine asked.

"I have a security penthouse," said Helen, smiling.

"Lucky you."

*   *   *

"My chief criticism of you, Miss MacIntosh," said Carmine in biting tones after they left, "is that you have no idea how the other half lives, even after some exposure. That leads you to speak before you think. The moment Miss dos Santos said she did some of her art as a hedge against an indigent old age, you should have put a censor on your tongue. Why are you so quick to inform the world that you have millions, when what you ought to remember is that extremely few people are in your boat? I haven't heard you contemplating giving any of your millions away to those less fortunate."

"I apologize, Captain. I knew it was the wrong thing to say the minute I said it, but I didn't know how to get out of such an awful predicament—I apologize, Captain, I do!"

"Why are you apologizing to me, Miss MacIntosh? You only offended me at second-hand. By rights you ought to go back and apologize to Miss dos Santos. This kind of apology is rather self-serving, don't you agree?"

"Too much time's gone by for me to go back," Helen said quickly. "If you like, I'll write her a note."

"Yes, do that," said Carmine, still simmering.

He spoke no more until they were in his office, where Nick and Delia joined them.

"How did he manage to get away?" Helen asked, still desperate to retrieve lost ground with the Captain.

"By being prepared for all eventualities, I suspect," said Carmine. "And helped by the Hochners, who should have stayed put and watched for him, not rushed to Catherine's door and impeded the cops."

"They're famous with the uniforms," Delia said.

"Ask Fernando Vasquez. He's inherited Danny Marciano's file on them. Eternal complaints, then they missed the Dodo."

Nick pulled the knapsack that lay on Carmine's table closer to him. "Cool," he said. "While the back of Catherine's apartment block seethed with cops, he hunkered down in a bush on Hochner property and changed his appearance. He left the Dodo's gear in the bush and emerged somewhere as a different person, I'm picking wearing gaudy clothes. But what was in these, Carmine?" Nick pointed to ruches in the knapsack's exterior.

"Struts that maybe kept the knapsack rigid?" Delia offered.

"Why?" Nick asked.

"Whatever they were, he took them out," Carmine said slowly.

"Unless they're an intrinsic part that hampered him?" Helen asked. "Something that stopped him hiding the thing?"

"No, the cavities are still distended by whatever was inside. Round pipes or rods …" He counted the ruched bulges. "Six. Added together, about six feet. But what would he do with something six feet long? Subtract one, and it comes down to between four and five feet, depending on the length of the components. Not all the cavities are the same length."

A conversation with two uniforms crashed into Nick's mind. "It's a crutch," he said.

The rest gaped at him.

"Ike Masotti and his partner found a crippled guy on Cedar Street hobbling toward Persimmon. Not far from Catherine's apartment. Crutch under his arm, dragging his right foot. He was wearing pants in that Scotch check that's almost all yellow, and a red windcheater. Ike got no joy out of him, wrote him down as mildly retarded."

"The Dodo!" Helen cried.

"He's good, Carmine," Nick said. "Fooled two smart cops nearly right outside where it happened. You know Ike Masotti—not easy to fool. It was early, mind, the sirens were still yowling because Catherine wasn't home. A little later, the cops would have been less confused."

For answer, Carmine picked up his phone and asked Fernando Vasquez if he knew how many cops had encountered a luridly dressed cripple.

"The guy's brilliant," he said, hanging up.

"Slipped through our fingers," Nick mourned.

"Yes, but Ike Masotti set eyes on his face," Carmine said, "and while he may have attempted disguise hiding in the Hochner bushes, he didn't have the time or the facilities to do anything dramatic. The cops who saw the cripple later might not have been so lucky, so it's Ike's description we go on. Who was his partner?"

"Muley Evans."

"What's he like?"

"Sharp. We'll get a good drawing."

It was long after midnight before *Didus ineptus* went to earth. The red windcheater had been turned inside out to display its black side, and the MacLeod tartan pants were now showing their black lining. Thank his lucky stars for the verdure of Carew! He had gone nowhere near his car, still parked on Persimmon; the walk to his *own* car wasn't impossible for someone who kept in shape by walking. When he hid to reverse his clothing, he dismantled the crutch and polished every inch of it outside and in. They'd not nail him with a print inside, even if they had the wit to think of it. Then he pushed the sections deeply into a bush and walked on, a man of ordinary mentality clad in black. Who wasn't accosted at all. The crutch and flashy clothes had been a part of Plan C, an escape which he wouldn't use again. When pulled up by three different sets of cops—one on foot (the first) and two in squad cars—he had given a sad, braying laugh that branded him as slightly retarded and been let go without being asked for so much as his name. It was worth noting for the future that a man in black who didn't want to be seen tended not to be seen, even if he didn't behave furtively. Black is better, black is definitely better! For flashy apparel, be retarded.

On the border of Carew and Busquash was his rented apartment; he let himself in, still wearing surgeon's gloves, and undressed. The stash of clothing was folded carefully and slipped through a manhole in the hall ceiling; they were too hard to get, necessitating a trip to New York City and theatrical suppliers, so while the apartment lasted, he'd hang on to them. After that he donned hiking gear and shouldered a new knapsack, filled with exactly the things a hiker would need for the Appalachian Trail.

On the border of Busquash and Millstone was his own car; he reached it without seeing a cop, got in and drove away. If a cop should stop him, he had his story straight.

But no cop did. Home at last, he realized he was ravenously hungry, took a Stouffer's lasagna from the freezer and used the forty minutes heating time it gave him to put out his pajamas, secret the knapsack in his special place, and revel in a shower. Refreshed, clad in silk, he opened a bottle of French claret and sipped the wine with relish; no guzzling for *Didus ineptus*! It had been a close thing tonight. He never wanted a closer. The killer in him slavered at the thought of putting paid to Catherine dos Santos, but the survivor in him was stronger. There were other names in his book, other lives to take. The fucking bitch had tricked him, and, in tricking him, had evaded him forever. He would not be going back to vent his rage on Catherine dos Santos. Thinking that, he raised his glass.

"Here's to the Holloman police," he said, smiling. "May they think me a vengeful man and waste their time!"

The police artist's drawing was interesting because no one recognized it. And that could not be.

It showed the face of a brown-skinned man in his forties, dark haired and dark eyed, with a beaky nose and a wide, thin mouth. There was a general impression of a damaged mind.

"This means he was in make-up for the attack," Carmine said, and, to Ike Masotti, "It really looks like him?"

"I'm sorry to disappoint you, Captain, but it's what my mom would call a speaking likeness," Ike said.

"Bearing no resemblance to the guy the Hochners had noticed creeping around."

"Yeah, but the Hochners are notorious," Ike said. "Their guy was probably reading meters. This is definitely the guy I saw."

"Ike, you did better than you can realize. Your drawing shows us what we're up against. Thanks a lot."

Ike departed, scratching his head.

"Why do you think this isn't the Dodo—or rather, that it's a Dodo in disguise?" Helen asked.

"Because Dr. Meyers has a general description of the charming man who had a long conversation with four of the rape victims," Carmine said. "He had light brown hair, light brown eyes, and a fair skin. His mouth was full and his nose only slightly beaky."

"Perhaps the man the victims saw was also in disguise," said Delia. "He's very clever, so he will have taken it into account that we might elicit descriptions from the Sugarman parties."

"He must present as bulky before he enters his victim's apartment," Nick said. "Combat fatigues, and under them, another outfit as brightly colored as he can make it without looking any more than dressed in bad taste."

"And under the gaudy outfit, yet another, I think," Carmine said. "He didn't seem to be on the street as retarded and lame for more than a few minutes, yet no one saw him enter a car and drive away. He must know the location of every tree and bush in Carew, and as soon as he saw no cops anywhere, he was back into the bushes for a quick change into something dark and inoffensive. Has a crutch been found?"

"No, despite a thorough search," Nick said.

"Did he abandon it? Or lug it home under his clothes? It seems he lugged it home, strange as that might be. His reasoning is beyond me!" Carmine slapped a hand to his brow. "To make matters worse, Sugarman himself can't identify any victim's drawings. He swears that he had no gate-crashers at any party. That means—no, it can't!"

"Means what?" Delia asked.

"That he made-up for one conversation—impossible!"

Delia squeaked. "Not really impossible, Carmine, if you think about it. Say he spots his quarry on a sofa grabbing a little rest from the bash, nips into the lav, makes himself up. If she's still there when he pokes his head out, he's on the sofa next to her as slick as a rat goes up a sewer pipe. If she isn't there, he nips back into the lav and takes his make-up off. He's full of gall—certainly he doesn't lack it, now does he?"

"Oh, that's too much!" Helen cried.

"No, Delia, I see where you're going," Carmine said. "It *is* possible, even if not very probable."

"He must have an ego bigger than Tokyo," Nick said.

"Well, we know *that*! How else can we fit all the pieces of this puzzle together? Parties, especially good ones, are about as easy to keep track of as the rails in a freight yard. They criss-cross perpetually. However, it does tell us one thing."

"It does?" Nick asked.

"Yes. It says that the Dodo is fair in coloring. All his make-up has been brown, including light brown. Come on, guys! We've all had instruction in disguise—felons do resort to it, otherwise we wouldn't have to sit through slides showing what blue contact lenses do to brown eyes—very little. Whereas if the eyes are light in color, it's easy to change them with lenses of almost any color. We can say that the Dodo's eyes are blue or grey or pale green, and his hair, at darkest, is a light brown. If he keeps a beak shape to his nose, then it's probably straighter than that. Narrower too." Carmine's voice had grown excited, his hands moving expressively. "Skin has to be fair, and the bones of his face prominent. This guy's cheeks are plump. Think of the Turks who shot Josef von Fahlendorf down in Munich—you know you're not looking for fair gunmen. But if fair gunmen wanted to give an impression of Turks, it would be easy. Just thick, black hair and brown skin."

"Oh, oh!" cried Helen. "The von Fahlendorfs could have been the gunmen! They were, Captain, they were!"

Carmine shot her a look of scorn. "No, they were genuine Turks. Why keep a dog and bark yourself?"

"Carmine, dear!" Delia exclaimed. "You've just widened the Dodo pool of suspects enormously."

"No, diminished it. Holloman's a place of many, many dark people—African, Mediterranean. There are far fewer fair." He sputtered, grinned. "Hard to say that! Far—fewer—fair."

"Where would you draw the line?" Delia asked.

"At Mason Novak, speaking of Gentleman Walkers. Don't forget there were bunches of them at every Carew party. He's basically red, which doesn't exclude him. His eyes are a very light brown."

"Or, at the other end, Kurt von Fahlendorf, though he's been busy being kidnapped," Helen said.

"Bill Mitski," said Carmine. "Arnold Hedberg. Mike Donahue. Though if the Dodo is a Gentleman Walker, he'll be easier to nail. We use the line-up. The rape survivors must have recovered enough by now to try identifying their attacker."

"No, Carmine, you can't do that," Delia said quickly. "It's too demanding for the women, who haven't recovered enough. I'm sure that's what Dr. Meyers will say. No, I'm right!"

"Of course she was right," said Desdemona.

"I was hoping you'd be on my side," he said, disgruntled.

"Not when it has to do with the effects of rape."

"Okay, I'll leave it."

She leaned over to kiss the top of his head. "Thank you, dear heart."

"How are things with you?"

"Much better. I don't break down anymore. Julian is turning into a human being, believe it or not, and Alex is just divine. The sweetest little chap, quite different from Julian—oh, he was sweet at six months too, but looking back, I can see the germ of Julian the defense attorney. It was in the way he looked at me—measuring me up. Alex slobbers."

"Slobbers?"

"Pools of drool."

"I haven't noticed," Carmine said, surprised.

"You don't have breasts, Daddy. Alex is far more like you than Julian is. Loves his food, does Alex."

"That *does* bode well! Not a defense attorney type."

Julian burst into the room, arms stretched out, and landed on Carmine's lap. "Daddy, Daddy!"

"Hi, Captain. How's the sub tonight?"

"Oh, *him*! I'm in the Wild West now, Daddy."

"Buffalo Bill and Wild Bill Hickock, huh?" Carmine asked, racking his brains for Wild West heroes not famous for killing people, and very conscious of Desdemona's presence.

"No, I'm Julian Delmonico, and I round up steers faster than anybody else on the Chisum Trail!"

Prunella flourished a large book. "It's hard to find one that's not full of shoot 'em up dead, but I try, Captain." Her voice changed to command mode. "Bed time, Mister Delmonico! I am the boss of the roundup and you are a mere cowboy, so ride 'em!"

Julian's goodnight kisses were entirely dutiful; he let out a piercing shriek. "That's me, rounding up!"

"It's a wild country with a wild past," Carmine said to Desdemona when they were alone. "He's half Calabrian, and you Brits haven't always been peacefully inclined. You even had a civil war. I know you find the prospect of raising two sons in America appalling—is that why you're depressed?"

Her rather plain face grew plainer, as it always did when she was unhappy; the pale blue eyes were teary. "No, I don't think so," she said. "I really don't, Carmine. After all, you stand for law and order."

He crossed to her chair and squeezed himself in it beside her, one arm around her shoulders. "Yet twice you've had to get yourself out of danger," he said, throat tight. "Lovely lady, that's a part of the law and order. We've been married now for nearly three years, and I can't live without you. Every time you feel blue, remember that."

"That's the trouble," she said. "I do."

Sitting up, he turned her head so that he could see into her face. "Does that mean you've thought about *leaving* me?"

"No, of course not, silly! More that I worry about you in your job, I think. You're right, this is a wild place. It's—it's gun-happy! You even had to teach me to shoot, remember?"

"That was common sense, Desdemona, nothing else. The odds are infinitesimally small, yes, but I'd rather be sure than sorry."

"I won't be able to deflect Julian from guns for much longer, will I?" She sounded desolate.

"Not when he plays with Ceruttis and Balduccis, I'm afraid. But you can't forbid him to play with his peers either. That would isolate him. And you can't tell me that British kids don't play with toy guns. Sure they do! Violence is entrenched."

"Yes, but how many kids find a gunman in their backyard?"

"That's unfair. Neither American nor British kids."

"Unless their father is an *American* cop."

"Not even then. It was a simple quirk of fate."

She got up suddenly and went into the kitchen; Carmine didn't make the mistake of following her to pick at her cringing flesh. Sweet Jesus, don't let a second wife desert me because of my job!

*   *   *

When all the election results of that very close victory were in, Richard Nixon was President and Hubert Humphrey the also-ran. "It's Humphrey's name," moaned Nick, a fanatical Democrat. "*Hubert!* The moral of the story is not, don't christen him that because he won't get the Democrat nomination, it's really because he won't get elected when his rival's got a name like Richard."

"At least Connecticut voted Democrat," said Delia.

"And all that's in the past," said Carmine. "More to our purpose is the fact that the Dodo investigation has foundered."

It hadn't seemed possible that the new slant on the Dodo's appearance would go nowhere, but that was exactly where it went.

"We have nowhere to go and no place left to look," he said to his assembled team on Monday, November 11. "It's a purely local Carew affair, in that nothing has ever come to light about it outside of Carew. The Dodo, the Gentleman Walkers and the victims are all based in Carew. His last chosen date was the nation's election day, which on the surface looks ideal, and he thought so too. His failure leaves us confounded—how is he going to adjust his timetable? His pattern to date has been at three-week intervals, but will he wait three weeks, bringing him to November 26, or go down to two weeks—November 19—or even one week—tomorrow? If it's tomorrow, we're shit out of luck, folks. Captain Vasquez wouldn't be amenable to saturating Carew with cops so quickly after a Dodo failure, and I'm not sure we should ask him for that on any date, even the twenty-sixth. We can definitely assume that this guy has a list of victims that isn't going to run out anytime soon, and, from what happened on election day, we might be excused for assuming that he

285

has a list of plans as long as his victims. If we were going to catch him by saturating the area with cops, we would have succeeded then. His contingency plan was better than ours. He escaped. We got egg on our faces."

"Maybe what we should be considering is his needing to blow off steam?" Nick asked.

"Yes, that's an element," Carmine said when no one else replied. "Not getting as far as first base with Catherine should cause a huge sense of frustration. But I think the Dodo is too cold-blooded for that kind of reaction. I read him as more likely to retreat into his shell and not try anything for months. Lull us into believing that he's moved on to an equivalent of Carew in another state."

"No, Carmine, he won't do that," Nick said.

"Why?"

"Because Carew is *home*. He's been living in Carew for a long time. If she's been in Carew for longer than a few weeks, he knows every Carew woman's face. Not that I think any woman who hasn't attended a Sugarman party is in danger. That's where he picks them. But he won't retreat into his shell—Carew is his shell. The drive is too strong for months of inertia. He'll go for another victim, probably in three weeks—the twenty-sixth."

"Could we set him up with a victim?" Helen asked. "I live in Carew, and I'm willing to be bait."

"Thank you for the offer," Carmine said, "but the Dodo works exclusively off his own list. We've been here before, remember?"

"How about trying to find his victims instead of him?" Delia asked. "We *have* to try, Carmine!"

"The pool is too big, it just is. He likes professional women who live decent but not celibate lives," said Nick when Carmine didn't answer. "Ethnic background, religion, physical type are all different, Delia. The pool's too big."

"Okay, the Dodo goes on a back burner," Carmine said. "From what Corey says, the Black Brigade is restive, and the Taft High weapons cache is a bone of contention between him and Buzz. He says there are no weapons left at the school, Buzz thinks there might be. Emphasis: *might be*. Abe and his team are going on general duty. Nick and Delia, you're going to Corey. The most important item to ferret out is the weapons cache—does it or does it not exist?"

"Corey has good connections with the Black Brigaders," said Nick. "What makes Buzz disagree?"

"It seems to depend on whether or not there's a splinter of the Black Brigade operating at Taft High," Carmine said. "A sub-group could exist without the parent group's full knowledge, given Mohammed's secretiveness. A couple of years ago he was militant, but he's never inclined toward violence for the sake of violence. I do know that some Black Brigaders get irritable at what they see as Mohammed's sloth, or even timidity. When the confrontation over Wesley le Clerc never got off the ground, Mohammed kind of retreated. That's why I'd be surprised if there isn't a splinter group forming."

"You think it's at the school?" Delia asked, grimacing.

"I don't know. Help Corey and Buzz find out."

He was wearing his navy suit trousers; out of his cupboard came his silver-braided dress jacket. "I have to go, and I won't be back today," he said.

"What do you want me to do, sir?" Helen asked.

"Go back over the rape victims, right back to Shirley, see if you can find something new or any points in common we've overlooked." Jacket on, he ran a finger around its high neck. "How I hate this neck!

All you can do, Helen, is read. If you get bored, read one of your textbooks." He left his office.

"He looks so splendid in his dress uniform—my heart leaps," said Delia, sighing.

"Thanks a million!" Corey said with a snarl when Carmine walked in two days later.

"Excuse me?"

Corey waved a sheet of paper back and forth under Carmine's nose. "This! You betrayed me. I thought you agreed to keep the Form 1313 business between ourselves?"

"Whatever gave you that idea?" Carmine asked, surprised.

"When we talked a few days ago, I thought we agreed that you'd brought up 1313 of your own volition, as a way of finding out how I felt about Morty. And I *told* you! He displayed no evidence of depression or suicidal tendencies, which is why I refused to submit the form. After all, it's designed so that a man's senior in the chain of command can't plot against him—*two* signatures, *two* statements!"

"Until you tell me, Corey, I don't know where you're going."

The paper flapped again. "I wish I could say this is a letter of commendation," Corey said, shaking in rage, "but it's not. It's a written reprimand!" His voice took on the tones of Judge Thwaites passing sentence on someone he deemed contemptible. "Do not let anyone else under your command eat his gun, Lieutenant Marshall, do you hear me? This time it's a caution, but if there is a next time, the full weight of the Law will fall upon you!" He dropped the letter. "A reprimand! *Me!*"

"No aspect of Morty's death should be the object of sarcasm, especially when you choose Judge Thwaites. The enquiry wasn't conducted under any Holloman public official, which should tell you that its findings are impartial," Carmine said.

Corey sneered. "Oh, sure!"

"I still don't get your drift, Corey." Make him say it out loud, don't let him suppress it to chew like a cow its cud.

"You and Silvestri have more pull than any other cops in the whole of Connecticut, including the Staties. You made sure I was reprimanded, you and *Cousin* Silvestri. All you had to do was pick up the phone. and call in a few favors."

"Jesus, Corey, how paranoid can you get? This was an enquiry into Morty Jones's death, not any alleged negligence on your or anyone else's part," Carmine said, stunned. "And you're right about Form 1313—it would have been considered and discarded as the right of two superiors to differ. What made the panel sit up and take notice was your own conduct, Corey. You harangued them about your innocence."

"You and Silvestri killed my chances of being exonerated," Corey interrupted.

Carmine stared, stupefied. "*Exonerated*? What a word to use! No one is persecuting you, Corey, and you weren't on trial. But you behaved as if you were, and that's what earned you the reprimand. The panel became convinced that at least some of the smoke originated in a fire. You talked for a full half hour not about Morty Jones, but about yourself, the demands of your duties, how difficult I, and ultimately John Silvestri, made your job. Have you been listening to Maureen? Have you? I'm sure she's an admirable wife domestically, but she knows nothing about police procedures.

Whenever she sticks her oar in, you're the one gets in trouble. And she's been worse ever since you became a loot, Cor. Much worse! Like that crap about Abe Goldberg and my favoring him over you—I could hear Maureen saying it."

"You can't bring my wife into this," Corey said aggressively. "It's the pot calling the kettle black—rumor says your wife is a basket case. You're passing the buck."

"My wife is ill," Carmine said, holding on to his temper, "nor does she try to interfere in my police business. I can't say the same for Maureen. And if I see it, Cor, so does everyone else. Including *Cousin* Silvestri. Tell her to butt out."

"She's got my best interests at heart," Corey said stoutly.

Oh, a lost cause! thought Carmine. "You deserved to be reprimanded," he said. "Morty was reaching out for help, and you refused to see it. I know why. For exactly the same reason that you can't be bothered writing a good report—there's too much pain in the effort. No one has demoted you. The reprimand will go on your record, and that's a shame, but it could only matter if you were moving on—"

Light dawned. Shit, Carmine, you fool! Maureen has made plans to move onward and upward, which means out of Holloman and out of the Holloman PD. Now it can't happen. Corey has spoiled her plans. Not me. Not Silvestri. Corey. She's known right along, but gave him the wrong advice—harangue the enquiry panel.

"If you wanted to look squeaky-clean, Corey, you should have blamed yourself a little. Tell Maureen no one's perfect."

Corey swallowed. "Why are you here, Carmine?"

"I've come to see why you're making no use of two highly experienced and intelligent detectives in Delia Carstairs and Nick

Jefferson," Carmine said. "They've been with you two days, yet you haven't even bothered to see them, let alone give them orders. What's going on?"

"No, I haven't seen them or used them," Corey said, waxing indignant. "They appeared out of the blue, and I've had no kind of written direction from you—any kind of communication, even a phone call. According to Captain Vasquez—" he held up a fat pamphlet "—I could be sued if either of them was injured on the job. I mean, what's the matter with this place these days?"

"I'm amazed that you read boring stuff like that," Carmine said solemnly. "One of the penalties of a captaincy, you may tell Maureen, is an overwhelming amount of paperwork that can't be avoided or postponed, plus a daunting number of conferences and meetings that achieve virtually nothing. And, if the captaincy is in the Holloman Police Department, it comes with a uniform coat whose collar could double for a guillotine. In the current landslide of duties that have little to do with Detectives, I overlooked the particular piece of paper that notified you about Carstairs and Jefferson, both of whom, for the purposes of shuffling paper, are *men*. They are now your men, Lieutenant, to do with as you please."

"Carstairs is a woman!" Corey protested.

"Does paper have a sex? Perhaps they should be its?"

"You're a sarcastic bastard, Carmine."

"I am indeed. If you think that my ability to slip the dagger between your ribs is formidable, Corey, almost six years of being associated closely with me should tell you how awful it is when I twist the dagger inside the wound. And the first twist of the dagger is this: make sure your wife keeps her place."

"Wives are off-limits for discussion, Carmine, you know that."

"I ought to—it's my own regulation. Sometimes, unfortunately, the rules have to be broken. You should be asking when, not why— you know the why. The when is now because this person who is vital for your well-being—your wife—has made your police business her business, and put a black mark on your career that would otherwise not have happened. Maureen's made herself the subject of this talk, which I find extremely distasteful. I have nothing to say about her apart from her police interference, which has got to stop. Do you see that?"

"How come you never talked to Morty about his wife, then?"

"Oh, come on, Corey! Ava wasn't my business."

"Nor is Maureen."

"She is, when she makes mischief within my division."

"She doesn't. It's your imagination."

"Okay, then I'll drop the subject. You've been warned, and so has she." Carmine leaned forward, looming. "If you don't improve your attitude, Corey, there will be other reprimands. You're going to have to learn what nearly a year of winging it hasn't taught you—how to be a *good* lieutenant. You're slipshod and careless, which you never used to be. How much of your apparent efficiency when you were on my team was due to Abe Goldberg's covering up, I don't know, but now you shape up, hear me? We're looking at a green winter, and that means trouble."

"You can't possibly be naive enough to think there are still weapons at Taft High, Carmine. Did Genovese go over my head? If he did, I'll crucify him!"

"No one has gone over your head, but in asking me, you've just revealed one of your deficiencies—you don't trust a man the moment his opinion conflicts with yours. Differing opinions are healthy, Corey, they indicate your men can think for themselves. Trust doesn't enter into it. Buzz Genovese is a new detective, he needs guidance, not derision. Or are you in favor of the trainee system and more Helen MacIntoshes?"

Corey looked horrified. "The old way is the best way!"

"Then don't fuck up. Whatever you do, *don't* fuck up."

Delia was waiting outside Corey's office door, which Carmine had closed on leaving. He stared at Delia in surprise.

"What's up? Isn't Corey treating you right?"

"If being ignored is incorrect, he isn't. But is there any way Corey can do without my talents?" Delia asked.

"Give me a good enough reason, and I'll cut you loose."

"Helen."

His brows furrowed, something stirred in his eyes that Delia couldn't assess, except that Helen worried him. "Expand."

"She's a very good girl, but younger and more inexperienced than she'll admit. That's the trouble with growing up in that particular household, I imagine. Stacks of success, money, power—and ego. It hasn't escaped me that you've chided her several times for arrogance and insensitivity, and I agree, she has too much of both. It's just that—" her long, red nails fluttered like the tips of flesh-colored butterfly wings "—my thumbs are pricking, as the Bard would say. Let me stay with her, please!"

Too much money, too much beauty, too much too soon … "I see. Well, you and Desdemona have already kicked my ass over the rape victims, so who am I to ignore God-sent warnings? If you think she might inadvertently cause trouble, Delia, then by all means stay with her. If Corey gripes, refer him to me."

COLLEEN McCULLOUGH

The bright red mouth broke open in a beam, revealing that Delia's teeth also wore lipstick; with a squeeze of his arm, she was gone, her clunky shoes booming up the stairwell.

She found Helen already surrounded by files, with what she privately called a "Joan of Arc" expression on her face, which lifted to see who came in, visionary, beatified.

"Oh, Delia! I thought you were going to Corey," Helen said, Joan of Arc replaced by Snow White choking on an apple.

"The boss changed his mind," Delia said artlessly, pulling up a chair and sitting.

"I thought he was finally trusting me!"

"He always trusts you, Helen. Try to climb out of that oversensitive skin of yours to see what I believe is called the big picture. No, let me put it another way. You interpret Captain Delmonico's actions and orders as pertaining exclusively to you, but that's wrong. He acts and orders to achieve maximum results from every member of his teams, highest to lowliest. Between his telling you to work the old rape victims on your own and his ordering me to join you, he must have seen that something would come up needing more than one pair of hands."

"But what could?"

"We have to find it. Surely you know me well enough by now to understand that if the credit belongs to you, I will gladly give it to you. I'm not greedy."

Yes, but you are, Helen. Second-string bothers you, your eyes have turned stony. Ambition! So much ambition!

Keeping her voice neutral, Delia embarked upon the story of the Ghost, who had abducted teenaged girls, tortured and raped them, then murdered them. It was a famous case which Delia went into more deeply than any of the filed reports did.

294

"You're saying that lightning won't strike in the same place twice," Helen said at the end. "I get the message" She shrugged, smiled. "So okay, any suggestions as to where we look?"

"Yes. We're going out. My Buick, or your Lamborghini?"

"Will it offend you if it's my Lamborghini and I drive?"

"Lord bless you, no, child! All those horses are fun."

"Where to?"

"Mark Sugarman' s, with every drawing of the Dodo we have."

He was not annoyed to see them. Just resigned. "I hope you realize that this is my *ninth* interview?"

"Lord bless you, no!" Helen cried, enamored of Delia's phrase. "Actually this isn't an interview, it's a collaboration."

It had been agreed in the car that she would take the lead; Helen used his big white table to spread the drawings. "The police artist did these, but he's not a patch on you, and we need more drawings. Would you do them?"

He was in love with Leonie Coustain, but who could resist those wonderful eyes when they held pleading? Mark Sugarman swelled a little. "I'm clay in your hands," he said, laughing. "Yes, I'll do them."

"Now?" she wheedled.

"Yes, now." He walked across to shelves and supplies for a sketching block of thick, raggy paper, then filled an empty jar with pencils. "I'm ready. From here on, you have to direct me."

Helen looked over the drawings and found one, full face, that showed a dark-haired, dark-eyed man with a beaky nose.

"This one first," she said, disappointed when he took it to his drawing board and pinned it in the left-hand corner, then tore off a sheet of paper and fixed it to the center of the board with what looked like plasticine.

"Oh, I can't watch unless I move one of your tables."

"I forbid it. Sit there, at the bar. You're as close now as I can bear. Do you want a better drawn copy?"

"No, I want you to work with the bones of this face and do as I say."

"For you, Helen, that's not difficult. Tell me."

"Make the nose straight and narrower, the mouth smaller but its lips fuller, and the brows more arched," she said. "He needs to be twenty pounds lighter, whatever that would do to his face, and his coloring should be on the fair side."

Silence fell. The two women watched, fascinated, as the new face grew below the one in the top left-hand corner. Mark kept working, it seemed oblivious, until he sighed, stretched, and turned on his stool to face them.

"Well? Is that what you want?"

It was difficult to credit that the one drawing had its basis in the other; Mark's version was handsomer in a Hollywood way, yet didn't look like anyone they knew.

"Shit," said Helen, "I was sure I'd recognize him!"

Mark had swung back toward the drawing board and was studying his work in a frowning concentration. "You know, girls, I am positive I've seen this guy somewhere," he said. He continued to look for some minutes, but in the end sighed in defeat. "It beats me! I can't place him."

Helen seized another drawing, of a fairer but fatter man. "Do you mind doing the same thing to him?"

"Of course not. If it can help, I'll feel that at least I did something for Leonie."

This progressed faster, as if the pencils, all sharpened, knew their route around the blank paper more unerringly. At the end, all three gasped.

"It's the same man!" Helen cried.

"Definitely," said Delia.

"And I'm no farther ahead with my memory, girls. I know him, I know I know him! *Where?*"

"A party?" Helen suggested.

"Could be, though I can't label him with a name, and every man at a Sugarman party is a friend, not an acquaintance."

"The mystery man who converses in a corner with victims?"

"Is *that*—?" Mark shook his head. "No. It's not unlike, but it's not like either."

"Okay, let's go through the Gentleman Walkers—the handsome ones," Helen said. "Sorry you can't help, Delia, but if you don't mind sitting there, I think Mark and I ought to do that."

"I can help," Delia said, going down on all fours to get at her huge briefcase. "I brought the relevant Gentlemen with me in photographic form." She shook the case like a dog a hard pillow; pictures cascaded out. "It's best if all three of us do this, because people's ideas of beauty differ so much."

For a moment Delia thought Helen was going to have a temper tantrum, but good sense won; she laughed. "You are so right, Delia! I'm dying to see your idea of handsome!"

A merry half hour ensued, at the end of which Mark admired Delia's choices more than he did Helen's; since he qualified in both women's listings, he couldn't be dismissed as biased.

"Your choices are all male models," he tried to explain to an incensed Helen. "You have no place for subtleties like charm or kindness. To me, they illuminate a face to beauty, whether they're men or women. I agree that Kurt von Fahlendorf is very handsome, but his face is Narcissus—no character."

"How can you say that, Mark?" Helen demanded aggressively. "Delia picked him too—and you did yourself! But to say he has no character—oh, that's ridiculous! One day he's likely to win a Nobel Prize, yet his colleagues *love* him! Ordinarily they hate the prize winners. If you saw him with his sister or mother—!"

"That's not what I mean, and I agree, he has to go down in every list of handsome men. It's just that he's not near the top of my list, any more than he is of Delia's. I agree with you, Delia. Mason Novak every time, followed by Arnie Hedberg and Mike Donahue. Bill Mitski's ahead of Kurt. I put Greg Pendleton up there as well."

"Oh, go take a running jump!" said Helen, pouting.

"No need, Helen. None of the Gentlemen is my mystery man."

"Shit, triple shit!" said Helen.

"Time to go, dear." Delia turned to Mark and held out her hand, smiling. "Thank you so much for your patience, Mark. Um—may we take your drawings?"

"Oh, burn them!" Helen snarled, and swept out.

"She's been spoiled," said Mark, taking Delia's briefcase and staggering. "Man, this weighs a ton! Funny," he said as they waited for an elevator, "she got markedly nicer for a few weeks after she joined the Holloman PD. I'd begun to think that she had the makings of a wonderful woman."

"She still does." Delia got in, Mark following. "I put her relapse down to disappointment at not shining as brightly as the sun at the end of some time period she'd set herself. She didn't think her junior status would last. She's been with us for ten weeks now, which I imagine is the length of her tether."

Mark loaded the briefcase into the Lamborghini's trunk, and watched the car roar away.

"Poor Helen!" he said, then went back inside Talisman Towers.

Mason Novak was walking out. "Just the man I came around to see! How about lunch?"

"As head of two 'Who Is The Handsomest?' polls, Mason, how could a mere eleventh on the list turn you down?"

"Huh?"

"Wait while I get a jacket, and I'll tell you over lunch. It makes a marvelous story. Where are we going?"

"Up-market, or down?"

"Sea Foam, and I'll pick up the check," Mark said. "When the story's as good as mine, we don't need eavesdroppers."

Mason listened, entranced, then shouted with laughter. "My God! I don't know whether to shiver with amusement or fear."

"Neither," said Mark loyally.

"I think a lot depends on whether Helen MacIntosh likes me, don't you?"

"She likes you fine, but it's Kurt she has her eye on."

"Poor Kurt!" Mason said, real pity in his voice. "I'd hate to head any Helen MacIntosh list, from handsome to husband. Do you think Kurt fills both roles?"

"I have no idea, and you know what?"

"What?"

"I'm not going to ask."

* * *

I hate this year! thought Carmine as he trudged up the stairs to his office. Between Fernando Vasquez, M.M., John Silvestri and my own limitations, I haven't managed to get out into the field nearly as much as I want to. Delia and Nick can manage fine, but that's no consolation. I keep getting flashes of insight that go nowhere, one of my lieutenants is in a state of covert rebellion, and I have a rapist-murderer uncaught after ten months. Not to mention a glass teddy bear that's a museum piece and a bank robber cum vandal who seems to have disappeared in a puff of smoke. My wife's moving away from me into an ideal world where she can see her sons grow up untainted by violence, I haven't set eyes on my pre-med daughter since she started at Paracelsus, and Myron isn't visiting.

"What have I done wrong?" he asked Patrick O'Donnell later.

The blue eyes twinkled. "Nothing, cuz, nothing! You've hit a patch of doldrums, is all. Until the wind fills your sails again, you just have to sit becalmed."

"I wouldn't mind, except that I'm missing something, Patsy. Every time I think I've sunk my teeth into the Dodo, a distraction intrudes—Vasquez with some new scheme, or John in need of yet another report, or, or, or!" Carmine said passionately.

"I know the feeling. Now that I'm fifty-seven, John wants to know whether I'm going for retirement at sixty or sixty-five—how the hell do I know yet? A lot depends on Ness, whether she retires at sixty. We're the same age, our kids are grown and off our hands—work fills our lives, damn it!"

Carmine knew that his cousin's decision rested ultimately on whether he felt the empire he had built was built on solid foundations. When he had begun as Medical Examiner, forensics were virtually non-existent; now it occupied more floor space and staff than necrology, and more of his time too. And it kept expanding as new discoveries were made. Had Patsy prepared for them sufficiently? Would sixty-five be better?

"How's Desdemona?" Patrick asked.

"Recovering from the depression, but now she's got a new bogey—sons and guns," Carmine said.

"Oh, that one! Maybe you should send her to talk to Ness. Even primary school has its share of gun worries, but they have to be put into perspective. There's a huge cultural gap too."

"Tell me something I don't know! But actually it's not Desdemona worrying me as much as my detectives. When a man eats his gun, it's the culmination of a whole slew of problems that ought never to have been allowed get that far. Or that big. Any fool can see that, yet Corey refuses to—and he's no fool! I can't trust him to see what's under his nose in foot-high letters."

Patrick opened a filing cabinet drawer and removed a full bottle. 200ml beakers made great glasses, there was a carboy of distilled water, and every laboratory had an ice machine.

"The sun's been over the yard arm for hours, and John does not rule here. You've been in that uniform for days, so don't refuse me." He put a clinking beaker in Carmine's hand.

"I have no intention of refusing. Cheers!"

"Cheers! The trouble with Corey, cuz, is that the canker eating at him you can't remove—Maureen the snake, Maureen the scorpion. I hear he was reprimanded."

"Rumor does not lie. Unfortunately Maureen was planning on a move to police captain some place other than Holloman. Well, the reprimand kills any hope of that, which is good for Corey."

"I agree. He couldn't thrive out of his home town. Is he cooking any more reprimands?"

"It depends whose side you want to take in his little team war. Buzz Genovese says there are still weapons at Taft High, but Corey is adamant there aren't. I gave Corey Nick Jefferson and Delia, but he wouldn't use them until I told him in person. He thinks I've planted them as spies."

"Jesus, he's paranoid! As if you'd ever do that. You're quite capable of doing your own dirty work." Patrick put his beaker down. "Corey has to go, Carmine, you realize that. He's running a personal agenda and sees you as his enemy."

"I know, but I haven't worked out how to do it. Nor, more importantly has the Commissioner. We won't lose another man by a cop suicide, but there are other ways. Corey's not capable of looking after his men properly."

"Have you talked to John about it?"

"Only briefly."

"Time to sit down with John and get it all out in the open, cuz. If anyone has a solution, it will be John Silvestri."

"I can't be sure how he'll react, Patsy. He might jump too brutally. He's capable of great mercy and sympathy, but also of putting a man's head on the chopping block."

"When he decapitates, the circumstances are different. Corey is a seventeen-year veteran who's spent his whole cop career in the Holloman PD. The mercy and sympathy will be there. He knows dear sweet Maureen, just like the rest of us. Nasty bitch!"

"I guess you're right." Carmine drained his beaker and stood. "Thanks, Patsy. I'll lay everything out for John scrupulously."

* * *

On his way across the building, Carmine looked at his watch. Six o'clock. Too late for Desdemona to salvage her dinner, but early enough to put parts of it in the refrigerator. He disliked destroying her work, but he had a job to do that couldn't wait.

She behaved, as always, like the perfect policeman's wife. "Never mind, my love," she said over the phone, "it was only a beef roast. Prunella and I will have some tonight, and the rest can go into a shepherd's pie tomorrow. What flavor would you like the minced beef to have? Curry? Italian? Plain old Limey? I'd top a curry or an Italian one with risotto, an English one with mashed potatoes."

"English," he said promptly. "How's the kids?"

"Like runner beans—I can almost see them growing. Oh, I do hope they don't shoot to seven feet!"

"So do I. That means custom-made beds, mattresses, sheets, blankets, watching for round shoulders and sway backs—"

"Carmine, stop! They might inherit their height from you."

"Well, we're not short. I'm five-eleven, my pa was six-one, and the Ceruttis are taller than the Delmonicos. Whether you like it or not, wife, our sons will play basketball."

"Rather that than American football! Wake me up when you come to bed, please."

And that was that. He phoned Malvolio's and got Luigi.

"Do you ever go home, Luigi?" he asked, suddenly curious.

"Home is Malvolio's. I live upstairs anyway."

"Jesus! How long have I known you?"

"Um … 1950 or thereabouts, Carmine."

"So it's only taken me eighteen years to learn that you live upstairs. Any family?"

"Four boys, all in the armed services."

"And the wife?"

"Took off with a sailor in 1944."

"So you raised your boys alone."

"The family helped."

"I don't even know your last name!"

"Silvestri. What can I do you for, Captain?"

"Is there someone can bring me over meat loaf and rice pudding in about an hour, Luigi?"

"Sure thing. I got some juicy shrimps, want a cocktail?"

"Why not?"

He fetched all the relevant files—and some that only he felt were relevant—and put them on his table. The only way to tackle the case of *Didus ineptus* was to go through it from its beginning to its present end in the peace of a deserted office. After a pensive look at the number of files and the area of his table, he went to Stella Pulaski's office and took the two folding banquet tables stored behind her door. Once they were up, he decided he had sufficient room, and began the business of distributing the files widely separated enough to allow their contents space if they needed laying out. The last series of interviews Delia and Helen had conducted with the victims went into each victim's pile.

Then he proceeded to break the files up: uniformed reports, detective reports, witness reports, victim reports. By the time that he was satisfied that everything was arranged according to his needs, Minnie arrived with his dinner, which went on to his formal desk together with a giant thermos of Luigi's coffee.

He sat and ate—Luigi was right, the shrimps were juicy—until the plates were clean, then sent them back to Malvolio's in the custody of a desk cop. Under Danny Marciano, it would have simply happened; under Fernando Vasquez, he had to fill in a form explaining why he had used a uniformed cop as a personal servant. Jesus, how he hated the bureaucratic mentality! An imp whispered that he should fill out a form explaining why he'd ordered a uniform to shine his shoes, but he pushed the little devil away; he was too busy for pranks.

Stomach full, coffee mug steaming, he started work.

Considering that the first inkling the police had of the Dodo's existence was the rape of Maggie Drummond on Tuesday, September 24, and it was now Tuesday, November 19, Carmine realized that at no time had he been free to examine the case from its actual start on March 3 until this moment. But after tonight, that would change; he would have the Dodo at his fingertips. Even as he worked it nagged at Carmine that if the Dodo switched to two weeks, tomorrow they would have another victim, and she would be dead. Yet he couldn't seriously think that: the Dodo might tell himself that nothing temporal ruled his forays, but three weeks did.

Shirley Constable, the first victim, on March 3, a Sunday. An embryonic Dodo, not even named because she had been so terrified that she hadn't even remembered his notice. But in her last interview, after some weeks of treatment, she had told Liz Meyers that the man definitely wasn't Mason Novak. The Dodo's touch was alien. Mercedes Mendes, ten weeks later, on Monday, May 13. Even after weeks of therapy she maintained she had no boyfriend; Dr. Meyers had elicited an unknown fact about her that solved the puzzle. Mercedes was a lesbian. Leonie Coustain, raped on Tuesday, June 25, which was six weeks after Mercedes. The Dodo was growing into his final shape, gaining confidence. From then on his intervals were roughly three weeks; Esther Dubrowski on Tuesday, July 16,

Marilyn Smith on Tuesday, August 6, Natalie Goldfarb on Friday, August 30, Maggie Drummond on Tuesday, September 24, Melantha Green on Tuesday, October 15, and the attempt on Catherine dos Santos on Tuesday, November 5. Why with some victims he had varied by a few days Carmine couldn't begin to fathom. Personality traits, linked as they always were to career choices and life styles, were as varied as ethnic backgrounds, religions, family histories. Two were religiously motivated virgins, two were lesbians, the rest had fairly active sex lives without sleeping around. If they had anything in common, it was a professional career; apparently the Dodo was not drawn to women in menial jobs. All were strong personalities, if very different, and it occurred to Carmine that the Dodo harbored a degree of hatred for outgoing, independent professional women. Had he been publicly laughed at by one such? The first of his victims, for instance? The pre-rape Shirley Constable had been noted for her outspoken frankness. She had "caught" a much wanted fish, Mason Novak, who hadn't looked at another woman since they became an item, but she was one of Carmine's two religiously motivated virgins—a wedding ring came before sex.

Easy to see why Maggie Drummond was his last living victim; she had flipped him a more insulting bird than a dodo when she survived her rape unintimidated, despite its new horrors—his fist, the asphyxiations.

The Dodo murdered Melantha Green. She had a boyfriend steady enough to be gifted with a key to her apartment, and apparently enjoyed a safe, comfortable relationship with a fellow black in medicine. Why had the Dodo chosen her for his first killing? Her blackness? No, somehow that didn't fit. The Dodo did nothing unreasonable according to his lights. What was unique about her?

Catherine dos Santos was not a virgin, she had admitted, though she didn't indulge in sex regularly. Maybe she would qualify as a nun-like person, but only so far. She hadn't put up the bars on her windows, but she had hailed them in delight when she was looking for a place to live. Why was a mystery, but Carmine felt that a part at least of her defenses—the sirens, definitely—contained an element of the practical joke. She had been dying to try her sirens out! Well, they had done their job. That she had been spared the Dodo's attentions had to be attributed to her own ingenuity; the police had done nothing to help her, any more than had the abominable Hochners.

All of which, he decided at midnight, stretching painfully, pointed to a part of a motive for *Didus ineptus:* he intended to ruin the happiness and contentment of a number of professional women who irked him more than most of the breed. What Carmine couldn't come to grips with was the exact nature of the Dodo's sexual motives. No victim had been cut, hacked, mutilated, burned or endured the tortures usually inflicted by the multiple offender. He bruised, and with numbers seven and eight, he had used a rope, probably of human hair, to asphyxiate. If he wasn't caught, would he progress to other forms of torture? Carmine didn't think so.

Accepted thinking had it that rapists who murdered preyed on prostitutes because such crimes went almost unnoticed: who misses a whore? Whereas the Dodo preyed on women who were noticed. Nine women thus far, and we didn't know about him until the seventh.

What if this kind of predator is common? Police notice boards are full of the pictures of missing young women, pretty, from good families, pursuing careers. What if a number of them can be traced to a horrifying death at the hands of a raping killer? I am looking, Carmine thought, at the tip of an iceberg.

Our Dodo knows every single one of his victims, but whatever his victims do to be entered on his list, no one save he knows. At first raping them was enough; he used them, abused them, and left them emotionally handicapped for life. Until Maggie Drummond spoke out, exposed him. My two women, Delia and Helen, brought in Dr. Liz Meyers and the rape clinic, and now he sees the damage he inflicted start to heal. But no one can heal a dead victim, so he moved up and on to murder.

Whose is the next name on his list? He's left me no clue that I can see to identify her.

The Gentleman Walkers of Carew, he decided at one a.m., were no help to the investigation. Mark Sugarman led one group of Walkers; Mason Novak led the other group that walked on the alternate days. No name had sprung out as never walking on a Dodo night, which probably meant that the Dodo wasn't a Walker—or that the Dodo was listed as walking, but didn't.

There was a cross-link between the Glass Teddy Bear gift shop vandalisms and the Dodo case, in that Hank Murray, manager of the Busquash Mall, lived in Carew and, when he had the time, served as a Gentleman Walker. Then there were the Warburton twins, who also lived in Carew and seemed to lead lives of leisure. They were devious and shady, but any criminal activities in California had gone unreported, and in Connecticut they were simply dismissed as eccentrics, a type of person both prominent and tolerated in a university city like Holloman.

From there he went back to the victims and did the whole exercise again, this time using sources like Helen MacIntosh's journals, which he found informative, perceptive and amusing. She had put them in his custody a week ago, even including the one she was entering—in about nine weeks, she had filled no fewer than seven books!

Her colored inks amused him in one respect, but in another provoked sincere admiration: she was right when she said it was a help, and certainly the purple entries were something of a revelation. Her description of the glass teddy bear, his value, and Amanda's stubborn refusal to admit its worth were excellent; he was interested to learn that his cool, selfish, ambitious trainee had developed a fondness for Amanda that ripened into friendship; long after there was no necessity to put entries in her books about the Vandal case, a paragraph or two of purple ink would appear.

Then there was her work on the California connections of the Warburton twins, starting with Howard, their father.

"Howard Warburton was autopsied," she wrote in black ink, "not because he had died falling down his stairs, but because the examining doctor at the scene thought his body in an impossible posture. At autopsy he was shown to have a spinal column fracture at C2–C3. There were no other injuries apart from minor bruising. The police pathologist agreed that Mr. Warburton's head should have been closest to the bottom step, not his feet, and called the death suspicious.

"Then the twins—eight years old—admitted that they had been present when the accident happened, and had pushed and pulled at their father trying to revive him. His head had been closest to the step, but by the time they finished with him, it was farthest away. That left only one difficulty, the fact that there had been no cerebral or cardiac catastrophe to cause the fall. Then Robert said he thought his father had tripped, and Gordon, a parrot according to the San Diego police, said he saw his father trip too. After interrogating the twins intensively, the San Diego D.A. declined to pursue the matter. The year was 1945, and the cream of every crop was in the armed services. Howard Warburton hadn't been, thanks to poor vision and flat feet. Two reasons why he might have tripped."

In purple ink she had written: "They did it! In 1968 we're a bit more sophisticated about the capacity of children for doing murder, but in 1945 I guess people would have died of horror at the mere thought.

"I didn't think there was any reason why, provided I kept identities properly concealed, I shouldn't talk to Kurt about it, and he agrees with me. I made my killer one child, in case you're worried, Captain. I confess I only do it to get a rise out of him—he's so cool, calm and collected. Sorry, sir."

Smiling, Carmine put the book down. She was incorrigible! However, she had been dating Kurt exclusively for eight or nine months, and no one knew better than he that all human beings need someone to confide in. According to her lights, Kurt was ideal—unconnected to her work, prone to take her side. What more could one ask? he thought, an image of Desdemona before his eyes.

Carmine ploughed on—black pen, blue pen, red pen, green pen, and that inevitable purple pen to put a very personal, highly biased slant on everything that swam through her little part of the huge police ocean.

Sometimes there were irreverent remarks about her father—purple pen, of course! and one perceptive comment about her mad-in-an-uncertifiable-way mother, who had seen three ghosts in the Chubb House sitting room fireplace. Which wasn't enough to make it into Helen's report book: what was? The fact that all three stopped playing some antique game of cards, complete to wigs and buckled shoes, and stared at Angela MacIntosh in utter terror. 'A ghost! Can you see her?' asked one. Then all three disappeared. Written in red overwritten in purple: "Mom strikes again. No one's safe."

And what do I do? he asked himself at three in the morning, finished at last. What she says is so interesting, though she has no idea of it. And the spontaneity of those little stories about her parents, Kurt, and Amanda Warburton—wonderful!

Desdemona was awake, watching New York television on the little set that stood atop the bureau in their bedroom; she tended to be insomniac if he hadn't come home by bedtime. Even knowing he was sure to be safe—if he wasn't, they'd race to tell her—couldn't compensate for the fear in a cold bed.

"Did you do what had to be done?" she asked, sitting up.

"Yes. I just needed to see all of it in perspective and from every viewpoint." He threw his clothes over a chair, too tired to put them away.

"Do you know whodunit?"

"Yes, I'm fairly sure." He crawled into bed and cuddled. "The trouble is, there's not a shred of evidence."

"I love your hair," she said, running her fingers through it. "Mine's so flimsy."

"Wrong genes, my giant English mouse." He kissed her neck. "I hope you're not in too much need, love. I'm past it."

"So am I, actually. I'm just glad you've seen the trees as well as the forest. Are you sure there's no evidence?"

"Positive."

"Will you confide your suspicions to anyone other than me?"

"Not this time. There are all kinds of complications, too many sensitive egos … " He was mumbling a little.

"Yes, it's not a terribly happy division at the moment, I know." She looked brisk. "You sit on it, love, no matter who tries to probe." A giggle. "Or with what."

He forced his eyelids open. "I'm just glad, Desdemona, you're not in danger from a killer." The words came out a trifle slurred.

She grabbed his hair again, but painfully. "Carmine! Don't you dare tempt fate! Take that back, or cross your fingers, or—or—or something!"

"I crossed my fingers," he murmured, and was asleep.

Good, she could leave the TV on; it would take her some time to grow drowsy. Twisting, she looked down at his face in the dim, flickering light. The lines had smoothed away, he was at peace. How awful to think I have to wake him again four hours from now. He'll be mad at me for letting him sleep an extra bit, but I don't care. The world won't end if he's not sitting at his wretched kitchen table by eight o'clock, and so I'll tell Delia. What would I do without her?

CHAPTER VII

"I've worked our strategy out, twinnie dear," Gordie said, waving a thick artist's paint brush dripping crimson gore.

"Do tell!"

"To get the blood right, we have to witness a slaughter."

Robert swung around from the typewriter; the exasperation on his face was exactly mirrored on his brother's, and he gave a whinnying laugh. "Gordie, your face is perfect! We're getting so good that we won't even need to be in the same room together."

"Shall we continue our rhymes a little more?"

"Why not? Um—slaughter … Rhymes with daughter, caught her, bought her, fought her, sort her—"

"Yes, yes, that's plenty!"

"Party pooper! All jokes aside, Gordie, I do like your sketch. It's new, it's different—a novel concept for murder. Why don't we make more of it?"

"Will Amanda like it if we do?"

"Who cares, twinnie-winnie?" Robert asked, tittering. "She is our aunt, and small potatoes."

"Don't forget that we need Captain Delmonico to dig our biggest potatoes, Robbie. Will he like the blood?"

Robert leaped to his feet and executed a stylish pirouette across the black-and-white crazed rug; Gordon joined him at his halfway mark, and they finished together with an *entrechat.*

"Oh, we haven't lost our balletic skills!" Gordie cried. "Here's a harder one—Aubergine."

"Margarine. Ne'er was seen. Long string bean. Not that keen. Fast machine. Primp and preen."

The elfin face looked sly. "Ah—Dodo?"

"HoJo. No—no. Old crow. So-so."

"Darling, you are brilliant!" Gordie went back to his work station. "We will go through with this, Robbie, won't we?"

"Yes, Gordie, we will. I promise we will."

"I can't, Hank," said Amanda Warburton wretchedly. "I'm so sorry, but while I esteem you as a friend, I'll never think of you as anything else. I stopped loving a long time ago, and the scars are too many and too deep to eradicate." Eyes full of tears, she gazed at Hank piteously. "Please understand! It's impossible, but that's no reflection on you. I'd like to keep you as my friend, but you may find that an insult."

Hank's chief reaction to this rejection was a profound thankfulness that he hadn't gone down on one knee to propose; it had occurred to him to do so, but something had restrained him—a subconscious knowledge that she would refuse him, probably. So he leaned back in his chair, released her hands, sighed, and tried valiantly to smile.

"No, I'm not insulted, and yes, I'd be glad to continue as your friend. We'll forget that tonight ever happened. I'll never refer to it again unless you do, not by look either." He took a breath and managed to make the smile more genuine. "You're fun to be with, Amanda. I'd hate to lose our dinners, games, times with Marcia and the animals. Is that all right?"

"Yes, Hank, of course it is! But for tonight, would you prefer that we called off dinner?"

"Good lord, why? Lobster Pot, Solo's, Sea Foam, Jerry's? Take your pick," he said, sounding quite himself.

"Lobster Pot, please. Would you mind taking me to the Mall afterward? A new shipment from Orrefors came in just as I was leaving, and I'd like to get it unpacked. I left my car there and walked home, so it's just the ride."

"It's more than the ride. I'll help you unpack."

And so it was arranged.

Amazing how life goes on, Hank thought as they settled into their customary booth; he ordered broiled scrod, she went for soft-shelled crab, and they both had a vinaigrette dressing on their salads. Their talk was perhaps a little stiffer than usual, but Hank held his end up heroically, and by the time they left for the Mall she was relaxed on one drink more than she normally had. Yes, they would get through this.

He was kicking himself for trying to move their relationship up a notch, though his sensible side insisted that if the answer was no, there was no propitious moment. The idea of her was stronger in him than her reality, but had it not been, he would never have dreamed his dreams or fantasized about their love-making. And it was true, hope did spring eternal; by the time they reached the back door of the Glass Teddy Bear, he was able to believe that at some time in the future, she would change her mind. Women always did, especially bolstered by the fact that a suitor had declared himself, then stuck around as a friend. What did they call such men? *Cicisbeos*, that was it. Education, he reflected, keys jingling in the lock, was a wonderful asset.

He stood back for her to enter first.

"Oh, bother!" she exclaimed. "The light is out, and I can never find the switch panel for the others."

"Here, I know." Hank pushed her into the back room and flicked at the bank of switches Amanda could never find. "Gee, there must be a major fuse blown," he said. "They're all out."

The blow fell on the side of his skull and crushed it in the manner of an eggshell—still in one piece, yet shattered to smithereens. Hank Murray was scarcely conscious what had happened, the blood poured into his cranium so rapidly. He was dead even as he hit the floor.

Dazed by a much lighter blow, Amanda was on all fours and crawling toward the shop when the black clad intruder straddled her, put a gloved hand in her mass of hair, yanked her entire trunk upward, and cut her throat clean to the backbone. The blood jetted out at arterial pressure, fine drops showering boxes and the wall behind them like paint from an air brush. The attacker stepped away to let her bleed out, a matter of scant minutes. Then, the business ended, he went into the shop. There, on a dolly and wrapped in padded cloths, the glass teddy bear waited. He swung the apparatus around and wheeled it through the back room on the far side from the blood, out the back door; glancing at Hank's keys, he removed them and put them in a pants pocket. Despite the security, there was no one in sight; the attacker made sure his silenced pistol was where he could reach it in a hurry, then went to the service elevators. One opened the moment he pressed its button; he wheeled the dolly in and pressed the basement parking level. Again he was in luck; no sign of a guard.

Inside the door to the garage was a bank of alarms. Out came a paper; the attacker consulted it, punched one alarm. It was followed by a shriek and squeal of sirens three floors up, but before the guards in the garage could gather, he and his dolly were hidden in the janitor's closet. As soon as the pounding feet died away, he wheeled his treasure trove through the door and into the garage, where his van stood parked only feet away. An electric platform carried the dolly up to the level of the van floor, where it was strapped into place. That done, the attacker wormed his way forward into the driver's seat, started the engine, and was a mile away before anyone checked that entry to the garage. False alarm—wasn't that typical?

It was noon on Thursday, November 21, before anyone thought to query Hank Murray's absence and Amanda Warburton's unopened shop. When Hank's secretary couldn't locate him or his keys, she phoned Captain Carmine Delmonico, whom she knew from the days of the Vandal. Oh, pray there wasn't more trouble!

"Something's up, sir," she said. "I have spare keys—could you check the Glass Teddy Bear for me? Miss Warburton and Mr. Murray are great friends, now neither of them can be found."

His detectives were out; Carmine decided to visit the Mall on his own. Why the secretary was so worried he couldn't work out, except that some people have a nose for disaster, and he couldn't afford to ignore someone with a nose whose accuracy he didn't know. Alarm bells were ringing in him too, that was all.

On his way to the back corridor he passed the Glass Teddy Bear's window, and his heart sank. The glass teddy bear wasn't in it, nor were the dog and cat. At the back door he pulled on rubber gloves and examined the lock: no tampering. A turn of the key and he was inside, an almost dark expanse that reeked of blood. When no lights came on he backed out, keeping within his own footprints. Two security guards had turned up; he beckoned them over.

"Stay here and don't touch a fucking thing," he said. "I need a phone. Where?"

"The shipping desk, Captain—in there."

"Where are the fuses for this shop?"

"In that wall cupboard, Captain."

When he opened the cupboard door with another key he found the Glass Teddy Bear's fuses in the off position; when Carmine did the up-down-up to switch them on, they stayed on. Someone had probably turned them off here.

At the shipping desk he found a phone. "Stella, tell Dr. O'Donnell I need an M.E. and a forensics tech at the Busquash Mall a.s.a.p. Where are my team?"

"Nick and Delia are here. Helen's with the Judge."

"Good. Send me Nick and Delia, please. It's urgent."

When he flicked the lights on this time, they revealed a shambles, though it was poor Amanda Warburton who had done the bleeding. Fourth time unlucky, he thought. Amanda had survived three attacks, but they were just the thief softening her up. Hank Murray had died because of his devotion to her. Fifteen big, sealed cardboard boxes said a new shipment had arrived; she and the faithful Hank had probably come in to unpack them. It looked like a huge amount of stock, but undoubtedly wasn't. Glass came surrounded by relative oceans of packing materials.

Her face was distorted by terror, mute evidence of her last moments, but he didn't think she had seen her attacker. He came at her from behind while she was crawling, Carmine deduced. Hank had died without a fight; never saw it coming, in all likelihood. There were no bloody footprints, no marks to say who the Vandal—was it the Vandal, or another, more violent predator?—might be. A different man, Carmine decided. His conviction that he knew the identity of the Vandal hadn't budged. He went outside to speak to the guard.

"Was there any kind of fuss last night?" he asked.

"The alarms went off in Hood's Antiques about half after ten," said the guard. "False alarm, Captain. Some clown of a practical joker triggered it at the alarm bank inside the basement garage door."

"Did that require a key?"

"Sure. They're in a wall cupboard, same as fuses."

"And the fire chief is satisfied wall cupboards are safe?"

"With our kind of fuses and alarms, yes."

Patrick came himself, with Paul Bachman in tow.

"Thanks for the personal touch, Patsy. Anything?"

"No, nothing. Both attacks were incredibly savage. The temporal and parietal regions on the right side of Mr. Murray's skull were pulverized, like gluing uniformly small fragments on to a sheet of plastic—it's only the scalp holding the bone together. Miss Warburton's throat was cut to expose the ventral surface of the vertebrae—only the spinal column kept her head on her shoulders, poor thing. I don't think I've ever seen a more brutal assault, yet it had to have been done in seconds. The fellow wouldn't have made contact with the blood. He stayed behind her. He used a knife on her throat, not a razor, because he needed a proper grip for traction to go that deep."

"A hunting knife, you mean?"

"Yes, or a military version of same."

"He didn't leave it behind?"

"If he did, we haven't found it so far. Want to see his blunt instrument?"

Patrick held up a curious item almost two feet long. Made of clear glass, it was a tube that flared at one end into an open, lily-like shape; its other end was a round, closed bulb.

"By rights the pipe should be a yard long, but this one is only half a yard. It's a British device for drinking beer, and it's called, would you believe it, a yard?" He pointed to the wall, where a similar but much longer item sat on a bracket. "The one on the wall is the real thing, very thin glass, but this one is purely an ornament, not intended for use. It's heavy."

Carmine grimaced. "You mean anyone can drink that much?"

"For a beer drinker, not a problem. Miss Warburton stocked a good range. The shorty would make an efficient weapon if the bulb is used as the club. The glass is thick enough to have weight and durability. The skull didn't have a chance."

"Inventive. Of all the heavy objects in a shop full of them, that half yard makes the best concussive weapon."

"The whole set also makes an ideal decoration for a wall you don't want cluttered with yet more paintings. Designed to appeal to expatriate Limeys."

"The killer didn't have to know its proper function to see its concussive potential," Carmine said.

"I agree, I agree! Just tossing theories around. You don't think he's an Englishman, Carmine?" Patrick asked.

"Take my word for it, there are no Englishmen in this case."

Delia came up, unable to hide her distress. "Carmine, this is frightful! That poor woman! She didn't even believe the glass teddy bear was worth stealing."

"So why kill her for something he might have gotten by more peaceful means?" Nick asked. "Tied them up and taken it."

"That's the question I ask myself," Carmine said.

"Mind you, she loved it," said Delia.

"So much that she wouldn't have parted with it for any sum, Delia. It had other meanings for her than money. After Helen established its true worth, I communicated with my opposite number in the Venice PD, thinking the glass teddy bear had been stolen. But it hadn't. It was legally Amanda Warburton's property, bequeathed to her in the will of Lorenzo della Fiori, the glass kingpin. Amanda was his mistress. Unfortunately he had a very jealous wife, who invaded the love nest and stabbed della Fiori fourteen times with a kitchen knife. Amanda was stabbed too, but survived. The glass teddy bear— including its eyes—was made especially for Amanda, and was already en route to America when the fracas happened. His kids inherited his money and all his property except the glass teddy bear. It happened eleven years ago, when the eldest child, a girl, was nine."

"Then the kids are grown enough for revenge!" Nick cried, having heard Carmine's explanation.

"No, the kids are in Venice too busy with their education to worry about the past. Having a mother in prison is no picnic. The eldest boy, another Lorenzo della Fiori, is now seventeen and determined to be the next glass kingpin. Kids don't live in the past unless they're brainwashed, and the only person who would have done that is in prison."

"Then where did Amanda's money come from?" Delia demanded.

"Sale of other Lorenzo della Fiori pieces. She'd acquired a lot over her years with him, and after his death she sold the lot. They'd never been inventoried, he'd freely given them to her, and it never came out at the time. His work is gorgeous and she got top dollar for every piece," Carmine said.

"What about the star sapphire eyes?" Delia asked.

"Legally an intrinsic part of the work of art. My Venetian counterpart knew nothing about them, and no theft of a pair of star sapphires answering their description has ever surfaced in Europe, let alone in Venice. The theory he offered me was that the stones came from the USSR, which is a source of fabulous treasure and gems. If old Queen Mary of England could buy some of the Russian crown jewels at auction for relative peanuts, who knows what else has been smuggled westward to obtain hard currency?"

"It sounds like a fairy tale," Nick said. "How did Queen Mary know the jewels were for sale?"

"They were auctioned at one of the great auction houses," said Delia. "She bought diamonds and pearls, as I remember, and used her own money—she was awfully rich, and laden with ropes and ropes of pearls." She chuckled. "Now the pearls you buy in a cheap shop outshine the real ones!"

"How do you know all this gossip?" Nick asked.

"It's not gossip, Nick dear. Cleopatra thought you could dissolve a pearl in vinegar. Of course you can't."

"Theft of the bear aside, any evidence?" Carmine asked.

"No," they said in chorus.

"He's crafty and clever as well as shockingly brutal," said Delia. "He also has luck."

"Luck?" Nick asked. "Expound!"

They guffawed until Carmine's glare sobered them.

"Consider! Security here is pretty good, yet this chap—*not* the original Vandal, is my guess—got in and got out again without ever being seen. There's a strong element of luck in that. Equivalently, Miss Warburton and Mr. Murray ran out of luck. He seizes his moments, yes, but the moments were there to be seized. Thus far, our killer has led a charmed life," Delia said.

"Then we're going to proceed on the assumption that our luck is more potent than his," said Carmine. "Are we finished here?"

"Yes," Nick said.

"Did Paul give you her keys, or are they missing?"

"No, they were on her, I have them," Nick said. "Mr. Murray's keys are missing, so every shop in here will have to change its locks, not to mention the Mall itself."

"Our killer is not coming back," Carmine said positively. "He took the keys to create havoc, no other reason. Maybe make us think he's a valuables thief. He's not. He's a killer."

"What about notifying her next of kin?" Delia asked.

"The Warburton twins? They can wait," Carmine said. "I'm going to inspect her apartment without that pair breathing down my neck. They give me the creeps."

"Did they do this?" Nick asked as they used the elevator.

"Possible, but not probable."

"This is gorgeous!" Nick said, gazing around the spacious luxury of Amanda Warburton's apartment. "If she owns this, we have to reconsider our estimates of her worth."

Carmine was already at the desk, which contained no locked drawers or compartments. He held up papers. "Deeds. She owns this free and clear, no mortgages."

At which moment a pathetic meow came from the bathroom.

"Her animals!" Carmine said. "Jesus, I'd forgotten them!"

They were huddled in the bath as if they knew what had happened to their mistress, the cat pressed into the dog's belly between its front and back legs, the dog hunched with its nose on the cat's sleek skull. A water dish was empty; cooing and clucking, Delia refilled the bowl and found canned food in a cupboard. They drank and ate ravenously. Nick, it turned out, was more afraid of dogs and cats than of criminals, and Delia seemed to frighten them; when Carmine went back to his examination of the desk, Frankie and Winston sat at his feet and refused to be banished. He decided to ignore them.

"Her will," he said, brandishing a single sheet of paper. "Everything to the twins except the glass teddy bear, which she wills in perpetuity to Chubb on condition that it's displayed in a suitable manner. Wow! Wait until M.M. finds out! God help us if we don't get it back."

An accordion file held a portfolio of stocks and shares.

"Blue chip, the lot," Carmine said. "Robert and Gordon are going to be wealthier than I'd expected, so we move them up on the list of suspects." A wry grin. "That gives us two names." He bent down and got a face full of dog hide as well as a sloppy tongue. "Cut that out, Frankie!" To his surprise, the dog desisted at once. A snide smile his team exchanged irritated him: he lashed back. "Delia, don't stand there decorating the place! Call Marcia Boyce and get her here yesterday. Nick, go back to County Services and ask for someone from the pound with two animal carrying cages."

Nick and Delia scattered, but not before they flashed each other another snide smile. The chief was being conned by two real experts.

*   *   *

Marcia Boyce was shocked but not rendered speechless. "I don't know why, but I've been expecting something like it," she said to Carmine in Amanda's sitting room, its glass wall showing the tree-filled beauty of Busquash Inlet like a landscape painting, complete to mirror-bright water and dreamy little fishing shacks.

"Why, exactly?" Carmine asked, pouring her more tea.

"You'll laugh at me, but sometimes I see penumbras around people, and Amanda has always had one. Black, laced with the red of fire—or blood, I guess. It's waxed until lately it's all but obscured her face and body—kind of like a shroud."

I hate people like this, Carmine was thinking. They always have after-visions they're convinced perpetually existed. I bet Miss Boyce consults a ouija board and goes to séances. But I also bet she never showed this side of herself to Amanda, who would have derided it—and her. "Can you tell me anything more concrete, Miss Boyce?"

"Only that, from what Hank Murray and I pieced together, she had had doubts about making the twins her heirs. But then she suddenly announced that she was going to leave them as her heirs because she had no one else. She wasn't too happy about it, I add." Marcia sipped her tea, then supplemented it with a dollop of Amanda's costly cognac.

"How do you feel about the Warburton twins, ma'am?"

"I detest them! Though I wouldn't have thought they had the guts or gumption for murder." She looked down at the dog and cat, glued to Carmine's feet. "Oh, poor babies! What will become of them, Captain?"

"Unless you want them, Miss Boyce, they go to the pound."

"Oh, no! That's *awful*!"

"The solution rests with you."

"I can't possibly take them! Amanda managed fine because she could take them to work with her, but I can't possibly do that. I'd come home to find that Winston had shredded my best upholstery and Frankie had torn the drapes down."

"Do they do that to Miss Warburton?"

"No, they like her. Would you believe that Amanda trained Winston to perch on the toilet to go for his number ones *and* number twos? Frankie wees in the shower stall and does his number twos on newspaper. Amanda was a very patient person."

He kept Marcia Boyce a little longer, but learned nothing new that wasn't connected with penumbras. The Warburton twins had chameleon penumbras, never the same color for more than a day at a time, and Carmine's penumbra was amber with a purple edge.

After Miss Boyce departed a little unsteadily for her own apartment on the same floor, all Carmine had to do was wait for the guy from the pound. He arrived fifteen minutes later, a small animal carrying cage in either hand, and a hollow pipe ending in a rope noose tucked in his belt.

Frankie and Winston took one smell and retreated behind Carmine, the dog growling, the cat hissing.

"You never said the dog's a pit bull, Captain!" the pound guy said in horror.

"He only looks. For a dog, he's a pussycat."

Out came the rod. The noose, as Carmine knew, could be loosened or tightened once slipped over the animal's head; with visions of the insult to these sheltered, much-loved house pets chasing through his mind, Carmine stood watching as the pound guy decided to start with Winston.

"Your cats is worse," the guy said, preparing his noose. "Your cats got your four sets of claws and your teeth. Your dogs just have your teeth, even your pit bulls."

Ten minutes later the cat was behind a credenza and the dog vigorously defending it.

"Fuck off," said Carmine tiredly, "and take your gallows with you. Leave the cages. I'll deal with the animals myself."

It was too much. He had made up his mind as the pound guy fruitlessly pursued the gigantic marmalade cat. Amanda Warburton had been a thoroughly nice woman whose life, cruelly shortened, had seen more unhappiness than bliss, and he had liked her. Now she was dead, and no one wanted her beloved animals. The pound? That couldn't be allowed to happen. Like a totally innocent man thrown without warning into an overcrowded jail cell.

"Butter! Grandmother Cerutti always used butter," he said, going to the refrigerator.

Diet margarine. No, grandmother Cerutti wouldn't have had it in her house. So he went down to the corner store, run by two young Nepalese, for a stick of butter. Their cold storage wasn't very efficient, so he didn't have to hang around too long waiting for the stick to soften.

"Come on, Winston," he said to the cat, which had emerged, "I won't let anyone hurt you. Butter sticks, not gallows sticks."

It lay upside down on his knees and allowed its paws to be buttered, then walked into its cage when he lifted the door. The dog was just as easy. What was it with the pound guy?

The cages went on the Fairlane's back seat; Frankie and Winston took a ride in a car that smelled of babies, detectives and assorted evidence.

When he marched into Desdemona's work room carrying two animal cages, she gaped.

"Two fully house trained, adult pets," he said in tones that indicated he wasn't prepared to concede the tip of his finger. "They belonged to a very nice lady who was murdered last night, and there's no one to take them except the pound. It's time Julian learned that he can't pull a cat's tail without getting scratched, and the dog's loyal. They are now members of the Delmonico family."

Desdemona shut her mouth. "Um—am I allowed to ask their names, sir?"

He laughed, hugged her. "The cat is Winston. He sits on the toilet to piss. The dog is Frankie. He goes in a shower stall, but if we have a flap cut in the back door, they'll probably prefer to go outside except in snowstorms. I buttered their paws, so they can't go home."

Desdemona was on hands and knees, opening cages. "Oh, how lovely! Prunella was just saying we should go to the pound for an adult animal as a house pet—puppies and kittens behave like the babies they are, adults are better. Did you bring them food? Does the cat drink milk?"

"Water and canned stuff. I brought what Miss Warburton had in her cupboard. It will cost a bit more to feed us, but two animals will be a help in occupying the kids."

And that, he thought as he returned to County Services with two empty animal cages, was well done; he didn't even grudge filling out the form that enabled him to commandeer a uniform to drop the cages at the pound, way out of town.

"The half yard blunt instrument revealed nothing except scalp secretions from Hank Murray and hair lacquer from Amanda Warburton. However, when the killer used it on Miss Warburton, it was a gentle tap to stun. Murray got the full force of a very strong man—massive internal hemorrhages," said Patrick O'Donnell. "I think he was prepared to encounter Amanda, but Hank came as a surprise. He didn't really care how Hank died as long as he did. Amanda's death was planned, I believe. A hunting knife sharpened to split a hair used when the head and neck were up but not stretched—if the neck is stretched by pulling the head way back, the carotid arteries are hard to get at. Most of the traction occurred after he'd done the cutting, to direct the blood spray well away from himself."

"How did he move the glass teddy bear? Any ideas?"

"First off, he was alone. Paul went over the shop and the back room minutely, and there are no signs of an accomplice. One set of footprints in the shop carpet—size tens or thereabouts, but no chance of a sole pattern or a full outline. From the solid tire tracks, he used an upright dolly to move the bear, which means he's very strong physically. Of course the dolly might have had a platform raised and lowered by an electric motor—that would help him move the bear off the window shelf on to the dolly. But think of the gall, Carmine! The bear must have been out of the window, wrapped and on its dolly before Amanda and Hank appeared at ten-thirty. Security everywhere!"

"Luck. I also think that he should have put a notice in the window saying the bear had gone for repairs," said Carmine. "Though his luck is phenomenal, as Delia rightly pointed out."

"He hadn't gotten as far as moving the bear out of the premises," Patrick said. "In the back room the dolly tracks travel clear of the blood even when that necessitated a slight detour. What might have happened if he'd run into a guard?"

"Dressed all in black? A shot between the eyes from a .22 with a silencer. Or he might have been in coveralls by then, had a sheaf of papers, and bluffed his way past the guard."

Something in his voice made Patrick look up quickly, to meet innocent yellow-brown eyes. "Any other questions?"

"No." Carmine glanced at his watch. "I have to see the Warburton twins and break the news."

"Do me a favor, Carmine?"

"Anything, Patsy."

"Before you let the Warburtons loose in the glass shop, how about sending Helen up there to have a really good look at the contents? She was the one spotted the value of the glass teddy bear, and I notice she seems to have an eye for glass art."

"Good idea. I'll do that."

Helen was waiting in his team's room, looking flustered and upset. "I wish you'd pulled me out of my teaching session!" she greeted him. "I missed it, I missed it!"

"There are times, Miss MacIntosh, when you remind me of my least favorite queen, Marie Antoinette. You can't always have what you want, and Judge Thwaites for one would agree with me. His time is more valuable than yours, little though you may care to hear that. Don't grumble, and bear his crotchets with a good grace. I understand that you feel a special interest in Miss Warburton, but you can still do her a big favor."

"Yes, yes, anything!" Helen cried eagerly, the crux of Carmine's homily scarcely impinging.

"Go out to the Busquash Mall and examine the glass shop with a very sharp eye," Carmine said. "I want to know if anything else is missing, down to the last china-headed pin or glass tear drop. Don't miss a thing."

"Yes, Captain." She was on her feet. "Where are Delia and Nick going?"

"Through Hank Murray's office and apartment. You stick to the glass shop—is that clear?"

"Yes, sir." And she was gone.

The Glass Teddy Bear had emotional connotations for Helen that even Carmine, so perceptive, had not really grasped. It was the workplace of a woman who had become a genuine friend, and genuine friendships were scarce in Helen's world, for she had as yet not formed one properly—who was real, who was not? Amanda, she had divined, was a woman who hadn't had things easy: sweet but iron-hard. They had looked at each other, and clicked.

So when she entered the shop she found it filled with echoes of someone undeservedly dead; Helen had to blink the tears away.

Black shops were extremely rare, perhaps limited only to glass; the lighting, she realized now, was so cunning. Every spotlight or lamp fell upon a treasured piece, with the more economical lines clustered so that they blazed pinpoints of fire. On a slim black pedestal stood a magnificent prism; beside it was an atomizer of water that, squeezed, liberated a cloud of droplets that lit from within as a perfect rainbow. Gorgeous!

The yard and the half yard beer tubes, so different in construction, sat above Lalique and Murano glass picture frames; an exquisite glass teaset, dazzlingly plain, sat in pride of place atop arrays of wine glasses, and a Baccarat crystal ball of solid glass spun the world upside down. How beautiful everything was! If the Warburton twins had a sale to close the shop down, she would be here to buy the prism and the crystal ball.

But this was not doing her job, and she owed the dead woman her very best. Up and down Helen prowled, concentrating hard on the arrangements; what luck that she had paid for Dad's urn and borne it away a week ago—why had she done that? Clairvoyance?

The counter contained a shelf on which sat jewelry and tiny objects: animals the size of thumbnails, buttons, strings of crystal beads, some faceted, some round globes. Why the buttons in particular made her smile she didn't know, except that some were suitable for the most ornate of wedding gowns, while others, austere enough to please monks, would look great on a man's yachting jacket. Though the ones she liked best were dark blue glass on which were gold glass cameos of lions. I'll be buying Kurt a set of those for Christmas, she made a mental note, and saw a choker of glass beads shading in color from pale pink to deep burgundy. Oh, how perfect for Mom, with her swanlike neck! So ideal! Scorpion hues for a Scorpion lady.

No, no, this wasn't doing the job!

Back to the shelves, until finally she came to the paperweights, a wonderful collection. One beauty, she was horrified to see, had a

label that said $5,000! And there, in the middle, was a vacant space.
A space that, Helen was sure, Amanda would have filled immediately
after its occupant had been sold.

The insurance company was stringent and Amanda had obeyed
their dictates. The paperweight display, thirty in all, was laid out in a
plan. The missing one, she was bewildered to discover, wasn't
expensive at $300. Clear glass containing tiny trails of colored glass.
According to its photograph, it looked like a map of some metropolitan
subway system in a city that gave each route a different color.

Had the killer broken it? Or did something about it appeal when
others, far more valuable, didn't?

"Nothing else is missing," she said to Carmine on Friday morning,
giving her report.

"But you think he took it," Carmine said.

"If he didn't, Captain, then it was sold so late in the day that Miss
Warburton didn't replace it," Helen said. "My hunch is that he's
responsible. I searched the storage drawers until I found an identical
one, and left a receipt." She reached into her capacious bag and
withdrew it, put it on the table.

"It looks like a 3-D map of a city subway."

"It does indeed," Carmine said, picking it up. "Maybe it's a dead
ringer for his way home?"

She looked shocked at the joke, but wisely held her tongue; the
Captain could sometimes be facetious for no apparent reason. Best
change the subject. "How did the twins take the news?"

"About as I imagined. Squawks, shrieks, crocodile tears, a fit
of hysterics from Gordie that Robbie dealt with by emptying a vase of

dead daisies over his head. Underneath, gratification to find themselves Aunt Amanda's heirs. I gave them the will, since she doesn't seem to have employed a lawyer, wise woman. But when I told them about the glass teddy bear, they were as chagrined as astonished. If it comes to light, it belongs to Chubb. I'm picking they've rushed off with the will to see if they can challenge Chubb's right to the *pièce de resistance.*"

"I'll back Chubb," said Helen with a grin. "Though it's irrelevant at the moment, sir, not so? First, get your teddy bear back, then worry about ownership."

"Exactly."

"What happened to her pets, Captain?"

A peculiar look came over his face; Delia could have told her that it was embarrassment. "Er—well—er—I took them home for the kids. Mature, already house trained, you know."

"That's great, sir! What a relief! I've been racking my brains how I could talk my father into taking them, but now I don't need to bother. I envy you."

This reception made Carmine feel much better, especially after a rather traumatic night with a howling dog and a puking cat. Desdemona had changed her mind and wanted them gone, but Prunella scorned such intolerance. In two or three days the worst would be over; the Delmonicos would wonder how they had ever gotten on without Frankie and Winston, said Prunella staunchly, then called the carpenter to make an animal flap in the back door. Maybe, thought Carmine with a faint ray of hope, Frankie and Winston would run away and his household could go back to normal. The worst of it was that he had been appointed cleaner-upper of cat vomit.

*   *   *

When Robert and Gordon Warburton discovered that Amanda's estate, even minus the glass teddy bear, was worth in excess of two million dollars, they were ecstatic. It didn't hurt nearly as much when their lawyer, a sharp fellow, informed them that they could forget challenging Chubb for ownership of this museum piece that only Chubb could afford to house.

"Where shall we live, dear one?" Gordie asked his brother. "Here, or in that divine apartment?"

"Oh, here, beyond a shadow of a doubt," Robbie said. "I'd hate not having a garden, and while we've improved this so much it would sell for a hundred thou, the apartment will sell at auction for ten times that. Cash in the bank! We need cash in the bank! If we sell the apartment, we can keep Amanda's blue chip stocks, yet still have plenty of ready money to splash around. Our plans are forging ahead—who was to know that Amanda would contribute so much in death? We hoped for a donation, but—oh, it's a wonderful, wonderful world!"

"Death has always done well by us, sweetest," Gordie said, smiling. "Look at Mommy."

"Thank you, I do not want to look at Mommy!"

"I'm fed up with drawing and painting!" Gordie said suddenly.

Robbie hastened to offer comfort. "There, there, twinnie my love, I know. Just remember that you're the rock on which our enterprise stands. Do you want to leave no more durable epitaph on our tombstone than '*The Acting Twins*'? Well, do you?"

"No," Gordie admitted, but grudgingly. "On the other hand, I am fed up with drawing and painting!"

"Oh, saints preserve me!" Robbie cried. He sat down beside Gordon and took his hands, chafing them. "Listen, my darling one, we can't move on to the next phase until you've finished. I was not exaggerating, it's your work will get us there, and it has to impress Captain Delmonico! How can it, if you won't finish?"

"He refused to show us the photographs of Amanda with her throat cut," Gordie said sulkily.

"I couldn't push too hard, you know that! We *need* him! If he refuses a far greater request, we're nonentities, has-beens—"

"Would-be-if-we-could-bes," Gordie said helpfully.

"I do not need more synonyms!" Robert snapped. "Think of being immortal, Gordie! Of taking reality to a new height!"

"Reality," said Gordie, "can always be improved on."

The atmosphere in Carmine's office on Monday, November 25, grew more anxious and tense with the arrival of each team member. By the time that Delia, the last, put her puce-pink and apple-green body on her chair, it seemed hard to breathe. They had all visited the premises over the weekend, astonished to find no Carmine; now, so close to the Dodo's due date, he wasn't here again!

When he did arrive at a quarter after eight he looked well, rested, even cheerful.

"You've had a good weekend," Delia said accusingly.

"A very good one. The two new family members have decided to settle in," he said, "and it's going to work better than I'd hoped." He sighed, smiled. "Desdemona's come around."

Nick stubbed out his fourth cigarette. "If we knew what you were talking about, Carmine, that would be a help."

"Oh! I took Miss Warburton's pets home last Thursday, and we had a minor crisis that I was afraid might turn out major. But it didn't. The dog fell in love with Desdemona, and you know what she's like. About as much aggression as a caterpillar. Besides, she's English and the English adore dogs."

Delia's eyes were twinkling. "What happened to the cat?"

"Attached itself to the real ruler of the house—Julian."

Nick lit up his fifth. "All well and good, Carmine, but have you forgotten that the Dodo's due tomorrow?"

"Won't happen," Carmine said positively.

Three pairs of eyes stared.

"Won't happen?" Delia repeated.

"No. He may strike next week or even the week after, but not this week."

"How can you be so sure?" Helen asked.

"Because this week is Thanksgiving Day, and it spoils his plans. He's escalating, and there's only one way he can go—to a longer, more complex process. That means choosing a victim who won't be missed for three or four days," Carmine said.

"Of course!" Nick exclaimed. "Even the most solitary person is invited to someone's Thanksgiving dinner."

"There's that, yes, but he himself will be expected to eat Thanksgiving at someone's table."

Delia jumped. "You know who he is!"

"I think so, yes."

"Tell us!" Helen cried.

"I can't do that, Helen. I have no evidence—not a shred. Until I do, his identity has to remain my secret."

"That's ridiculous!"

"No," said Delia, answering when it became obvious that the Captain wouldn't. "It's ethics, Helen. What if word should get out? All observation changes events, but if the Dodo has an inkling that his identity is known, the game changes in all sorts of ways. What the Captain knows as fact is still merely suspicion if there's no evidence to back his contention up."

"I wouldn't tell a soul!"

"Of course you wouldn't. But this is a relatively public place, dear."

"End of subject," said Carmine, picking up a sheet of paper. "The Hollow is starting to boil worse than Argyle Avenue, and no one wants a repeat of last summer. We're not going to have snow before Thanksgiving Day, which means we have to plan for a warm, green winter. Arson and looting can't be allowed to happen, it's too hard on the majority of ghetto residents. Captain Vasquez has asked for two-pronged preventive measures and Commissioner Silvestri thinks his ideas are right." The amber eyes rested on Nick Jefferson. "The uniforms are not going to get much rest—they have to be ready for riot duty in literal minutes. The role of Detectives is to dig for information, which means Mohammed el Nesr and the Black Brigade. Without information, we won't be able to nip riot nuclei in the bud. Abe Goldberg's in charge of our contribution, but you, Nick, are going to have special duties. Abe feels you can be disguised—provided, that is, that you're willing to take on something so risky."

"I'm willing," Nick said, looking eager.

"You have a family, and you owe them a duty too."

"If it hadn't been for luck and one itty-bitty fire extinguisher, Carmine, my mother and father would have lost their house last July, and again in August, when they had six fire extinguishers. My uncle's shop was looted. My wife and children won't stand in my way. I'm up for it."

"Captain Vasquez has brought in this movie make-up artist—not all his uniforms are staying out in the open with riot gear, but they're not trained in detection. So a lot rests on you, Nick. This make-up guy swears he can make you look six inches shorter and twenty years older. Go see Abe, okay?"

On the echo of Carmine's last words, Nick was gone.

"I wish I could do something like that," said Delia, clearly regretting both her sex and her color.

"How would you like to join the whores behind City Hall? The pimps are black, so are most of their girls. Information, Delia, as much as you can glean. Whores and pimps talk, and I've heard your various American accents. Go mulatto, your skin will take that, and your hair color's perfect."

"I need a pimp," said Delia, wriggling in anticipation.

"One of the new academy graduates is black, fortyish and has a perfect face for disguise. Jimmy the Pooch."

And Delia was gone.

"What about me?" Helen asked, voice steely.

"You have a forensics class from nine until noon, with an afternoon in the autopsy room."

"I want to be in the field!"

Carmine's face set. He clasped his hands together and gazed at her sternly. "You've entered a predictable phase in your detective training," he said, "and you have to get through it, Helen, without derailing your career. You're finding the classes frustrating, even though they are by far the most important part of your curriculum. Later on you'll see that I'm right, but now, while you're blind to that fact, you simply obey orders. What do you expect me to do with a twenty-four-year-old apprentice who looks like Jane Fonda, huh? Dye your skin and put you in the Hollow or Argyle Avenue to gather information? How stupid can you get? You'd be kidnapped and raped, and not by the Dodo! By some junkie off his face or some hate-crazed Black Brigader! If I could use you safely in a field job, I would, but there's nothing that suits your talents or your appearance. Your ambition is boundless, but next time you pass a mirror, *look* in it. You'd be ideal for corporate crime or thousand-dollar call girls, not work in ghettoes on the verge of riot or tawdry poor-white dives. Class is bred in the bone, never forget that, and accept your limitations without blaming the boss."

Speechless, she sat with her mind in turmoil, hating the fact that she had exchanged her father for a man who could have doubled for him. Of course he was right, there wasn't an argument in the world could make him wrong. Fantasy was fine and dandy, but it had no business intruding on reality.

After what she gauged was an interval long enough to save a little face, she got up and went to the team's room, there to sit at her desk and enter her journal until ten of nine.

His paperwork organized, Carmine went to Corey's office, a walk that these days felt like a thousand miles of slogging, and always made him feel sick to his stomach. The poor girl! He had hated to do it, especially given that he had reprimanded her on other occasions in recent days, but it had to be done. And, as he had known, Helen MacIntosh possessed sufficient strength of character to realize that the boss was right. Passion had driven her in her perpetual quest to belong, to have an equal chance to shine. But when brutal fact was pointed out, she could step far enough away from her passion to see the truth.

Unfortunately, he thought, entering Corey's office, Corey Marshall had nothing like Helen's intelligence. Life for him was a crueler arena, and at this moment his most formidable opponent in it was his boss. A no-win situation.

Sure enough, Corey was on his feet in a second, knuckles on his desk, head snaked forward. He was going to get in first.

"I have my own methods, my own style, my own goals!" he said with lips peeled back from his teeth. "If you're here to preach me another sermon, don't bother. I get the work done, I even fill in all Vasquez's forms! What's with all his paperwork, tell me that? The guy's not a cop, he's a paper-shuffler!"

He left the desk and began to pace up and down; Carmine, face expressionless, took a chair and watched him.

"You look down on me," Corey said, "but I can't figure out why. Except that you're an obsessive who can't bear the tiniest loose end, even if it's an end that doesn't matter a fuck. The whole world has to be squared up! No wonder you love Abe—you're so like him! A pair of obsessive-compulsive freaks!"

Maureen's vocabulary, phrases, thinking.

And here I am, Carmine thought, still wondering how I missed this side to Corey. Yes, I was aware that he and Abe were two very different kinds of men—detectives too—but I didn't see Corey's incipient paranoia, his lack of tactical planning, the underlying weakness, and the sheer enormity of Maureen's hold over him. I guess they didn't exist, at least to their present extent. While ever he took orders he could keep his chin above the rising flood, and the rivalry with Abe was there only as an equal's chance at a sole lieutenancy. His independence was finite, and the responsibility was mine. He could function at the peak of his talents. Now that he has the responsibility, one part of Corey has filled with overweening pride, while most of him is wandering, lost. And he's shut me out.

"I wish you'd let me help," Carmine said suddenly.

"*Help*? With what?"

"Your difficulty coping with the job."

Corey closed his eyes. "I seem to remember our having this conversation, or one like it. I don't know where you get your ideas from, Carmine, but they're mistaken. What do you want?"

"The Hollow is about to go ballistic, and I need to know that the Taft High weapons case is properly closed."

"I've submitted the paperwork saying it is."

"Buzz still doesn't seem so sure."

"Buzz is an old woman. When am I getting my second-stringer, and who is it?"

"Donny Costello. He's on his way up."

The discontented face didn't lighten. "Costello? He's as big a nit-picker as Buzz."

"You need all the nit-pickers you can get, Corey, because you're not one," Carmine said. "Watch out for your men."

"Oh, fuck off, Carmine! Your trouble is that you keep trying to teach your grandmother to suck eggs!"

"It's clear that you never knew my grandmother Cerutti."

"Fuck off!"

"Corey doesn't appreciate the value of routines," Carmine said to John Silvestri at five that evening. "While Maureen is in the driver's seat, he won't improve one iota either. I hadn't incorporated her into the equation, more's the pity. She's gotten delusions of grandeur, as the psychiatrists say."

"Funny how we tend to overlook a man's domestic situation. Can you imagine two women farther apart than Maureen Marshall and Ava Jones?" Silvestri asked. "They've both worn their knees down, but for different reasons."

"I can't get rid of Corey, can I?"

"No. We can see the express train roaring down the tracks at us, but until it hits, we have to assume it won't."

"Gossip says Buzz Genovese is still insisting the Taft High business isn't closed, and that worries me."

"Has he gone over Corey's head to you, Carmine?"

"Who, Buzz? Not in a thousand years. Too honorable."

"Who does Corey get as second-string?"

"Donny Costello."

"Better him, than the kind of recruit a Helen MacIntosh trainee system would give him. Costello doesn't mind paperwork."

"How about putting a brake on Fernando's paperwork, John?"

"Funny, he's not that much younger than you, but his attitude to the job says every police department he's ever worked in must be a yard deep in paper. How can you be so relaxed, with the Dodo due to strike tomorrow?"

Carmine rose to his feet. "Want to stroll down to Malvolio's for a drink?" he asked. "Then I can tell you about Thanksgiving Day. Incidentally, how are you and Luigi related?"

"First cousin, but no Cerutti."

"I'm improving. It's taken me a mere eighteen years to find that out. Some detective."

What Carmine couldn't know was the ferocity involved in the difference of opinion between Corey and Buzz about Taft High.

Two weeks ago Buzz had confronted Corey yet again.

"Let me continue," he had begged Corey. "Everything at Taft indicates that there's a splinter of the Black Brigade operating—and that the Black Brigade is about to go to war against it. You know as well as I do how much black militancy gets wasted on in-fighting, especially places like Holloman, where there are two ghettoes separated by a university campus and a business center. It works to our advantage, but the Black Brigade is entrenched in the Hollow, while something new is going on in Argyle Avenue. And Taft seems to be the ham in the sandwich."

"It sounds great, but where are your facts, Buzz?"

"Thin on the ground," Buzz had admitted. "That doesn't mean I'm imagining things, Cor. There are still weapons at Taft High."

Corey had flicked the report in his hand. "Your argument is as flimsy as the paper it's written on, Buzz. I have very reliable snitches in the Black Brigade, and they say that the Taft High business was a genuine mistake, never a part of a plan."

"But this is not the Black Brigade itself!" Buzz persisted. "It's a splinter group with a more violent agenda, and its aim is to spread revolution in the style of Lenin—terror first and foremost. One of its cornerstones is high school violence. The Black Brigade soldiers don't know the splinter group exists, it isn't something Mohammed el Nesr wants spread about."

"This report is pure supposition, Buzz. If I were to be guided by it, I'd be laughed at," said Corey.

"And being laughed at is more important than the chance that there's violence brewing at Taft?" Buzz demanded.

Flushing, Corey had put the sheets down as if they burned. "That is uncalled for! Give me facts and I'll be happy to believe you, but I won't act on hunches. Can't you see it now?" His voice had taken on tones of hysterical drama. "Taft High School parents sue the city of Holloman for discrimination and defamation! Go away, Buzz! Do the job I've just given you—nail whoever held up the Fourth National Bank out in the Valley. It's both tangible and important."

Unable to do more, Buzz had left it. There was some justice in Corey's stand; only the thought of a tragedy involving children had spurred him to such effort.

His report went into the Taft High weapons cache file, but on two Thursdays, when Carmine, Abe and Corey met to discuss the cases of the week, Corey had not produced the report, or even mentioned it in passing. It sat in the back of the file, unread.

Tracking down the Fourth National Bank robbers had taken time, but Buzz Genovese was a good detective, albeit inexperienced. The crime had all the earmarks of a funding exercise rather than self-profit, but Corey's Black Brigade snitches were very young and very junior in the hierarchy, so knew nothing of Mohammed el Nesr's thinking, and swore it wasn't the Black Brigade—with complete truth. A $74,000 take would buy a lot of firearms up to and including fully automatic weapons, but if Mohammed was innocent, who else was there with the organization? A question Corey didn't ask. Buzz went to his splinter group, and, eventually, to an address: 17 Parkinson in the Argyle Avenue district.

At noon on Tuesday, November 26, Buzz, Nick Jefferson and four uniforms entered the house to find two black men watching a Lakers replay on television; neither man was armed, and a rigorous search of every cranny on all three floors revealed no firearms.

17 Parkinson was a three-family house that had been gutted and completely lined with mattresses, every window boarded up. Milo Washington and Durston Parrish clearly lived in it, but Buzz's snitch, vouched for by Nick, swore that Milo and Durston were the heads of the new splinter group. So where were the caches of weapons?

Posters had been pinned to the mattresses extolling bloodshed, black supremacy, the slaughter of whites, and, many times over, three capital letters: BPP. It was a new acronym to Buzz.

He stared at Milo Washington, a more commanding figure than Durston Parrish. Well over six feet, a good physique, a handsome face, milk coffee skin and hip threads; the eyes, large and an interesting shade of green, regarded him with contempt. He must, Buzz reflected, be feeling an utter fool—watching a Lakers replay!

"What does BPP stand for, Milo?" Buzz asked.

"Black People's Power," Milo said proudly, defiantly.

"So that's it! Who're you, man?" Nick asked.

"I am the founder and leader."

"And articulate when you need to be. Where are the guns?"

"Wouldn't you like to know, Uncle Tom pig?"

A frisson of fear shot down Buzz's spine; they hadn't been quiet about raiding 17 Parkinson, thus giving those in the houses nearby time to evacuate before the bullets started humming.

"Something's wrong," Buzz said to Nick when the search proved fruitless. "Milo didn't deny the guns—he's stupidly articulate, needs time inside having talks with Wesley le Clerc."

"We've got nothing on them," Nick said. "Watching the Lakers win isn't a crime, and there were no stashes of any kind."

"Don't hold your breath, Milo," Buzz said to him on the porch, a corner of his mind wondering why the uniforms, clustered around one squad car, looked so upset.

They had all been inside the house when the fracas at Taft High occurred. Two students, two teachers and a riot cop were dead, and another thirty-three were wounded, all but two slightly. Someone on Parkinson had run to the school to alert the kid who led Black People's Power there; spoiling for action, he gathered his troops, broke out automatics and spare clips from the BPP cache, and set off to bust Milo and Durston free. If the pigs thought they were taking Milo in, they better think again! But one of the BPP kids was a spy, there to tip off the Black Brigade kids when the BPP arsenal surfaced. The BB kids tapped their own cache, and a gun battle developed within the school. Only the intervention of riot police had stopped the hostilities.

Why hadn't Corey Marshall believed his report? It all hinged on that, thought Buzz, wandering desolately across the courtyard blaming himself—and Corey. He'd *known* the guns were at the school! Trouble was, he didn't have enough evidence to lay before Captain Vasquez, who might otherwise have hit the school at the same moment as Buzz hit the BPP house on Parkinson. No, no, it was all wrong! Corey Marshall was the necessary link and—

Someone was pacing the courtyard: Carmine Delmonico. His face was grim, nor did Buzz need to ask why he was out here, pacing. Sometimes a man needed to have space and open air.

Carmine saw him and strode over.

"Do you *believe* this?" he demanded. "Two rival black power factions, two thousand hapless kids of every color God makes a human skin—shit, shit, *shit*! How did one faction think it could bust Milo Washington loose, and why did the other faction decide to stop them inside the school? My wife is right, it's guns! And drugs! Why can't they use a classroom as a place to learn instead of as a place to come down off of smack?"

The two men turned and began to walk together.

"I knew I was right," Buzz said at last, clenching his fists. "I kept telling Corey there was a splinter group, but he wouldn't believe me. I didn't have any facts, just my cop instincts. I was conned too, Carmine, by Corey's Black Brigade snitches. They talked me into thinking that the Black Brigade wasn't worried by the formation of Black People's Power. Whereas the truth is that Milo was making significant inroads into Mohammed's army, and war was in the wind. The trouble is Mohammed's ordinary soldiers are not in the picture—I should have seen it, but I didn't. Jesus!"

Another silence fell, again broken by Buzz Genovese.

"I put in four hours writing that report, busted my ass, but I didn't have facts to back up my cop instincts. Just little signs—stray remarks, sidelong looks, interrupted whispers—not facts, facts, facts! The Valley bank holdup went down to finance BPP weapons purchases, but tell me why—just tell me why they had to hide the weapons in a school? *A school!*" He stopped, recollecting himself. "Well, too late now. Five lives! I am haunted, Carmine."

"What report, Buzz?"

"The supplementary one I submitted about the Taft High arms cache. Corey closed the case for lack of evidence a month ago—well, I guess you know that. But I knew it wasn't over. So I watched and listened for another nearly two weeks, then I wrote this second report." He looked embarrassed. "Sorry, Captain, I didn't mean to snitch, and Corey was right. There wasn't a shred of evidence."

* * *

"What do we do about it?" Carmine asked, holding up the second report. He was staring at Commissioner Silvestri and Captain Vasquez, whose faces were carefully neutral.

"If so much as a whisper of this gets out, the media will have a field day. The death of kids in a school is *world* news," Carmine went on. "Holloman is full of journalists. The Black Brigade and its splinter, Black People's Power, are local black power groups with no national impact. To the journalists in this year of riots and terrible violence, the BB and the BPP are peanuts. Martin Luther King Junior dead, then Robert Kennedy—it's an awful year! But what if it leaks that the Holloman PD had warning of a second weapons cache at Taft High, and didn't so much as look for it? It's known now that both groups had a cache at the school, but nothing indicates that the Holloman PD didn't do its job. Except this." He put the seven sheets down on Silvestri's coffee table.

All three men had read Buzz's report, pulled from the back of the Taft High file by a terrified Corey Marshall. What Carmine didn't know was whether Corey had intended to bring him the report, or burn it. His cop instincts said Corey intended to burn it, but just as he pulled the sheets, Carmine had walked in.

"You said one of my cases would come back and bite me," said Corey, handing him the report.

"I'm sorry that it's so terrible, Lieutenant."

"What's going to happen to me?" He sounded petrified.

"I don't know. But if you have any brain at all, don't so much as mention it to Maureen. That's your only hope."

"I told Corey not to confide in Maureen," Carmine said now. "He might even obey that order, because I don't think he could face the tongue-lashing she'd give him."

"You're very smart, Carmine," Fernando Vasquez said.

"If I were, this wouldn't have happened. I knew that Corey Marshall was weak, but so was I for not acting."

"That's aftersight speaking." Fernando's beautiful hand indicated the report. "You kept this unduplicated, and you guys in Detectives haven't caught up enough with modern policing to keep copies of everything. For instance, did Sergeant Genovese keep a copy for himself?"

"No. Why would he? It's in the file."

"In future, he should. The world increasingly belongs to the lawyers, Carmine, and some of them are more ruthless than any journalist. I don't increase paperwork for no reason. I do it to protect my men. With the Dodo on your back, I haven't gotten around to Detectives yet, but it's coming."

"I gather that the existence of one copy of this is a good thing?" Carmine asked.

"A very good thing. What happens if Buzz goes poor Morty Jones's route, huh? Guilt, depression, a steel meal? Without a copy of his report, he'll be seen as confabulating," Fernando said, black eyes like two glistening stones.

"It won't come to that," Carmine said. "This time, I'll make absolutely sure." He felt sick, pressed his midriff. "John, you haven't said a thing. Fernando has left me in no doubt of his solution to our troubles—burn the report. What do you say?"

"That God moves in mysterious ways," the Commissioner said, "and that you've acted for the greater good of the Holloman PD. It's not even a question of blame—attitudes vary. Is Corey's hard-nosed attitude more reprehensible because five people have died? He had every chance of being right."

"If you'd read Buzz's report, John, would you have pulled your men out of Taft High?" Carmine demanded.

"No," Silvestri said flatly.

"And you, Fernando?"

"I would have blitzed the place, no matter what the parents and teachers said in objection. That was the only way to do it, Carmine. Empty the entire school, then search the cockroaches and fleas to see if they were packing."

"Lessons for the future," Silvestri said, sighing. "I am going to maintain that the school was scrupulously searched and all the weapons it contained were confiscated. Luckily the kids involved all went to the juvenile courts, so it's not our fault if they're already back at Taft High. As for the BB cache and the second BPP one, the guns had been placed in the school so recently that we'd had no word of it. Like so many other places, we've had a bad year with race riots in Holloman."

"You intend to burn it," Carmine said, voice flat.

They look like father and son, he thought as Vasquez and Silvestri went to a glass-fronted ornamental cupboard. John took out a big silver tray while Fernando hovered at his side. Trim, in silver-encrusted navy uniforms, very dark of hair and eye, flawless features and a certain catlike grace of movement. Thank God! John has finally found his heir. Not that he intends to retire for some time to come. He has to groom Fernando.

Buzz Genovese's report burned while Carmine watched the two uniformed men make sure no flake remained unblackened.

"I'll see Buzz tomorrow morning," the Commissioner said when Fernando took the tray off to the private bathroom. "It's sad but simple—when Lieutenant Marshall looked for the report, it had gone. Too suggestive, you think, Carmine? Well, I think Corey deserves to wear the odium, especially in Buzz's eyes."

"I appreciate your having me here, John."

Fernando returned.

The three men sat down again.

"We still have one problem," said Carmine.

"Corey, you mean?" Silvestri asked.

"I mean."

"It's a hard one."

Fernando leaned back, satisfied that he had done his part; Carmine continued to speak to Silvestri, as if he too thought it.

"I have a solution, John."

The Commissioner sat up. "You do? Hit me!"

"First of all, Corey's not suited for his present position. He's too anti-routine in a job he thinks should have no routine, not to mention that he paints himself into a corner. A more secure man would simply admit that he was wrong, but Corey's not secure. He's also dominated by his wife. What he needs is a job having equal status but none of the responsibility—no human beings as individual human beings, just as ciphers."

Fernando was bolt upright, wary and annoyed. "No!"

"Oh, come on, Fernando, he's perfect, and you know it. By Christmas you will have completed your reforms—three lieutenants, remember? After pushing Mike Cerutti through one department after another, you intend to put him in as lieutenant in charge of anything with wheels—well, it's logical, and you're a logical man. Of course you need a lieutenant in charge of personnel, but a guy very much under your thumb. For that reason it won't be Joey Tasco, it will be Virgil Simms. Mike and Virgil are good men who can't afford to forget that you promoted them over a lot of heads, that their income has zoomed, and that they get to wear silver braid. However, you need a senior lieutenant, and whom can you trust in the Uniform Division, tell me that? Ideally you need someone from outside, but you haven't been here long enough to survive the palace revolution that would provoke. Whereas Corey Marshall has been in the Holloman PD for seventeen years, eleven of them in uniform. Everybody with seniority knows him, and he's well liked. His being awarded the top job will be seen as shrewd and inarguable. On the other hand, what you know about him chains him to you. He'll have to work from a list of do's and don't's that you write in letters of stone—he'll have absolutely no room to maneuver. Nor will his wife have the smallest share in his power. Corey is the perfect senior lieutenant. C'mon, Fernando, admit it!"

"I agree it's my best answer," Fernando said. "Damn you!"

"So do I agree, and mine's the deciding vote," said Silvestri.

"You told me I had too many lieutenants, and you were right," Carmine said, grinning. "In future, Detectives will have one lieutenant—Abe Goldberg, and one captain, me. One fewer loot, a lot fewer headaches."

But, thought Carmine later, driving home, today has been an awful day. Not every death at Taft High was an innocent one, but even a flesh wound is too high a price to pay for a troubled peace. And I have colluded at the destruction of a document that indicts one of my own men and should be published to vindicate another. What might have happened if I had refused to collude? If I had insisted on publication? John Silvestri wears the pale blue ribbon, and he colluded. It's Vasquez, of course. The new breed, the modern cop.

What good would publication have done? It could only have worked did it happen beforehand, and for that, I blame Corey Marshall. He knew the report existed, but no one else did except its author. It's a terrible dilemma, and both of its horns are cruel. To have published his findings, Buzz Genovese would have had to go over his boss's head, and he had seen that as lacking honor. Well, so would I. Honor is preserved, but at the cost of five lives and a bunch of wounded. I can see why John Silvestri has chosen to make Corey Marshall the villain of the piece, but are the three of us—himself, Fernando, and I—innocent?

"One of my worst days," he said to Desdemona, telling her everything save the collusion.

"Oh, Carmine, a horror! And I do understand why guns are such a large part of it," she said. "Male creatures are genuinely combative, it's a part of the sex. Now that we're busy making war so unpalatable, a different sort of war is breaking out on our streets and in our schools. Or else some kid's crashed his bike at a hundred miles an hour. Whatever. Young men die violently. When young women do, it's mostly at the hands of a man."

"Shall we mourn together, Desdemona?"

"Better together than apart, dear love." She led the way to the sitting room and got busy at the little bar, so that when next she spoke, it sounded offhand, casual.

"I'm starting to go to church with Maria," she said.

He took the glass carefully. "Why?"

"It can't do any harm, can it?"

"No, it never can."

MONDAY, DECEMBER 2

to

END OF YEAR

1968

CHAPTER VIII

When Helen asked Captain Delmonico for the return of her completed journals, he denied her request. "They're locked up and they stay locked up until you've finished your training," he said. "One question before you go, please. Why did you show part of them to Kurt von Fahlendorf? My instructions were explicit."

"Sir, I showed Kurt the parts relevant to his kidnapping, in the hope he'd offer me a clue," she said—well, it was half true.

One eyebrow rose, but he said nothing.

"I admit I didn't preserve its security properly when I began my journals, but I have learned, sir. Delia chewed me out because my gun and badge were in my bag too—she was right, of course." Her laugh sounded unconcerned. "But no one burgled my bag, sir."

"Did you have an enjoyable little vacation?" Carmine asked.

"More enjoyable than you could know, Captain. I managed to avoid Dad's Thanksgiving table."

"That can't have impressed him."

"Well, no, it didn't, but I had an excellent excuse."

She really must have had a good excuse, Carmine thought, for M.M.'s Thanksgiving dinners were huge and required the whole of his rather meager family. His practice was to have his bursars find him fifty poor freshman students on scholarship who wouldn't be able to afford to go home. Helen's loss would have been felt.

"The Dodo didn't strike," she said, heading for the team's office. "He's way overdue."

"Yes, he's done what he intended to—confuse us," Carmine said. "You're on your own, Helen, I'm afraid. Nick and Delia are still on special duty. I know it's not glamorous, but your most valuable occupation will be to man the phones and study. Stella only fields my calls, so the team phones are unattended. Fred has linked all three team offices plus Lieutenants Marshall and Goldberg together, which means you'll be busy with messages."

He was smiling; the least she could do was smile back. But as she went to sit at her desk, Helen was fighting annoyance. How dared they? Oh, why wasn't she older and plainer, why did her hair have to be the famous apricot?

The phone rang.

"Helen MacIntosh taking messages for everyone!"

This was greeted by silence; then came a laugh. "Helen? Isn't this your phone?"

"Oh, Kurt! I'm sorry, just—oh, it doesn't matter."

"I've been trying to get you for over a week."

"The Captain gave me leave. They've got something going on that I'm not equipped to participate in, and since I had a private matter to attend to, I applied for leave."

"I went around to Talisman Towers," he said, "but no one was ever home. Thanksgiving Day, I suppose. But when your father didn't know where you were, I was *worried*!"

"Oh, poor Kurt! I'm sorry."

"You keep saying that. I'll forgive you anything if you come to Solo's with me tonight."

"What a brilliant idea! I can tell you everything."

"I'll pick you up at six forty-five," he said.

"Uh—no, that's too difficult. I'll meet you there at seven, okay?"

"It will have to be," he said, and hung up.

Typical Kurt: he was there to welcome her. Sometimes Helen contemplated arriving somewhere an hour earlier than the appointed time, just to see how early Kurt arrived. Not only was he dreamy to look at, he was also a total gentleman. And a genius besides.

"Did you finish your equations?" she asked, accepting a glass of French chambertin.

"Yes, I did, then went back and rewrote the ones on the tank wall." He added sparkling mineral water to his own glass.

"Honestly, Kurt, how can you ruin a wine this good by diluting it? Sometimes you don't make sense."

"It's heavy, darling Helen, and I want a clear head." The icy blue eyes gleamed. "I want to hear your news, for instance."

"No, let's start with your news," she said.

"How do you know I have any?"

"I can read you like a book."

"Ach, so … It is stale news by now, but you are entitled to know it, I think. Josef was indeed married to the Richter woman, which made his marriage to Dagmar bigamous."

"I am so sorry!"

"Sorrow is not necessary. No one will ever know. Frau Richter and her son were shot dead just minutes after Josef—isn't that amazing? Such a coincidence!"

Helen threw her head back and laughed. "About as amazing a coincidence as Roosevelt, Churchill and Stalin meeting at Yalta!"

"That is ironic," he said placidly, starting on his shrimp cocktail. "This is delicious! You are not shocked?"

"No, Kurt, I'm not shocked. Who did it?"

"Turks, I believe."

"Who are now on their way back to Turkey to live the life of lords," she said, still chuckling.

"About that, I cannot postulate."

"Did the Munich cops make the connection between Frau Richter and Josef von Fahlendorf?"

"How could they? Josef was careful to leave no evidence, and the Frau, who had all the documentation, kept it in her desk—not even locked, can you imagine that?"

"Yes, actually I can," said Helen, who felt no pity for the Richters. What if she had been fool enough to fall for a con man and foisted him into the MacIntoshes? It wouldn't have happened, of course, any more than it would happen in the future, but she understood the von Fahlendorf predicament completely. Dagmar had the flaws of genius: she could conceive new formulae and processes and she could administer a multi-factory company with all the shrewdness and knowledge of a born business person, but she couldn't judge people or manage her private life. How like her was Kurt? Very different in most respects, but …

"Would you fall in love with the wrong person?" she asked.

He raised his head from his food, smiling. "You tell me."

"If I could, Kurt, I wouldn't need to ask."

He put down his fork, took her hands. "Helen, Helen! I am in love with you. I have been in love with you since I first met you at that party of Mark's ten months ago."

"Oh, rubbish!" she cried, removing her hands. "You only think you are. It's not real."

And like that, he gave it up! "Have it your own way," he said, pushing the empty shrimp cocktail bowl to one side, a habit that was not etiquette, perhaps, but some people couldn't bear to look at a dirty plate, and Kurt was one such.

"When did Dagmar tell you?" she asked.

"The day after we returned here."

"Thus making sure baby brother Kurt wasn't incriminated."

"How could any von Fahlendorf?" he asked, eyes wide. "There was nothing to connect our family to Turks on a rampage."

"How many *did* die?"

"I have no idea."

"Another question, Kurt—how wealthy are you?"

"I have more than enough for my personal needs."

"As much as I have?"

"No, Helen. One-fifth of it—ten million."

"Safely invested?"

"Absolutely."

They settled to eat the main course, neither with the temperament to grieve over dead Richters, dead Turks or dead innocents. Dagmar had done the cleaning up her own incompetence had made necessary, it was as simple as that.

"Now," he said over coffee, "I want to hear your news."

Her face lit up. "I bought a new apartment," she said.

"I wasn't aware you were unhappy at Talisman Towers."

"I wasn't, but then I had a chance at an eighth floor condo on Busquash Inlet," she said, speaking in a rush. "They are so divine, Kurt! The owner of this one was murdered—had her throat cut. I happened to know her a little, and enough about her heirs to think that if I got in fast, they'd sell to me. I offered them one-point-two million, and they jumped at it. Of course probate hasn't been granted yet, but it's tied up so that they can't get out of it. You know them— the Warburton twins."

He had listened with intense concentration, and nodded when she had ended. "Yes, I know the building, it is beautiful, and the view must be superb. But Helen! So much money! It isn't worth a quarter of the price you paid."

"I agree, if it were not for the fact that no more high rises will ever be built on Busquash Peninsula. It would have gone for a million at least at auction. The twins were well aware of that. Everyone is happy!"

"Have you moved in?" Kurt asked.

"Yesterday, finally. I wanted to buy all new furniture—by that I mean some very old, some middling, and some very modern."

"I 'd love to see it."

"Abandon your coffee and follow me to my new home. I'll make us Jamaican Blue Mountain."

Amanda would not have known her apartment, Helen had wrought so many changes. The carpet and the upholstery were cobalt blue, the walls and ceiling lime-green, and interesting antiques were scattered about. Her lamps were Tiffany and her chandelier 1910

Murano glass, a collection of magnificent paintings adorned the walls, and two bronze slave-girl lights six feet tall provided the first illumination once the front door was opened. Had she paid attention to her mother, whose taste was famous, she would perhaps have chosen a less strident theme, but Helen had her own ideas and Angela hadn't been able to budge her. Mom was a source of New York shops and galleries, nothing else.

Kurt hated it, except for the Matisse and the Renoir, which, she admitted, were on loan from her father.

"They do not belong," Kurt said. "They are too delicate."

"I see what you mean, and anyway, I think I have to give them back," she said, sounding displeased. "Dad says my security isn't good enough. *I* say, why should anyone know they're here?"

"I know now, and as time goes on, more and more people will. Come, Helen, your papa is right! There is a black market for work of this caliber."

"Come and have a look at the bathroom" was her rejoinder, leading the way through a big bedroom containing an enormous bed and into a bathroom tiled in Norwegian Rose marble. "See? It even has a Jacuzzi, and I didn't have to change a thing, I liked it just as it was."

"I like the Jacuzzi," he said, smiling at her, "but I would like it better if you and I were in it minus our clothes."

She gave him a considering look. "I'll think about it. Come and see the kitchen. It's so perfect that I'm thinking of taking cooking lessons."

"Every woman should know how to cook."

She gasped. "You male chauvinist pig, Kurt!"

His eyes flashed. "I do not mind the reference to my sex, or to being called a chauvinist, but I will *not* be called a pig!"

"Pig, pig, pig!" she shouted.

He turned and left her; she heard the front door slam.

"Holy shits!" she said, only half inclined to laugh. The other half was angry—was he *that* German, that he had no sense of humor? Why did "pig" insult him more than the rest of a famous phrase? For a moment she thought about racing downstairs and begging his pardon, but then the MacIntosh stubbornness cut in; her chin lifted. Fuck Kurt von Fahlendorf!

A Jacuzzi—she'd immerse herself in its bubbles all alone. Not that she would have consented to sharing it with Kurt or any other man. Delia laughed and called her a "professional virgin", and she had admitted the truth of that to Delia. It didn't mean she was a physical virgin, it meant she was a cockteaser who pretended to outraged indignation when a man tried to have sex with her, convinced that she wanted it.

"You invite rape, Helen!" one man had said, frustrated.

"Go on!" she exclaimed. "I'm not the one at fault, you are!"

What she suspected about Kurt was certainly true of her: emotional coldness. Never having experienced a strong sexual drive, Helen could only ape its externals, and wondered how many other women were the same. The few men who had attracted her were all dark in a Silvestri way rather than a Captain Delmonico way, and she knew who her next target was going to be: Fernando Vasquez. That he was married and the father of children didn't enter into her calculations: ethics and money never did, for she had none of the first and too much of the second. Christmas would see her make her move on Fernando, who was surely ripe for an affair, a deduction made for the crudest of reasons: gossip said he'd been faithfully married for a very long time.

Now was the right moment to get rid of Kurt, who was proving hard to get rid of. Which von Fahlendorf had commissioned the Turks, Dagmar or Kurt? It could as easily have been Kurt. In fact, in some ways Kurt made more sense. Would a Muslim culture accept a commission from a woman? Dagmar knew what was afoot, yes, but had she enacted the plan? Probably not, Helen concluded. No, Kurt did that before he boarded the plane, and in such a way that these foreign thugs had obeyed orders to the letter. How did he find them in a basically law-abiding immigrant populace? Kurt might be Nietzsche's Superman, but he was also mild-mannered Clark Kent, America's alter ego.

Having solved all that to her satisfaction, Helen stepped into the Jacuzzi and lay being gently pummeled by streams and jets of water for twenty minutes before emerging to wrap herself in a towel and go about her very last chores—bag and gun.

Her handbag went into a Chinese coromandel cabinet inside the front door; in the early days she had left it lying around anywhere, then Delia had objected, explaining that, since the bag held a firearm, she must conceal it. Looking back, Helen knew now that more than her gun had been vulnerable. So had her work journals. Not that anyone ever read them, but Delia had been right, it was better to be sure than sorry.

Her 9mm Parabellum pistol never remained in the bag these days, hadn't in many weeks. It went under a pillow on her bed and stayed there until the morning. If, as tonight, she came home with someone, she left the person in the living room or, in Kurt's case, the study, while she used her private bathroom—an excuse that let her enter the bedroom so she could park her weapon. She readied the gun for firing: safety off and a round in the chamber. If an intruder woke her, she didn't have to fiddle. Tomorrow she would eject the round, insert it in the magazine, and put the safety on. That way, no accident.

I'm tired, she thought, wandering toward the bed.

Something cannoned into her back so forcibly that she went down in a heap on the floor, her face in the white bedroom carpet, her arms behind her back. The towel had gone in the initial attack, but Helen forgot all about modesty as she fought to free herself. He had her face downward and was sitting on her ribs; part of her fight was just to breathe, and she couldn't seem to use her legs above the knees. Cold metal closed around her ankles and fettered her, then came the click of handcuffs on her wrists. Arms and legs were almost immobilized.

He yanked her on to her back so that she could see him, at the exact moment that she opened her mouth to shout for help. She didn't seem able to scream, but she could shout, she could definitely shout! Too late. He had the duct tape over her mouth. You fool, you fool! Why didn't you shout?

She didn't need to see his face to know it was Kurt. In a weird way, her subconscious had always known Kurt was the Dodo. At dinner tonight, for sure. The paperweight … Why hadn't her consciousness seen the truth of its significance? She *had* known, but something in her mind refused to let her admit his name, let her see what tonight had made manifest. After his frankness at Solo's table, he had nowhere to go except to this.

"Your bed is hedonistic," he said, looking disgusted. "How many pigs can fit on it at one and the same moment?"

She tossed her head about furiously, drummed her feet on the carpet, made noises of frustration, while her eyes blazed up into his devoid of fear. Take off the gag, let me talk!

Jerking her to her feet, he propelled her to the bed with a series of vicious kicks on the buttocks—he hurt, he hurt! At the bed, he dealt her an even stronger, harder kick that saw her upper half land three feet up the mattress. But her feet and legs didn't make it, nor could she summon up the traction to move them in any direction; however she tried, they slipped. Then he grasped the ankle chain and lifted her legs himself, arranged her on the bed to please some idea of his own. Tears slid from the corners of her eyes, but he couldn't know why: she wept because he had put her on the far side of a king bed from her gun. Now she had to cross an acre of bed to reach it.

Her mimed show of defiance had produced a reaction; he ripped off the tape.

"Scream, and you will wish you had not," he said.

"I'm only crying because I can't kill you."

A statement that made him laugh. "You are unique, Helen! I am delighted to talk to you. You are so interesting."

"Thank you, kind sir," she said mockingly. "How many of those marvelous disguises did you use, Kurt?"

"I did not count. I enjoy acting."

"Why switch from rape to murder? Why kill Melantha?"

"Boredom, as much as anything. I needed fresh stimulus."

"Catherine dos Santos must have stimulated!"

"Yes, I enjoyed that. A close call, but I was alive."

"You're crazy, Kurt."

That stung. "I am not insane! I am a genius!"

"Yes, you are a genius, but in a limited way," she said, deciding to humor and insult him simultaneously. "A Renaissance man you're not. Really, all you are is a mathematician with a passion for sub-atomic particles. You couldn't even get the Dodo's taxonomic name right."

"My choice of the Linnaean name was deliberate," he said loftily. "The bird is an extinct species, therefore inept indeed. What kind of bird walks up to a hungry man and begs to be eaten? The modern taxonomic name is ludicrous! *Didus ineptus* it was, and *Didus ineptus* it is to me."

"But why call yourself a dodo?" Talk to him, talk to him!

"My species is extinct."

"What species is that?"

"*Didus ineptus.*"

He won't tell me that, she thought. Whatever his reason, it's locked inside his mania. "Tell me more about the dodo."

"Women have made men so ineffectual that they are extinct! What man is master in his own home anymore? Even a physics bunker is not safe from women! Women are taking over!"

"That's a load of crap, Kurt, and you know it! You're manufacturing reasons you think will sidetrack me, and they won't. I want to know the real reason for being a dodo."

"Yes, you are intelligent. I have always known that, but never as positively as I do tonight. Why do you waste yourself on a police career? It is vulgar."

"You're a snob, Kurt, you couldn't understand. I don't *waste* myself—it's the stepping stone to a public career that could take me to the White House if I wanted. The problem is that I don't think I want that. What I know is that the Dodo can make me famous, win me decorations and a lot of media exposure."

He looked incredulous. "You truly believe you will win?"

Her eyelids lowered, she sneered. "I know I'll win."

The chain made a dull, clunking noise as he brushed his hand across it. "Trussed up like a dodo? Like an unbelievably stupid, ugly bird? You cannot win, Helen. In a few hours you will be as dead as a dodo." He tittered. "I am like the Pope, I am infallible!"

He began pinching, poking, punching and squeezing her flesh; she had to endure it without making the slightest noise, or he would gag her. Whatever happened, she must keep her mouth free! It was her best, her only weapon.

His erection had grown huge; twice he fitted its tip against her entrance and she stiffened, but on each occasion he muttered something in German and positioned himself away from the bed, muttering in German, staring at her.

"You can get it up, but can't you get it in?" she asked.

"Stupid! Of course I can—if I want to. But the question is, do I want to? I like probing you better."

"I bet you do!" she said. "It's more disgusting."

"Hasten slowly," he said in her ear, applying tape to her mouth. "You must be silenced whenever I am not in the room. Good for me that you have a new apartment—no one will visit you." And he flipped her over on to her stomach.

Wriggling desperately to turn over again, she reviewed all her options. She could bite his rubber glove to shreds, but if she did—no. He wouldn't leave a fingerprint, he was too smart, and he might kill her in a rage. She had to reach her gun, and in order to do that, she had to talk. Talk constantly herself and keep him talking. Talk and her gun were her best options.

Eating a slice of cold pizza, he strolled in.

"Look at you! You've turned yourself back again, you clever little dodo! Well, no matter! Why do young American women starve themselves? Their refrigerators are empty. Cottage cheese … Diet this and diet that. I was amazed to find half a pizza in your refrigerator, but it is on its last day of edibility. Don't you like my big words? You, Helen, are a tough bird. Your every movement tells me that you will not easily succumb to terror."

He finished the pizza. "Lie there and think of death while I find a book that can teach me a new word or phrase—how I love that!—and entertain me as I wait."

The books! Her eyes followed him as he walked toward her study, where three thousand books lined its walls. When he came back, he held a book she couldn't identify. *Take off the tape*!

He tore the tape off and sat down in a white velvet chair.

"What's the book, Kurt?"

"H. Rider Haggard. *King Solomon's Mines*," he answered. "I greatly esteem Victorian and Edwardian novels, provided that they are of the adventurous kind," he said, apparently not averse to more talk. "The prose is excellent and the subject matter lurid. I have found that there is always an example of the genre on the shelves of a bookish woman, and I am not interested in women who are not bookish."

"What would you do if you didn't find an example of the genre?"

He laughed. "That cannot happen. I pay several visits to a woman's apartment to check her out."

"You haven't been in this apartment before."

"Ah, but many times in Talisman Towers!"

"I've changed a lot of things, Kurt."

He opened the book and started to read while Helen continued trying to free her hands, safely hidden behind her back. These, she had realized, were her own cuffs, though the ones connected by a chain on her ankles were his. The Commissioner had taken some of these cuffs as an experiment, for the salesman claimed they tightened the more the prisoner struggled. Helen had been issued a pair to try on Nick and Delia, who soon learned how to immobilize the ratchet. So did Helen.

Kurt the Dodo had put the cuffs on quite efficiently, but hadn't pushed them cruelly tight, perhaps because he wanted the focus of her pain to be what he did to her.

Her joints were slim and supple, her willpower immense. Pray that her book continued to hold his attention! The short chain held her hands close together; she grasped the fingers of her right hand with her left, clustered them, moved her left hand up to her right's knuckles, then crushed them until her right hand was nearly as small as its wrist. Oh, the pain! The cuff slid off. Easier to work her imprisoned left hand, a little larger, with the right one liberated; closing her mind to the pain, she forced its knuckles through the cuff and now was completely free. She was in the middle of the bed, what seemed a day's journey from the pillow, but she made herself lie ostensibly still and worked her way across the bed a millimeter at a time, so slowly that his peripheral vision saw no movement. The book was holding his interest, but if he turned to look at her, she was caught—her position had definitely changed.

She was petrified, understanding that this was her only chance at winning. From the moment when he had stood forth in all the glory of his alter ego, he had cast her into paroxysms of fear. Cold and dark as outer space, he was a creature inhabiting a lightless human body, obsessed with the spectacle of terror and the ecstasy of someone else's suffering.

But her fear was not for her own torture and death. It was terror that she might fail. She couldn't fail, she couldn't!

"Do you take the rests so that you can get it up again?" she asked, interrupting his concentration.

He looked up, startled, and, as she had hoped, didn't notice how far she had moved.

"Even you cannot inspire me to frenzy," he said, sneering.

"Have you ever achieved orgasm?"

A look of horrified prudery came over his face. "Disgusting! You are disgusting! Things like that are not your business!"

"What utter crap! Do you come, Kurt?"

Now he was really angry, past noticing that she was moving.

"Immoral! You are immoral!"

A few more inches. Nearly there, nearly there …

He rose from the white velvet chair and stormed toward the bed, face contorted in fury; it was then that Helen saw the silenced .22 on the bedside table next to him. But it was her advantage. Even as she twisted her body up to a sitting position while he, astounded, gaped at her, Helen's hand came up holding her gun, safety off, round in the chamber. She shot him in the right chest. He leaped backward to sprawl on the fluffy white floor, staring up at her as the pink bubbles gathered on his lips.

"You're going to be as dead as a dodo, Kurt," she said, swinging her legs on to the carpet well clear of the growing, wet red stain. "Can you still speak?"

He tried, but coughed instead; his hands flailed.

"Afraid of dying, Kurt?"

That provoked extreme agitation. "This is an excellent apartment, quite sound-proof," she said in a relaxed, chatty voice. "No one will hear my gun as anything except far-off backfires. I will call the police, of course. When I feel like it. I'm going to make you suffer first. A gut shot. My, it will hurt!"

The squat, ugly muzzle came up; the pistol roared.

Kurt screamed, a thin, fluid sound.

"I don't think that hit a major artery," she said, "but you can always hope it did. No, no artery! Just liver and gut."

His screams were dwindling, the pink foam spilling from his mouth, the blood from the gut shot dark and venous.

She kept talking to him, though whether at the end he heard her, Helen didn't know.

Only after the last life died from his eyes did she shoot him in the heart. "Show's over," she said, looking at her naked body. "No way any cops are going to see this." She went to her dressing room and slipped on a silk robe, then went to her study and picked up the phone.

"Captain Delmonico? This is Helen MacIntosh. I've killed the Dodo in my new apartment at Busquash Inlet. It belonged to Amanda Warburton. Will you organize things, please?"

When Carmine arrived with Delia, she was sitting on the far side of the bed from Kurt von Fahlendorf's body, composed and displaying no symptoms of shock.

"What happened? The full story," he said, standing where he could see her, but not too close.

She told him lucidly and plainly; it was, he thought, the most exemplary narration by a killer that he had ever heard; she had learned her lessons well.

"The Commissioner was right not to switch to these cuffs, Captain. Kurt saw them in my study and used them—lucky for me! I did a Houdini while he read his book. My hands are much smaller than yours. I knew how to work them so the ratchet didn't move."

"Irony in operation," Carmine said.

"You knew he was the Dodo," she accused.

"After reading your journals, yes. That can be your first examination, next Monday morning. Go through them and find out what gave Kurt away. It's all there."

"The paperweight?"

"Yes. The little colored glass trails going in all directions look like the tracks of sub-atomic particles. I saw it because I read science magazines."

"And I saw it because Kurt had shown me photos, but then I forgot until tonight. My memory needs honing." She looked disapproving. "Why didn't you arrest him, Captain?"

"It had better be Carmine from now on, Helen. There was no tangible evidence. My big mistake was in thinking he'd never put you on his victims list. You didn't fit the stereotype in so far as he had one. For example, you were too aggressive. You were a source of information—he read your journals until I saw the light and locked them up. My last mistake," Carmine said, "was in underestimating the depth of his madness."

"What about girls who did fit the stereotype, Carmine?" Delia asked. "We had so much trouble finding them."

"That was because we never managed to refine our list of qualities that appealed to him," Carmine said. "You and Helen exhausted yourselves looking, but always in something of a fog. Even now, do we really know all the qualities?"

"No," said Helen. "He gave himself away to me over dinner tonight. I don't know if he intended to, or not. It also came as a shock to him that I'd left Talisman Towers, moved out of Carew. Living in Carew is a definite, I believe now."

This little madam is as tough as old army boots, thought Delia as she listened. Oh, she'll undergo a reaction later on tonight, but nothing a battle-hardened veteran wouldn't. She is going to be one of those cops around whom criminals steer a wide berth. Dainty and deadly, that's Helen. I'm glad I like her, but I understand why none of our male detectives do.

"You're a crack shot, Helen," Delia said suddenly . "Why didn't you go for his head?"

"I was so awkwardly positioned," Helen said, a falter creeping into her voice. "He and I were on almost the same plane, it was like standing sideways to a target. The second shot went into his belly because right at the moment I squeezed the trigger, he leaped in the air. Finally he was right—that was the heart shot."

"You won't go to trial, but there will be an internal police enquiry," Carmine said. "Just tell them that, and don't lose any sleep. When an officer lethally discharges a firearm, it's inevitable."

Her eyes filled with tears, she shivered. "I know all that! Don't forget that I've been a police officer for three years."

Ah! Signs of tension at last. Thank God for that. Carmine had begun to wonder at her self-control, forgetting she was M.M.'s daughter. Much steel there. "Kurt's house can wait," he said.

"I won't be able to participate?" Helen asked.

"No. The Commissioner hasn't taken your badge and gun. You can work anything except the Dodo—*as a trainee*. However, by the end of January I think you can start looking for a proper job."

Her face lit up. "Captain! Carmine! That's wonderful."

"Take comfort from the fact that I'll never have another trainee half as good. Which makes me doubly sorry for this shooting."

"You mean there's no vacancy for me here, sir?"

"I'm afraid not, Helen. We still have a pool of eligible men to wade through. Where would you like to go from here?"

"I'll have to think about that."

"You do pick odd moments to dispense earth-shaking news," Delia said as they put their coats on in the hall.

"She's not nearly as composed as she looks," Carmine said. "She needed a boost, and her fate is decided."

"I offered to stay, but she wouldn't hear of it," Delia said. "She announced that she'll sleep on a living room couch—apparently she hasn't furnished the other bedrooms yet. Knowing she's still in the throes of decorating makes me hope she does take my one piece of good advice."

"What advice, Deels?" Carmine pulled the fur flaps of his Russian hat down; it was way below freezing outside.

"I told her not to have a white carpet."

There was a further job to do that could have been done from Helen's apartment, but Carmine waited until he was back in his office. He picked through the contents of her bag, surrendered as part of the investigation, and found her private notebook. Dagmar's phone numbers were under F for Fahlendorf; he hadn't expected Helen to get that wrong, nor had she. Eyes on the railroad clock, he decided Dagmar might have opened her office. The workload must have increased after Josef's death, unless he had done a literal nothing for his fat pay check.

She answered with her first name: a very private line.

"Frau von Fahlendorf, this is Carmine Delmonico of the Holloman Police."

"Yes, Captain?"

"I'm very much afraid I have bad news, ma'am. Your brother, Kurt, died a short time ago."

When he ceased to speak, only the curious wrongness of the silence told him she was still listening; a broken connection was different, deader.

"Frau von Fahlendorf?"

"Yes, I am here. Kurt died? *Kurt*?" The incredulity was very apparent. Then, "My little Kurtchen? How?"

"He was shot, ma'am, trying to kill a police officer."

"You imply Kurt was trying to commit murder?"

"He had already murdered, ma'am. Professor von Fahlendorf was the rapist-killer known as the Dodo," Carmine said.

Another silence ensued, one Carmine for the life of him couldn't find words to break; it stretched on and on.

At last she spoke. "Are you sure the name is Dodo? Are you sure Kurt and this Dodo are one and the same?"

"Positive, Frau von Fahlendorf. Positive."

"How strange that Kurt would choose *Didus ineptus!* That is the bird you mean by dodo?"

"Yes, it is. Why is it strange?"

"When Kurt was a dunce at chemistry, our father always called him a dodo, too stupid to prevent his own extinction. He meant that Kurt was too stupid to perpetuate the family."

No use! Carmine was thinking. Kurt's psychopathology dates from an earlier age than his teens and chemistry. But I'll ask.

"How old was Kurt at that time?"

"Three—four. He had a brain, we knew that, but Papa was convinced his destiny lay in chemistry," said Dagmar.

Too flip, far too flip. Why is she lying?

"And that's it, Frau von Fahlendorf?"

"It is all I can think of."

He cleared his throat. "Er—the funeral, ma'am. Do you wish the body sent home?"

"I will make the arrangements, Captain. Privacy is all."

The most intriguing thing he had learned was that the Frau hadn't really been surprised. Grief showed, then flickered out; Kurt's sister had been waiting for news like this since—when? His flight to Chubb? Or the chemistry dunce? Though the question that plagued Carmine most was why Kurt the Dodo had attacked Helen.

As always, his only confidante would be Desdemona.

The guest annex at Kurt von Fahlendorf's house was not where he stored his operational gear; when it was searched at the time of his kidnapping it must have had the Dodo's souvenired books on display, but no one had known their titles, so their significance wasn't understood. Now they were joined by a glass paperweight and the glass teddy bear, both exhibited against a black background.

"I wonder why he stole the teddy bear?" Delia asked. "He had no intention of selling it, did he?"

"His original intention was simply to remove it from any location where Helen could see it," Carmine said. "None of us knew exactly how friendly Helen had become with Amanda Warburton, but Kurt knew. Don't forget too that he read her journals, in which she admired the glass teddy bear enormously. She was very proud of her skill in discovering the nature of its eyes."

"But we did know how friendly she was with Amanda," Delia objected. "She acted under your instructions."

"Maybe I instructed her, but the friendship wasn't counterfeit. Kurt was insanely jealous, so much so that his imagination turned her journals into diaries written in a code he couldn't crack."

"But they weren't diaries in a true sense!" Delia cried.

"No code either. Just the tortured thinking patterns of a madman. By the time he broke into the glass shop to steal the teddy bear he was hardly able to keep up a front of sanity. I had his boss, Dean Gulrajani, on my phone at the crack of dawn this morning begging for help. He put the change in Kurt down to the kidnapping, but then admitted it had started when Jane Trefusis, a woman physicist, joined the lab. Kurt hated her."

"Why murder those two nice, harmless people?" Delia asked.

"My theory is that he thought Amanda was really Helen, and Hank Murray was a new boyfriend. He'd read Helen's early notebooks, where she'd raved about the glass teddy bear."

"I know he squired Helen around," Nick said, "but did he honestly love her? Was he capable of that much reality?"

"No, but he thought he was. His fixation on Helen was multi-layered, and a big section was devoted to his family, how they would react to an American wife. Helen was the only one who fitted. By definition, the teddy bear was hers."

"Then who was the Vandal?" Nick asked.

"Hank Murray. It couldn't have been anyone else. He used the Vandal to establish a friendship with Amanda, to whom he was strongly attracted. The trouble was, he had nothing to offer her financially, and his past was shady—no one seems to know whether he took a knife to his wife, or she took it to him. It does seem that he was scared stiff of a trial and its verdict."

The three of them emerged from Kurt's house to find Robert and Gordon Warburton lying in wait for them.

"We hear Kurt's as dead as a dodo," Robbie said, giggling.

"That joke is worn out by now," Carmine said wearily.

"Is it true? Is it really true?" Gordie squeaked.

They look like gnomes, Carmine thought, though they aren't small, or ugly, or misshapen. Other-worldly? No, more sub-wordly. Then it hit him: they were from Mars.

Since it would be on the news, Carmine nodded. "Yes."

"Didn't I always tell you?" Gordie asked Robbie. "A villain! A dyed-in-the-wool villain!"

"A dyed-in-the-synthetic villain, from that background."

Carmine had to smile: they were witty.

"A professor of physics named Kurt

Played with radioactive dirt;

Even God on high

Got some in his eye,

And cast Kurt into Hell for the hurt," said Robbie.

"You're probably right about Kurt's ultimate destiny," Carmine said. "Do you coin your limericks on the spot?"

"Of course," said Robbie. "That's why 'radioactive' doesn't scan properly. Never mind, never mind!"

Gordie rushed into speech. "Captain, Robbie and I had this genius idea for an original screenplay!" The greenish eyes slid sideways in a remarkable suggestion of cold and ruthless passion; a quick glance at the other twin revealed the identical look. "Even now it's finished and copyrighted, a few weeks can see a stolen version out before we could get ours off the ground. We don't know any real moguls!" Now there was a hint of persecuted desperation in his voice, and his eyes were wild with fear; the other twin's look was identical. How *do* they do it?

"Oh, shut up, Gordie!" Robbie said irritably. "Not that Gordie's picture is too pessimistic, Captain, it isn't. It's more that he bewilders rather than enlightens."

"Correct," said Carmine, settling to enjoy the situation. "Enlighten me, Robert—if indeed I address Robert?"

"You do because I am," said Robert. "Gordie isn't wrong, Captain, I do assure you. Our screenplay will be pinched, tweaked and bowdlerized out of all recognition, especially the legal kind, leaving us with something no longer original." He drew Carmine farther away from Delia and Nick. "It has come to our attention, Captain, that Myron Mendel Mandelbaum is your best friend. In fact, that you share a wife. We have been working maniacally to finish our Grand Guignol, which we beg you to read. It's complete down to the story boards—Gordie is a brilliant, *brilliant* artist."

"Story boards?" Carmine asked blankly.

"Yes. Imagine your favorite movie drawn as a gigantic comic book—they're the story boards. Film is a visual medium, and its purveyors are not fond of reading words. In fact, words are enemies. Reduced to a comic, any Hollywood dodo—oops!—idiot can grasp its plot and substance." Robbie pulled a face. "I fear that characterization is another matter."

"You want me to ask Mr. Mandelbaum to grant you an audience?" asked Carmine, loving it.

"Yes, exactly! Our screenplay is perfect for him, but we can't even get through his outer defenses. If we could just see him in person, I know he'd go for our project! *Blood out of Stone* may not win any Academy Awards, but it will make gazillions!"

"That's sure to appeal to Mr. Mandelbaum," said Carmine with a grin. "If I get you your audience, will you promise to keep out of my way?"

Robbie gave a theatrical gasp and wrung his hands together. "Captain, Captain, if you do that, you won't even see our dust!"

"Then it's a deal." Carmine glanced at his watch. "By now he'll be at his office. Can I use your phone?"

"Does a fat baby fart? Of course you can!"

The Warburton twins cavorting in joyous circles around him, Carmine entered their house and stopped. A ghastly head, bloated and greenish, was fixed to the wall in front of him.

"That's Arthur de Mortain," Gordie said. "Number one in the Stone Man's trail of victims. They are all descended from King Arthur and his legitimate French wife, Ghislaine."

"Aren't you in the film yourselves?"

"*In* it? Captain, we *are* it!" Robbie cried. "Behold the Tennyson Twins, sleuths extraordinaire!"

"Ah! The action takes place around 1890."

"Amid London fogs and gloomy graveyards a-drip with dews and yews. The Stone Man will look like a cross between the mummy and Frankenstein's monster."

"Why not make him smooth and handsome like Gregory Peck?"

That didn't go down well; they were creatures of habit.

"I guarantee you'll love the Warburton twins and whatever they've written," he said to Myron some minutes later. "It's pure Hollywood." He flicked over the pages of one of a number of massive albums. "The movie makes a great comic, which I gather also makes it ideal. Not to mention that the Warburtons are refugees out of a comic … Well? Do I tell them to climb on a westbound plane, or not?"

He hung up. "Climb on a westbound plane today, gentlemen. Mr. Mandelbaum will give you a whole morning, and if he likes your comic, lunch afterward at the Polo Lounge."

"Courted for my connection to a Hollywood movie mogul," he said with disgust when they arrived at County Services.

"They sure fell on their feet," said Nick, not approving. "Innocent of all wrong-doing, the richer by whatever poor Miss Warburton left, and now selling their ideas to Myron Mendel Mandelbaum in person." His lip curled. "They're crooks."

"I agree, Nick, they are," Carmine said, "but they're a great example of what can happen to borderline people. Fortune favored them, so crime isn't necessary."

"Yeah, like lawyers," said Nick.

"Someone suing you?"

"No. I'm in Shakespeare's camp, is all."

"He must have had the tights sued off him," Delia said. "Probably by that twister Bacon."

"No, no, we are not going down this road again!" Carmine yelled. "Just because a couple of cases have resolved themselves doesn't give us an excuse to celebrate. Too many bodies."

That's the part of this job I hate the most, he thought, damping down their enthusiasms and elation at the close of a long and very hard investigation.

Helen came in. "Am I allowed?" she asked.

"Sure. It's lunch in a minute anyway."

"Was Kurt the Vandal?" Helen asked.

Carmine went through that again, with some amendments; she didn't need to know that Kurt saw her, not Amanda, as his victim.

Then she changed the subject abruptly.

"Has Dad seen the glass teddy bear?"

"I'm taking him this afternoon."

"And I can't go, right?"

"I'm afraid not, no."

She drew a breath. "I know it's off-limits, Carmine, but I don't see how it can stay sequestered from me," she said. "It's a brain-teaser, really, and I can't come up with the answer. If you know, and you tell me, I promise I won't mention the Dodo ever again."

"Curiosity killed the cat, Helen."

"But information brought her back."

"Okay, one question. Ask."

"Kurt was at every Carew party, but he certainly wasn't the sympathetic guy on the secluded couch. I mean, he was up front! Bold as brass, nothing sneaky or anonymous. So what's with the stranger no one can identify?"

"None of us has an answer. Kurt could easily have gathered sufficient information to fuel his plans, that's not an issue," Carmine said. "Who the other guy was is a mystery."

"Does that mean another Dodo is hunting?"

"If he were, he would have struck by now, and I doubt that

Holloman will ever see women concealing rape again, at least in such numbers. Since the victim drawings all show the same man—well, more or less—we have to assume that he did go to the Carew parties. My guess is that he's a psychologist writing a thesis or a book. As he didn't announce any intentions in that direction, he's sneaky and unethical. I understand that Carew is back in party mode, but all the Gentleman Walkers are looking out for the mystery man. If he shows up, he's under arrest."

"Even if he's done nothing?" Helen asked.

"Only for long enough to be interviewed—and warned, if it seems necessary. No one wants Son of Dodo taking over."

"I never thought of that." Helen turned to Delia. "I thought you said lightning never strikes twice in the same place?"

"It depends on the lightning, dear."

"No, that's too much! Son of Dodo! You're surely not serious?"

"Then who is he?" Delia asked. "*Not* a sneaky psychologist."

M.M. was staggered. "It's the most extraordinary thing I've ever seen," he said, gazing at the glass teddy bear. "Helen's right about the eyes, they're mesmerizing."

"You should have seen it in the shop window, properly lit," said Carmine. "Took the breath away."

"I hear you commandeered the dog and the cat."

"With infant children, I thought it was a good move."

"Until one of them dies." M.M. groaned. "What a circus!"

"The voice of experience?"

"Several times."

"Where are you going to put this beauty?"

"The Aubergs have been nagging me to fund some wonderful art building, but they want it small—intimate, said Horace Auberg. I'm having terrible trouble finding somewhere to put Blue Bear—that's his classy new name—so I think I'll ask Horace for Blue Bear's house. Just one room, with some other pieces around the walls in niches, and Blue Bear in the middle. He'll have to be ten feet away from the nearest spectator in case some maniac tries to swing a hammer at him." M.M. sighed. "The world is full of maniacs! Look at Kurt von Fahlendorf. I even hoped my daughter might marry him. You can't trust anyone anymore."

"That you can't," said Carmine gravely.

"Blue Bear can't stay here either."

"He's off to a bank vault this afternoon, sir. I'll bring the paperwork around for you, then you can put him in your own vaults."

"What do you think, Carmine?" M.M. asked as they departed.

"About what, Mr. President?"

"Blue Bear's house."

"Ask your wife to chair the approval board. She'll know."

"You have a beautiful house," said Fernando Vasquez to his host that Saturday night, ensconced in Carmine's leathery study. "So much oriental art, such rich colors."

"And like the men of ancient Rome, I deal with the decor," Carmine said, smiling contentedly. It had taken longer to have a dinner for Fernando and his wife than was strictly polite, but Desdemona had to want to do it, and she was only now, in early December, really getting back to her old self.

She was in the kitchen with Solidad Vasquez, leaving the two men to their port and cigars in peace.

"Maureen Marshall thinks that Corey's been promoted," said Fernando with a grin.

"His pay is up some," Carmine said, "and he's got a very pretty uniform. I give it six months before Maureen starts chewing about some new imagined slight."

"Know thine enemy," Fernando said.

"She won't get through your defenses, will she?"

"Nope. She doesn't know me the way she knows the rest of you. A large part of your difficulties was due to familiarity, and you know what they say about familiarity—it breeds contempt. My strong suit is the sheer number of my men."

"I can see the point and the strength of your argument, but don't forget that Corey was a uniform for eleven years. Some of your most senior men know him very well."

Fernando laughed. "I can handle Corey—and Maureen."

Solidad Vasquez was a willowy beauty with that iron backbone most wives of ambitious men seemed to own. It hadn't taken Desdemona long to discover Solidad's metal, or to admit that her own backbone was of the ordinary kind. But then, thank God, Carmine was not an overly ambitious man. Though it ate at him sometimes, he liked the job he had. Listening to Solidad's artless but crafty chatter, Desdemona found it easy to trace the upward rise of the Vasquezes, and, reading what wasn't said, understood the prejudices and insults that followed those of Hispanic origins. Fernando and Solidad Vasquez were going to get there, hand their children an upper middle class existence.

Desdemona's extreme fairness and height fascinated her guest.

"Your skin is like milk!" Solidad exclaimed.

"Comes of no sunshine as a child," said Desdemona, smiling. "The part of England I come from gets a lot of rain and little sun. As for the height—my ancestors were Vikings."

The Vasquez children, two girls and a boy, were older than the Delmonico pair, but not by enough to kill a burgeoning friendship. For the first time in her American career, Desdemona was choosing a friend for herself, someone unconnected to Carmine's huge family. Solidad too was a stranger, it made sense for them to stick together, and they liked being opposites in so much, from size and coloring to background and nationality.

The Vasquezes had bought a house on East Circle four doors down, which meant a jetty and a boat shed.

"I liked them, especially Solidad," Desdemona said to Carmine after their guests had walked home.

"Good," said Carmine, not blind. "How's your mood?"

"Back to normal, I would say. No, leave the dishes. Dorcas is coming in tomorrow morning to tidy up." She huffed. "I can't thank my Aunt Margaret enough," she said in a whisper as they passed through the nursery to check on the boys.

"You've decided what to do with your legacy?" Carmine asked as they reached their bedroom.

"Yes. It's going on domestic help. By rights it should go on college fees, but I have a funny feeling that domestic help is more beneficial. I'm such a hygiene freak."

"Anything that gets you through your days more happily is better," he said. "I love you, Mrs. Delmonico."

She snuggled close. "And I love you, Captain."

"How are you coping with the guns?"

"Quite well. The Taft High business opened my eyes a little. New countries take people from so many different places. Slavery was a part of the people movement too, involuntary though it was. Eventually it will all settle down, just not yet."

He held her tightly. "You won't leave me?"

Her head reared up in shock. "Carmine! Whatever made you think that? My goodness, I must have been depressed!" She slid into bed. "Now that Alex is weaned, I'm a box of birds, truly."

There was no more talk. Words were simply sounds. Passion, tenderness and a delicious familiarity of touch and sensation sometimes meant more than any words.

December wore down toward Christmas in racial discontent and several attempted riots provoked by Black People's Power; that they came to nothing was due to the city's small size and careful management. But the BPP continued to create persistent disturbances that no one wanted publicized by arrest and arraignment. The Holloman PD was very busy.

And, as is perpetually the way with people, individual griefs, problems, troubles and dilemmas outweighed the larger picture; a family's budget was more important than the national one, its members more treasured than anonymous millions.

For Carmine the year tottered to an end in an inevitable mixture of the personal and the cop. Desdemona was commander of her domestic ship again; there were no more attacks of despair, no more delusions of inadequacy, but, having had her fingers burned, Carmine's wife lost the last of her beloved independence. She was inextricably bound to her family, she would never be free again. Wishful thinking to yearn for it, yet sometimes, in the very remotest watches of the night, its ghostly summons sounded, a tattoo from a distant, youthful battlefield. For Carmine himself this life of watching his sons grow and his wife change was near idyllic, for he sensed that their need of him was greater.

His people settled down in their new configurations, though some of the senior uniforms noticed that the men of Detectives avoided Corey Marshall as if he were a leper. Memories were long; he would always wear the odium of Morty Jones's suicide and the unhappy fate of Morty's children. He was, however, a good chief lieutenant for an autocratic martinet like Fernando Vasquez; as he had a staff of his own, paperwork was a breeze.

The problem Helen MacIntosh posed was solved thanks to her ability to suck up huge amounts of professional information; when Carmine told the Commissioner that he thought her ready to move on at the end of January, Silvestri blandly agreed, readying himself to do battle with Hartford over a replacement. As he would have M.M. on side, he anticipated victory.

Judge Thwaites had her measure.

"She's feral," he said over Christmas drinks in his chambers.

"Interesting word," Carmine said.

"As wild as she is cunning, and capable of evading every trap set for her." His beady old eyes glittered; he sipped his Kentucky bourbon. "A fantastic instinct for the kill."

"You make her sound a criminal, Doug," said Silvestri.

"She would be, given a different upbringing. As it is, I predict she'll be governor of the state before she's forty-five."

"Or governor of someone else's state," said Carmine. "She's going to one of the New York Manhattan precincts."

"Vindicated," His Honor said with a chuckle. "All of this was only to return from whence she came—as who she wants to be."

People were looking at her differently since she had shot and killed Kurt von Fahlendorf; Helen was never as conscious of it as when she was with the male detectives. Not overtly from Abe Goldberg, so immensely professional that he could subdue every emotion. And not at all from Carmine Delmonico, who understood her predicament, Helen sensed, because his wife had twice been threatened by a killer with a gun. Some superstitious atavism, buried deep, told Carmine that Helen's peril had deflected evil intent away from Desdemona.

The rest of the men were a lost cause. Nick, Buzz, Liam, Tony and Donny eyed her warily, avoided one-on-one situations if they possibly could, and dried up conversationally whenever she hove in view. Privately she despised them as specimens off the Ark; they believed women belonged to the kitchen and their children. Well, let them be male chauvinist pigs! She was protected by Captain Delmonico, and she stood on better terms with him than they did.

Delia was Delia, a good friend, a staunch supporter, the loyalest of fellow women. Never having fired her .38 or her Saturday night special save at the range, she couldn't fit herself into Helen's shoes, was the trouble. Since her secondment to Abe Goldberg, Helen didn't see enough of Delia, a pity.

Most astonishing change of all to Helen was that in her parents. Her mother waffled about "bad karma" and was having sessions with her swami or guru or whatever he was called—just like the Beatles, really. Though Angela was very happy at the resolution of a quincunx in Helen's natal horoscope—it had bothered her ever since, she told Helen, now she knew that it was Helen's ability to shoot people dead. Her father, one of the nation's great liberals, found himself on the receiving end of remorseless sarcasm at producing a killer-cop child, and hadn't thanked her for the adverse publicity.

In fact, Kurt's death had changed everything, Helen thought as she stared down at Busquash Inlet from behind her glass wall. The Warburton twins, briefly owners of this apartment, were moving back to the West Coast, having struck a fabulous deal with the movie mogul Myron Mendel Mandelbaum to write, direct, and star in a blood soaked film about murder and twin detectives.

It hadn't taken any steel on her part to continue living here. The white carpet had been replaced by a rust-red one—Delia was right, no snowy bedroom vistas for Helen MacIntosh! The trouble was that now the rust-red carpet was down, she found she didn't like it. Purple would look better. This debate over decor, she was astonished to discover, was seen by people like the male detectives as callousness! She was supposed to be cringing in fear! *Why*? Hadn't she achieved a great victory? She, a weak woman, had put paid to the existence of a man who had raped, tortured and eventually murdered fellow women! They should give her a medal, not subject her to an enquiry. Of course that had exonerated her; she had acted in self-defense.

Some of the consequences were exasperating, like the one that compelled her to see Dr. Liz Meyers and attend the rape clinic sessions devoted to Dodo victims. How she hated those sessions!

After she spent two of them insisting loudly that the Dodo had not raped her, Dr. Meyers dismissed her as unsuitable for group therapy of this nature; after another one-on-one session, Dr. Meyers referred Helen to Dr. Matthew Worthing, who specialized in difficult cases. But Helen never saw him.

What a profound experience it had been! The thrill of the kill ... When she closed her eyes she could see, as if in slow motion, the crimson flower bloom in Kurt's bare chest, followed by another in the right upper belly, and a final one over the heart. Not huge blooms, but tight little buds that had slowly unfurled. The sight of him on that white carpet! The look in his eyes! That was best of all. Amazement and terror, absolute incredulity. And then he died. Poof! Lights out.

How often dare I kill? Not here—never again in Holloman! Not even in Connecticut. I'll be able to kill at least once in Manhattan, maybe twice or three times before I have to move on. Three million square miles of police departments, so many that I can wander from place to place at my whim. I'll get better at it. To dispose of a body would be a tremendous help ...

The look in his eyes! Watching the life vanish from his eyes, I came to climax. Now, even thinking of it, I climax again.